I0651291

They Hosed Them Out

THEY HOSED THEM OUT

John Bede Cusack

Wakefield
Press

Wakefield Press
16 Rose Street
Mile End
South Australia 5031
www.wakefieldpress.com.au

First published by the Australasian Book Society in 1965
This revised, expanded edition first published by Wakefield Press, 2012
Reprinted 2016

*The characters in this novel have no relation to any persons, living or dead, for they
are composites of typical airmen who fought and died in the European Theatre
in the Second World War.*

Cover designed by Lanz+Martin, lanzmartin.com
Typeset by Wakefield Press

National Library of Australia Cataloguing-in-Publication entry

Author: Beede, John, 1908–1979.
Title: They hosed them out / John Bede Cusack.
Edition   Revised and expanded.
ISBN: 978 1 74305 105 4 (pbk.).
Subjects: World War, 1939–1945 – Aerial operations,
                    British – Fiction.
                World War, 1939–1945 – Personal narratives,
                    Australian – Fiction.
Dewey Number: A823.3

CORIOLE

McLAREN VALE

CONTENTS

Editor's dedication:
'Whether he told me the truth or not I never knew'
– John Bede Cusack

Author's dedication:
To all Air Gunners
who fought and died
in the Second World War

From my mother's sleep I fell into the State,
And I hunched in its belly till my wet fur froze.
Six miles from earth, loosed from its dream of life,
I woke to black flak and the nightmare fighters.
When I died they washed me out of the turret with a hose.

'The Death of the Ball Turret Gunner',
Randall Jarrell

Editor's Acknowledgements

Without the assistance of these people this book would not have happened.

Michael Bollen; Nick Hector; Clive Jackson; Kerry and Phil McCouat; Nick McCouat; Joan Pugh; James, Michael and Susan Treloar; Mandy, Porta and Voula Tzaras, Paul Wilkins and Bradley Williamson.

EDITOR'S INTRODUCTION

If you have never read John Bede Cusack's rollicking ride of a story, *They Hosed Them Out*, I can only envy you, discovering for the first time an addictive work to which you will return, re-experiencing this remarkable man's telling of a little-told part of the wider battle for a free Europe.

First published by the Australasian Book Society [1] in 1965 under the pseudonym 'John Beede', *They Hosed Them Out* is published here under the author's real name for the first time. Despite numerous reprint editions which remain difficult to locate second-hand, the book has never been regarded as an Australian Classic in the wider sense.

Cusack tells the idiosyncratic story of an Australian air gunner, a lightly disguised version of his own adventures in England and over Europe in World War Two. Written in a simple, distinctive voice, *Hosed* is highly entertaining; in some aspects Homeric, occasionally almost super-real. Cusack's pithy, sardonic Australian humour shines through, allowing us to see a long-gone world through a vivid prism. Whether you are an aficionado of aviation memoirs and Australian militaria or not, the sheer range of subjects referred to and experienced by one man in the course of his flying career as a not-very-humble air gunner is nothing short of remarkable.

Although a pragmatic lightness of tone prevails throughout, there are comments of dark bitterness which bring to life the twisted, topsy-turvy life of the aviator in and out of battle. Cusack spares us nothing; war's ugly civilian underbelly rubs against its RAAF and RAF counterpart in a way few military biographies approach; the black market and exploitative underground industries in England are encountered and passed on – and in one case escaped from – just as the reader has gawped at them in disbelief. This is not the usual bomber memoir, nor an overview; this is the view from the outsider underdog.

Described as fiction, yet clearly drawn from the author's experience,

Hosed has the benefits of both; fiction frees Cusack from truth's requirements of naming names, yet allows him to write the truth partly as he remembers it, partly to thrill.

The distance of time and the requirements of the original publishers mean that a modern publisher required editing to produce a fuller, more complete book than the original. The main goal has been to preserve Cusack's story, his voice, his 'ring of truth'. His chatty style and unique choice of word and phrase was an extra delight.

In this edition you will find newly-restored sections (including some full chapters) left out by the original editor but kindly provided by Cusack's daughter, Kerry. The addition of these chapters has also helped balance the book; the mostly unpublished chapters are 2, 23, 24, 36, and 38; chapters with noticeably extra material are 11, 13, 17, 19, 25, 26, 28, 30, 32, 37, 39 and 42.

The second goal has been to follow Cusack's lead of topicality; through his fiction a complex web of history peeps out. The first time I read the book (in 1974) I was fascinated, but badly wanted to know more. Pursuing that ring of truth can be addictive. So now, while the non-specific nature of squadron and personnel details remain in the text, leading notes on factual matters and pointers for further investigation are available for those whose further interest is piqued. Individuals have only been identified in the notes where the event or individual seems significant (for example, Len Trent VC or Basil Embry). However, a veil has been drawn over some possible or likely identities where facts cannot be known (and may even lead to unjust accusation). Cusack was not beyond exaggeration for effect.

In preserving the story as Cusack intended I have not corrected the occasional inconsistencies (many made for the sake of the story) or quirky descriptions. A little of the text has been smoothed out, perhaps the characters are a little clearer. I have tried to keep the referencing unfussy and unacademic. Cusack's logbook confirms much of the fictitious Beede's experience – however that is no reason for us to assume that the rest of the book is accurate; in the final analysis Cusack produced a story for publication as fiction.

The original list of characters has been extended and may be found at the beginning; the glossary of terms has been expanded and can be found after the story proper. The appendices include articles written by Cusack while still in RAAF service and published in Australian magazines of the day. He later reworked these articles for inclusion in the book, and you may like to compare the book versions with the originals. The final appendix puts Cusack's – and Beede's – war into a wider context while Kerry McCouat's brief biography of her father rounds out the book.

If you are new to this book, do not expect the contemplative nature of that classic of Australian literature, Don Charlwood's *No Moon Tonight*. As Charlwood himself explained, he was an exception to the breed of bomber pilot; his book does not represent the average Australian in the RAAF or RAF. Similarly, Beede is neither a Clive 'Killer' Caldwell nor a Weary Dunlop.[2] Beede is neither a hero nor a villain, but a stranger in a dangerous, swiftly moving world.

That *They Hosed Them Out* has been reprinted in so many editions world-wide is testament to its lasting significance; this 'fictionalised memoir' deserves to be placed where it belongs, on civilisation's shelf of military classics. Now, perhaps, it can be.

Robert Brokenmouth

DRAMATIS PERSONAE

Part One – Preparatory

The Mob: Eight Gunners (of the original thirty-two trained at Winters)

Aub 'Gunner' Aarons: 'dark-haired … a bubbling sense of humour and fund of witticisms'

John 'Johnny' Beede: based on John Bede Cusack, 'the eighth member', the author

Arthur Hally: The Mob's leader; 'a 16 stone block of a man … the strongest man I ever met'

Fred 'Happy' Henderson: 'chief bitcher, political propagandist and bush lawyer of the group, who knew his King's Regulations backwards'

Blondie Henschell: 'Hally's cobber … 6 feet, 14 stone, with an aggressive jaw and a deep, rasping voice, the unlikeliest bank clerk ever'

Harry 'Smiler' 'Mac' Macdonald: 'an insurance clerk, whose pendulous jowl reminded you of a sad-looking bloodhound … could see nothing happy in anything, but relieved his griping with an unconscious dry humour'

Norman 'Bourke' Malloy: 'ex-Brisbanite, the best-equipped man in matters that keep the weaker sex happy that any of us had ever met; a perpetual female chaser'

Bryan 'Smithy' Smith: 'handsome … with the crinkly brown hair and irresistible smile, who hailed from the Clarence River'

Allied to The Mob

Bill Driscoll: 'a tall and good-looking chap from Sydney with a flashing smile'

Tom Hedge: 'a South Australian farmer'

Sid Pascoe: 'a natural comedian'

Peter Poast: 'a nineteen-year-old Sydneyite with a cherubic face'

Jimmy Sullivan: 'ex-naval type … who had transferred to the air force and, having failed honourably as a WAG, had ended as a straight air gunner'

Colin Tempe: 'red-headed, irrepressible … ex-NSW police cadet'

Bill Gorman: close cobber of Johnny's: 'a big, easy-going, pleasant fellow who had been a budding solicitor in civilian life'

Other Gunners

Kiwi: 'a fair-headed, happy, effervescent New Zealander with a perpetual grin' – assimilated into The Mob

Ron 'Clarkey' Clarke: 'a sallow complexioned bloke who made no secret of the fact he did not intend to fly … in any crew position. His stated intention was to build up a list of fake illnesses'

Dagworth – 'lurks artist'

Ray Steer: 'an unpredictable, foul-mouthed half-wit that no-one bothered with'

Place Getters from the Gunnery School in Wales – assimilated into The Mob

Drake: 'a tall, studious South Australian'

Martin: 'a dark Italian-looking joker'

Sherwin: a bloke 'so good-looking he was almost effeminate'

[No Name]: 'a skinny little fellow from Western Australia'

Part Two – Bomber Command

Beede and Kiwi's crew

Flight Sergeant Peter Snowden: Pilot, a tall fair-haired solicitor

Flight Sergeant Williams: Co-pilot, 'a Welshman with a big-toothed grin'

Stan Jones: WAG, 'a little sharp-faced Cockney'

Bill Ninnes: Navigator, a tall, dark thin bloke

Barnes: cleaner and message boy, former observer

Maxie: little Cockney WAG

Fred Bliss: Australian burns patient

Mrs and Mr Weston and their daughter Helen: provided a place of rest for airmen and soldiers

Part Three – Tactical Air Force

Air Vice Marshal Sir Basil Embry: Commander of 2 Group (which included 464 Squadron) from June 1st 1943 to August 8th 1945

Beede's crew

Flying Officer Jack Parr: a tall navigator

Flying Officer Wilbur Cronin: a shorter, pleasant-looking pilot

Flying Officer Bill Fogg: open-faced, bubbling, enthusiastic

Tom Hedge: South Australian, one of the original ITS gunners

Parker: pilot of the aircraft Blondie flew in

Ian Potter: a sprog Aussie gunner

Dr Stanton: Beltwell squadron Medical Officer

Claude: 'in charge of the preparation of food for the mess'

Maria: 'a tousled red head'

Rip: 'a young gunner'

Bob: 'a big Maori'

Tommy: 'a long stove-pipe of a gunner'

Long 'un and Snowy: gunners

Vincent 'Bull' Collins: Pilot, and 'the roughest bloke … any of us had ever met'

Part Four – Boston Interlude

The Five Gunners from 464

Flying Officer Bryan 'Smithy' Smith: 'handsome … with the crinkly brown hair and irresistible smile, from the Clarence River'

Flying Officer John Beede: the author's pseudonymous creation

Tommy: 'a Kiwi'

Tommy: 'a small Australian from Sydney'

Stan: 'a big farmer from the Riverina'

Smithy's crew

Tom 'the Yank' Ryan: 'a hawk-faced flying officer with slightly buck teeth'

Stan Bell: 'a six foot five giant ... English navigator'

Beede's crew

Flight Sergeant Bill Thomas: Pilot, 'a chunky, serious-looking joker'

Jock McAlister: Thomas' 'navigator, a soft-voiced Scotsman'

Fred 'Basher' Williamson: WAG, 'a tough-looking little Geordie with a broken nose'

464 Odds and Bods

Squadron Leader: 'a big man with a prominent hooked nose and grey, piercing eyes'

Squadron Leader's navigator: 'the picture of the upper-crust Englishman who, because of his class rating, had no need to be anything but himself'

Squadron Leader's WAG, Des Holstead: 'a Londoner with a wide-mouthed grin'

Squadron Leader's straight AG, Jack Stokes: 'a quiet, easy-going Canadian'

Pearl: 'a well-dressed, good-looking woman of twenty-five or so'

Beryl: 'a journalist ... in her thirties and ... endowed with all the things that make a woman a woman'

Tubby Evans: 'a little Australian gunner'

'a major who had won his commission in the Western Desert'

Boofhead: 'a colonel in the quartermaster's department; the scion of a noble English family'

Part Five – Victory in Sight

Pete: 'a quiet, likeable Canadian navigator'

Scotty: Pete and Beede's batman, 'a middle-aged Scotsman'

'the DFC and Bar English gunner' (who was in the crew who went in last at Brest)

Beede's new crew

The Skipper, Wing Commander Smith: 'a tall Wingco ... [with] dark wavy hair, stood over six feet tall and looked like a matinee idol.'

Ted Allington: Navigator, 'a six-footer with a lean, tanned face [and] a shy smile'

Fred Archer: 'a well-set-up WAG with a DFM and an aloof English air'

The Tour of Soho

The Guide: 'a little podgy Cockney called Charlie'

Six AIF types from Perth (one is Big Bill, another is a captain)

Flying Officer Bill Fogg: WAG. 'an open-faced, bubbling, enthusiastic Australian', last seen in Beede's 464 crew.

W/O Chief Mechanic: Chiefy, a hard-bitten Australian Warrant Officer

Bluey: 'A lanky Australian pilot'

Murph: 'a little Aussie gunner'

PART ONE

PREPARATION

CHAPTER ONE

The convoy which moved out of Halifax Harbour on that cold April day in 1941 comprised ships of a wide variety. There were merchantmen, tankers, several cargo-passenger ships, slick refrigerated cargo ships down to dirty old tramps all assembled to run the Nazi blockade and get their cargoes to England.

Our escort, two destroyers and a corvette, bustled around getting the ships into line. When everything was sorted out, we found the convoy was sailing in four columns – eleven ships on the two outer lines and ten each in the inner. The *Karamac* was in the second starboard, along with the tankers and vessels carrying the more valuable cargoes. On our left was a merchantman flying the special red flag indicating munitions and explosives. The closeness of this dangerous fellow-traveller didn't please the crew. 'If the fugger goes up', said one, 'she'll blow us all to bloody hell'.[1]

The *Karamac* was nearly three months out from Sydney, Australia. In that time she had travelled to Christchurch, New Zealand, across the Pacific and through the Panama Canal, much to the wrath of Goebbels who declared her a 'ship of war'. Having evaded the U-boats in the Caribbean and South Atlantic, she was now on the last leg of her journey.[2]

She was an old ship. A plaque on her foredeck testified that she had been born in the Clyde in 1908, had served through the First World War as a troopship, and had again taken up the job in 1939. Her gross tonnage was 17,000. It was claimed that she was the longest cargo-passenger vessel in the world.

When she passed through Sydney Heads three months earlier, she had been loaded to the plimsoll.[3] At Christchurch, sweating watersiders had still further crammed her holds with urgently required cargo for war-torn England till it was assessed she held twenty thousand tons of vital goods in her bulging belly. During buffeting from a three-day gale in the Pacific the *Karamac*'s cargo had shifted slightly so she now had a ten-degree list to port which gave her a rakish air, like a plump housewife returning from market with one too many under her stays.

In addition to the urgently needed supplies aboard were a hundred and eighty-two members of the Royal Australian Air Force, comprising a hundred pilots, fifty navigators and thirty-two straight air gunners bound, like the cargo, for England; reinforcements for the sorely-pressed Royal Air Force.

On this particular day, eight gunners known as The Mob were gathered on the fo'c'sle[4] watching the navy get things organised.

Over the three months' voyage the gunners, particularly The Mob, had been an oppressed minority, for even in this tight little world the 'class distinction' of pilot, observer and gunner was already firmly established.[5]

To understand this, it must be realised that ninety-nine per cent of pupils who entered an Initial Training School, or ITS, had their hearts set on being fighter or bomber pilots. In the inevitable sorting and culling that goes on after examinations, those who missed out on the pilot's course hoped for a posting as an observer. The mathematical wizards got first preference here. Bods who did not make these two grades were then posted as wireless air gunners – WAGs for short. There was usually no direct posting as plain air gunner.

When a pilot failed, he slipped a cog and could carry on as an observer. If he still missed out he descended one down the ladder and became a WAG. If he couldn't make the grade here, he was given the choice of some twenty-odd postings, such as PT instructor, driver, military policeman, motor boat rescue crew, air gunner, clerk, etc. If he wished to remain aircrew, he became a gunner or, if he was fed up with the RAAF he could give it away, and, according to his inclinations, choose whatever position suited him. In other words, he had reached the end of the line and the nature of his postings offered in lieu of an AG testify to the low official opinion in which he was held.

With the AG's who sailed in the *Karamac* there was a big difference. They considered themselves very hardly done by, for they were compulsory volunteers of the 'You, you and you' system, a subject that always raised the blood pressure and fighting spirit of the meekest member of this little band.[6]

CHAPTER TWO

An hour out from Halifax the first swathes of fog and mist swirled in from the Atlantic, and in a matter of minutes the entire convoy was blotted out. Only now and then could a ship be seen. How they kept station was anyone's guess. Strangely enough, they did not move quietly but wailed and booed to each other in every imaginable fog horn key, not unlike a lost herd of brass-throated cattle. One of the crew explained the noise didn't matter as U-boats could pick the churn of the collective screws miles away on the hydrophones[1] and would have to fire blindly, so would be more hindered than we were.

The gunners had long before been placed on two-hour gun watches, a duty performed with ill grace because they felt that pilots and observers should do their share too. Now that we were in these dangerous waters, the guns[2] themselves were manned by professionals from the ship's crew. We were only there as extra eyes.

For seven days and nights we sailed in this cold, cloying, cotton-wool world; then on the eighth the wind rose, blowing away the fog, and in a matter of an hour it was blowing a gale.

As the seas came up amazingly fast, the ships behaved in their characteristic ways. The *Karamac*, with her slight list, rolled ponderously. The tankers wallowed, often going straight through the waves. The destroyers and corvettes bobbed like corks, disappearing completely out of sight in the big seas. How they lived, slept and ate in these slender cockleshells it was hard to say.

That day, a small cargo boat which had struggled to keep up with the convoy developed engine trouble and started to drop steadily astern. It was then we learnt the cruel law of the convoy; no-one waited for anyone. We could imagine the feelings of its crew as it was left to its own devices, gradually dropping back into the inhospitable vastness of the Atlantic.

As darkness came, the waves tumbled and the winds shrieked

through the rigging and I asked Spider, the bar steward, what would happen if we were torpedoed. His advice was 'break into the bar, get yourself a bottle of Scotch and swallow it', as it would be impossible to launch boats and no-one would stop to pick us up. 'You drown quicker if you're drunk.'

Next morning it was still blowing like hell, then at about ten o'clock the wind stopped and amazingly enough in an hour the seas were almost normal. This was in direct contrast to the Pacific where, after a storm, the seas ran high for days. By nightfall we were sailing in almost calm waters, visibility was good and it looked like a quiet night.

Somewhere about midnight, there were two simultaneous explosions that rattled our eardrums, followed by the jangling of alarm bells. We had been warned to have everything ready and I was into my clothes, overcoat and onto the deck in sixty seconds flat. Just as I reached my boat station, there was a tremendous flash of light, followed by a muffled explosion ahead. Even before the flash had subsided, a glow that slit the darkness grew in intensity and brightness till it bathed the entire convoy in a blood-red light. Someone said in an awe-stricken voice, 'Good God, one of the tankers has been hit.'

By the time we came opposite the stricken vessel, she was a mass of flame from bow to stern. From the midst of this inferno came a medley of screams and shouts, and figures could be discerned rushing frantically about. Even the sea was afire and a boat that was being lowered, possibly because its davits³ burned through, suddenly precipitated its occupants into the burning water. A flaming human figure raced along the deck, then in an agony of despair, threw itself like a burning torch over the side.

Even though the tanker was some five hundred yards away, the heat jumped across the intervening space in a searing blast and in the two minutes it took us to pass the burning vessel, the horror-stricken airmen looked into this glimpse of hell with open and unabashed fear. It was a sudden belly-chilling introduction to war. Gradually, the convoy passed this grisly torch that marked its own passing so brightly and the sounds of its unfortunate crew faded with the distance, although the fire continued to burn and flash in the darkness of the ocean for a long time.

So intent had we been on this horrible spectacle, we had for a moment forgotten the battle which continued to rage around us. Depth charges were exploding continuously. Two further flashes followed by an awesome dull rumbling showed that two more vessels had been hit. The action continued until early morning when, as though by a signal, the subs broke off their attack. The loss was five cargo ships, a tanker and, we heard later, the poor little ship that had drifted so far astern.[4]

At breakfast, Hally expressed the opinion of all when he said, 'I reckon every bloody seaman who sails in a tanker should get a VC. Fancy sitting on that bloody stuff. I wouldn't do it for twenty thousand pounds a year.'[5]

We were an edgy and quarrelsome Mob that day. I was on the midday watch. At about half-past there was a boom of gunfire as the leading destroyer fired on a strange plane which appeared suddenly out of the clouds and disappeared just as smartly.

Half an hour later a general alarm went as signals flashed throughout the convoy. Then, from the east, came the drone of aircraft and at about one o'clock, out of the cloud on the starboard quarter appeared three four-engined Kuriers[6] flying a widely-spaced 'V' formation at about 6,000 feet. It was obvious their intention was to make a diagonal bombing run across the convoy. As they came into range led by the front destroyer, every large gun in the convoy barked defiance. Black puffs dotted the sky around the attackers. The shooting was accurate because the sea was remarkably calm.

Jumping with excitement, I said to Bill, a phlegmatic Geordie who was sitting quietly, his eyes glued to the sights, 'Have a bloody go!'

'May as well piss against the wind,' he replied, 'range be too far.'

While attention was centred on these fast-approaching black crosses, the guns of the alert destroyer dead on our starboard flank suddenly switched to a fourth plane which was coming in at a swift dive at about two thousand five hundred feet, obviously intending to bomb while his higher-flying companions created a diversion. Instantly, the guns of the ships in our quarter were switched to this intruder but despite concentrated fire he came swiftly in.

'That bastard's after us,' said Bill, his Oerlikon chattering like a pneumatic drill as it spat tracer and incendiary in a graceful arc.

We saw the bomb-doors open as it passed over the first line of ships. A hail of light and heavy flak reached up to pluck it from the sky. Later on, we were to appreciate the bravery and singleness of purpose of this fanatical Nazi pilot who held his straight and steady course at this suicidal height, to make certain of hitting his target.

Just as it seemed only a matter of seconds before the bombs started falling, a Bofors found its mark. Three near-direct hits threw the plane almost on its side. The pilot wrestled it back but in that brief second, both plane and crew were doomed. Two more direct hits blew the port wing and its two engines almost completely off, and the huge plane, still plucked at by a web of tracer, trailing smoke and flame, went into a vertical dive to hit the sea in a welter of foam and a tremendous whoomph, as its bomb load exploded. Pieces of plane, bomb splinters and flak churned the sea white and everyone ducked at the angry buzz of these bits of flying death. On the death rattle of the Nazi came an ear-splitting shriek as the bombs from the three high-flying planes came plummeting down. At the sound, the convoy swung sharply to starboard as the towering white pillars of water marched diagonally across the turning vessels. Bombs fell in front and to the side of the *Karamac*, and although they rattled our teeth, did no apparent damage.

It was here I was to learn my first lesson in aerial warfare. A piece of shrapnel the size of a duck's egg smacked into our position and rolled onto the deck. I thought, 'here's a souvenir,' and grabbed it – but let it go almost as fast because it was red hot.[7]

Other ships in the convoy were not so lucky. We passed a small cargo vessel of about three thousand five hundred tons which, with no apparent deck damage, was already settling in the water. Her siren blew mournful long and two short blasts, the signal to abandon ship. 'Near miss,' said Bill, 'enough to spring her plates.' We saw the crew tumble helter skelter into the boats as she rolled sluggishly into the swell. On the port quarter, a cargo vessel, its bridge completely wrecked and afire, was careering around in a wide arc, its steering apparently jammed. The rest of the convoy scattered out of its uncontrolled path.

Above, the Kuriers turned for home, one with black smoke pouring from the starboard outer engine.

I looked at my watch. It was three minutes past one. In three hectic minutes ships had been sunk, a plane and crew blown out of the sky and death had brushed closely by every member of the convoy. It was then that I noticed that Bill was patting the deck of our ship. 'She's a little bloody beauty,' he kept saying, 'No bloody Nazi is ever going to get her, she's a lucky ship. She be a little bloody beauty.'

The crew were firmly convinced that their ship was a lucky ship. They would point out that she had survived the first war and despite innumerable close shaves in this one, was still going strong. Little did they know that her good fortune was to hold for only one more year before deserting her in one horrifying half-hour; torpedoed in a raging storm in the Indian Ocean, the *Karamac* was to plunge to the bottom with all hands.

The result of this little skirmish was two vessels sunk and three so badly damaged that they could be written off. Thus Hitler in twelve hours had reached out across the ocean from his fortress in Europe to display his might, both under and above the water, and to give us a preview of what stormy paths lay ahead.

Just before I went off watch the alarm bells went again as a strange, pot-bellied plane appeared at about five hundred feet to starboard. Bill said, 'Christ, it's a bloody Sunderland from Coastal Command.' The pilot kept a safe distance as the Aldis lamps[8] winked and presented his credentials. Obviously, he had a deep respect for itchy-fingered convoy gun crews, who were liable to fire first and ask questions afterwards.

A few minutes later a second plane came into view and carried out a similar routine. It was then we knew the dangerous centre of the Atlantic had been bridged and from then on during daylight hours, we would have the protection of these wonderful Coastal Command work-horses as they flew their interminable circuits, veering off to drop a depth charge, circling a spot to bring an escort racing in. So good was their protection that we did not have any further attacks.

On the fourteenth day we sighted the northern tip of Ireland and later sailed into the protection of the outer channel. Here we were safe from both sub and air attack, for minefields guaranteed the first, and proximity of shore-based fighters the second.

CHAPTER THREE

We landed at Liverpool at 4.30 pm. The city had been bombed the previous night and, although it was reportedly a light raid, work squads were still clearing up the rubble. What impressed us was the way ordinary citizens, despite new and old damage, roped-off streets, dangerous buildings and so on, seemed to be going about their affairs. Buses and trams still ran and businesses, despite the lack of glass, were open. In fact, we appeared to be the only ones disconcerted by the signs of aerial savagery.

We were met by the mayor and a committee of public-spirited citizens who tendered a welcome at an afternoon tea in the Town Hall. Hally, Blondie, Smithy and myself slipped out in the middle of the speeches to sample the local hops. We selected a small, unpretentious hostelry near the hall so we could hear any sound indicating that the party was breaking up.

A surly, beetle-browed barman who looked on us with no favour, served four pots of beer without even a bubble on them. Smithy said, 'It looks like bloody cold tea.' Hally said, 'Hey, mate, your beer's flat.' This bloke must have been one of the Liverpool Irishmen, or perhaps his nerves were on edge with the bombing, because he took a dim view of this remark. For several seconds he couldn't speak and then he spluttered, 'Me bleedin' beer's flat, is it? Let me tell yer it's a new keg I just put on and if you bleedin' Orstralians don't like it you can get to bleedin' hell.'

We jointly told him what he could do with his 'bleedin' beer' but found when we entered a second pub we had done him an injustice, for the beer here was just as flat as the first lot. A friendly bystander overheard our remarks and explained that English beer did not have a head or froth like its Australian counterpart, and what looked like flat beer to us was, in fact, quite fresh.

Things looked like developing into a nice little party when we heard the bark of orders and tumbled out, just in time to join our comrades lining up to march to the station. On the way, we saw a marvellous cathedral perched on the brow of a hill – a picture of medieval architecture. As we came closer, however, we saw it was battered and scarred and completely burnt out. We learnt it had been a victim of a bomb raid the previous week.

We boarded a special southbound train and, even though it was only early spring, it was still light at nine o'clock so we were able to catch our first glimpse of rural England. What amazed the Australians was the vivid green of the grass and fields. The countryside, divided into innumerable pocket-handkerchief fields or paddocks, separated by stone fences or hedges, was one of luxuriant fertility. Nearly all of it was under crops of some kind. It was difficult to believe these same fields had been tilled for centuries, yet continued to give an abundance of food and fodder.

Another interesting point was how towns and villages seemed to start and stop, the tilled fields marching right up to the walls of the towns. Along the train-lines, near towns and villages, were neat little vegetable plots, apparently tilled by diligent citizens.

We arrived at Bournemouth at 5.30 am to be greeted by air raid sirens but as far as we could see, no-one took any notice. The citizens were not yet about but this coastal city looked a serene and peaceful spot untouched and untroubled by the Blitz and horrors of war. A bus took us from the station to the sergeants' mess, a spacious two-storied building at which well-to-do citizens had holidayed prior to the war.

We had expected meals to be skimpy and short but our breakfast was as good as we would have received in Australia. Afterwards we were marched to our billets, which consisted of two beautiful six-storied blocks of flats situated on the eastern side of the town with an unsurpassed view of the bay and the coast. These, we understood, in peacetime cost from twelve hundred to fifteen hundred pounds a year unfurnished, which was money in anyone's language.[1] Hally, Blondie, Smithy, Gunner and myself were allotted to a front room on the sixth floor. We thought someone must have blundered, as it was too rich for gunners.

It was a lovely day, the sea was blue and serene; far away, the sun flashed on the white cliffs of the Isle of Wight. 'Now, I could really settle down in this little burg and let the bloody war go by,' said Blondie. 'This place will do me.'

Lost for a moment in contemplation, my mind went back to that windy November afternoon nearly six months before. The course had lined up for the afternoon parade after the first month's exam at Winter's RAAF ITS.[2] Black, the CO, had taken the microphone. After a short preamble on patriotism and the necessity of bashing the Hun, he called for volunteers for thirty-two air gunners who would go almost immediately to England, offering the inducement of missing the monotonous round of examinations connected with ordinary postings.

I recalled again the scene as the four-hundred-strong course stood lined up in their blue dungarees, felt hats pulled down over their eyes against the glare of the sun and the dust whipped up by a squally southerly; a hush that fell over the parade ground after his appeal. No-one volunteered, for even in those early days rumours of the unhealthiness of this particular calling had filtered in from twelve thousand miles away. To a man they stood fast. After a second impassioned plea one lone figure was netted. Later, this bod was discharged as mentally unsuitable.

The CO then called for the roll and declared, 'The following airmen whose names I call, will take one step forward.' After a preliminary clearing of his throat, he called the first name, 'A.A. Aarons.' I could still remember Aub's anguished ejaculation, 'Christ, A for bloody Air Gunner.' The smile was soon wiped from my face as my own name was called. So down through the roll that authoritative, brassy voice continued till thirty-one stunned young men stood not two feet, but twelve thousand miles apart from their course comrades. As the last name came over the public address system, a sound soft and sibilant as wind passing through a field of ripe wheat arose from the packed ranks as the lucky ones let their collective breaths go.

With the exception of the first volunteer, the chosen thirty-one, plus one other, were still together, despite the string-pulling of influential parents and relatives. In this regard, as there were one Federal and four State parliamentarians numbered amongst the fond parents, the pressure must have been great. However the RAAF stood fast to the decisions made by the CO on that blustery afternoon.

From Winter's, the unhappy group had been transferred to a tough rookies' training school for a month, where we were passed over to the tender mercies of two tough drill instructors known as The Animal and The Louse.

After these two characters had done their best to break our spirits and instil some air force discipline into our rebellious souls, we had been passed on to a gunnery school in New South Wales.

Here the lone volunteer had shown signs of mental aberration and had been replaced by an ex-naval PTI by the name of Jimmy Sullivan who had transferred to the air force and, having failed honourably as a WAG, had ended as a straight air gunner. During the three weeks' course, we had learnt some of the elementary phrases of gunnery, flown for an average of two hours in the open cockpit of an ancient Fairey Battle[3] and fired some five hundred rounds from an old Vickers machine gun at sandpit targets. As the course progressed, it was revealed that twenty-six of these budding gunners had never fired a rifle. I'll never forget the look on the grizzled range sergeant's face as he watched these amateurs handle a .303 rifle which, as anyone knows who has used it, has a weighty firing kick.

It's true saying that birds of a feather flock together. At ITS, friend-ships had already been formed that were to continue at the rookie's training school and beyond, for these young men had early in the piece formed themselves into four separate groups.

Number One Group was The Mob. Arthur 'Art' Hally, a 16 stone block of a man, was the leader. He was the strongest man I have ever met. Next in line came his cobber, Blondie Henschell, 6 feet, 14 stone, with an aggressive jaw and a deep, rasping voice, the unlikeliest bank clerk ever. Then there were dark-haired Aub 'Gunner' Aarons, with a bubbling sense of humour and fund of witticisms, whose father owned half a dozen Sydney hotels (Gunner, because of his name, was a moral first on every roll); twenty-year-old, handsome Bryan 'Smithy' Smith, with the crinkly brown hair and irresistible smile, who hailed from the Clarence River in New South Wales, where his people owned a farm; Harry 'Smiler' 'Mac' McDonald, an insurance clerk, whose pendu-lous jowl reminded you of a sad-looking bloodhound (Smiler could see nothing happy in anything, but relieved his griping with an uncon-scious dry humour); Fred 'Happy' Henderson, chief bitcher, political propagandist and bush lawyer of the group, who knew his King's Regulations backwards (any bod's fight was Happy's meat; the greater the injustice, the more bitter the defence, so he was constantly in strife with the powers above); Norman 'Bourke' Malloy, ex-Brisbanite, the best-equipped man in matters that keep the weaker sex happy that any of us had ever met; a perpetual female chaser. I, John Beede, was the eighth member.

Closely allied with The Mob was the second group of five kindred spirits. These included red-headed, irrepressible Colin Tempe, an ex-NSW police cadet; his cobber, Tom Hedge, a South Australian farmer; Sid Pascoe, a natural comedian; Peter Poast, a nineteen-year-old Sydneyite with a cherubic face, and Bill Driscoll, a tall, good-looking chap from Sydney with a flashing smile. The two groups frequently amalgamated and assisted each other. They were almost as one, but thirteen made an unwieldy crowd.

Completely dissociated were three characters; a little fellow called Ray Steer who was such an unpredictable, foul-mouthed half-wit that no-one bothered with him; Dagworth, a lurks artist;[4] and a sallow-complexioned bloke by the name of Ron Clarke who, since we left Australia, had made no secret of the fact he did not intend to fly as a gunner or, in fact, in any crew position. His stated intention was to build up a list of fake illnesses and he had started his campaign from the time we left Australia by reporting every Thursday on Medical Parade to the ship's doctor.

Our crowd treated Clarkey with a contemptuous rough humour, and when the mood took us, we would solicitously enquire as to his health. One day, out of curiosity, I enquired if he genuinely intended getting out of fighting. He assured me that he did, but would give no reason, only stating flatly that he was not going to fly. What intrigued everyone was that he made no secret of his intentions and I think it was generally felt he was putting on an act and when it came to the test he would be in it.

The third group consisted of the younger and nicer fellows. They came from a slightly higher social stratum, were college educated and did not smoke, swear, drink or associate with bad women. They were not softies and in sport could more than hold their own.

The fourth group comprised five members of well-to-do families. They were all stacked with cash, drove modern cars, and were much in demand in the young social sets wherever we were stationed.

The pilots and observers were an even younger class group and already their responsibilities and training had placed the service stamp on them. They were, in fact, an elite class who had gone into the air force in 1940, when the qualifications were exceedingly high. The pilots had their wings, the observers their flying 'O'; thus they had been sub-jected to a year's intensive training and showed it in their bearing and behaviour.

Two or three of the older types, attracted by the free and easy behaviour of our crowd, joined The Mob. In this way I palled up with a Western Australian pilot called Bill Gorman and we finally became inseparable cobbers. A big, easy-going, pleasant fellow who had been a budding solicitor in civilian life, Bill used to say; 'There's no doubt, you gunners have the right slant on this service life. You have no worries and you don't give a bugger about anything or anyone.'

Despite the spontaneous bitching, I felt our group was not unhappy. For my part I had nothing to whinge about, because to get into the air force I had had to put my age back six years. I had done this by stating I was born in Cork, Eire, and signing a statutory declaration to that effect. As far as the air force was concerned, I was an Irishman. Actually, I was a dyed-in-the-wool Australian.

At thirty, I was far removed from school and the study habit. At the initial examinations I knew I had not done well, so if I wanted to stay in aircrew I realised I was a certain candidate for a gunnery berth. Hally's contention that 'it doesn't matter if you fly in the front or the arse of the plane, you're still fighting the Nazis' was generally accepted.

Happy Henderson, with his strong left-wing political inclinations, worried much about the couldn't-care-less attitude of the boys. 'You know, Johnny,' he would say, 'they haven't a bloody thought in their heads except food, beer and women. I don't think they even know what they're going to fight for.' He used to try hard to get his message across: that the ones who survived this mix-up[5] should band together and see that no individual or group of individuals could ever plunge the world into war again.

Happy must have thought I had some grey matter but then he thought I was twenty-four. If he had known I was thirty, rising thirty-one, he would have written me off as a complete no-hoper for, when I came to look at myself I found, despite the difference in age, I wasn't so far removed from Happy's condemnation of my cobbers.

During the Depression, I spent four years roaming Australia like thousands of other young fellows, doing all kinds of jobs – gold mining, working in shearing sheds, timber cutting, navvying, fighting; in fact doing any kind of work I could pick up.[6] In 1934 I had joined a large electrical organisation as a salesman and, mainly because I had known hard times, had the gift of the gab and was not afraid of hard work, had by 1940 risen to the position of sales manager. This was not the high title the name implied as I was more or less a glorified commercial traveller, but it paid a thousand pounds per year, which was good money in those days. Also, the fact that I was single meant I had no objection to transfers, so that at some time or other I had worked in every state in Australia. I ran an expensive car which I used in my business, was a member of a leading Sydney surf club, so surfing, beer and females occupied about equal amounts of my leisure time.

Bournemouth was a town of contrasts. Only the waterfront showed evidence of a country at war. The beaches were barbed-wired and barricaded. Concrete tank traps stood shoulder to shoulder along the sea walls. The pier had been wrecked in sections so that invaders getting a foothold would not be able to use it. Barbed-wire entanglements stretched along the fore-shores, headlands and seashore parks. We were advised under no circumstances to attempt to go beyond these entanglements as the area was mined. There were rumours of lovers who had foolishly ignored this advice and come to a sticky end.[7]

All that day we spent in reviews, examinations and general service routine. There seemed to be an air of urgency in everything. Though there was a certain amount of bullsh,[8] the English officers possibly felt we were dangerous cattle and used tact and firmness to accomplish their ends.

At 4 pm we had what the English term 'tea', which seemed a little early from our Australian viewpoint. It was our first experience of the quaint old English custom, the forerunner to a supper that commenced about 8 pm and was the main meal of the day.

After the 4 pm effort, we started a sightseeing tour. What interested us was that, despite the fact that the enemy coast was not eighty miles away, there was an absence of air-raid precautions and, in contrast to Liverpool, no damage. This place had never been raided, so the shops were unboarded and the windows untaped.[9] It appeared to be a carefree holiday town. The parks and streets teemed with children and holiday-makers. It appeared as if the Nazis had declared an unofficial truce on this very tempting target. Rumour had it that there was an unofficial agreement; 'you don't bomb X and we won't bomb Z'.

They knew we were there, because Lord Haw Haw in his

'Germanaire Calling' broadcasts, to which everyone seemed to listen,[10] declared, 'We know you're there, Aussies, but you'll keep.' It was not until a year later that the Jerries raided the parade ground one morning, causing a number of casualties.

We certainly liked the English drinking arrangements. In contrast to our own 'six o'clock swill', here the pubs opened from 10.30 am to 2 pm then closed till 6.30 pm. Some varied their trading hours by opening at 11.30, closing at 2.30, opening again at 5.30 and remaining open until 10.30 pm, thus you got a drink at reasonable hours. Instead of rationing beer as in Australia, they cut down on the alcoholic content till you could drink a gallon of it and not get full. Blondie said in disgust, 'All I get is bladder exercise.' Women drank on equal terms with men in bars, which was a civilised arrangement.

There were literally thousands of girls in the city, comprising WAAFs, ATSs, WRENs and hundreds of holidaymakers from London and nearby towns. They took the Australian, New Zealand and Canadian servicemen to their individual arms and hearts and most of these young fellows were overwhelmed by the attention they received.

At that time there were over two million surplus women in England, so that Bournemouth, with its plethora of servicemen, was the answer to a young girl's prayer, the Mecca to which they flocked. What intrigued us was the friendship and good fellowship of these English lasses. Most of them insisted on standing their shouts[11] in bars and they were also exceedingly generous with their charms and favours. As Blondie rumbled, 'Anyone who isn't getting his share must be a moron'.

Most of these women had been through desperately anxious days. They had seen their armies shattered on the European mainland and their island undergo one of the most sustained and vicious air assaults in history. From a seemingly hopeless position they were still in the fight and hitting back. The arrival of these airmen from all parts of the Empire gave life and hope to the words of Winston Churchill, so they rewarded these young fellows in the way the soldier has been rewarded throughout history.

Air alarms were frequent, but nobody seemed to take much notice. Enemy planes often tracked in over Bournemouth on their way to London and more important targets, so that when the sirens gave their banshee wail, people merely stopped and looked skyward to see if the planes were on course.

Within a few days we were all broke but in many instances, our various girl friends offered to pay expenses and, where this was refused, extended loans. Bourke was in his element. He had three beauteous females fighting for his favours, and the boys generally agreed never had they had it so often or so easy.

During our six days at Bournemouth, we were given, among other checks, colour-blindness tests. We wondered why they had not been given before we left Australia, because if an airman could not pass he was out of aircrew. Actually, one observer and a pilot were scrubbed and another observer was a borderline case. Clarkey failed dismally, not that it did him any good, because there were traps to catch the shrewdies.

Bournemouth was a sophisticated, interesting and lovely city, yet not twenty miles away was a little fishing village with a tiny stone harbour on which the fishing boats rode at anchor as they probably did in Drake's day. Bill Gorman and myself were accosted by child prostitutes of thirteen and fourteen years of age, escorted by harridans, who we were later advised were usually their mothers.[12]

CHAPTER FOUR

We were given five days' leave. The gunners were advised they would be posted to a gunnery school in Wales on their return. Hally, Blondie, Bill, Smithy and myself decided to go to London. A marvellous service bureau known as the Lady Ryder organisation provided an efficient service and booked us in at a Lions Club near Knightsbridge.[1]

Hundreds of books have been written about London at this particular period in her chequered history, but what impressed us newcomers was its tremendous size and the miles and miles of drab roofs and chimney pots that flowed past the train's windows as we rode towards the centre of the city. We had expected to find it completely devastated but found that, because of its size, London had been able to absorb the punishment. In fact in the city proper, quite large areas were completely untouched by the Blitz, except where a burnt-out or bombed building made a gap amongst its untouched neighbours like a missing tooth. The area near St Paul's Cathedral, however, was completely flattened.[2]

Our first three days were given to visiting well-known places such as Westminster Abbey, The Tower, etc. We also made the acquaintance of the Boomerang Club, situated in Australia House. This was exclusively for the use of Australians and without a doubt one of the best service clubs in England. Through its doors at some time or other passed every member of the RAAF to partake of excellent fare, read Australian newspapers, play ping-pong or billiards or just sit down and talk of cobbers in faraway Australia.[3]

The first night passed without incident but on the second, as we were doing the usual rounds of the pubs, there came the faraway nerve-torturing wail of sirens which swelled and grew as thousands more joined in. Then, like the rumbling notes in an orchestra, softly at first, but growing in intensity, came the growl of gunfire. Gradually it increased in intensity as the enemy planes moved up the estuary towards the centre of the city.

At the first warning sound the well-trained Londoners moved towards the public shelters and underground entrances in orderly file. There was no sign of panic or haste. A Cockney paper seller remarked, "Ere come the bastards again'. Searchlights poked inquisitive fingers into the darkened sky, swinging and groping with their silvery beams. The gunfire worked itself into a crescendo. High above, you could see the burst of shrapnel and shells as the gunners attempted to throw the planes off their bombing run.

Soon the streets were silent except for the patrolling police and members of the National Fire Service and Air Raid Precautions. These stalwarts, ordinary working men, white collar workers, business executives, remained to face the danger from above, alone. Well-fortified with dutch courage, we had intended to watch the fireworks from the shelter of a doorway but a policeman caught us in a flash of his torch and put an end to this. ''Ere,' he said, what are you doing out 'ere; do yer want to get yerselves killed?'[4]

Hally countered with the obvious, that the bobby himself was as likely to be killed, adding that it was our first air raid and we wanted to see what went on. The bobby was adamant. 'Better get into the shelter over there, boys,' he said. 'We don't want to be picking you out from under a building.'

A high-pitched shriek and a tremendous whoomph not so far away added force to his arguments and haste to our steps as we made for the shelter, a squat brick structure set in the centre of the street. Someone struck a match as we came around the brick blast front into the pitch black interior. The place was full, its silent occupants sitting on wooden seats that ran around the walls.

A voice said, 'Why, it's bleedin' Orstrylians. Come and sit down, boys.'

There was a general reshuffling as room was made for us to squeeze in. In the brief glow of a matchlight I found a place between a fat old dear with a black shawl draped over her head and an English soldier who had his arm around a girl. Our arrival was the sign for a few facetious remarks but as the gunfire rose to a new pitch and the whoomphs grew in intensity silence fell on the gathering, the only sign in the darkness being the faint glow of cigarette ends that briefly lit the faces of the smokers. After each crash and whoomph my fat neighbour shook like a jelly and from her came a tortured, 'Holy Mary Mither of God, pray for us sinners now,' trailing off into an unintelligible finish.

The soldier, however, had his mind on more earthly things and from the darkness came giggles and half-hearted 'don'ts' followed by slaps.

The drone of planes seemed to pass directly overhead and a couple of nearby explosions shook our shelter. In the darkness you could gauge the tenseness as everyone followed the menacing drone; cigarettes were held in motionless fingers; even the soldier ceased his endeavours; the wheezy 'Holy Mithers' grew in intensity.

Gradually the sound of the planes and the gunfire seemed to move from our area. The cigarettes glowed again, the giggling resumed, and the 'Holy Mithers' dropped to a whisper.

The sirens finally, mournfully announced the All-Clear and as we came into the sulphurous night, we found to our astonishment the raid had lasted an hour – and the pubs were closed. We took the Tube back to Knightsbridge. I will always remember the sight of those thousands of Londoners huddled on the platform, sleeping in all sorts of positions right up to the edge. It was difficult to force a way through the groups. It reminded me of a giant casualty clearing station. The trains did not stop running till 11.30 pm, so these unfortunates, young and old, had to put up with the roar of the carriages and the passing of indifferent travellers till close on midnight. Most had come through the long and dreary winter dragging their bedding and blankets underground, emerging early in the morning to carry on their everyday tasks.[5]

CHAPTER FIVE

Back in Bournemouth the gunners were immediately mustered and advised to pack. Hasty farewells to our friends amongst the pilots and observers jolted us out of the happy holiday mood we had lapsed into and reminded us that the war was still on.

The training station was situated on the coast of Wales, near Cardiff.[1] On arrival we were told by the CO we were in for an intensive three weeks' training that would take priority over everything else. In the interests of concentration and study the sergeants' mess was placed out of bounds.

On the first day we were joined by a New Zealander, a fair-headed, willowy type who had missed the previous course through illness. He was immediately christened Kiwi. He was a happy, effervescent bloke with a perpetual grin. Hally and Blondie took a great shine to him and he immediately joined The Mob. In a matter of a week he was so completely accepted you'd have thought he'd been with us from the beginning.

Classes started at 8 am, really 6 am as English summer time was two hours ahead of standard time.[2] On the first day the squadron leader in charge of the course announced that special postings would go to the first twelve on final examinations. He didn't state what this particular prize was but intimated that it would be worth going for.

That night Happy had a brainwave. He called our crowd together and said, 'Why don't we sew this thing up, because if we can get among the first twelve we can all stick together.'

Only Mac and Bourke weren't sold on the idea. Mac reckoned there was a catch in it somewhere. He was finally won over, but Bourke flatly refused to do any extra study as he declared he could find more interesting things to do. Thus the final line-up was Hally, Blondie, Smithy, Gunner, Happy, Mac, Kiwi and myself.

The main subjects were air technique, aircraft recognition, the hydraulic system of an aeroplane as affecting turrets, a complete study of the .303 machine gun, practical gunnery and firing at targets from aircraft. The latter was supposed to cover a third of the course.

Aircraft recognition consisted of throwing photographs of various aircraft from a projector onto a screen, where they were left for a matter of two or three seconds. In this period you decided what the particular plane was. To confuse the issue, the photos included German, Italian and a number of our own planes. But I never by night found an aircraft that obligingly silhouetted itself so that I could say with certainty, 'Ah ... a Messerschmitt 109.' However, no-one knew this at the time and we laboured diligently to commit the photos to memory.

In every gunnery course I ever attended, one main subject was the detection and rectifying of the twelve stoppages of the .303 machine gun. Mechanically minded air gunners took these in their stride. The procedure was that you carried out a series of tests which, like Sherlock Holmes's deductions, covered all possibilities till the correct stoppage was found, then applied the counter to correct it. I had no mechanical leanings whatsoever and found that my endeavours usually meant barked knuckles and, in many instances, the danger of losing the end of a finger. Actually, I never heard of anyone rectifying a stoppage in the limited space of a turret, because while you were struggling to fix the stoppage, who was supposed to do the watching?

In flying tactics, we learnt that fighters had a well-defined plan of attack called a curve of pursuit, in which they followed certain steps. In theory, this consisted of, first, the positioning period, when the attacker flew a parallel course some fifteen hundred yards behind to the right or left of the aircraft, estimating the course and speed of the other plane.

Having assessed this, if he was on the bomber's starboard or right wing he would bank, drop his port or left wing, and start his attack towards the tail of his target. At approximately eight hundred yards he would straighten up, pull his sights on to the target, drop his right wing and come in for the attack proper. To nullify this, as soon as he banked the second time, the gunner who had been watching and giving a running commentary to his pilot, knew the enemy was committed to attack and ready to open fire.

At six hundred yards the gunner would give the command 'Turn starboard, go' at which the bomber pilot threw the bomber into a violent right turn. If everything had been estimated correctly, the fighter pilot, already launched on his final thrust, would be unable to turn, and travelling at a hundred and fifty miles per hour faster than the bomber, would go skidding past its tail. The gunner, estimating distance on his illuminated sight at six hundred yards, was supposed to open fire ahead of the plane so that it passed through his fire.

An easily understood simile would be a greyhound coming in from the right rear of a rabbit making a vicious burst intending to pick up the bunny which immediately swerves right. The dog, already committed to his lunge, cannot stop his rush and skids past the victim's rear.

In addition to his running commentary while all this was going on, the gunner, in an endeavour to down his adversary, had to estimate the attacking plane's overtaking speed; that is, if the bomber was doing two hundred miles an hour and the fighter three hundred, this was a hundred miles an hour, so that he allowed two complete radials of his gunsight for every fifty miles an hour ahead of the attacking aircraft. In such an instance he would allow two radials and when the fighter did his final roll seven to eight hundred yards out, he would open fire.

To bring his target into his cone of fire he had to allow for proper deflection, and in addition to making corrections for bullet trail and gravity drop (the bullet, as it left the aircraft and met air resistance had a tendency to swing away from the target and naturally had a downward gravity pull) the competent gunner would allow a certain amount of radials in front or ahead of his target and shoot upwards so that the bullet trail and gravity drop were compensated for.

I would say it was in deflection shooting that ninety per cent of gunners failed. It must be borne in mind that most of these young fellows came from cities and had never handled a firearm before.

In the lull between shearing seasons during the Depression, I had once joined up with a professional shooter who was employed on a western New South Wales station clearing out what was termed 'vermin'. For this work we got our tucker and the bounty which went with the heads of eaglehawks and ears of wild pigs. We also shot kangaroos for their skins. Economic necessity dictated that you got the maximum result for a minimum of bullets, and I reckon it took me six months to become a really accurate shot, where I could both hit and drop a fast-moving target.

Even with this experience I found when it came to 'towed target practice' (a fighter plane towing a canvas drogue behind it on a long rope), in my three efforts my results were only twenty, twenty-three and twenty-five per cent of hits. The gunner sat in the tail of an antiquated

Whitley bomber and had to estimate the approach of the target and fire bursts at it. This result didn't seem particularly good to me until the instructors informed me that half of the course didn't score a hit, and a lot of the others had less than five per cent. With these results, how the hell could you expect these young fellows to hit a plane moving a hundred to a hundred and fifty miles faster and manned by an experienced pilot bent on blowing them out of the sky?

On their practical gunners' training we were supposed to do a total of nine flights and fire approximately eighteen hundred rounds of ammunition. However, nearly every day fogs and mist rolled in from the cold Irish Sea and either stopped these flights or caused their cancellation when the planes were already in the air. Thus, at the end of the course, I had completed only three trips and fired six hundred rounds. In addition, the course comprised the use of a cine-camera gun against actual attacks by fighter aircraft, but due to poor visibility and the bad weather this was never carried out. These restrictions meant we did only approximately one-third of practical gunnery.

Despite the nose to the grindstone technique we still had time for pleasure. On the first weekend we were granted leave for the Saturday and Sunday and found some eleven miles from the camp was a holiday watering place that, although not as large or as beautiful as Bournemouth, combined a lot of the attractions of that place, together with a few extra ones. I was later to find it was like a miniature Blackpool. Here the boys found themselves as popular as ever with the local and visiting females. Some of the Welsh gallants, however, took a dim view of these foreign intruders who dallied with their girl-friends and expressed their resentment in the use of toil-toughened fists so that a few bloody noses and black eyes resulted.

In spite of the local skirmishes that often involved the innocent and guilty alike, we grew to like and respect these hard-working Welshmen, who, once honour was satisfied, extended a warm welcome to us in their working-men's clubs and in the local pubs.

Over the last week of the course, under Happy's tuition we forsook the fleshpots and concentrated on extra study. We had the blessing and assistance of various instructors who were taken with our group's idea of sticking together. When the exams came off we sat together and gave each other a little moral and unofficial assistance. When the results were announced it was found all except Mac were in the first twelve.

The special prize was then announced as a direct posting to an operational squadron in Bomber Command. Hally, on learning this, said to Mac, 'I'll fix this for you. I'll have a word with Tait (a tall serious South Australian) and see if he'll change with you, as I feel certain he won't want to come with us low-heels.' Mac didn't seem enthusiastic. Hally, however, went ahead, and after some discussion got Tait to agree to the exchange provided the CO was willing. We expected Mac to show deep appreciation of these endeavours on his behalf, but he reacted in the opposite direction, backing and filling and showing a marked disinclination to join the crowd.

Finally Blondie exploded, 'You're mucking about like a girl with no pants on. Do you want to be with us or not?'

Put on the spot, Mac then agreed diffidently to be in it.

Hally said, 'I can't make this bastard out. Here's me working myself to a standstill and all he's done is mess around.'

As Mac and I were walking back to the mess, I said, 'What the hell's wrong with you? Anyone would think you didn't want to be with us.'

There was silence for a while, then he said, 'To tell the truth, John, I don't.'

I looked at him in surprise. 'You're kidding,' I said.

'No, the main reason why I don't want to go to this particular posting is that I'm not a fighting man. I'm not like Hally, Blondie, Smithy and yourself and the rest of The Mob. I've never had a fight in my life. I'm such a coward I faint at the sight of blood.'

I looked at his long sad face and mournful eyes and said, 'Arr, balls.'

'No,' he said, 'that's fair dinkum. I'm no hero. I wish I had enough guts like Clarkey to try to get out of this bloody mess.'

Listening to my companion I realised he was dead serious and said, 'For Christ's sake cheer up, Mac. You'll feel different when you get on to the squadron and into a crew.'

'That's another thing,' he declared, 'We shouldn't be going on to an operational squadron. What type of training have we had? Two weeks in Australia where we learnt nothing and three weeks here with practically no gunnery work. Why, it's the equivalent of giving a foot-slogger a three week course leaving out the rifle drill, and sticking him into the front line. I never scored a hit on the target and neither did seventy per cent of the others. We've done an elementary course on air gunnery, left out the essential practical parts, and they're posting us direct to an operational squadron. It will be sheer bloody murder.'

'But,' I protested, 'we'll get more training there.'

'Do you think we will?' he asked mournfully.

'We're a moral to,' I declared, 'only it'll be with your own crew. Cheer up, you old bastard.'

Afterwards I gave his words some thought and decided there was a lot of truth in them. An interesting point, I realised, was that whereas they would scrub a pilot, observer or WAG at the drop of a hat, no matter how poorly a gunner performed he still stayed on course.

Clarkey, I knew, had made no attempt to pass the examination and, prior to this had pleaded air-sickness, vomiting on the few flights he had been on. With his record of malingering, the medical staff had sent him off in an Anson with a doctor on either side. Unable to put his fingers down his throat he had shown no signs of sickness and was passed.

When the course was completed, due to our lack of practical training, the squadron leader made an application for an extension of the course from Training Command, which was refused. He was so angered at this decision that in the remarks in our log books at the end of the course report he wrote: 'Extension of course requested but refused.'[3]

The other four place-getters, making the dozen, were a tall, studious South Australian named Drake, a skinny little fellow from Western Australia, a bloke called Sherwin from Melbourne who was so good-looking he was almost effeminate, and a dark Italian-looking joker called Martin. They were a quiet quartet. We soon found they were brothers under the skin, however, and they were assimilated into The Mob.

A week prior to our exams, Gunner had captured a harmless green grass snake about 14 inches long. This little fellow, which he nicknamed Pancho, had round googoo eyes and took kindly to captivity, lived in the pocket of his master's battle jacket, and at a whistle of command would poke his head out to see what was going on. He drank milk and beer with complete impartiality and swallowed with gusto the various insects the boys collected for him so that at the end of the course he had developed a spare tyre. A deal of amusement was had by his owner with WAAFs and other females who crossed his path.

The morning after our exams were completed we were mustered for a full medical. The procedure consisted of passing through various check-points, the last being a short-arm inspection, before a very near-sighted medical corporal, with the thickest pair of bifocals we had ever seen. When we got to this myopic, we had to drop our strides, pull up our shirts and he would then conduct a minute examination at about two inches range of the chest, tummy and finally the privates, the latter being held up to facilitate examination.

Gunner was in the middle of the parade and word got around that he was going to offer Pancho for inspection. When his turn came the corporal started his usual close-sighted viewing of his chest and stomach, then brought his glasses within a couple of inches of Pancho's wriggling head.

For a few seconds, his head and eyes moved with the undulating snake. Then, as he suddenly realised that this penis was behaving in a most unusual manner, he let out a startled squawk and fell backwards.

At this the whole course collapsed in screams of laughter and even the head medical officer, who was an irritable old cuss and had 'had' Australians, laughed too.

When Bourke followed, the corporal viewed his generous offering with obvious distrust. Someone said, 'He must think it's a python,' and there was another roar of laughter.

PART TWO

BOMBER COMMAND

CHAPTER SIX

Late that afternoon the chosen dozen said goodbye to the rest of the gunners and entrained for a station somewhere in Norfolk. We travelled to London, arriving early in the morning, and then had to wait till 4.30 pm before our train left.

Night travelling in England was a nerve-wracking experience. All stations were blacked-out and, except for a shaded light over the name-board, there was no indication of where we were. At some stations, a voice speaking the dialect of whatever area we happened to be in called the name; as we were unable to understand these blurred and unintelligible announcements, they might as well have been calling in Chinese or Czech.[1] If no-one in the carriage knew the locality, it entailed someone getting out and racing along to see just where we were. As the train stopped only a minute or so, this could be hard on the nerves, particularly if the scout came panting back to announce, 'This is it!' As our train stopped at every station it was 11 pm when we finally arrived.

We were met by an English flight sergeant and the usual RAF blitzwagon and driven to the station. It was so dark we were unable to see what kind of place it was. A supper was waiting and after this was consumed we were conducted to an igloo hut with a promise that accommodation would be sorted out in the morning.

One very obvious feature of the place was the almost continuous roar of plane engines. Like lions roaring, the stillness of the night would be shattered by the sudden starting up of a motor, closely followed by a second. These would run in unison on a gradually increasing note, fall away, and start again, then sometimes splutter to a stop. We soon found that this was a diapason that was to become a part of our lives, sometimes muted, sometimes ear-shattering, day and night.

We were so tired that despite the lack of luxury we slept like logs. In the early grey morning we woke to the din of returning planes. Mac querulously complained, 'Can't they show some consideration and cut out some of the bloody racket?'

That morning we were paraded first before the adjutant, a dapper, middle-aged squadron leader who welcomed us to the squadron and informed us that it had a long and illustrious history, having been formed during the First World War, and he felt sure we would worthily uphold its traditions. He further stated that the aircraft we were to fly in were Wellingtons and that on the previous night the squadron had been on a strike into Germany. Preliminary checks had shown it to be a successful one.[2]

He then handed us over to a gunnery officer, a thin-faced flight lieutenant with a DFC. He didn't prove as matey as the adjutant and informed us, in no uncertain terms, what was expected of us and even made an inspection in which he made several biting criticisms as to our general military appearance. Blondie growled, 'I don't think I'm going to like this bastard.'

Smithy, Hally, Blondie, Mac and myself found quarters in a Nissen hut.[3] At lunch-time some of the crews that had been on the previous night's operations appeared. They looked a tousle-haired, taciturn group, eating their meal in silence, although now and then one would make a remark regarding the night's operation.

'Glum lot of bastards,' said Hally.

It was not till later we realised the reason for the silence – four planes had failed to return and two dozen faces had disappeared from the mess.

After lunch, five of us cadged a ride and went out to the hangars to look at the planes in which we were to fly. They appeared to be solid kites in comparison to the ones in which we had previously flown – twin-engined black-fuselaged monsters that squatted in their bays like huge black crows. The Wellington was an unusual bomber; its structure was termed 'geodetic', that is, its fuselage was made of ribbed latticed duralumin covered by a tough fabric. Its crew consisted of six men: pilot, co-pilot, navigator, wireless operator, front and rear gunners.

We palled up with some ground crew who were working on one of the planes in the hangar and they let us look it over, first warning us to be careful not to step off the catwalk leading down to the rear turret as one misstep would mean a foot through the cloth covering and this was a chargeable offence.

Next morning we were allocated to crews. Kiwi and I were told we were flying with a Flight Sergeant Snowden. Blondie and Hally, like ourselves, were lucky enough to be together, but the rest were placed singly. We were amused to find there was some competition to obtain our services due to the idea that because we came from Australia, the land of great open spaces, we must all be crack shots. One WAG informed Hally and Blondie that they would make 'top-hole gunners with all the practice they had had shooting wallabies and kangaroos'. We thought he was being facetious but found that this was a generally accepted idea.

After lunch in the mess a tall, fair-haired pilot came up, introduced himself as Peter Snowden and said, 'I believe you're in my crew.' He had a clipped, incisive speech, his handshake was firm and I liked him from the start. I called Kiwi over and after introductions he said, 'You'd better come and meet the rest of the crew.' He led us to a group of three airmen and said, 'This is Williams our dickey pilot[4], Stan Jones our WAG, and Bill Ninnes, our navigator.'

Williams was a Welshman with a big-toothed grin, Jones was a little sharp-faced Cockney, and Ninnes a tall, thin bloke, almost as dark as our Skipper was fair. He spoke the same good English. We found the Skipper was a solicitor and Ninnes was doing an engineering course at Oxford. He and the Skipper had been close friends in civvy life and were inseparable companions in the squadron. There was an awkward air of reserve between the six of us, mainly because we didn't seem able to find a common subject of interest. Jones broke the ice a little by suggesting a trip out to see our kite, S for Sugar.

We then learnt each aeroplane on a squadron had a particular letter of the alphabet which coincided with some well-known word, i.e., A for Apple, F for Freddie, C for Charlie, S for Sugar etc. Jones explained the crew had only done one operation, a pamphlet run over France. This was a way of breaking crews in before sending them on the hazardous German trips. Generally they were uneventful ops in which, apart from some flak, nothing much happened. However, on this journey a surprise burst had severely wounded the rear gunner who was still in hospital. The front gunner had broken a leg the previous week in a game of football, hence the two replacements.

S for Sugar was a comparatively new machine, her paper run into France having been her first trip. 'Not that they last too bloody long,' said Jones. 'There isn't one kite on the squadron with more than twenty ops up.'[5]

'Why don't they do more than twenty ops?', Kiwi enquired in all innocence.

'They get "the chop",' our companion said grimly.

It was soon evident we were not going to get on with the gunnery leader. Our first difference of opinion arose the following day when we were told we were to go to Group Headquarters some twenty miles away for a week's schooling. We mustered after lunch with our personal effects at the flight.

The day was raw and cold, a biting wind blowing in from the North Sea, with sharp intermittent showers. 'If this is spring I wouldn't like to see what winter's like,' someone commented. As we waited, a wagon with a covered top but open sides arrived to take us to our destination.

'Christ! They don't expect us to travel in that, do they?', said Smithy. 'We'll freeze to death.'

Someone suggested that perhaps it was to take our baggage. Hally checked with the WAAF driver, a Lancashire lass, who said it was transport for gear and bods. Just then the gunnery leader arrived and barked, 'All aboard'.

Acting as spokesman, Hally said, 'I don't think we should have to travel in that truck, sir. Several of these men, including myself, have colds and we'll freeze.'

For a second he looked as though he couldn't believe his ears, then shouted, 'I'll give the orders around here. Get aboard that truck or I'll place you all on a charge.'

The boys jacked up, and eventually the exasperated officer, after a lot of bluster and threats, obtained a bus. There were three English gunners with us who were also doing the course. These blokes were flabbergasted at this flouting of authority. Gunners, it seemed, just didn't do these things.

Training headquarters was situated in a permanent station; our quarters were large, dormitory-like affairs; the mess and surrounding buildings all had the appearance of a well-run club.

'Here, Bournemouth apart, is where I could fight this war from,' was Mac's reaction.

Next morning we marched to our classroom where we were met by a rather scruffy-looking Warrant Officer with a DFM who set the ball rolling by remarking that he understood we were troublemakers and we might as well know from the beginning where we stood with him. He added that gunners were known as 'the shit' of the air force and had a flying life-expectancy of one hour. He added sourly, 'Most of you will be hosed out of your turrets before you're much older.'

Hally said he hadn't come twelve thousand miles to be referred to as 'shit' and was immediately backed up by the rest of us. Happy then kept the water boiling by adding fuel to the fire.

'You state we have a life expectancy of one hour. What's the average duration of an operation?'

The W/O didn't see the trap. 'Seven to eight hours,' he replied.

'That means,' said Happy, 'most gunners don't live to see the enemy coast.'

The instructor must have complained to his superiors, for next morning Hally, Happy and myself were told to report to the chief gunnery officer. He proved to be a conciliatory flight lieutenant who told us we were here to fight the Nazis, not our instructor, and, after a five-minute talk on co-operation, dismissed us.

The course was a rehash of the previous one, although we were given some instruction on night fighter tactics. This lost value when we found that our instructor had never done a night operation!

The W/O, after our initial difference, proved not a bad type. We reckoned he'd been so used to putting the boot in without resistance that it shattered him when he ran into some opposition. In this respect we found the average English aircrew took all that was handed out to them without complaining. The Australians, New Zealanders and Canadians, however, kicked hard against injustice.

On this course we did air-to-air firing, four flights of half-an-hour each for a total of twelve hundred rounds. At the end of the course, Happy and Mac complained bitterly that we had learned nothing new and we still hadn't done any practical night flying or fighter affiliation.

On our return to the station, Happy, Hally and myself were again paraded before the Wingco, a middle-aged chap with cold grey eyes and a thin strip of a mouth. We had decided in advance that we would make an issue of our dispute with the instructor and not the bus incident. When he stated that he understood we had caused trouble with our instructors, Happy said that we objected to being referred to as 'shit'. This forthright statement shocked both the adjutant, who was present, and the Wingco. 'What do you, ahem, mean by that, flight sergeant?', he demanded.

Happy elaborated, advising how the dispute had arisen, adding that he personally objected to being referred to in this manner and he spoke for the rest of the contingent.

The Wingco then said there was certain air force jargon which though strange to our ears was nevertheless universal in the RAF. His manner implied he could not understand why we had taken umbrage at an appellation that had common usage on all squadrons.[6]

Happy then declared he was not having this description applied to himself and, if necessary he would take the matter to our Australian headquarters at Kodak House. This we found was a trump card, as no CO likes tangling with headquarters, particularly an overseas one, so after a lecture on discipline and co-operation we were dismissed. We afterwards heard, but were never able to substantiate, that an order was issued to instructors that air gunners in future were not to be referred to as excreta.

CHAPTER SEVEN

Immediately on our return, all new crews started on night-flying exercises. For a fortnight we stooged around England on four- and five-hour trips. The one who really worked hard on these do's was the navigator as the two pilots merely followed his instructions. The rest of the crew, particularly the gunners, were just there for the ride and on odd occasions took a little nap. It was certain we obtained no useful practice to fit us for what lay ahead.

At the end of this period five crews were called one afternoon and briefed for a pamphlet op into France. On these raids the planes carried nothing more dangerous than large bundles of propaganda pamphlets. Each plane was given an area to cover. We were directed to the Pas-de-Calais area, which meant only an approximate three-and-a-half hour journey. The fact that the rear gunner had been wounded on the previous sortie didn't add to my peace of mind.

Strangely enough, the complete darkness and absence of any searchlights or flak from the time we left our coast was more disquieting than later trips where there was plenty of both.

The only conversation was Ninnes' instructions to Snowden and his terse comments of 'Enemy coast coming up', and 'Crossing enemy coast'. After approximately twenty minutes' travelling, Ninnes said, 'Wireless operator, get ready to unload those pamphlets.' The procedure was to cut the rope and then toss the propaganda down the flare chute, a funnel-like contraption in the middle of the aircraft.

I knew we had some eight large bundles for spreading and estimated it would take Jones at least six to eight minutes to cut the packages and jettison the pamphlets. It seemed next to no time when he reported, 'Pamphlets gone, sir.'

Snowden was so surprised he said, 'You sure you got rid of them all?'

'Definitely,' said Jones.

'You were damn quick then,' the Skipper commented.[1]

It wasn't until a week later, with a few beers on his chest, Jonesy confessed he had thrown the completely intact bundles down the chute, his explanation being, 'I didn't think the bloody pamphlets would do much good but I might have hit a bloody Jerry on the head with one and that would definitely have left an impression.'

The trip back was uneventful. We saw no flak, no enemy fighters and arrived back smack at 4.30 am. We were interrogated by a sleepy officer who, after a few questions, told us that all crews had returned safely.

Next day the weather turned bad and blew a half-gale from the north-east. All flying was out for the next two days. On the third morning there seemed to be an unusual amount of activity about the station. At lunch time it was accepted by the older members that it would be a full petrol load. We found that the ground crew could tell the approximate distance of the coming op by the amount of petrol that went into a plane. A three-quarter load meant a reasonably short one, a full load a long one. Happy said, 'they could count us out as we hadn't got to that stage yet.'

At about four o'clock the Tannoy spoke, asking all crews to report to operations at 4.30 pm. Snowden and Ninnes came around and collected Kiwi and myself. The front gunner said, 'What the hell do they want us for? We won't be going.'

Snowden and Ninnes exchanged glances but didn't say anything. It wasn't until later we found the navigators had already been briefed and Ninnes had been in it.

When we arrived at the ops room, a separate stone building capable of seating over a hundred people, most of the crews were already there. Service police checked us in. Then, when all crews were seated, the doors were shut and locked. It was a long building and the bottom part of the wall was covered by a large green curtain. Both the Wingco and the Groupy were present.

The latter spoke. 'Well, boys, I guess you're wondering where you're going. Here it is.' With that, he pulled the drawstrings and two curtains rolled back from the centre, something like a miniature theatre curtain. There, covering the entire wall, was a huge map of Europe from the Baltic to Spain. Red tape stretched from England across the North Sea, deep into Germany.

For a while the significance of those vivid red lines escaped the newcomers, then as various exclamations came from those in the know, we suddenly realised this was the route and the end of the tape was the target.

As the buzz of conversation increased in intensity the Wingco held up his hand for silence. 'I know it's a tough one,' he said, 'but this is a general two-group bash. We are putting up every available aircraft. I am aware there are some crews here who haven't done a fully-fledged operation but this will be a good one to cut their teeth on.'

Kiwi and I looked at Snowden with questioning eyes and he nodded his head. 'Jesus,' said Kiwi, 'I don't like this one little bit.'

The Wingco explained our objective was a factory area in Essen, which meant we had to penetrate the Ruhr. This, we gauged from a variety of comments, was considered to be a decidedly unhealthy place.

The Wingco covered the main points of the attack. The meteorologist then gave us a resume of what we could expect to and from the target. The navigation officer said a few concise words, stressing the necessity of missing the bad flak areas, both going in and coming out. These were marked in red. The wireless leader gave some points on special jamming techniques the Germans were using.

Although the gunnery leader was present he had nothing to say. After the general briefing was over, he called us to one side and gave us this terse advice: 'Keep your eyes open and don't go to sleep.'

'That bastard should have a record made,' said Blondie, 'and he could go to sleep for all the use he is.'

As we were taking our gear to the bus, an English pilot was saying to his navigator, 'Eighteen thousand arseholes! They bloody-well know none of these kites can get to seventeen thousand. With the load, we'll be lucky to get to sixteen thousand.'[2]

'That right?', Kiwi asked Snowden, who gave an embarrassed smile and said, 'I can't really say, old fellow; haven't tried the old bus out yet.'

It's hard to say how the crew felt about the coming op. The atmosphere was one of almost painful silence. We were such a completely untried and inexperienced crew, I guessed everyone felt it was wisest to keep his mouth shut.

The rest of the crews had little to say in the bus trip around the perimeter. Here and there the bus would stop, the driver would announce A for Apple or whatever plane it happened to be. The crew would clamber out, someone would say, 'Good luck,' and on we would go again. We were the second-last crew out. The night was pitch black and the ground crew were moving about the aircraft which towered above us like some prehistoric monster.

Inside the Wimpy the air was heavy and filled with the smell of oil and petrol. I moved down the catwalk to my turret, parked my 'chute and closed the doors behind me. Seated there, I experienced a feeling of complete isolation and loneliness that I was never able to lose while I flew in Wimpys, even though I was only thirty feet from the rest of the crew and could speak and hear them over the intercom.

I heard the pilot giving his instructions, then each member reported he was in position and ready. Away somewhere in the darkness I heard a muffled roar as engines came to life. Our own, after a few preliminary coughs, started with a shattering roar that shook the plane. I tried the control stick and swung the guns in an arc to see they were working. Before I knew it we were moving.

The red lights slipped by as we bumped along the perimeter and in what seemed seconds, S for Sugar was rattling down the runway. Even in daylight it is difficult to tell when a plane leaves the ground; in the darkness of night it is completely impossible, so for the rear gunner there was always that feeling of suspense that the plane had not lifted and perhaps was rushing to its destruction.

We did a circuit of the station and I saw the perimeter lights twinkle. The navigator gave a course and we were on our way.

As on previous trips all the work and conversation was shared between the navigator and the Skipper. The rest of us, particularly the two gunners, sat there, listening, and looked out into the darkness. I know I had no clear conception of what was expected of me, nor, as I found out afterwards, did Kiwi.

We heard Ninnes say, 'Crossing coast', and then later 'Enemy coast coming up,' disquieting words that conveyed but little to me sitting with my back to the engines. 'Crossing enemy coast,' said our navigator. So dark was the night, sea and land merged into one indistinguishable black mass. Looking down trying to pick some line of demarcation I suddenly saw a line of bright flashes twinkling below. Almost immediately dead astern a series of dark red flashes appeared. The lights twinkled again and the flashes danced a little bit closer.

Almost in embarrassment I heard my voice say in the earphones, 'Think there's flak behind us.' At the word 'flak', our pilot who was evidently more tee'd up on such matters, acted with creditable alacrity and shoved the plane into a steep dive. Above us, the vicious bracket of three danced and he said tersely, 'Haven't you been told to report height and position of flak immediately?' I did not answer and in an uneasy silence we flew towards our target.

'Half an hour TOT, Skipper. The height is only fifteen thousand feet; you will have to push her if we are going to get to eighteen thousand,' reported our navigator.

'I've been pushing her ever since we got over the coast,' replied Snowden, 'but she's not making it. May be able to get to sixteen thousand.'

'Briefing said eighteen thousand,' replied Ninnes.

'I know that,' said our pilot, 'but unless we get the crew out to push her we'll be damned lucky to get to sixteen thousand.'

God or someone rode with us in the sky over the Third Reich that night for never was a crew less fitted to defy the might and cunning of Hitler. Like tourists on a sightseeing trip the gunners gazed in wonder as the flak curved gracefully skywards and the searchlights probed, trying to catch an unwary adventurer in their silvery threads. What added to the armchair ride of S for Sugar, although we didn't know it then, was that we had a first-class navigator. We had been routed to miss bad flak areas, but less fortunate crews who wandered from the path attracted Guy Fawkes displays that caught our attention. If this was any indication, there were a lot of sprog navigators flying that night.

Sitting in my rear turret I was at a disadvantage as comments came to my ears, since I could see only to the rear and about forty-five degrees to either side. I spent half of my time swivelling the turret in an endeavour to look at the matters under discussion.

Our navigator said, 'Ten minutes TOT'. I was still trying to work this out when Kiwi asked, 'What's TOT?'

'Time On Target, you clot', answered Ninnes. 'Don't they teach you blokes anything?'

Then Kiwi said, 'Jesus, look at those searchlights and flak. Have we got to go in there?'

These ominous words sent a creepy feeling up and down my spine. It would be hard to describe the next ten minutes as we came into the defence perimeter. The sky seemed to turn into a sea of molten flame. How it was possible to live in this inferno I did not know. S for Sugar was buffeted wildly and shook like a sapling in a storm. Flashes of light mushroomed for a few seconds and plummeted downwards, marking the passing of a plane and crew.

Strangely enough, no noise came to our ears while we rode this man-made storm except the navigator's voice giving calm and precise directions. 'Tracking in on target,' he said. 'Left, left, steady. Right, steady, hold it, steady, bomb doors open, bombs away.'

The plane, released from its four thousand pound load,[3] seemed to leap with joy. Snowden, as per instructions, held the plane straight and steady for twenty seconds after the bombs had gone so that the camera would operate. Then he said, 'Let's get out of this place.'

As we did a tight diving turn I had a full view of the destruction down below. Fires seemed to be burning everywhere. To my inexperienced eyes, it looked as though the entire city was alight. For a while I thought of the women and children cowering there, many of them possibly enveloped in this holocaust. Then a terrific whoomph which nearly threw the plane on its back brought me back to reality. 'Bugger them', I thought in angry self-justification, 'they have brought this on themselves.'

Once clear of the city the flak fell away. This should have been a sign for extra caution as fighters rarely operated in flak. However, I continued to spoil my night vision by watching the fires drop slowly behind. The navigator was applying himself to plotting our return course and a constant stream of instructions and alterations ensued between him and the pilot. Now and then bright horizontal lines of light would break the darkness. These often culminated in an orange flash. Kiwi said, 'They must be tracer from fighters.'

Combats seemed to be going on all around us but we flew serenely on. After what seemed like an age, our navigator said, 'Enemy coast coming up.' Crossing it we ran into some desultory but inaccurate fire which soon fell behind.

By this time the excitement and concentration of the trip was beginning to take its toll. I found the rocking of my turret extremely comforting, then over the intercom came a weary yawn.

'Hey, you blokes, don't go to sleep; keep your eyes peeled,' said the Skipper. As fighters were known to chase bombers back over the Channel, the reproof was justified.

As we came back over the station, the skies were already full of orbiting fellow-travellers. Someone was calling for an immediate landing and was given a green. Control gave us a height and we flew a circuit for forty-five minutes. Feeling that I had faithfully carried out my watch-dog duties, I slumbered peacefully, to be awakened by the bump of wheels as we touched down. Dawn had already broken as we came back to flight. Someone said, 'You want a rum?' This, I found, was a RAF custom to loosen the tongues of crews at interrogation.

The gunners had not been informed of the intention of this briefing and wondered what all the questions of a pimply-faced intelligence officer meant. If we had known he was trying to get as much information on defence establishments in enemy territory and other general information as he could we might have been of some assistance, but as one of the boys stated afterwards, 'I thought the bastard was checking up to see if I'd done my job.'

With the rum working on empty stomachs there was soon a babble of chatter and a little line-slinging. Someone said, 'we had four combats but lost them every time'. Another said, 'we had three'. We couldn't rightly claim any, but away from our crew, Kiwi and I modestly claimed two. What with the grog and the release from eight hours of anxiety the boys certainly let themselves go. Our jubilation was short-lived when it was rumoured three Wimpys had not returned. This started a search around the crowded room to see if any of our mob was missing.

The Wingco stopped speculation by announcing three planes had not returned, that a signal had come through stating one had made a forced landing just over the coast and all the crew were safe, but there was no news of the other two.

'What were the crews, sir?' There was a complete silence as he paused as though weighing the question. 'The two that are missing are A for Apple and J for Johnny. C for Charlie is safe,' he said.

Kiwi, who was standing beside me, said, 'Christ, Aub was in J for Johnny.'

We waited at the flight until we were told if we didn't catch the bus, we would have to walk back to the mess. At breakfast we learnt that the reward for our night's flight was two eggs. I have never been partial to cackleberries so couldn't say that I was impressed. The English boys seemed to think that this was a more than adequate compensation.[4] The discussion centred on the loss of J for Johnny and the op in general. Some of them had had exceptionally rough trips, possibly because they strayed off course and ran into the flak areas.

It did not seem possible that Aub had gone. In those early days we were willing to grasp at straws. We conveniently forgot about those plummeting comets that fell earthwards, trailing their golden tails. The lively little Gunner couldn't be dead. He would have bailed out before they went down or perhaps they had ditched or had landed somewhere else, with damage to their wireless. We sought every reason rather than admit that he was dead. We had no yardstick to measure whether it was a good or bad trip but everyone agreed the chances of surviving thirty such trips did not look particularly bright.

At midday we were awakened by orderlies and the Tannoy announced special lunch times for navigators, which didn't mean a thing until Snowden said, 'Looks as though we're dicing tonight. Ninnes has gone to the special briefing.'

'Christ!' exclaimed Kiwi. 'Not again tonight! I haven't got my blood pressure under control from last night's do!'

Ninnes came back and said, 'It's on all right.'

Bomber Command was evidently taking advantage of the good weather. The fact that the crew's nerves might be in a jangle didn't mean a thing. Briefing was substantially the same, only the Wingco prefaced it by complaining photographic reconnaissance had revealed that bomb results were poor. Only approximately twenty per cent of hits had been registered on the target area.

Someone said, 'Balls!' and that was the consensus of opinion. The memory of that inferno of flame below was still vivid in our minds. The Wingco's statement didn't seem to tie in with the facts. He let the angry murmur of dissent die down, then said, 'It's essential that this objective be destroyed. The target is the same again.'

The curtain fell apart and there, stretched across the map were the same red indicator tapes. Target for the night is rarely received in silence. There is always the inveterate wit who has something to say, the same buzz of comment, but today there was complete silence as the crews gazed at this identical track. They felt they were having one put over them. It didn't seem possible they had endured so much – two crews lost with another plane written off – for such lousy results.

Again the leaders went through their paces. When briefing was finished, our gunnery leader called us together. Before he had time to open his mouth Blondie said, 'Keep your bloody eyes open and don't go to sleep.' This raised our sunken morale a little. He was nonplussed for a second. 'I'll see you in the morning – that's if you get back, Henschell,' he said.

When we were going out Blondie growled, 'One day I'll bomp that bastard.'

This op was almost a repetition of the first. The same uneasy feeling as we took off. The flak came up. This time we reported it. Ninnes plotted his competent course as flak and searchlights reached up to the left and right to pluck the off-course stragglers from the sky. Bright lights blossomed and faded. Over the target the great cones of searchlights, twenty to thirty lights bonded together in one great pillar, probed and searched. The flak was worse, if anything, than on the previous night but we rode through it, dropped our load and flew a virtually straight and level course home. Although we saw the horizontal flare and tracer around us indicating aerial battles, we never sighted a fighter and finally landed at base without trouble.

After briefing, we learnt another two bombers had not returned but, as they were two crews unknown to us, the impact was only slight.

Kiwi said, 'These ops don't seem to be too bloody bad. When I first saw that flak I didn't think you could live in it but now I think all we need is a bit of luck.'

Bearding Hitler in his den successfully two nights running had engendered some confidence and hope.[5]

CHAPTER EIGHT

Mac was our unofficial meteorologist. At the first sign of daylight he would be up, peering through the blackout curtains. If the weather was lousy he would report it with a note of cheerfulness. If it was clear he would declare mournfully, 'Not a bloody cloud; looks like we'll be dicing again tonight.'

When we awoke the next morning Mac reported overcast sky and rain. This drizzle increased in intensity later in the day and washed out all thought of operations. That night a pleasant holiday feeling prevailed. No ops coupled with the fact that most of the crews had successfully completed two do's in three nights started a series of sessions in the mess, which as the night wore on and the grog took effect, gradually amalgamated all the crew into a happy singing mob. Snowden and Ninnes retired early, but Williams, Jones, Kiwi and myself kicked on well into the night.

The following day, Mac glumly reported the rain had gone and prophesied it would be on again. This proved true, because just before lunch the Tannoy brassily announced a special navigator's lunch time. That afternoon, before the main briefing, Williams went to make a phone call to his wife and found the mess telephone with a neat chain and lock on it. Thus we learnt the station was completely cut off from the outer world.

At briefing, in addition to the Groupy and Wingco, was a middle-aged florid officer with bags of rings who was finally pin-pointed as the Group Air Vice-Marshal. An English pilot called Granger, with twenty ops to his credit, remarked, 'I don't like the look of this. These bloody AVMs mean a lousy target.'

The Groupy introduced our distinguished visitor, who informed us he had come along to briefing because this was a special do. At a sign the Wingco drew back the curtains and there we saw the tape running through the heart of Germany. Someone said, 'Cologne? Gee, that stinks!'

The Wingco then took up the briefing. He explained that this was a momentous occasion: tonight history was being made – Bomber Command was going to launch the first thousand plane raid on Germany.[1]

Someone raised a laugh by enquiring if they were going to use Ansons (a twin-engined plane used for training).

Casting a withering glance in the direction of the interjector, he continued, 'Every Group is to take part and every available kite is to fly. Your bomb-load will be mainly incendiaries and because of the distance and weight of the bombs to be carried there will be only a small petrol safety margin. Navigators will have to be on their toes and evasive action will have to be cut to a minimum. The whole operation is scheduled to be carried out in ninety minutes. This will necessitate careful timing, so see that you arrive over your target in your allotted time.'

A voice from behind said, 'Christ! A thousand bombers in ninety minutes! What a schemozzle.'[2]

The Wingco gave some details. There would be approximately a hundred heavies, that is, the new four-engined Halifaxes. The balance of this mighty air armada was to be composed of Wellingtons, Whitleys, Hampdens and any other kite that could go the distance.[3]

'Might be worse,' said a Canadian pilot. 'We could be in Hampdens.'

The squadron, the Wingco continued, was to go in at eighteen thousand feet; the attack was to start at 1 am and finish at 2.30. The navigators had their attack times and heights.

'Eighteen thousand!' said one pilot. 'My old bomb will be lucky to hit fourteen.'

On the way out in the bus Snowden said, 'I don't like this bomb-load. It's five hundred pounds up on the last two do's. We'll be lucky to get to sixteen thousand ourselves tonight.'

'Seventeen thousand, five hundred,' said Ninnes precisely.

'I know it is,' said Snowden, 'but I'm telling you we won't be able to bloody-well make it.'

His use of the great Australian adjective for the first time was a sign our pilot was reaching maturity. In fact, it was one of the few times I ever heard him swear.

The last of the twilight still hung over England as we climbed into the evening, covering the drome and surrounding countryside in a soft translucent haze that gradually deepened as we crossed the coast and started to climb. Gradually the sea and the sky merged and the stars twinkled dimly as S for Sugar strained mightily like a weight-lifter trying to do the impossible. The engines beat a frenzied tune, the wings fluttered, the whole plane shuddered.

'Enemy coast coming up,' and almost in the same breath a whoomph of shells beneath us indicated that the enemy gunners were on their toes. Normally Snowden would have dropped the nose and dived a few hundred feet to throw the predictors off their scent, but tonight, conscientiously following instructions, he continued his climb. Strangely enough the gunners, anticipating a change of course, dropped the next bracket below and before they could correct, we were out of range.

On this night the Germans did not lack for targets and they must have looked at the radar screens in amazement as the bombers streamed across their frontier.

Our plane shook and vibrated as she struggled to get height, but like a pregnant dachshund the ironmongery in her belly dragged her earthwards. Petrol is consumed, but a bomb-load is with a plane until it is dropped. Added to this, a second and more serious problem intervened, for the overloaded plane was unable to get the speed necessary to reach the target on the stipulated time.

For some time after crossing the enemy coast the navigator and the pilot had engaged in a near-argument, with the former calling for more height and speed and Snowden tersely stating he was getting every foot and ounce of speed out of the plane. This finally culminated in Ninnes declaring that if this continued we would be twenty minutes late on the target. No pilot likes to have his flying ability questioned and Snowden was near to exploding when he retorted, 'I'm doing the best I can, navigator, so get off my back. I can't help it if we're twenty minutes late and three thousand feet out. This kite is flat out and I'm doing my best.'

Ninnes said, 'Sorry, Skipper. I know you're doing your best.'

As we vibrated our uneasy way across the heavens the flak arose in its deadly splendour on all sides as sprog pilots blundered off-course to run into the dangerous areas. How many were lost in this way would be hard to say.

We came to Cologne twenty minutes late and three thousand feet short of altitude. In the glare of the searchlights planes flittered like moths and the sky was a mass of smoke and flame. Strangely enough, the bulk of the Jerry hate seemed to be bursting well above us. The reason for this was suddenly discovered by Kiwi who exclaimed, 'Gawd! The heavies are up there, that's why the flak's so high.'

Williams asked, 'What about when they bomb?'

Jonesy said, 'Let's drop our bloody bombs and get out of here,' but sure and steady our navigator's voice came over the intercom, 'Target coming up, left, left, steady.'

The air reeked of cordite and gunpowder. S for Sugar lurched like a drunken sailor in the grip of shell-blast and the slip-streams of other late-comers like ourselves.

'Right a little', said Nav.

'Drop the bloody things,' I said silently.

Then those blessed words, 'Bombs away.' A cone of light groped for us but Snowden steadfastly held the plane on that straight course for twenty seconds to let the camera take its picture, then as the great pillar of light touched the port wing, he swerved violently to starboard. Suddenly around us like falling raindrops dropped the thousands of incendiaries as the heavies five thousand feet above let their loads go. Close behind, the sky was suddenly lit by a brilliant flash as a bomber, hit by the falling bombs, exploded. High above, crippled by flak, a heavy plummeted, slowly at first, then with ever-increasing momentum towards the earth.

Our guardian angels surely rode with us that night for the sky seemed to be filled with burning planes. As we turned to battle our way home, Cologne burned, its fires fed by thousands of incendiaries and burning bombers that fell to help the fires, as though avenging the crews that died in them.

Then, like hawks loosed on a flock of pigeons, the German fighters climbed to wreak their hate on the planes that had devastated their city and on the untrained and inexperienced crews. Horizontal tracer and gunfire filled the night as the shaken crews battled for home. We seemed to bear charmed lives, for although continuous combats were going on all around us, nothing came our way.

A hundred miles from the target, I was admiring the glow of the fires when it happened. A stream of white-hot ingots seemed to suddenly materialise out of the night from the port quarter and fly straight at me. I can honestly say I never saw the fighter and it didn't conform to the tactics I had been taught. In that split second between surprise, fright and panic, I rose to the occasion and bellowed, 'Turn port, go!'. The pilot, already alerted by the crash and the flight of tracer, obediently threw the plane to the left which meant we flew straight into the path of the attacking fighter.

For one brief moment it looked as though he would crash into us and I felt that I could have touched the black shadow as it banked violently by us. My correct order should have been, 'Turn starboard!' Perhaps I fluked the right order! Perhaps the close shave our attacker had from a collision so frightened him he flew home and changed his pants. Or perhaps he, like us, was a sprog and being only human decided to call it a night. Anyway he did not attack again.[4]

After the panic was over the Skipper checked all crew and found nobody had been hit. Jonesy shoved his head into the astrodome, reported damage to the port wing but the motor seemed OK. If ever there was an alert-eyed gunner on the rest of the way home, it was me.

Going over the enemy coast the flak flickered and the search-lights probed. Over the dark sea I reported numerous flares rising from the water.

'Looks like someone in the drink,' said Williams.

'Judging by the flares half the bloody air force is in the North Sea,' commented Kiwi.

Just as we reached the English coast the port motor started to go on the blink. Over base, Snowden asked for an urgent landing. We were told to orbit as there were more urgent cases than ours. Finally, just as things were looking desperate we were given the okay from control and came in with five minutes' petrol left and three massive holes in our port wing.

Our losses that night were five planes with roughly forty per cent of the remainder unserviceable. Amongst the missing crews were Drake and the little skinny bloke from Western Australia. I remember asking what was the latest a plane could expect to make base. 'Five minutes,' said an officer.

Kiwi and I went outside and strained our ears for the drone of returning planes. The five minutes came and went, and with heavy hearts we climbed aboard the bus for the mess.

The ground crew took this mass of planes and men to their hearts even more than aircrew. Without a doubt these under-paid, over-worked men, with none of the glamour or perks that went to fliers, played a major part in the final victory. Without this untiring work, endless servicing and loyalty of the erks, the air force would have soon ground to a stop.

It was a glum breakfast. Thirty flying mates had gone and everyone had a tale to tell of combats and danger. How many planes were lost that night we never knew, but rumours persisted for months that over two hundred and fifty planes had been lost on this operation.

It was stated Air Sea Rescue had been completely swamped and were not able to cope with the special emergency of dozens of aircraft either damaged or out of petrol that had had to ditch. Remembering the forlorn rockets that arose from the inhospitable North Sea, we thought of the unfortunates either in rubber dinghies or struggling in the icy grip of this grey waste.

Afterwards, we went across to the huts of the two missing crews to see if there was any further news. Three officers were piling belongings on a bed. 'What the hell's going on here?', Kiwi demanded.

'We're the Committee of Adjustment', said a sad-eyed individual.

'What's that?'

'We look after the deceased's belongings.'

At this, silence fell over the hut. That statement, 'We look after the deceased's belongings,' had a terrible finality. It was hard to believe that only yesterday these two had laughed and joked.[5]

CHAPTER NINE

I had a horrible feeling of guilt. They say conscience makes cowards of us all. I could not get out of my mind that I had given a wrong order the previous night. It was only a miracle my belongings were not being checked too. What if there was an enquiry? I had given an order; 'Turn port', and yet all the damage was on the port wing. Added to this was the disquieting thought that I was not competent to do my job. What was the good of having a highly trained efficient crew if the rear gunner was a drongo? I felt with a certainty this is where the others had failed; that their first sudden attack had been their last.

I knew there was a certain uneasiness amongst the crew. Kiwi voiced this as we were having a shower by asking, 'Did you see that Jerry before he attacked last night, Johnny?'

'Only a second or two before he opened fire,' I replied.

After an uncomfortable pause he asked, 'Do you reckon you gave the right order?'

'Of course I bloody well did,' I declared, 'and if you think you can do better you can take my place.'

'Don't get your shirt off, I was only asking.'

'You can go and get fugged,' I said with feigned indignation, and walked out.

I have always felt attack is the best form of defence so, as we were going in to lunch with the crew I said, 'Kiwi wants to know if I gave the right order last night. What do you boys think?'

Ninnes replied, 'Well, we're all here. Must have been fairly right.'

'I've been giving it some thought, but I can't make out if the attack came from your starboard how he came to pepper our port wing and then apparently broke to port,' said Snowden.

'I'm buggered if I know. Perhaps he was a sprog, too.'

This had the effect of clearing the air, and I found that my fears with regard to an enquiry were unfounded as the squadron had so much on its hands with the number of unserviceable planes that not a question was asked. Because the station was virtually immobilised through losses and damage we were all given forty-eight hours' leave.

Though insufficient to take us to London, this still placed Norwich within our reach so our crew, together with most of the squadron, caught a local train.

There was little talk as we chugged through the flat countryside. It was as if I could feel that fighter's breath down my neck as he swept by, only a few feet away from us just a few hours before. Three of our crowd gone. It was a miracle Kiwi and I hadn't joined them.

On arrival at Norwich we booked our beds in the local Lions Club and started the inevitable pub crawl. After a few drinks with us, Williams, Snowden and Ninnes, who had little accord with our drinking habits, decided to see a show.

Later in the evening, as we were getting well and truly on the way, Mac broached the subject that was at the back of our minds. 'We might as well get blind,' he said. 'It'll be the last chance some of us will get.'

'Balls,' said Blondie. 'I reckon I'll be around for a long while.'

'That's what Gunner and the other two thought last week,' countered Mac; 'three out of twelve is twenty-five per cent in four operations. On that average there won't be any of us left in another twelve.'

'Mac's right,' said Hally. 'I don't like our chances. The whole bloody trouble is that while they train pilots, navigators and wireless operators, they don't give a damn about gunners. What training have we had? None of us had more than ten hours' flying up before we joined the squadron. What the RAF hasn't woken up to is when a plane is attacked it's completely in the charge of the rear gunner. He's the bloke who gives the orders and tells the pilot what to do. Why, it's only a miracle that Johnny and Kiwi didn't go last night too. That would have been five out of twelve.'

Kiwi started to speak but, catching my jaundiced eye, changed his mind.

They say a drunken man speaks a sober man's mind, so I said, 'I'll admit I didn't see the Jerry until he opened fire. To tell the truth the attack was virtually over before I could say anything. This bloke certainly didn't conform to all the bullsh I learnt at the training schools. I agree with Mac; we're dead ducks unless we can smarten ourselves up.'

The grog may have helped. It swept away all pretence of reserve and false pride. We admitted we were mug gunners, and in a spot; the problem was what to do about it. During the discussion we found we all suffered from the same thing: embarrassment to say or report anything for fear of showing our ignorance.

'I think we all want a good talk with our crews to get a better understanding,' Hally declared. 'It's team-work that eventually counts.'

On the way back in the train next day, Kiwi and I had a talk with Snowden and Ninnes on our discussion. I said, 'We seem to fly like strangers and I, for one, don't like opening my mouth for fear of making a blue.'

Kiwi remarked, 'I haven't said a dozen words in the three ops.'

Snowden said, 'Could be something in what you say. Looks like we'll have to get together.'

One good result was it made us think and talk over our problems. We all agreed it was obvious that night-fighter tactics were completely different from what we had been taught and that night-fighters obviously stalked their victims and then moved in for a quick kill. The only protection against this was constant vigilance.

Another advantage was we all openly discussed our greenness with the rest of our crews, which had the effect of overcoming the initial barriers of silence that had ridden with us on operations. This in turn started to develop the first signs of a good team spirit that was necessary for survival. Previously I considered that, apart from the navigator and pilot, we had been virtually flying as separate units, but now these talks were helping to weld us into a crew. It was stated that sixty per cent of mishaps occurred in the first four or five operations, so if a crew could survive this critical period, their chances of survival were greatly increased.

Another point that emerged from the discussions was, why the hell we used the nautical terms 'starboard' and 'port' in an aircraft, remembering that the gunner was sitting with his back to the pilot, so that his port was the pilot's starboard. We agreed the use of these terms was likely to lead to error because, first of all, the gunner had to think which was port and which was starboard, and having decided that, he then had to think in reverse as far as the pilot was concerned. By the time he's sorted it all out, they were all dead ducks.

Happy said, 'I don't know why they don't use "left" and "right".'

It was Ninnes who came up with a solution. He asked, 'Why don't we treat the plane as a clock; make the nose twelve o'clock and the tail six? Thus the right wing would be three and the left wing nine, so that a plane coming in, say, on the gunner's left quarter, could be quickly placed at four or five o'clock and, if dead astern, at six o'clock.'[1]

The gunners discussed this new plan and declared it to be a good one. They in turn talked it over with the pilots who agreed it was much better than the old patter that must have been born in the days of the First World War.

We referred it to our gunnery leader, who said he felt sure the Wingco would not agree, but said he would refer it to our headquarters. The CO, who by this time had 'had' gunners in general and us in particular, jumped on it with both feet.

But Hally said, 'Who the hell's going to know what orders we give? I reckon this is easy. I'm going to talk my crew into using it; it saves those precious seconds that are the difference between copping the chop and getting home.'

Our crew conferred. Nav was for it. Snowden was uncertain. He had the Englishman's ingrained dislike of going against authority.

Kiwi's bright suggestion that we take the kite out for a training flight and try out both systems was killed when the navigators were called to an early meal. This meant it was on again and all planes would be grounded while they were got ready for the night's op.

This called for some fast decisions. Ninnes said, 'I reckon we'd better decide. The easiest way would be to take a vote on it. How about you, Johnny?'

'New one,' I said. 'Simple and easy. We can give it a try as we're going across the sea to get used to it.'

'How about you, Kiwi?'

'I'll go with Johnny – he's the bloke that cops most of the attacks.'

Jones voted with the gunners. The second pilot said, 'I think it's a matter for our captain.'

'I don't intend voting on my own idea, but I reckon we should follow the gunners,' said Ninnes.

Snowden said, 'You know I stick for regulations, but I'm out-voted by my crew and will abide by the vote. Let's try it going out. I want to live, too!'

There were only eight crews at briefing, this being the maximum number of planes the squadron could muster. The target was Bremen; this, the briefing officer explained, being selected as an easy target. The lights were switched off and the epidiascope[2] became the only illumination. The met officer gave the weather forecast, a high-pressure system over the Midlands which could mean fog on our return.

An aerial photograph of our target was projected onto the screen. They say Bremen is the second port of Germany. As I looked at the clustered buildings, the mass of streets, I thought fleetingly of the unsuspecting citizens and women and babies who would die that night. This thought passed quickly as I remembered London, Coventry, Rotterdam and the French refugees strafed on the roads. I saw the groping searchlights, the flak, the fighters who would rise to pluck their percentage of bombers from the sky.

In dozens of rooms such as this throughout England, hundreds of eyes would be looking at this self-same photograph; twenty-five bombers would mean one hundred and fifty pairs of eyes would not see the sun rise in the morning.

The voice droned on: there was information for pilots, navigators and wireless operators. The gunners sat in silence. 'We may as well be back in the mess for all the bloody notice they take of us,' Blondie remarked.

As we careered down the runway and took off into the darkening evening, a new spirit was evident in the plane. Gone were the awkward, strained silences of previous ops. The calls from each crew member were clear and alert. Kiwi reported flak ahead just as Ninnes said, 'Enemy coast coming up,' and almost simultaneously, 'Searchlights at eleven o'clock.'

Down below, over what should have been the sea, I saw red lights twinkle maliciously. At ten thousand feet it meant seven seconds before those hurtling trajectories burst. 'Flak at seven o'clock,' I reported.

Our pilot immediately dropped the nose into a sharp dive and bursting flak jolted the plane, but as the main burst was upwards we missed the full effects of the explosion.

'Where's that flak coming from?' Ninnes asked. 'We're not over land yet.'

Below, the lights twinkled again, and dead astern a light blossomed suddenly, illuminating the sky and sea for the duration of its death-sentence descent. It was then I saw the flak-ship well out from shore – a deadly trap to catch the unwary.

Kiwi said, 'I think I see the target ahead.'

'That would be it,' said Ninnes. 'Six minutes to target.'

'Christ,' said Kiwi, 'do they call this an easy target? Look at that bloody flak.'

I felt the usual creep of hair on my neck; the rear gunner having no front view could only listen to these disturbing remarks.

'Going in to target,' said the pilot and then we were in a maelstrom of flak, searchlights and bombs. It always baffled me how you could live through such violence. The only conclusion was that there was so much air that it took a lot of shells to fill it. Cordite and smoke filled the plane.

'Bomb-doors open.' Then, after an eternity, 'Bombs away!'

Snowden threw the plane into a steep turn as we turned for our run out, and I saw the nightmarish glare of fires and explosions. A search-light gripped us for a second but, with a vigorous flick of its tail, S for Sugar slipped from its grasp. Gradually the lights and flak lessened and we were out. Glowing behind us arose the flames of the bombed city.

From this supposedly easy op two sprog crews, both on their first flight, failed to return. They had come to the squadron only fourteen days before.

Next day a special parade was called and the CO announced that we had a new ally, for that morning Hitler's Panzer divisions had smashed into Russia. He made it clear that he didn't have a very high opinion of the Russians and their fighting abilities. I thought Happy would burst a blood-vessel. 'Listen to that one-eyed, bird-brained bastard,' he declared. 'If brains were dynamite he wouldn't have enough to blow his cap off.'[3]

Despite the CO's lukewarm acceptance of our new fighting partner, we shared Happy's view that it was the only bright bit of news that had come from the fighting front for many a long day. Happy pointed out that the all-conquering Napoleon had fallen on his face over a similar project a hundred years before. In addition, anything that split the Nazi's aerial fighting strength was something our way.

Two nights later it was on again and Jonesy complained bitterly it was time they gave him a break. Met reported that fog would develop just after we left, but would clear by the time we returned. If not, we were to divert to an aerodrome in the north-east. We would be advised of these locations later.

As we flew over the coast, the plane seemed to vibrate more than usual and the climb seemed less steady. Finally, Snowden said, 'I don't like the look of the port engine. The pressure seems to be down.'

Approaching the enemy coast it was evident something was wrong.

We had only reached eight thousand feet instead of the anticipated ten; not that a thousand or two was unusual in this worn-out kite, but we copped quite a pasting going on.

Snowden reported the pressure was falling rapidly and, after a discussion with our second dickey Williams, a decision was reached that we return. This was not an easy decision on the part of our pilot because he would have to bear the brunt of any enquiry on our return. Coming back we again copped a pasting, for in addition to the wham of the heavy stuff we were bashed by light flak.

S for Sugar was virtually flying on one engine, but with her nose down and her tail up we soon out-distanced the unwelcome attentions of the coastal defenders.

Coming back over our coast we crossed a northbound convoy and, despite Jonesy firing the colours of the day, those itchy-fingered coots must have decided any plane coming in from the east could have nothing but bad intentions, and they got stuck into us.

To add to our problems, Jonesy then reported base was out and we had divert to a place called Claxstone. Williams said he knew the place; it was headquarters for 4 Group. As we were scheduled to arrive by approximately 9.30, this conjured up hopeful thoughts of frivolity, for headquarters were noted for their sumptuous surroundings and luxurious appointments.[4]

CHAPTER TEN

We were not disappointed. The sergeants' mess was a beauty; it had an entrance like Claridge's and inside was even more inviting. A palatial reading room with comfortable chairs stretched to the right. From the left came the click of billiard balls. Jonesy had a look and said, 'Jesus, four billiard tables. This is like the Union Club. What a bloody difference to our mangy mess.' [1]

Our arrival in our awkward flying boots carrying our gear caused a furore, and by the surprised and annoyed looks that came our way it was evident airmen arrayed in such war-like accoutrements were not regular visitors. We asked for the president of the mess and, after a period, a fat, red-faced W/O came bustling up. Snowden explained that we had been forced to return from an op and because our own station was closed, we had been diverted. He requested we be allowed to have a drink at the bar.

The W/O said he knew we were coming, but would have to find out first if it was okay for us to go into the bar, and left us standing like shags on a rock. [2] After a period, he returned and told us he had been unable to contact the president and until he received his permission he was sorry we would not be able to have a drink.

'But we're sergeants,' I replied, adding tactlessly, 'fighting ones at that.'

The W/O was adamant. We could, if we wished, have supper.

'But I want a drink,' Kiwi protested.

'I'm sorry,' said our interrogator, 'but we have our rules. Perhaps after you've had supper everything will be all right.'

Calling the steward, he instructed him to take us into the dining-room. This was a surprise packet, too. There were separate tables covered by tablecloths and tastefully decorated with bowls of flowers. Jonesy stared at the decorations in disbelief. 'Different from our trestles. These bludgers don't half do themselves well.'

The supercilious orderly took pains to let us know that supper had been served over half an hour or more. Snowden coldly advised him we had been sent in by the W/O. We were then informed we could have tea and sandwiches.

'Gawd, could I do a grog,' moaned Kiwi. 'Wonder if they've found that bloody president yet.'

There was quite a delay and finally the sandwiches and tea were brought in. The sandwiches were tastefully laid out on a cut lettuce dressing. It was the first time I had seen lettuce in England as salads were made with cabbage, so after we had eaten the sandwiches we ate the lettuce. When the orderly returned he stared at the empty plates.

'Hey, where's the lettuce?' he demanded.

'We ate it,' said Kiwi.

This shook him to the core. At this shameless confession he staggered off and we heard him say to a fellow orderly, 'They ate the dressing!'

'Christ, you'd think we'd eaten my bloody grandmother,' said Kiwi. 'Now for that grog.'

When we trooped out we were met by a red-faced flight sergeant who said the bar was closed.

'Well, you can stick your beer,' said Kiwi. 'It's unfortunate you bludgers don't know there's a war on.'

Snowden said in his precise English voice, 'I presume you can offer us a bed; or do we sleep on the parade ground?'

The flight, obviously embarrassed, called a grey-haired orderly who was standing by and said, 'Show these sergeants to their rooms, will you please, LAC.'

'Rooms?' said Jones.

'This way, please,' said the orderly, and led us along a wide gleaming corridor. The three rooms were a revelation. At least twelve feet by ten, they contained two beds with sheets and pillow-cases, built-in wardrobes and two tasteful writing desks.

The orderly who was arranging the blackout curtains, turned and said, 'What planes do you boys fly?'

'Wellingtons, Pop,' replied Kiwi.

'Were you on a raid tonight?' he asked.

'Yes, but we only got as far as the enemy coast and developed engine trouble and had to return.' Then, recalling our inhospitable treatment in the mess, demanded, 'Why couldn't we get a drink? Do these blokes think we're suffering from leprosy or something?'

'I couldn't say,' replied the orderly. Then, with a furtive look, he pulled a parcel from his tunic. 'But if you and your Aussie friend would like to have a drink on behalf of myself and the bar stewards we would be only too pleased.' I took the parcel from him, unwrapped it and found a three-quarter full bottle of Johnnie Walker.[3]

'I hope you'll be discreet, please,' he continued, 'as my friends and I could get into serious trouble should the higher authorities become aware of this gift.'

We looked at the bottle and the kindly donor in amazement.

'You bloody beaut,' said Kiwi. 'Don't you worry, we'll eat the bottle if necessary. Will you have one with us?'

'No, thanks,' he replied and, offering us his hand, said, 'Good luck, boys, we appreciate what you are doing for us.'

After he was gone, we sat down and looked at the Scotch and all Kiwi could say was, 'Well, I'll be buggered.'

After some discussion, we decided to ask Jonesy and Williams in and leave Snowden and Ninnes out. Neither were drinkers and both were liable to have an attack of conscience. We told the other two we had snitched it as we were coming out of the dining-room. They were so astonished they never questioned this most improbable explanation.

It was a happy little interlude. There wasn't enough to make us full but Jonesy, who wasn't a particularly good drinker, became convulsed with merriment and subsided into uncontrollable laughter every now and then and had to have a sheet stuffed in his mouth to quieten his gurgles.

Next morning the old boy came in with a cup of morning tea and carried off the evidence. Breakfast was served by smart WAAFs and we had the choice of an excellent menu. Ninnes remarked that the high life was evidently a bit too much as we all looked a bit fagged.

Kiwi, who never let any grass grow under his feet, arranged a date for the evening with the little blonde WAAF who was serving us – if we were still there – and she also promised to arrange a comrade for me. This put a new complexion on our stay, so that we prayed the fog would hold, or the port motor would require lengthy attention. A flight sergeant at our table said, 'You may be a bit stiff. That's the chief's girl you've dated.'[4]

We were informed that mechanics were testing our engines. It was our contention they worked overtime, for by 11 o'clock the fog had cleared and by midday we were told both motors were running normally and we would be able to take off immediately. So we didn't have a chance of seeing what the decision would be when we fronted the bar at lunch-time, nor what these hard-fighting boys ate for lunch.

When we arrived back at the station Snowden and Williams were immediately summoned for an interview with the Wingco. We never heard what actually happened, but in the afternoon when they arrived back, Snowden was white with anger. Williams said, 'Gawd, was that a bawling-out!'

We later found the Wingco had accused them of shirking their duty and failing to press the attack in the true traditions of the RAF. To Snowden's protests that the pressure had fallen on the port motor, he had countered that the chief mechanic at Claxstone had stated the engine had reacted normally. What apparently wasn't taken into consideration was that these worthies had worked on the engine for over four hours. The Wingco warned that should this happen again they would be both charged with LMF. This was the first time that we heard those dread initials, which we found stood for 'lack of moral fibre'. An NCO charged with this offence could be completely stripped of his rank and dismissed in disgrace from aircrew.[5]

Snowden said very little about this interview, but we knew that he was deeply hurt by the unwarranted accusation.

That night in the mess we learnt an interesting point about this charge. Although non-commissioned officers could be charged with lack of moral fibre, it could not be applied to an officer. It also appears at about this time the RAF had found, through a series of incidents, there was some collusion amongst air crews, and there was definite evidence that some of them were not even crossing the enemy coast, but instead dropped their bombs in the sea and then stooged in comparative safety over the North Sea until their allocated flying time was covered, then returning with concocted stories and falsified flight plans.

Just how true this was we never knew, but shortly after this an order came out that every bomber, if not already fitted with a camera, had to have one installed and no excuses would be accepted for a crew returning without a photograph of the results of their bombing runs.

Jonesy stated that as far as he was concerned, collusion was a damned good idea and it was a pity we couldn't get some into our own crew.[6]

CHAPTER ELEVEN

Shortly after this episode, an unusual figure appeared in our flight room. He was a rather short young fellow in a blue Australian battle-jacket, the only insignia showing was an Observer's 'Flying O', commonly known as 'the flying arsehole'.

This fellow swept floors and seemed to lead a quiet introspective existence. His duties appeared to lie between cleaner and general message boy. He had no signs of rank and domiciled with the ground crew, who seemed to accept him readily enough. Obviously he had been aircrew, but had suffered a terrific fall from grace. What intrigued us was that he went his unconcerned way oblivious of the inquisitive glances of fliers, particularly from the Australians.

Enquiries finally revealed he had been an observer, had been appointed to a bomber crew on another squadron, had done all his initial training, and then, after briefing for his first op, had calmly sat down and declared he wasn't going to fly, despite the pleading of his crew and the threats of his superiors.

For this, he was court-martialled and stripped of everything but his observer's insignia. If he had been a member of the RAF he would have been shot. The Australian, New Zealand and Canadian governments would not permit the shooting of aircrew for cowardice. Thus, a kind of social outcast, this little fellow did the menial tasks and went his unobtrusive way.

After a while, he blended in with the station and mixed in with the gunners, probably because they were more democratic and easy-going, and often joined us in our card and dice games as we whiled the hours away up at flight. We discovered his name was Barnes but as he never discussed any of his private business, no-one enquired into the reason why he had refused to fly, and strangely enough I never heard of any of the hard-boiled gunners, or, for that matter any aircrew, tease or deride him. Mac expressed our viewpoints in a nutshell when he said, 'I'd like to do what Barnes is doing, only I haven't got enough guts.'

Periodically, it seemed, this reluctant flyer was subjected to a brain-washing by the Wingco, who ran through the full gamut of honeyed words, promises, abuse, threats and finally complete frustration in his endeavours to convert and rehabilitate this affront to the prestige of the RAF. We understood he made frequent representations to have Barnes removed from the Squadron as he was considered bad for morale.

Probably because I was older than most of the others, and was interested in what had prompted this stubborn little fellow to make his stand, I often had a word with him and built up an accord so I could talk to him.

One night, while we were having a few beers at the local pub, I asked him straight-out why he wouldn't fly. Whether he told me the truth or not I never knew, but he stated the night before his first op, he had a most vivid dream in which he saw his plane with all its crew crash in flames and felt then, if he once flew, he would not come back.[1]

This phobia was given further impetus when his crew were all killed on their second operation. His words were grimly prophetic when he said, 'There are lots of men in the RAF who would like to do the same as I did, but they haven't got enough courage. This war won't last forever, and I will be living when thousands of the men on this station and others like it will be dead.'

As long as he was on the station, he never flew. Not long after-wards the Wingco's endeavours were rewarded, and he disappeared. We understood he had been transferred to the Tactical Airforce where, after a period, he agreed to train with a crew, did all the initial training and then, after they were briefed for their first op, repeated his act again, sitting down and refusing to fly. For this he was stripped of even his 'Flying O', and transferred to a RAF prison 'somewhere in England'.[2] I afterwards heard he had been released and, strangely enough, killed by a flying bomb in London towards the end of 1944.

The advent of Barnes had a forceful impact on Mac. If it were pos-sible, he genuinely debated his intention of refusing to fly, just like the little observer. 'He's got the right idea', he declared, 'he'll be bloody-well alive when we are either pushing up daisies or feeding the fish.' The boys listened to him with a kind of disinterested sympathy. Generally, after one of his doleful sessions, someone would tell him, 'Aw, for Christ's sake go on strike. At least we won't have to listen to your whingeing then.'

One morning, Mac arose and reported with a slight note of pleasure, that ops would be off because it was blowing half a gale. For once his predictions were wrong for, to our surprise, at midday the usual announcement of early meal times was given and it was on again.

The met boys stated that, despite the inclement weather at the station, it would improve over Germany and we could expect clear skies over the target. It was the lousiest weather we had ever flown in and the Wellington behaved like a bucking bronco from the time we took off, quivering and shaking, rising and falling in two-hundred-foot bumps, so that I spent most of my time clinging desperately to the guns to stop cracking my head on the top of the turret. As we came into the target area, a great expanse of cotton-wool covered the ground and the German gunners, secure in this all-enveloping security, kept their guns silent.

Ninnes reported, 'Should be over target now but I can't see anything.'

We stooged around for a while and then he said, 'Think we'll have to return.'

'Well, drop your bloody bombs,' said Kiwi.

'Can't do that,' he replied, 'unless we can see a worthwhile target.'

'Well, what are you going to do with them?' asked the incredulous gunner.

'Take them back, of course,' replied Ninnes. 'Those are orders.'

As the bomber stream turned for home, the fighters arose en masse, fortified with the knowledge that the bombers were still heavily laden and hindered by the prevailing headwind. They would be easy victims.

We received three attacks, but each was beaten off with timely evasive action. The last proved one dedicated bastard, and this fighter made four separate passes before he either ran out of ammunition or petrol.

On this abortive op, four planes failed to return. Hally said, 'Four kites and twenty-four crew just to bring all our bloody bombs back. It doesn't make sense.'

If possible, with the passing of time, Mac had become more doleful. He seemed to hold me responsible for the fact that he was on the squadron and would come to my bed and bleat out his fears. He was a coward, he declared. 'It's impossible for anyone to complete a tour.'

In the afternoon, Mac sat on my bed again. His voice was querulous, his jowls quivered, there were bags under his eyes and he looked more like a melancholy blood-hound than ever. 'This bloody racket,' he declared, 'is just plain suicide. I'm going to the MO to tell him I'm not going to fly again. They can classify me as LMF if they bloody-well like, but in five years' time I'll be alive, sunbaking at Bondi while the rest of this outfit's bones are bleaching somewhere in Europe. What's an LMF anyway? Did you know two weeks ago? If you told someone in Australia you had got an LMF they'd congratulate you. They'd think it was a bloody decoration. Barnes had the right idea. He had the guts to tell them he wasn't going to fly. Everyone is packing them, only they're too bloody frightened to say so.'[3]

Perhaps he was right and I knew I only had to say, 'well, go and see the MO. Tell him you are not going to fly', and he would have done it. All he wanted was someone to give him that nudge, but I was edgy and irritable. Consciously or subconsciously we felt his piking would cast a reflection on the rest of the Australians in the squadron. So I did nothing to help him.

Talking to Hally I said, 'I know I pack them while I'm out in the blackness and I feel that, although you talk tough, you do too.'

He was completely frank. 'My bloody oath I do, but I'd sooner be dead than let anyone know.'

'Supposing,' I continued, 'a man packs them a thousand times, perhaps ten thousand times more than we do. If you were in his shoes, how would you face up to it?'

'I'm buggered if I know, but if it was as bad as that I'd get off ops.'

'That's the way I think Mac is.'

'Then tell the silly bastard to give it away,' he said, 'but don't worry me about him. I've enough troubles of my own.'

I thought, 'Mac'll raise the subject again and I'll not only advise him, I'll take him up to the MO.'

We were both on the battle order that night. We sat together in silence going out in the bus. As we got out, I gave him a reassuring pat and said, 'We'll talk about it tomorrow.' I couldn't see his expression in the glow of the little blue light but he gave a sepulchral laugh and said, 'Perhaps there mightn't be any tomorrow for either of us'.

It was a hell of an op. The weather was lousy and Jerry turned it on from the time we crossed the coast and kept it up all the way to the target and back. It was seven hours of hell and suspense.

As we came back over our coast, Kiwi said, 'What a bloody night! I'm completely fugged. Will I be glad to get into bed!'

Somehow I couldn't get Mac out of my mind. 'This', I thought, 'will be the end. He'll give it away after this.'

Hally was already in when we arrived. 'What a bloody op', he said, 'I was beginning to wonder if you'd made it.'

We searched around to see who was missing. He said, 'I can't see Mac.' We stayed long after the time limit for the plane and crew to arrive. The bus waited until the occupants and driver grew impatient. After sundry tootings and irritable queries, one of them said, 'Let the silly bastards walk.' The driver called, 'Are you blokes coming?'. 'No,' replied Hally, shortly.

As we walked back, a new day was breaking. The mists were rising from the flat, grey countryside and a cold breeze from the east blew in our faces. I didn't sleep for a while, wondering and worrying how the reluctant gunner had met his end, three miles up in the blackness of the night. Fatigue finally took over and I fell into an uneasy slumber.

CHAPTER TWELVE

In late autumn we heard that some of our former course mates were operating in Halifaxes. They had done a conversion course first on Wellingtons and then on to Hallies. Bomber Command had set up a new training gunnery station centre at Skellingthorpe, Lincolnshire, which was really something. Apparently someone had awakened to the fact that sending half-baked gunners out with well-trained crews was a costly business. This, after almost three years of war!

Despite this advantage, both in training and planes, news of casualties started to come in of RAF crews battling into Germany in rapidly worsening weather conditions.

We got five days leave every six weeks. At the end of this period three crews were granted leave, including Hally, Blondie, Smithy, Kiwi and myself. Because our crew were English they all made for their families. We decided to go up to London.

There we ran into Bourke who told us ten of the gunners had completed a conversion course from Wellingtons to Halifaxes at Lichfield and were now on operations. Pascoe, Poast and Driscoll were already posted missing, presumed dead; all going in their first three ops. Due to a false alarm on a social disease scare Bourke had not yet entered the fray but said that in the last month of the training course, thirteen planes had been lost. He blamed this on the worn-out training Wimpys and poor flying conditions. 'I tell you,' he added seriously, 'it's as bad as ops.'

'Like bloody hell it is,' said Kiwi. 'We fly into Germany on those same worn-out Wimpys. You wait till you get on ops, boy, then you'll know the difference.'

One interesting bit of information was that Clarkey's crew had been amongst one of the lost training planes. They had run into a mountain top, the rear turret had broken off and, although the rest of the crew had been burnt to death, he had been miraculously saved because his turret had rolled away from the fire. Strangely enough he had suffered nothing worse than bruises which, however, gave him a good excuse for a neurosis and he was now off ops and recuperating at some hospital.

Bourke told us he had not regretted missing our special posting as they were doing intensive training and he felt they would be immeasurably better prepared than we had been.

That night, Bourke, Kiwi and myself started off with the intention of seeing a show but ended up in the inevitable pub. Later Kiwi attached himself to a brunette and disappeared into the night with the information that he would see us later. Somewhere along the line Bourke and I picked up two females. One was a little Cockney, the other a well-developed Lancashire lass. The Cockney went for Bourke, whilst the well-developed female, who was as tall as myself, found an accord with me. By the time the pubs closed we had come to a suitable arrangement. My partner stated that she wasn't going to have a knee-trembler or a do in the park, but if we liked to get a room it was on. She added she could take us to a place where such arrangements could be made.

A cab took us to a tenement-packed street. A greasy proprietor answered the door and offered no objections when we said we'd missed the last train, and could he put us and our wives up for the night.

The rooms were the usual lodging-house type with a rickety double bed, dressing table and wardrobe. Some doubts assailed me when I looked at Mary, the little Cockney, standing beside Bourke with an artificial coyness. She was, I decided, in for a surprise.

My partner was unashamedly keen. 'Come on,' she said. 'Let's get cracking. I've got to start work at 6.30 am.'

In the morning we made arrangements to meet the girls again that night, but during the afternoon ran into Hally, Blondie and Happy at the Boomerang Club. They told us that Martin and Sherwin, with their crews, had been posted missing the night after we'd left. This cast a gloom over the party, and when the pubs opened we started a session in which we finally forgot all about the girls. Later in the night, Bourke remembered our appointment, but it was too late to do anything about it. 'To tell the truth,' I said, 'I couldn't care less. In fact, I must be getting as old as I feel. I'm not as interested in women as I used to be.'

'Neither am I,' said Hally. 'They must be putting something in the food.'

This brought up the serviceman's pet subject that the food was doctored.

'That's all bullsh,' said Happy. 'It's just that you're so occupied keeping alive you haven't got any thoughts for sex.'

'I still reckon they put bromide in our food,' Blondie declared.

We arrived back at the station the next day at 5.30 pm. As soon as we reported to the guard we were told we were wanted at flight.

'What the hell do they want us for?', demanded Kiwi.

Our crew were already there when we arrived.

'What's the panic?', I asked.

'We're on tonight,' said Snowden. 'We were afraid you two mightn't get back on time. You'd better hurry up and get into your battle jackets.'

'But we weren't due back until 5.30,' Kiwi stated. 'What clot's put us on the battle order anyway?'

The pilot and observer exchanged glances. We thus learnt the Wingco had us set. It was not usual for crews to go on battle order after they'd just returned from leave, mainly because they wouldn't be very bright.

Williams expressed some doubts as to whether Wingco's parents had ever been married. It didn't alter the fact that we had to spring off our tails as briefing was in thirty minutes.

The target was Hamburg. As we flew out over the darkening countryside with that feeling of loneliness and fear I pondered Happy's words in London – we were certainly preoccupied with the thought of keeping alive. 'How long,' I wondered, 'could we keep going?' It was bad enough fighting in these antiquated, worn-out bombers, but to have a hostile station-commander made it worse.

Next day we learned the squadron was to be equipped with a new type of bomb. Previously our load had been made up of 1,000 pounders. This new dealer of destruction was a huge 4,000 pounder called a 'cookie'. It looked like an oversized 44-gallon drum and we noticed the armourers treated it with the utmost respect. It was a horrible-looking piece of ironmongery. In the afternoon the entire squadron was treated to a special lecture on the care and handling of this newcomer. When we learned that we were under no circumstances to land with it, we liked it even less. The reason for this instruction and the unreliability of this monster were indicated a few nights later when a plane carrying one blew up with a mighty roar before it even left the runway.

The terrific blast blew in windows and made a tremendous hole in the ground, but what really shook us was the rain of shrapnel, pieces of plane and other debris that were scattered over the entire squadron. Next day bits of human anatomy were found spread over an amazingly wide area. One of the boys found a thumb sticking upwards in a little shrub near one of the huts. It was a ghastly gesture. Inspection of this gruesome war souvenir provoked some macabre jokes till it was appropriated by the orderlies who were picking up pieces suitable for burial.

This illustration of the unhealthy reaction of this bomb added immeasurably to the fears of take-off. While I flew with these 'cookies' rumbling under us, that thirty-second run till we lifted off the runway seemed an eternity.[1]

With the passing of the short autumn, freezing winds blew from the North Sea across the flat countryside. The days shortened, the nights lengthened and though we had thought it cold before, we now came to realise just what cold was. To combat this new enemy we were issued with silken padded flying-suits which were donned over every possible piece of warm clothing we could lay our hands on. What the well-dressed gunner wore during this period was a thick woollen singlet, long woollen underpants, commonly known as passion killers, one or two outsized woollen sweaters and battle dress. All this was then covered by a silken padded flying suit. Our fleecy-lined boots and a pair of silken-lined gloves completed the outfit so that even Happy, with his skinny frame, looked like a fat waddling penguin. With all this flying finery aircrew, particularly the gunners, still froze. With the coming of early frosts and the first snows, we grew to dread the cold as much as the flak and fighters.

As winter progressed, flying conditions over Germany deteriorated in exact ratio – to the multitudinous dangers of operational life were added new ones: sleet, snow, and wing icing. It was rare to get good weather over targets. The met forecasts were rarely right. We afterwards found that each Group was likely to issue a different forecast as the RAF had not yet learnt to synchronise meteorological reports. Because of this, bombing became mostly a matter of guesswork. In addition, the Germans, with their colossal capacity for guile and camouflage, built satellite towns away from their cities and 'defended' these imitations with searchlights and flak and, as the bombers came droning in on the cold night air, set tremendous oil fires burning. Is it any wonder that young, inexperienced crews and even old ones, seeing the glow of fires through the cloud and fog, bombed those apparent signs of an important centre and, after battling back to their stations with a steady loss of planes and air crew, were berated next day by their station commander for poor bombing results?

The Germans were later found to have completely covered – with boards, imitation grass and trees – a lake that had previously acted as an indicator for one of their main towns. They then built an exact replica some forty miles farther east, so that bombing crews, when they used this imitation as a marker, were forty miles out in their calculations.

One remarkable feature of this aerial warfare was that we saw no bloodshed, corpses or other evidence of war. Now and then a plane would return badly shot up with some of its crew either wounded or dead. On such occasions corpses and wounded were quickly whisked away and evidence of their passing erased, as such sights were considered bad for morale.

One morning a Wellington returned with a dead rear gunner. He had taken an explosive cannon shell in his chest and from the waist up had been literally blown to pieces. When the facts became known the plane exercised a morbid fascination for air crew, particularly the gunners, and most made their way out to view the grisly scene. When Kiwi and I got there, the erks were trying to remove the evidence of the fellow's passing with scrubbing brushes and hose. This, I think, is how the story about hosing gunners out of their turrets originated. It was the only way to remove the blood and guts splattered in the confined space.

After a while, damaged planes and battered turrets lost their interest unless you were closely connected with the dead or wounded airmen. Generally a crew would just disappear out of the mess, so that if three planes were lost and the crews were sergeants, as most of them were, eighteen persons whom you either knew to speak to or by sight, didn't show up any more.

On the other hand, when we returned safely from a flight we wanted for nothing. We slept in good beds, food was good and you could drink when you liked. I never heard of an airman being charged with drunkenness. In addition we had nearly every amenity we could ask for. Cigarettes were plentiful. We received regular parcels from home. Feminine company was there for the asking. On an active squadron bullsh was cut to a minimum, there was no saluting and we had few parades. As Hally said, 'This is a bloody good life, all you've got to do is stay alive to enjoy it.'

As time progressed our operations gradually increased. In our log books appeared such names as Essen, Kiel, Duisburg, Munich, Stuttgart, Bremen, Wilhelmshaven, Hamburg, Dusseldorf and Nuremberg.[2] Every entry was a memory of nerve-racking take-offs with the unpredictable cookie and fear that could raise a cold sweat despite the freezing conditions; the concentration of watching and searching for the black shadow, darker than night itself, that would mean annihilation and flaming death; the searching cones of the searchlights; flak that jolted, rattled and shook the plane; the interminable battle to gain height; the frightening Guy Fawkes displays over every target; the dragging trip back with prevailing westerly winds seeking to retard the plane as its crew members urged it home; the struggle after leaving the target to keep tiredness at bay and keep a high standard of concentration; fear of the vengeful fighters, directed by instruments and radar, that roamed the skies to bring down in flames the bombers that so arrogantly rode the German skies in direct contradiction of Goerings' boastful words that 'no bombs would ever fall on German soil'.[3]

In late November we had our first snow – the first sighting for most of the Australians. For a while we revelled in it. Then the novelty wore off and we cursed the damn stuff as we slipped and slithered in the slush around the station.

At the same time icy gales blew in from the North Sea and the crews looked with dread and fear at this hundred-mile water hazard. It was said that any unfortunates unlucky enough to bail out over it had fifteen seconds to divest themselves of their harness and inflate their rubber dinghies when they hit the water. After that they would be paralysed by cold. From the tales we heard of survivors who performed this seemingly impossible feat and were rescued frozen and frostbitten after drifting around for days, it was considered by some better to take it easy for those initial seconds and accept the kinder fate of freezing to death immediately. However, my guess was that every man would battle valiantly till overcome by the numbing cold.

In December 1941, the crushing news of Japan's entry into the war sent a wave of unrest through the Australians and New Zealanders on the squadron. At the end of the first week a strong rumour developed that we were to be returned home. This persisted and to counter its unsettling effect, an official announcement was made that bomber crews would remain in England.

Christmas 1941 was, for the Australians, the most miserable ever. The disquieting news of Japanese progress, the poor bombing results, the heavy losses in men and planes, and the appalling weather all contributed to create a feeling of gloom, frustration and defeat, a conviction that we were on the losing side and that on the law of averages it would be completely impossible to survive thirty operations. By the New Year we had completed fifteen ops, which was half-way and were looked upon as a veteran crew.

About this time, two incidents connected with crew members occurred which did not help to lift the morale. The first concerned Maxie, a little Cockney WAG whose white, peaked face and skinny frame were the result of malnutrition from Depression days, for it appears that from the age of ten to fifteen he had existed mainly on bread and dripping.

Despite the fact that he always had a prodigious appetite and ate at a breakneck speed Maxie remained as pale and as skinny as ever. He was an inoffensive, quiet little fellow who should never have gone to war, and we noticed as the ops increased, a nervous little mannerism that developed, a kind of involuntary fluttering of the muscles on the right side of his face.

Men got rid of their tensions in various ways; some drank, others became cantankerous, some brawled, but Maxie seemed to have no outlet for his emotional stress except this continuous nervous twitching of his facial muscles. There was speculation as to how long he would last.

After a particularly tough op his plane was badly shot up by a fighter and the rear gunner killed. He had been instructed to go down and take over the dead gunner's place. We could readily imagine Maxie's nerve-racking journey down the catwalk after the tension of the fighter's attack. It appears, as he released the catch and groped in the darkness to remove the dead man, his hands had met a horrible ghastly mass of blood, guts and flesh. Despite the shock and horror of his find he had dragged the smashed remains back into the plane and crawled into the reeking battered turret and for three hours had taken over the dead man's duties.

We never discovered what transpired after they had landed but he had acted quite normally at interrogation. The first indication anything was wrong was while we were having our meal and Maxie came into the dining-room.

Blondie, who was sitting beside me facing the door, exclaimed, 'Christ, have a look at this joker. He looks as though he's seen a ghost.'

Suddenly he came over to our table, slumped into a seat and, clutching his head in his hands, began to rock backwards and forwards, uttering a high-pitched cry intermingled with some gibberish.

We had never seen a man's nerves break before. For a moment there was a shocked silence. Hally was the first to recover. 'He's broken down,' he declared. 'The poor bastard's nuts.'

With some difficulty, Hally, Blondie and myself got him out into the open air, but despite our efforts to calm him he became more hysterical and distracted.

'Better get him to the Doc,' Blondie advised. 'I think this bloke has had it.'

After some delay we got a wagon and carted Maxie down to sick bay. Except for routine inspections we had never had much to do with the medical officer, who was a supercilious young Englishman with an Oxford accent. He came into the room, looked at our broken patient and said, 'Well?'

'This man's nerves have completely gone,' said Hally. 'He's broken down.'

'Broken down!', mocked the medico. Then, moving across, he jerked the twisting face upwards. 'I think he's putting on an act.'

'Putting on an act?', we exclaimed incredulously, in unison.

'Or perhaps a slight attack of hysterics,' he replied, and slapped his patient's face with two stunning backhanders.

Hearing the explosive expelling of Hally's breath and reading the baleful message in three pairs of eyes, I think the medico realised how close he was to being flattened. He moved smartly to the door and called his orderlies. 'Take this man away,' he ordered. Then, turning to us he added maliciously, in his affected, bored voice; 'The man's an obvious malingerer. If he persists with this ridiculous behaviour I will charge him with LMF.'

We never heard what happened to poor little Maxie. We hoped that, when he got away from our half-baked medico he fell into more sympathetic hands and received proper attention.

The action of the doctor bore out the contention of most aircrews that operational squadrons were staffed by young doctors who were generally just out of University. They naturally mixed with and swallowed the doctrines of their superiors so that if a CO was a bastard so was the MO.

The complete anomaly and blatant injustice with regard to cowardice amongst aircrew was that whilst a sergeant or W/O could be charged with LMF, this label could not be tagged on to an officer.[4]

We had an instance of a flying officer pilot who had done a tour on Blenheims and was on his second tour with our squadron. The pilot, on four separate occasions, gave non-existent technical reasons why he could not take off, all of which were exploded by the mechanics. He was finally taken off ops and classified as unfit for flying duties. We contended there was no difference between this case and that of little Maxie.

The second occurrence was just after Maxie's departure. A most unusual gunner was posted to the squadron. He was an elongated beanstalk over six feet tall and thin as a match. His pallid, freckled face was surrounded by a carroty thatch. How the hell they came to make him a gunner we never knew and how he fitted his long frame into the confined space of the rear turret was anyone's guess.

This poor devil, in spite of his fiery hair, was obviously not a fighting man and showed all the outward signs of mental upset before he had ever done one operation. The day after his crew had done their pamphlet run he vomited continuously and was such a case of nervous tension that Hally and Blondie unsuccessfully tried to get him to see the MO.

Blondie said, 'You can't blame the poor bastard for not reporting to sick bay, particularly with a MO like that.'

On his crew's first op we were on the same battle order and I sat beside him at the meal table and noticed that he did not eat anything. On the way to briefing Kiwi and I walked with him and tried to get the message across that the real thing wasn't as bad as it was rumoured to be. 'All you've got to do is keep your eyes open,' we advised.

Getting out of the bus, Kiwi said, 'Jesus, that poor bugger's got the breeze up. Anyone would think he's going before a firing squad.'

We had a reasonable trip and in between worrying about flak, searchlights and fighters, I kept wondering how he was going. On our arrival back we were greeted with the astonishing news that he had bailed out before crossing the English coast. His skipper had made a routine check just before he left England and, receiving no reply from his rear gunner, sent the WOP to see what was wrong. The WOP returned to report that they had no rear gunner.

Naturally, the plane had to return and the Wingco made no secret of the fact that the proper authorities had been alerted and that the deserter was as good as dead.

Next day he made a short announcement that the errant gunner had been picked up early that morning, had been court-martialled and shot within twelve hours. He made this statement with a kind of relish, as though to warn others who might have similar thoughts.

For many days we discussed the attitude of this man who had the guts to bail out in the dark over an area of treacherous tidal flats and quicksand, in the sure knowledge that if he escaped one of these, when he was caught, which was a certainty, he would be shot.

CHAPTER THIRTEEN

With the progress of winter the weather deteriorated to such an extent that, towards the end of January, we were told that half the squadron was to be transferred to Northern Ireland to help counter the U-boat threat. Everyone hoped they would be in the transfer, for anything seemed preferable to the grind of operations into Germany. When the transfer was rostered, it was found that Hally's, Smithy's, our own and eight other crews were to remain while seven were to be transferred.

Jonesy said, 'I knew that bastard wouldn't give us a break.'

Early in February, on a wild night, Happy's crew failed to return. Nothing was ever heard of them. Happy was a man who was willing to stand up for his convictions and fight for his fellow-man. He was that rarest of specimens, a practical idealist who fought for the underdog, and his going knocked our morale even lower.

During February and March, despite being on battle order almost daily, we did only six operations. Day after day we would go through the routine of briefing, then wait, ready and tense, while the operation was deferred hour by hour. If the briefing was at 4 pm for a seven hour trip with a take-off at, say, 7 pm, it meant a return to base at about 2.30 am. But if the operation was deferred hourly to, say, midnight, then it was obvious the return trip could not be made without being caught over Europe in daylight.

The waiting, suspense and late hours were worse than the actual flying and the crews became nervy and irritable. Also, because a big proportion of Bomber Command had been switched to the Battle of the Atlantic, it meant less bombers and a hotter reception from flak and fighters during the period you were over Germany, for the Nazis concentrated to make night raids so costly that Britain would have to call them off. During this period it was not unusual to have up to six fighter attacks on a normal trip for, whereas the bombers were subjected to continual wastage, the German fighters increased in number and efficiency. This usually meant short shrift for new crews that came to the squadron.[1]

Over the targets, in addition to the greatly increased density of flak, the Germans introduced an amazing variety of scare pyrotechnics. These included flashes, explosions, exploding stars, and other ingenious contraptions that looked like a bomber blowing up, so that it appeared as though the entire force was being annihilated, and crews who weathered the buffeting of flak started their homeward trip with jangled nerves.[2]

With their abundance of fighters the Germans introduced a new diversion. The planes of the squadron had completed their trip and half a dozen were orbiting at different heights under instruction from control. Z for Zebra, piloted by a pleasant Canadian named Thompson, had called for an emergency landing with one engine feathered and the plane badly shot up. Control immediately placed the rest of the planes at different heights and gave instructions for an immediate landing.

We were circling at about fifteen hundred feet and I was watching the runway with some doubt. A badly punctured Wimpy with one dead engine was not the surest bet to land. I felt the tension existing in that plane as it made its run.

In the darkness for a brief moment I saw the glow of its exhausts as Thompson flattened out Z-Zebra for its landing and imagined the crews at crash stations, tense and fearful. Then suddenly the night lit with a stream of tracer. All hell seemed to break loose.

Over the intercom a voice screamed, 'Snappers, snappers, disperse, disperse!' Z-Zebra seemed to explode in mid-air. Close by there was another blinding flash. Snowden's reaction was immediate, executing a split-second turn away from the drome and, without waiting for instructions, started a violent weave.

A stream of tracer behind showed his manoeuvre was a wise one. Like startled pigeons the squadron fled into the night. Behind, the darkness was lit by the glow of fires. We were directed to a station some hundred miles away and landed safely.

Next morning we returned and found three intruders had infiltrated. In addition to Z-Zebra, two other planes had been shot down. The intruders had also shot up the hangars and control tower and altogether had a very successful visit. Later we learnt this intrusion had been planned on a wide scale and at least fourteen other dromes had been strafed with just as serious results.[3]

This meant from then on we could never relax. Previously, when we had got within reasonable distance of England, crews had taken it easy. Afterwards, however, gunners stayed at their posts, watchful and anxious till the plane actually landed. And so another little imp was added to an already oppressive load.

A week after this intrusion Jerry paid us back in our own coin with a bomber attack. When the smoke and confusion cleared there were twenty to thirty delayed-action bombs lying around the place, which mean the squadron was completely immobilised.

Between 6 and 8 am four of these went off, so the CO, probably on Group instructions, gave aircrew three days leave while they sorted things out.

We decided to go up to London, Blondie declaring he wished the bastards would come over twice a week. Leave was rather a problem in those days; most of the pleasant spots were out-of-bounds; travelling was as difficult and unpredictable as the Second Front; and London reached an all-time high in prices for accommodation.

However, in a little side street off Fleet Street we made the acquaintance of an unpretentious cafe with tabletops of grey marble, euphoniously known as 'Dirty Dicks'. Dick himself was a lean, hawk-nosed character obviously from the Middle East, who at various times stated he came from Malta, Greece, Albania or Egypt. He had evidently been told of the Australian and New Zealander's liking for grilled steaks. With meat rationing it was impossible to get a steak in London at any price but somehow Dick served fairly good imitations that, though a bit tough, still smelt and looked like steaks. From what particular beast they came from we never knew, but this drab little cafe became in time a meeting place and rendezvous for the meat-hungry Australians.

Rooming quarters on the top floor housed a diversity of adults and a motley collection of children. Whether all or a portion sprang from Dicks' loins we never knew but it was generally conceded if only a part were the result of his night work, he was a pretty good boy in bed.

Eating in England was a problem, particularly in London. The Boomerang Club offered light refreshments, excellently served by a bevy of charming volunteers. Every pub had its sandwich bars where you could get a variety of sandwiches. Restaurants and dining houses offered a collection of substitute meat dishes such as the repulsive spam and other unappetising concoctions. To get a roast dinner, a steak or even a grilled chop, was a complete impossibility. These substitutes were poor fare and the mere mention of a juicy underdone steak was liable to set any Australian drooling.

Restaurants run by shady characters offered on paper such tempting dishes as roast or grilled spring chicken, grilled steaks, etc. Generally, you were only caught once.

During my stay, I sat down to a grilled chicken you couldn't even get a fork into. I later learned the rooks or crows as well as seagulls suffered grievous losses to satisfy the insatiable appetites of London's wartime millions.

On another occasion I was served with what seemed genuine steak which looked all right, smelt all right and what was more surprising, tasted all right. After I had mopped up the last remnants I tried to assess what kind of beast it had been cut from; the darkness and coarseness of the meat indicated venison, probably poached from some nobleman's park. Pondering this problem, a notice in exceedingly small print at the bottom of the menu took my eye. Out of curiosity, I deciphered a message that stated; 'Under Health Regulations, this restaurant has permission to sell horse meat'. I know the horse is a clean animal, so is the cat, but I suddenly felt squeamish.

One night I was groping my way along the blacked-out streets when the banshee-like wail of the sirens sounded. It's something that never fails to chill the blood.

The organisation that this great city had to combat the raids was incredible. People disappeared like magic from the streets. In a surprisingly short time the scurrying of footsteps was replaced by almost complete silence, broken now and then by a sharp command as police and wardens took over, and the bleat of lost pedestrians in belated search of shelter.

I lodged myself in a big doorway and decided to see the fun from the civilian angle. In the period preceding a raid, a feeling of hushed expectancy hangs over the city. The policemen, wardens and others tread softly and speak quietly. The first white fingers of light begin to poke and probe in the black canopy overhead. You can sense the lifting of every face, and hear the quick intake of sharply-drawn breath. Then far away at first come the dull boom and the thud as the coastal defences open up. This swells and swells and swells, like some note begun on a mighty organ, increasing in intensity and volume that transcends all description as the raiders battle towards the centre of the city.

The searchlights have by now increased to hundreds, some swinging alone, others in great cones that sweep the sky in pillars of white light – all combining to make an intricate pattern of luminous lines, reaching far up into the blackness of the night. For all their fantastic beauty it's the barrage that creates the greatest impression, assaulting the ear in one tremendous, stunning burst of sound.

As the raiders were coming in very high, thousands of feet up, you could see shrapnel exploding in a brilliant display of fireworks. Then came one of the most exciting moments of all. A plane was 'coned', and though it tried desperately to rid itself of this unwelcome limelight, the searchlights held it.

I could imagine the fear that gripped that crew twenty thousand feet up as their pilot twisted and spiralled in a frantic endeavour to save his plane. As soon as it was caught in the lights, the guns seemed to work themselves up to a new pitch of frenzy, till literally hundreds of shells began to burst round the luckless raider. I held my breath. I knew how they felt up there.

Then suddenly the plane started to dive, trailing a silvery plume of smoke; faster and faster it fell, spinning like a burning leaf, for it was now completely out of control, and I watched till the tall buildings in front hid it from view.

I was so engrossed in the spectacle that I quite forgot the other raiders. A blood-curdling whistle that seemed to be coming straight down on my unprotected head woke me to reality, and I went to earth, wishing fervently that I was a mole, a rabbit, anything but the most prominent target in all London's streets. In those moments of suspense, when the shriek develops to a veritable scream, followed by a thud and then a mighty who-o-o-mp, I knew the meaning of the phrase 'his bowels turned to water'. I was certain the bone-shaking, breath-taking crash was just beside me, but it turned out to be in the next street. Further whoomps mingled with the crack of guns, then the battle moved away as the raiders sought to battle their way out again.

Slowly the barrage lessened and slackened till it died in the distance. Within seconds of the first bomb, fire engines and ambulances were clanging their way through the city. The shrill call of whistles and the scurrying of many feet showed that the complex and amazingly efficient rescue organisation that London had built up was swinging into life, and I took myself off to the nearest public house.

Later, at the Boomerang Club, Smithy and I met Dagworth, the lurks artist who had come over on the same boat as The Mob, and who was as bullshy as ever. Somehow he had got himself a commission. He said the RAF had recognised his worth and he was transferring to Ferry Command to fly planes across from America via Newfoundland and Greenland. He hinted that it was a job fraught with some peril but the dangers were alleviated by the fact he would spend some time in America on each trip and he understood there were some profitable rackets that could be worked from both ends.

After we got rid of him Smithy said, 'He's a bludger all right. If he's good enough to fly across the Atlantic he should be on ops. He's just too ruddy smart, that's all.'

Later in the evening we met a couple of females who were willing enough but as they had to catch the last train we had to content ourselves with an affair in the blackout.

'Funny thing about these girls,' said Smithy. 'A naughty seems to be placed in the same category as a kiss would be back home. How the hell they miss getting into trouble I don't know.'

When we got back to the station the bombs had been cleared out by two bomb disposal boffins. One bespectacled, quiet and unassuming fellow was still there. It was unanimously agreed that it took real guts to go to work on bombs that were liable to go off and blow you to smithereens at any time.

What really intrigued us was his statement, eventually substantiated, that at least sixty per cent of German bombs were defective.[4] This he attributed to sabotage on the part of conscripted European workers. But for that fact, the damage would have been much more extensive. Thus appeared one of the internal cracks of the Reich facade that could possibly have some bearing on the future conduct of the war.

In our absence runways had been repaired, damaged kites patched. As one disconsolate gunner said, 'All that you require to put a Wimpy back into fighting order is a pair of scissors and a roll of adhesive tape.'

CHAPTER FOURTEEN

By April a tardy spring showed signs of breaking through, but it was still freezing and the weather was lousy. Despite an almost constant alert and briefing nearly every day, we had done only twenty-one ops. As we got over the twenty mark a new spirit permeated the crew. Whereas we had previously fatalistically accepted that it was impossible to complete a tour, now a small ray of hope shone through the gloom. If it was possible to do twenty-one ops, Kiwi argued, with our experience and skill we should do the other nine. It was a thought that no-one except our exuberant front gunner felt like discussing. Every time he brought it up he was told to shut up. Still the hope was there. We were now the senior crew on the squadron and were pointed out to newcomers as the lucky ones who had completed twenty-one missions.

The Tannoy announced our twenty-second. Going up to briefing Kiwi said, 'This should be a soda.'

Jonesy said, 'Shut up, don't bloody-well talk about it.'

'Ah, bullsh,' said Kiwi. 'I know we're going to make it. I feel it in my water.'

'Shouldn't talk like that,' remonstrated Jonesy, 'should he, Johnny?'

'Better touch a bit of wood,' I cautioned. 'Remember it's not you but all of us, boy.'

I was rudely advised what I could do with my piece of wood and all of a sudden a feeling of doubt came over me and I said, 'Shut your mouth, you bloody fool, or I'll shut it for you.'

Snowden looked at me in surprise and said, 'Now break it up, boys!'

The target was Munich which, though well defended, wasn't so bad. Met forecast bad weather for the first three hundred miles but clearing from then on. The target would be clear. This raised the usual cynical laugh from his audience. From experience we knew these forecasts were usually eighty per cent wrong.

The op started badly as we nearly collided with another kite going around the perimeter which had got out of line and some terse words were passed between pilot and Control before we untangled ourselves. 'Some bloody sprog', commented Snowden, and I could imagine the collective eyebrows of the crew going up. It was only the second time we had heard him swear.

In the preliminary warming-up period, Snowden said to his co-pilot, 'I don't like the look of the port oil pressure.'

'No,' the second dickey replied, 'it doesn't look too good.' And then, after further test he asked, 'Do you think we should go?'

This two-way conversation was listened to by the crew in complete silence, whilst the plane shook and vibrated under full test. After what seemed an age, Snowden said, 'She's okay. We'll go.'

It's bad enough taking off on an eight hundred mile trip with a four thousand pound cookie and two sound engines, but with the expressed doubts of the two pilots in our ears, that hurtling rush down the runway was murder. When we lifted, Jonesys' fervent 'Thank Christ for that' expressed our combined feelings.

Complete darkness had already fallen and land and sea had merged as one black indistinguishable blob as we crossed the coast and set our course. S for Sugar shivered and shook as we strove for height and the two pilots took up their conversation.

'Pressure on that motor is still not rising,' said Snowden. 'I don't like the look of it.'

'No,' said Williams, 'Give her a bit of boost.' Then, after a period, 'Doesn't seem to make much difference.'

Ninnes's voice then cut in with, 'Forty minutes to enemy coast, our speed is only a hundred and eighty mph, height four thousand feet. We will not reach required altitude of ten thousand feet unless you increase climb rate.'

There was a silence for a while, then Ninnes said again, 'Did you hear me, Skipper? We are not maintaining either speed or climb rate to cross enemy coast.'

'Of course I heard you,' declared Snowden. 'I'm doing my bloody best.'

Someone said, 'My, two in one night!'

There was a long, pregnant pause, then Ninnes said in his clipped English accent, 'I am merely giving you information. If you cannot reach desired speed and height, I recommend we return to base.'

'We continue to our objective,' declared Snowden, and a heavy silence fell on the fearful crew.

It was evident to everyone that with a dicky[1] port motor we should jettison and return, but Snowden, with memories of his last interview with the Wingco, obstinately preferred to carry on. And when it came to final decisions, the Skipper made them.

We crossed the enemy coast at eight thousand feet and drew every damned gun in range. Safely over this obstacle we were left with the comforting thought that, unable to make height and flying at reduced speed, we would stick out like sore toes on the radar screens and, as well as being a target for ack-ack, would draw every fighter in the area. The only thing that saved us that night on the trip in, I think, was that the weather was so lousy the snappers could not pinpoint us.

Two hundred miles from target, Ninnes and Snowden had an argument, Ninnes stating that at our rate of climb and speed we would not reach twelve thousand feet and would be arriving at the target forty-five minutes late – a chilling thought because 3 Group Hallies were timed to arrive nine thousand feet higher and with double our bomb-load.

When Snowden obstinately declared we would continue, Ninnes said, 'I think the crew should have a say in this. It's their necks, too.'

Kiwi, myself and Jonesy immediately voted for a return. Williams, sticking by his Skipper, said he would leave it to him. This was a four to two vote, but Snowden squashed this by stating flatly 'I'm in charge of this plane. We will proceed to target.'

As forecast by Ninnes we arrived at twelve thousand feet, forty-six minutes late over Munich and copped hell. Luckily the Hallies had gone in a few minutes ahead of us and had drawn most of the hate. There was still enough left to toss us around the sky. Saint Christopher must have been with us that night, for we rode a sea of bursting flak from below and missed the falling bombs from above by minutes.

As we came off the target a greatly increased cold draught and a sound of flapping cloth above the engines was evidence we had lost some skin, but by some miracle S for Sugar, after dropping her load, not only held her twelve thousand feet altitude but improved it slightly, although because of a fifty-knot wind our ground speed, the real indicator of progress, dropped appreciably. Because we were thousands of feet below the main bomber stream we knew we would stick out on the enemy radar, so that when trouble came we were prepared for it.

Fifty miles on the long trip back to safety we struck our first fighter, a decoy with all the lights ablaze, flying a thousand yards astern. This was strictly for the birds and, instead of catching us unaware, alerted the entire crew so that when the fighter who was tracking us on instruments started his attack from five o'clock, we turned smartly into it and he ran through a long burst which so disillusioned him he disappeared into the night. His decoy also doused lights and possibly went in search of more gullible victims.

Our next encounter was from a fighter that came in dead astern. I didn't see him, but perhaps because he was a sprog too, he opened fire at about a thousand yards and, by the time he had closed to the dangerous distance of six hundred yards, our pilot had thrown S for Sugar into a wild corkscrew. Mainly because I had to cling to my guns during these wild gyrations I didn't have time to retaliate, but got in a short burst as he broke to port upwards just to show I was awake.

In these two attacks we suffered no apparent damage. All around us there were signs of conflict. Now and again brilliant flashes would indicate direct hits or a plane with one or two engines afire would fall slowly at first, then, with ever-increasing momentum, towards the darkness below.

I noticed these things only in an abstract sort of way, endeavouring if possible to miss the glare of the explosions but at the same time to use them to pick the glint of the night-fighter, guided by radar instructions and using instruments, which could be tracking somewhere in the dark behind.

Whilst concentrating so intently on this alien dark sky my mind still had time to listen to the impersonal discussions, almost like a radio play, that came through the earphones: Nav's' precise instructions as to course and height, Snowden's discussion with Williams on the ailing engine, which had lost so much compression they were trying to decide if it should be cut and feathered. WAG's laconic advice to 'let the bleedin' thing go on as long as it turns' was shared by the rest of the crew.

Any decisions in this regard were decided by our third attack. This bloke came in at five o'clock. A brief explosion somewhere in the sky silhouetted the dark hurtling shape and Snowden's split-second reaction to my screamed, 'Turn right!' probably saved the bomber and crew. This Jerry was a fighter. He tightened his turn and poured a red-hot stream of tracer and cannon fire at his rapidly-skidding target. How close the first burst went to my turret I'll never know but I'd swear six inches would be an over-estimate.

Something warned me that this bloke was no piker and even before we had straightened from our turn he swung in a circle and made a vicious head-on attack which was nullified by Kiwi screaming, 'Dive! Go!'

That bastard was a dyed-in-the-wool Nazi. Perhaps he had lost his home, wife and family, or had some grudge eating at his guts; or was a champ who always got his plane. Whatever it was, he stuck to us like porridge to a blanket. Like a rabbit in the family way pursued by a kangaroo dog we zig-zagged around the sky. We knew by the bangs and shudders that we had received hits but as the engines still functioned and the plane answered our pilot's masterly handling, we still survived.

A fighter only has limited endurance and ammunition and I think this was what really saved us, for his final attack from almost dead astern was a sizzler. Snowden had thrown the Wimpy into a violent corkscrew and despite the violence of the motion I poured a stream of lead at our attacker as he broke upwards to starboard. As he disappeared came Williams' blood-chilling announcement, 'Port engine on fire.' This looked like the end. It was only a miracle we had missed being blown to pieces with two engines, but with one on fire what chance would we have?

Kiwi's anxious voice came over the intercom. 'Do we bail out, Skipper?' I could well imagine his anxiety, for the front gunner had to have his door catch released by the second dickey, otherwise he went down with the kite. The fact that a number of front gunners persistently failed to survive bail-outs gave credence to the belief that they were often left to their fate by panicking crews.[2]

Snowden's voice, concise and calm, stilled the panic with, 'We're diving to port. I'll have the fire out in a jiffy. Watch for the blasted fighter. Is everyone okay?'

Everyone reported in. A short while later he announced, 'Fire out, feathering engine.'

Nav said, 'Down to seven thousand feet', and gave a course.

We did not know the fighter had broken his attack, but felt he was somewhere in the darkness, tracking us, ready to pounce.

'We're losing height, Skipper; can you keep her up?'

'You're lucky she's flying at all,' was the terse reply.

Somewhere at the back of my turret was a wild flapping; with the cessation of the fighting, I realised I seemed to be getting more than my share of the breeze. This was partially explained when I put my hand out and struck nothing. The perspex had either been holed or blown off.

'Six thousand five hundred feet,' said Ninnes. 'We'll be coming over enemy coast in ten minutes. If we continue losing height at this rate we'll cross at approximately five thousand five hundred feet.' A chilling thought with the best of ack-ack crews and radar ready to raise the score for the night's report.

When we came within range, Snowden said, 'I'm going to put her into a dive. It may mean we'll lose another thousand feet, but it's better than being blown out of the sky.'

'Flak dead ahead', Kiwi reported, his last prophetic words. The next second we were in a world of bursting flame, a criss-cross of brilliant lines as the heavy and light guns strove to pull us to the ground.

Our strategy seemed to be paying off for already the tracer, instead of climbing vertically, was beginning to arch as the gunners endeavoured to follow the diving plane.

'By Christ,' I thought, 'we're through, we've made it.' Then there was the most terrific crash I have ever heard. You never hear flak; the noise of the engines, the earphones, all help to drown it out. They say if you do hear a burst that's the last thing you ever hear.

We had crossed the coast when that bracket of three from the lurking flak ship hit us. They must have been just over the engine on the starboard quarter, luckily in a way, for eighty per cent of the burst is upwards; three feet lower and they would have blown the plane to pieces.

That something was wrong was evident by the steepening of our dive. Among a jumble of strange unintelligible headphone noises, I heard Snowden say, 'Quick, Nav! Quick!', then through the earphones came the most blood-chilling, agonised groan of pain I have ever heard. This was followed by a series of gasping rattles, as though two people were gargling their throats in unison. There was silence for a while, then Snowden's voice, on a strange key, said, 'Let WAG handle him. See if you can help me with the stick. You will have to help me.'

Through habit, whilst listening to this disquieting conversation and noises, I had automatically continued to operate the turret. It took me a while to realise it was not working. Then I realised the oil supply that operated the rams must have been cut.

'Rear gunner to pilot', I reported, 'Turret out of operation.'

'Oh, you still there,' came his weary voice. 'I'd almost forgotten about you. Put your turret on manual control. We've been badly hit. Two crew members are badly injured. We will try to reach base. If we ditch they won't have a chance.'

WAG's voice then broke in with, 'Have set on emergency, Skipper.'

It was hard to say what thoughts coursed through my mind. Two badly injured; that must be Kiwi and Williams, as I hadn't heard their voices since that terrific crash. Ditching? Gawd! What chance would I have if we ditched? I toyed with the idea of asking permission to go to ditching stations, then remembered the fate of the planes as they were going in to land; what was the use of being in the belly of the kite if some marauding fighter blew you to pieces?

Nav asked, 'How are you, Skipper?'

'Bloody awful,' came the reply, 'but follow my directions.' Then, to WAG, 'Better pull the front gunner out. He won't have a chance if we go in.'

It was an hour's trip back across those black waters and I will remember it to my dying day. The sky was beginning to pale in the east as we came to the coast. It must have been bloody cold in my turret but all I can remember was the clammy sweat that ran in rivulets down my back.

As we came in towards base Nav made a request for immediate permission to land, stating S for Sugar was on one engine, co-pilot and front gunner dead and the Skipper seriously wounded. 'I will assist with the landing,' he reported, and as an afterthought, 'Petrol dangerously low.'

The WAAF's voice came back cool and efficient. 'Permission granted, ambulance and fire engines alerted. Use centre runway. Good luck.'

This was the first indication I had that Kiwi and Williams were dead. I thought, 'this can't be right. Nav must have gone off his rocker.'

After a short silence, Snowden's voice, as though from a long distance, said, 'Unable to release landing gear, we will have to pancake. Rear gunner take up ditching position immediately.'

My first thought, 'Why doesn't he let us bail out?', was followed almost immediately by, 'Perhaps he can't move himself.'

I came out of that turret like a rabbit out of a burrow and halted momentarily as I glimpsed the aerodrome lights shining up through the denuded fuselage.

It looked as though S for Sugar had lost all her clothes. That trip back along the catwalk was hell. Every moment I expected to put my foot through a hole and plunge parachute-less earthwards, and ended up crawling the last ten feet on my hands and knees.

Arriving at my ditching position, the cross-bar, I saw for the first time two recumbent figures stretched on the passageway. 'Silly bloody place to ditch,' I said aloud, and then nearly jumped out of my skin as a hand grabbed me by the trouser cuff. It was Jonesy, with his head braced against the cross-bar, gesticulating madly for me to get down.

I felt the nose dip steeply, and as I braced myself, put out my hand to warn the inert figure nearest and came in contact with a sticky pulpy mass. Self-preservation made me grab my neck as the plane did an uneasy wobble and then hit the runway with a resounding whack, then commenced a tummy-turning slide up the runway with a screeching and screaming of tortured metal as though we were running over ten thousand cats.

Towards the end of our run we did a neck-jolting loop and S for Sugar, like the gallant lady she was, slithered off the runway, sheared the starboard wing nearly off and came to rest with her bottom facing forward, a complete write-off. That she didn't catch fire was possibly due to the fact there wasn't enough petrol left.

The organisation certainly worked that day, for in a matter of seconds after our violent halt, three fire engines, two ambulances, plus three staff cars were at the wreck. Someone smartly hacked their way through the side of the plane and stopped in horror at the ghastly sight of Williams' almost decapitated head and Kiwi's smashed face.

The two lifeless bodies were placed in one ambulance and the rest of us in the other. I wondered why everyone was so solicitous for myself. It wasn't till afterwards I realised that when I had stuck my hand into Kiwi's gore I had transferred it to my own head as I automatically braced my head and neck before we touched down.

Snowden looked dreadful. His right eye appeared to have been gouged right out by a splinter and hung from its socket like a squashed grape; his flying clothes were caked with blood. That he had remained conscious and able to fly was a triumph of will. He lay on a stretcher on one side of the ambulance, his good eye closed. Ninnes had attempted to sit beside him but the attendant had ordered him over with Jonesy and myself where we crouched uncomfortable and inarticulate.

As I looked at Snowden's ashen face I had a premonition he would not live. This gallant young Englishman had used his blood, determination and guts to get his crew home. Now that the job was accomplished he lay only semi-conscious.

At sick headquarters Doc took one look at Snowden and said, 'Crothers.' It was the only time I ever saw him concerned.

Due to the urgency of the case and because we were all covered in the two dead men's blood, it must have looked as though the four of us were seriously wounded. From here things really did move. We were transferred out of the ambulance which departed at speed with the Doc and Snowden towards Crothers, a large RAF hospital some twenty miles distant.[3]

Jonesy, Ninnes and myself were bundled into a second ambulance which took off after the first, their reasons for the hasty departure were twofold, the first being that badly wounded airmen were never left on the station – bad for morale; and secondly, as previously mentioned, we all looked cot cases.

On the way I tried to take my flying helmet off but found it was stuck to my head. I thought, 'It must be Kiwi's blood; I'll leave it till I get to hospital.'

Crothers was a model of efficiency. In a matter of minutes after our arrival we were stripped of our flying clothes and were being examined. Jonesy and Ninnes, except for a few abrasions, gathered apparently while they were dragging Kiwi and Williams from their positions, were unscathed.

I was in the same boat except that my stuck helmet was explained by about a dozen small flak splinters in my neck and shoulders. How the hell they got there I'll never know; general opinion was they were from a twenty mm shell, either from the plane or ground. This could possibly have come from the second head-on attack.

It wasn't till I got into bed that I realised how done-in I was. During the examination the doctor had learned what a shaky do we had gone through and said, 'I think I'll keep you two here for observation. This fellow will have to go into hospital while we get some of this ironmongery out.'

He was a decent bloke. I think he realised that a reaction would set in and his idea of keeping the others there was to give them a chance to get over the shock.

They gave me a couple of needles and a pert little nurse said, 'Here, Aussie, drink this.' I slept solidly for fifteen hours.

Next day they broke the news that Snowden had died during the night from loss of blood, shock and the eye injury.

About midday, Ninnes and Jonesy came in to say they were returning to the station. By the look on their faces, particularly Ninnes', I knew they had heard the news. We didn't say much. To my suggestion that he should get a gong, Ninnes said savagely, 'What's the use of posthumous gongs? He should not be bloody well dead at all. You know why he pressed on when he should have turned back.'

I found I had an exceedingly stiff neck and after they'd gone I underwent the most depressing period I've ever known – probably a kind of delayed action shock from all the violence, fear and death of those fateful eight hours. The stiff neck, a natural result of the pellets in it, received full attention. The doctor, no doubt well versed in the matters of shock, hit me with another bomb and I slept for another fifteen hours.

CHAPTER FIFTEEN

I had always thought there were no wounded from the air war. Here, however, the casualties from the whole of Bomber Command seemed to be congregated. They came, like myself, from the battles over occupied territory, the smashes and crack-ups, the hundred and one accidents that are part of a huge command with hundreds of planes and thousands of men.

They say if you want to really see war you have to see it from inside a hospital, for here were the wards of limb cases, the belly wounded, the eye cases, the head wounds; in fact every damned wound, injury and laceration you could conceive of.

With the dozen or so pellets in my skull I felt a bludger when I looked at the mass suffering of this flower of a nation's young manhood.

Yet despite the lightness of my wounds I was unable to get myself right mentally. Every night, as planes droned overhead, I remembered the suspense and fear of that last op; the horrible sight in the early dawn of those two mutilated figures, their blood and brains splattered on the floor; of Snowden's sightless socket and his hanging smashed eye.

During the week I underwent a couple of minor operations and they extracted some ironmongery. As a preliminary I found they intended shaving all my hair off. I kicked like hell, finally prevailing on the barber to shave only the back of my head, which he did with some misgivings, stating, 'I don't know what bloody surgeon's going to say about this.' Some dill said the back of my head looked like a baboon's backside! A couple of pieces of metal were tangled with certain neck muscles. These, it appeared, needed a more cautious approach. No doubt they considered a gunner with a permanently stiff neck would be a liability, not an asset. As far as I was concerned I didn't mind. The last thing I wanted to do was to go back on ops.

The doctor who examined me when I came in had a soft spot for me.

Most of the patients were young fellows hardly out of their teens. He was in my age group and insatiably curious about Australia. 'That's the place I'm going to,' he would say. 'Fancy all that sunshine, those golden beaches, blue sea and surf. It doesn't sound possible. You're not kidding me, are you?'

He was a fine doctor with a genuine sympathy for his charges. What a difference, I thought, to the station medico and his cynical attitude that everyone was a malingerer.

Once he said, 'You know, when I look at all these shattered young bodies I wonder if I'm really doing my part in this war. I often feel I should join aircrew and get stuck into those bloody Nazis.' I looked at him in amazement, then, when I realised he really meant it, said, 'You stay where you are, Doc. You're doing more for this war effort than any man I know.'

During the second week a specialist operated and took out the offending pieces and I could see an end to my stay in Crothers. Despite the fact that I was feeling okay physically, I could not get myself right mentally. The thought of flying again was enough to send me into a cold sweat.

It was then I really began to think I was lacking in moral fortitude. One night as we were having a yarn, Doc said, 'What part of Australia were you born in, Johnny?'

I answered unthinkingly, 'West Wyalong, New South Wales. Down in the Riverina in the wheat and sheep country.'

'Oh,' he said. 'I thought I saw on your records that you were born in Ireland.'

For a moment we looked at each other and then both laughed.

'Don't think I was prying,' he said. 'My guess is you're over age. I'd say you're thirty-one or thirty-two. Am I right?'

'Pretty close,' I answered, 'but does it matter?'

'No,' he said, 'but I'd say this. You've been really shaken up by this last do. I can get you off ops if you like.'

For a while I looked at him.

'How?' I asked.

'Oh, we'd give your right age and classify you as unfit for operations. Possibly get you into a training school.'

The temptation was there – no more flying, no more sweating out those lonely dark hours. 'Would they label me LMF?', I queried.

'Possibly,' he said. 'Only in a delicate way, of course.'

'Bugger that,' I replied. 'I'd be more afraid of having that tagged on me than I would of ops. Anyway, I'll think it over.'

'Pity,' he said. 'I thought you might teach me some day how to ride those waves,' then added sardonically, 'Now if you were an officer things would be simplified. We would merely classify you as USO – Unsuitable for Operations.'

'Guess I'll have to get a commission fast,' I replied.

I was a walking patient, free to adventure where I pleased. While wandering through the lovely gardens that surrounded the hospital, I came to a wicket gate with a notice, 'Out of bounds to patients'. The gate was slightly ajar and I do not know to this day what prompted me to push it open and peer in. On the other side was a smaller garden surrounded by a high fence.

A voice said, 'Come in, pal.' It was then I noticed the four patients attired in dressing gowns sitting at the small table playing cards. Three had their backs to me. The fourth, who had spoken, sat facing the gate. For a moment I thought he was wearing some grotesque mask, then as the others turned I stopped dead in my tracks, for the faces that looked at me were minus ears, noses, hair, eyebrows and eyelashes.

Their skins were puckered and scarred, one had a gaping cheek wound that was laid open like a sensual mouth. This same person clutched his cards in a pair of clawlike hands, through which the bones showed. These were burn cases, the men so scarred and warped by fire that they were segregated from ordinary patients. This, I found, was a kind of staging area before they went to the skin and bone-grafting hospitals. This was indeed the result of war in its most horrible form. I knew the shock must have shown on my face as I looked into these hairless scarred faces. 'How in God's name,' I thought, 'can these people live after what they have obviously been through?' The chappie with the gaping cheek wound said, 'Sit down, fellow. We don't often have visitors.' His nasal intonation meant one thing.

'You're an Aussie?' I queried.

'That's right,' he replied. 'Fred Bliss is the name, from Melbourne. These are my cobbers,' and introduced his companions.

'Where do you come from?'

'Sydney,' I said, then lamely, 'See you boys have had a bit of trouble.'

'Just a bit,' said Fred. 'What were you on?'

'Bombers. Wimpys,' adding apologetically, 'Copped a bit of flak in the neck.' Then, lamely, 'I'll be out in a day or two.'

'Half your luck,' said one.

These boys really had me at a disadvantage and knew it. I felt my eyes flinching as I spoke to them and tried not to take in their terrible burns. They were hungry for news of squadron doings and everyday life. These young fellows with their grisly mementoes were the unfortunates of war. They knew no-one could look on them without horror and pity; they had to be segregated from ordinary patients. Skin-grafting and face-building were not yet the miraculous arts they were later to become, yet these men could still laugh and have their sly digs at their obviously rattled visitor.[1]

I stopped and chatted with them for perhaps forty minutes, which seemed almost as long as the sixty back across the North Sea on our last fateful trip, then a bell rang and one said, 'Guess we'll have to be going.'

'Might see you tomorrow,' I lied.

'Fair dinkum?', said Fred.

'Why not?' I declared. 'That's if the gate isn't locked.'

'It won't be,' said Fred. 'We'll see to that.'

When I went out I quite truthfully had no intention of returning. I was so shaken I returned to bed and had a couple of really vivid night-mares in which I was being roasted and toasted in varying degrees. When I awoke next morning I felt as though a great weight had been lifted from my shoulders and mind. My worries seemed so infinitesimal that I was suddenly glad to be completely whole and alive. As I was going for my shave, I did something I had not done for months; I whis-tled a tune.

During the morning I decided to go back and honour my promise. If those poor devils can live with themselves, surely, I thought, I can overcome my squeamishness for half an hour. The gate was ajar as before and the four were sitting at the table as I walked in.

'We didn't think you'd come back,' said Fred.

'Why not?' I asked.

'Well,' he replied after a pause, 'no-one else ever has. Perhaps you're a tougher type.'

'Balls,' I said. 'You boys heard any good yarns?'

That day we really go to know each other, for they had lost their embarrassment and my tummy had ceased doing flip-flops. My earlier calling gave me a good repertoire of yarns, and I pulled out the best of them. We were all laughing our heads off at one of Fred's when a calm feminine voice said, 'That must have been a good one.'

I knew from her uniform she was a sister, with a pair of grey eyes as hard as agates. She looked me over and said, 'I thought this area was out of bounds, or are you one of our new patients?'

'Well, er, er …', I commenced.

Fred said, 'It's not Johnny's fault, matron. We invited him in.'

'I request that you leave this place by the way you came in,' she commanded.

I looked at the boys, their eyes glued to the table. 'She's a bitch,' I thought, and said aloud, 'Good luck, fellows, see you in London some time.'

It rained for the next two days, which disposed of the awkward problem of trying to see them again. That night I told Doc about my experience.

'No doubt about you, you get around,' he commented.

'Why do they keep the poor buggers to themselves?' I asked. 'All they want is someone to cheer them up.'

'It's not as easy as all that,' he replied. 'All who first meet them are visibly upset, some physically. It's not everyone has a stomach as tough as yours.'

I remembered my first belly-jolting view of them and thought, 'You could be right.'

'They have a long tough road to travel,' he continued, 'medically, surgically and psychologically, but there's an improvement in bone- and skin-grafting treatments. We are getting plenty of practice, you know. They'll be all right.'

'Well, I hope to Christ I go out clean. I'd hate to be burned like those poor devils.' I never flew afterwards without that ugly little imp of fear sitting on my shoulder.

'Anyway, it doesn't seem to have done you any harm,' replied the Doc.

'No.'

I paused. 'Ever hear of the saying, "I complained because I had no shoes until I met a man who had no feet"?'

We had a saying in my firm back home; 'How's your PMA?' Positive Mental Attitude, in other words, your mental outlook. Prior to my visit to the garden, mine had been dragging on the ground, now it seemed to have been magically restored.

That night I decided to give the night nurse a hand. She was a solid, tawny-haired Scotch lass with green, unfathomable eyes.

I don't know what prompted me, perhaps it was the direct way she looked at me, but while I was helping her to do some cleaning up in the room at the top of the ward, I suddenly put my arm around her, pulled her face around and kissed her. She returned my caress with an ardour that sent a thrill coursing up and down my spine and interest in things feminine revived with a rush.

I was impatient to get going. 'Wait a while. I'll see if the patients are okay.' A quick inspection proved satisfactory. In the small office was a night lamp and a couch on which the night attendant could rest. Returning, she looked at me with those inscrutable eyes, then turned and switched the light off. I got very little sleep that night and kept remembering a saying of an Australian cobber, 'Ever sleep with a red-headed girl? No, not a blooming wink.'

Next day, despite my lassitude, I was relaxed and almost contented.

Doc called me into his office at midday and said, 'Looks as though you'll be going out in two days. Sure you don't want to go off ops?'

This time I was certain. The contact with Fred and his cobbers and the earthly pleasures of the night nurse had raised my morale. My PMA was right on top.

'I've only got eight to go, Doc. I'll battle it out. Thanks for the offer though.'

'Okay,' he said. 'I'll get you seven days' leave. It may get you in nick for what's ahead. Though,' he added, 'you've made a remarkable recovery over the last couple of days.'

The next two nights were a pleasant repetition of the first, and it was with deep regret I departed Crothers. Before leaving I went around to the gate. It was locked. I called, 'Are you there, Fred?', but only the droning bees answered. I thought of those young fellows and Doc's words, 'They have a long, hard road ahead.' I felt glad to be alive.

I said goodbye to the Doc. He was a damn nice bloke who combined all the decencies of his profession with a deep and abiding compassion for his fellow-men. We renewed promises to see each other in Australia and I was off.

CHAPTER SIXTEEN

I went up to London and saw the Lady Ryder branch in Boomerang House. I had a desire to go to a quiet country spot and lie in grass and listen to the birds in the trees.

I explained to the middle-aged woman that I had been in hospital and what my thoughts were. She stated she had just what I wanted. An old friend of hers had a lovely home down in Surrey near Haywards Heath. She had a young daughter at school, one son had been lost at Dunkirk and another, a fighter pilot, had recently been posted missing in the Middle East; the third was fighting with the Eighth Army in the Desert.

'I'll give her a ring,' she said. 'You can wander around her garden and there are some lovely woods close by.'

Mrs Weston proved everything that had been said of her. A dignified English woman of perhaps forty-five, her home was a solid two-storied Tudor style house. Her daughter, Helen, a prim little miss of twelve, looked at me with wide violet eyes but kept her place like the little lady she was. Mr Weston, a solicitor who travelled up to London daily, was a quiet, reserved man. In his house I was at home. An English sheep dog called Shaggy, who looked the same at both ends, made the fourth member. The faces of three strong-looking men, two in Army uniform, one in RAF, looked at me gravely from a shelf.

None of us asked questions. I knew and appreciated the sorrow that lay over this home like a mantle. They felt I wanted to be alone and let me wander where I wished. By day I explored the lovely woods that lay close at hand or lay on the lush grass listening to the blackbirds and thought for the first time of Kiwi and the two pilots. It was the quietest and most restful week I had ever known.

Our leave taking was undemonstrative. I said, 'I hope you will have me again some time, Mrs Weston.'

'You will always be welcome here, Johnny,' she replied. 'Good luck and may God watch over you.'

On my way back I began to worry about Smithy, Hally and Blondie. I'd had a few notes from Smithy but nothing for the past ten days and in that time an awful lot could happen. Also, there was a new nagging worry as to what kind of crew I would cop to finish my tour. Perhaps they would make me a spare gunner or give me a new sprog pilot – a horrible thought.

On arrival I found my fears unfounded. Just before I had left hospital the powers that be had decided Wimpys were out and the squadron was to do an immediate conversion to Halifaxes.[1]

The boys had even more exciting news. The four Australian gunners were to be transferred to the Second Tactical Air Force, where a new Australian squadron was being formed. Kodak House had asked Bomber Command for some experienced gunners and Groupy had recommended our transfer. We couldn't find out what type of kites we were to fly, but what the hell did it matter?

I was astonished to hear that Ninnes and Jonesy had applied and been accepted for a transfer to a new force being formed, known as Pathfinders. Some rumours of this new striking force had been filtering through to the squadron for some time. It was to be composed of gen crews who would spear-head attacks and mark the targets with special flares. To the sceptics this appeared to be a sure way of committing suicide.

Later in the day I came across Jonesy who was rushing around like a bee in a bottle getting clearance.

'What's the bloody hurry?', I asked.

'Gawd! Am I pleased to see you!' he replied in his quick Cockney accent. 'Ninnes and I leave early tomorrow for our new posting. Ninnes particularly wants to see you. How about a session tonight down at the local? There's something we want to discuss with you.'

'Right! How about Smithy, Blondie and Hally?'

'Bring them too!' he shouted as he sped off.

We were waiting at the pub for the doors to open and again I felt that surge to be back amongst old cobbers. There was an unwritten rule in the RAF that after a particular friend or flying companion was lost you drank to his memory once only and then never mentioned his name again. The idea was a good one as it stopped maudlin reminiscences when the beer flowed. That night, despite the fact that it should have been a celebration for my return and that we were at least temporarily off ops, it was a sober gathering.

After I had given a lighthearted version of my visit to Crothers, I suddenly remembered Ninnes' and Jonesy's decision to go on Pathfinders.

'What's the guts on your new venture?', I asked.

'Well,' Ninnes replied in his precise voice, 'this is a purely voluntary show. They're calling for experienced crews. Fellow Australian of yours called Bennett is organising it. Appears these picked crews will lead the way to the targets, bomb, lay down markers and otherwise identify them for crews coming behind. It should do away with this bombing by guess or by God. Jones and I applied and have been accepted; I believe they will be using Hallies and a new plane called a Lancaster. They tell me it's a whizzer and can make thirty thousand feet.'[2]

'Sounds like another way of jumping off a cliff,' said Blondie. 'Do you think the Jerries are going to sit back quietly while you illuminate targets? You'll be a mark for every gun and fighter in the Reich.'

'Could be,' Ninnes agreed. 'But remember, there will be several squadrons and they'll all be gen crews with top-line equipment. I was hoping you'd come along with us, Johnny. We know each other's ways and could form the nucleus of a good crew.'

Before I could reply, Hally asked, 'Is it true you have to do a straight sixty ops for a tour?'

'That would be bloody silly,' I said.

Ninnes hesitated for a while and said, 'Yes, that's right.'

'What!', we exploded, 'Sixty ops for a tour? What dill thought that one up?'

'Sixty ops on twenty-two would be eighty-two!,' I exclaimed. 'You wouldn't have an ice cream's chance in Hell of getting through. Cripes, forget about it.'

For the next hour we drank, arguing on the merits and demerits of this new venture. We agreed that it was a wonderful idea, in fact one of the best that had come out of the war so far; if this plan could successfully be carried out it would mean the end of the old haphazard bombing and the senseless loss of lives and planes for little gain. But it was evident the top brass were not behind it, for why the imbecilic stipulation of sixty straight ops? This was enough to chill the enthusiasm of any experienced crew member. Thirty wouldn't have been so bad, but sixty – even with all the advantages that Ninnes offered it still looked like certain suicide.[3]

We tried to argue them out of their decision.

'Why, they'll be getting Hallies here,' said Smithy, 'and you've only got to do another eight and you're finished.'

But Ninnes was adamant and Jonesy followed him like a docile dog.

'I'll never be flying another op from this squadron,' he said, 'not under that bastard, anyway.'

We were all pretty full by this time, Ninnes more so than I had ever seen him. At this remark the four gunners looked at each other in awkward silence.

Then Hally said, 'Don't be bloody silly. Forget the past, do your eight ops and then you can tell them all to go to bloody hell.'

'No!', Ninnes replied with drunken obstinacy, 'I'll never fly from here again. If it wasn't for that unjust bawling out Peter got he would be alive today. If those dirty mechanics at Number Five HQ had made a true report and hadn't wanted us off their conscience and station those men would still be with us.'[4]

This was the first mention of our dead crew members and made a gloomy party even gloomier.

'Anyway,' said Smithy, more for something to say than anything else, 'he should get a posthumous gong.'

'He'll never get a gong,' declared Ninnes. 'He didn't crawl to the CO enough. You never see fellows like Snowden getting gongs, do you?'

'You're right,' said Blondie. 'You've got to be a crawler to get the odd gongs that are going. Peter wasn't built on those lines, he was a fine pilot and a gentleman.'

It was generally agreed in those days that a crew, when they finished a tour, should receive decorations. In view of the small number who achieved this distinction, this was well-merited. Yet every squadron knew instances where crews were denied this reward because they were not popular with the powers that be, while a crew whose pilot drank and played bridge with the Wingco or Groupy with less than thirty trips would be recommended for decoration.

It was apparent as the night wore on that Ninnes blamed the Wingco for the loss of Peter, also that he had shot his mouth off to such an extent that he would have very little chance of getting on in the squadron. His experience and ability merited that he be given at least a commission and, in the eyes of most navigators, it was considered he was the logical choice for the squadron navigator leader.

He had been informed if he wanted to finish his tour he would have to do it with a sprog crew. This was the deciding reason why he and Jonesy were transferring to the Pathfinders. In addition, I think he had a consuming desire to get even with Jerry for the loss of his friend.

Perhaps if either Ninnes or Jonesy had been close personal friends, or if I had their problems, I would have gone with them; but quite truthfully, when I came to analyse my associations I found the only one I had a close relationship with in the crew was Kiwi. In addition, I was going to a new Australian squadron along with three staunch and tried cobbers.

When closing time came we had to be thrown out, and later parted from Ninnes and Jonesy with drunken avowals to keep in touch.

That was the last I saw of either of them. I did hear from time to time of Ninnes' progress. His ability was quickly recognised and he became chief navigator for his squadron. Many months later we heard his crew were missing and as far as I knew, neither he nor Jonesy were ever heard of again.

PART THREE

TACTICAL AIR FORCE

CHAPTER SEVENTEEN

A cold wind was blowing from the North Sea and an icy drizzle was slanting across the aerodrome the day we left. As we drove through the gates Hally, Blondie, Smithy and I sang, 'Fugg 'em All', with fervour.

To get to our new drome entailed a five mile bus trip, a twenty-five mile train journey and then another six mile trip in a station wagon. This took five hours. Because there were no pubs near either station it was a cold and somewhat testy quartet that arrived at Beltwell.[1] We bucked up, however, when we saw the solid and imposing buildings that comprised the station.

The sergeant's mess was almost as imposing as the one at Group Headquarters, and we weren't surprised to hear this was a permanent station, and one of the best equipped in England.

We learned that the bulk of the squadron members had already arrived, so that all the rooms in the mess block were taken. The mess sergeant explained we could go into dormitories close by or take rooms in the double-storied cottages that had once housed pre-war permanent married couples, the disadvantage being the ten minute walk from the mess. Further enquiries revealed the disappointing fact that there were no femmes in married quarters.

Hally gave us a wink and intimated it would be a good idea if we looked them over. The more we saw of the station the better we liked it – bitumen roads, concrete paths, solid brick buildings – all gave the air of a well-laid out town. The 'married quarters' were a neat line of perhaps twenty cottages, all looking very much the same in design and very English. The bottom floor consisted of what was presumably a dining-sitting room and a kitchen, the top a large room which would have been a bedroom. Each room had a grate although all evidence of the kitchen had been removed. Both top and bottom rooms were equipped with sink and hot water.

We looked at each other and Hally said, 'Married quarters, eh! Tell you what, we'll try to get two of these. There may be a time when one or even two may wish to entertain a prospective wife alone.' He walloped Smithy on the back with a ham-sized hand.

As we sped back to the mess, Blondie said, 'Now, if we have any trouble we'll slip the Pom a couple of quid. They're as poor as church mice. Give me ten bob each.'

'Don't offer it all at once.'

The sergeant listened impassively to our protestations that each could not sleep with the other due to snoring, screaming and other less polite demeanours. 'The instructions,' he said firmly, 'are four to a cottage.'

Blondie said, 'But Sarge, our nerves are all shot to pieces. We've just completed a tour on Wimps. Here,' passing over a fiddly, 'be a good sport and help us.'

The Sarge wasn't too certain; after all, orders were orders. After further persuasion the second fiddly was passed over and the deal settled. 'Mind you,' he warned, 'should the accommodation position be grave, this arrangement will have to be changed. And make sure you keep some clothes in each room,' he said with a wink.

During our stay there we kept in his good graces and, as was usual with the RAF, once a place was shown as occupied, no-one worried.

Our arrangements were that Hally and Blondie took over one cottage and Smithy and I the other. We slept in the top room and used the bottom as a lounge-cum-bedroom, the advantage being if one had a prospect the other could retire to bed upstairs. If, say, Hally and Smithy had appointments and wanted to put on a little show, we would turn one of the cottages over to them and their visitors, ourselves retiring to the other. These turned out to be excellent arrangements and I never knew a cross word or lack of co-operation on anyone's part while we were there.

The completion of these matters left us with a holiday feeling. 'I'm going to like this joint,' Blondie remarked. 'I like the look of the mess and quarters, but what I like most is being off those bloody Wimpys.'

That evening when we went over to the mess, we were surprised to find Tom Hedge, one of the original thirty-two gunners, sitting in the lounge. In reply to our enquiries he said his crew had crashed on their return from their first op. Two had been killed and he had spent five months in hospital. He further reported Jimmy Sullivan, the ex-naval type, was on the squadron. Jim had been shoved into a training school but had kicked so hard he had been transferred to Beltwell. Tempe and most of the other gunners were dead, Tempe going on his twentieth operation. He had won fame by showing his complete disregard for superstition and air force instruction by flying on his thirteenth sortie without a parachute.

As far as he knew, only nine of the original thirty-two were left. Of these, Bourke had had a leg blown off. Whether it was the left, right or centre leg, no-one knew. Hally said there was only one like it in captivity and such a catastrophe was liable to throw at least a third of the femmes in England into mourning!

We found the planes were Venturas, two-engined jobs, an improved version of the Hudson, with a crew of four; pilot, navigator, WAG and straight gunner.[2]

The set-up of the mess building could only be described as magnificent. The reading-lounge room was better than Boomerang House. The bar had a quiet dignity. Efficient stewards flitted to and fro attending to our needs. I could not help thinking of that night at Group Headquarters. We sat up well into the night, talking of old friends, dead and alive.

Next day we went over to the hangars. These were massive, solid brick permanent buildings. Inspecting one of the bombers being repaired, it looked about half the size of a Wimpy, with a heavy underslung body and a mid-upper turret midway between the nose and tail.

Smithy summed them up; 'Looks like a pregnant Hudson to me.'

We had a look through one. There appeared to be bags of room. Armament was four .5s in front, two .303s in the top turret, with two guns pointing downwards from the tail. This one had us tricked until one of the erks explained, 'The WAG uses it when he's not otherwise engaged.'

During the day two flying officers, one a tall navigator, the other a shorter, pleasant-looking pilot, introduced themselves as Jack Parr and Wilbur Cronin. They mentioned that they were looking for a gunner; would I be interested?

I had decided to shop around before I picked my crew as ninety per cent of this squadron were sprogs and I didn't feel like going through those critical five ops again.

Yet somehow I liked the look of these two and all my prearranged plans of hand-picking a crew went astray. Instead of asking, 'How many ops have you done?', I found myself asking, 'What are the Venturas like?'

'They seem to be okay,' said Wilbur. 'Handle very well.'

'What's their endurance?'

'About five hours full up.'

'Can't be going to use us on any German do's then. Sounds like occupied Europe stuff.'

'Believe you've done a few ops,' said Jack.

'Twenty-two,' I replied. 'We lost three of the crew on the last one, including both pilots.'

They looked at me doubtfully. 'Both pilots!', they exclaimed incredulously.

'Yes,' I replied nonchalantly, 'one died later in hospital. Pretty grim show.'

Then, for a period, the bomber star was in the ascendant. We did not lose a trick in letting all concerned know we had been through the mill.

Later I met our WAG, a hearty Australian officer called Bill Fogg, an open-faced, bubbling, enthusiastic type.

Smithy said later; 'You've got a pretty posh crew, haven't you? All officers. You're the only bugger who's done any ops.'

'They seem all right,' I replied. 'In fact, we're doing a flip early in the morning. The keener they are the better I like it.' I added lamely; 'I was going to hand-pick my crew, but they all appear to be sprogs and the few experienced ones are tied up.'

We struck an immediate accord. Jack in civvy life was a barrister, Wilbur a BA and Maths teacher from Tasmania. Bill was an ex-Melbournite, an enthusiastic WAG, genuinely interested in wireless.

Next morning we went up for a spin. I liked the way Wilbur handled the Vent. We took off smoothly, went for a half-hour stooge and landed without a jar. The mid-upper turret, I found, had two .303 Brownings and rotated a full 360 degrees. Cut-out solenoids obviated the possibility of blowing the observer's head off as he looked out the astro hatch or of slicing off the twin tail-rudders.

That night the four old gunners were guarded in their comments as to the value of our new planes. From all aspects they seemed to be a backward step; endurance was only half the outmoded Wimpy; they could carry only two thousand-pound bombs or four five-hundred-pounders; top speed was in the vicinity of two hundred and seventy miles per hour, without a bomb-load. We speculated on what they were to be used for. Germany appeared to be out; perhaps Holland and occupied France.

In the next few days the rest of the boys joined crews; Smithy found a balding, quiet Australian pilot, Hally a slight, boyish-looking Queenslander who we were amazed to find was not only married but the proud father of twins whom he had never seen as they were born after he left Australia. Blondie teamed up with a Canadian called Parker, a slow drawling type with a smooth, bland face.

We all seemed happy with our choices. When I asked Hally why he had picked such an unlikely warrior, he said, 'Well, the poor little bastard wants a good gunner to look after him.'

We found the squadron, supposedly an Australian one, was only fifty per cent Aussie, the balance consisting of Canadians and Englishmen, with the odd New Zealander.

On the second day we found to our astonishment that an almost one hundred per cent Kiwi squadron was also housed on the drome. Such was the size of the place, they were installed in completely separate quarters. These boys were the best behaved crowd I'd ever seen. We frequently met them in our travels and the only thing that happened was a polite passing of the day. Blondie said one day, 'Surely these blokes don't come from the same place as Kiwi did – they're the politest lot of bastards I've ever met.'[3]

In addition to the six bomber gunners, we found fifteen Australian straight AGs who, like ourselves, had come direct from Stormy Downs Gunnery School without undergoing any conversion course. The same old racket had been practised on them; a promise that the first fifteen would go straight onto a squadron. They all had from six to ten hours flying up so it looked as though things hadn't improved much in gunnery training.

The Groupy was a permanent officer of the RAF, the Wingco a handsome blonde six-footer, an Englishman and a damn nice fellow. The officers, I would say, were hand-picked. Perhaps by this time it was agreed that Australians were difficult to deal with; they could be led, not driven. The squadron leaders were all good types; even our gunnery leader, a thin aesthetic young fellow with a DFM won in France on Defiants, was OK.[4]

He had his work cut out with the gunners under his charge. Most had had very little training and many of these young fellows couldn't've cared less. There was the usual smattering of complete dills. It was the old story over again of highly trained crews with uninterested untrained gunners.

After we had been on the place a week, we were sent across to the Group Training School. Because we knew from hard experience the unhealthiness of going out half-equipped against a well-trained deadly foe, we tried to instil into these young fellows the necessity of cramming every possible piece of knowledge into their heads. However, possibly because the first awe was already wearing off, our advice was treated with scant respect. In fact, they had already got to the stage where they felt we were line-shooting.

The bulk of these young fellows, we found, were aircrew who had been classified as WAGs and either couldn't do Morse or couldn't be bothered to learn. Counterparts of the original thirty-two, there was a percentage of wild men who had never attempted to learn anything and had inevitably gone off course and who couldn't have cared less; a middle group who had had a go and finally thrown in the sponge at the tediousness of a WAG's life; and finally the group of serious young fellows who had tried hard to complete the course but, because of their inability to take Morse and absorb the intricacies of the radio world, had finally had to drop to the lowly position of air gunner. They felt their position keenly and even now hoped for transfers to navigation schools with the remote possibility of becoming pilots.

Our statements that we had been drafted straight from Winter's as gunners and were not refugees from a WAG course were greeted with polite scepticism or outright disbelief. This was brought to a head one day by Hally declaring to an unbeliever; 'Call me a bloody liar, do you? Want to make something of it, hey?' The fellow hastily declined; henceforth any scepticism disappeared underground.

With the passing of time, the squadron gradually wore into shape and it was us who were finally absorbed into the squadron, rather in the fashion of the way the Chinese absorb their conquerors. This transition was not carried out without some upheavals.

One day at flight I was telling of how I had been rebuffed by two fighter pilots in a London pub. In the group was a sprog Aussie gunner called Ian Potter. This fellow was an angular whipcord type with a lantern jaw, a pasty complexion and was noted for his outspoken comments.

'Of course there's class distinction in the RAAF,' he said. 'The fighter pilot thinks his shit doesn't stink and won't speak to anyone below a bomber pilot, the navigators think they're Christ Almighty. Even WAGs think they're a class above the gunner and you bastards, because you've done a few ops, think you're a class above us.'

There was silence for a while, then I heard Hally growl; but as the remarks had been addressed to me, I said, 'What do you bloody-well mean?'

'I mean,' said Potter, 'you bomber gunners give me a bloody pain. All we hear is "in bombers we do this, in bombers we do that". It's about time you woke up to yourselves and realised you're not the little tin gods you think you are.'

These were fighting words. Blondie said, 'I'll take this bastard.'

'No, you won't,' I said, 'he's mine.'

We streamed over to the back of a hangar. Even though I was no champ, I was pretty confident of victory. When I was around 18–20 years-old I'd had a crack at the NSW Amateur Championships, and by the simple expedient of training like hell and dieting, I had been able to get my weight down under the light welter limit of 10 stone for the weighing-in. Once this was accomplished you had no further worry regarding weight, as under amateur rules you did not then have to weigh-in before each bout. This meant I fought at about 10–5, 10–6, which was the full welter division.[5] Despite this advantage, I was never able to get further than the last eight, and in getting this far copped some good hidings. Whether there were a lot of other bushy-tails like myself I never knew, but after my second effort and a super pasting from the eventual champion, I came to the conclusion I was no world-beater.

During the Depression, while working with a shearing team, I had palled up with a professional pug and had worked out with him. He had prevailed on me to have a go in the professional sphere on the Inverell circuit. Probably like every pug I had dreamed my dreams of some day being champion.

I had done all right while I stopped with the mugs in the four- to six-rounders. Ambition and bad advice had pushed me into the 10's. The blokes who got this far were no mugs, but generally cagey ambitious fighters. Two beatings in this class was finally climaxed by the father of all hidings handed out by a little Aborigine, all of 5' 3" tall and weighing 8 stone 6 and a half pounds.

Little was I to know that this tough little scrapper was, in twelve month's time, to be bantam and featherweight champion of Australia.

At the time, however, it was a blow to my ego and I thought, 'If I cop a hiding from this little joker, what will happen if I meet someone good in my own weight division?'

In the nine fights and six months I was in the professional ranks, I learnt more about training and fighting than I would have in a lifetime, as an amateur.

In my wanderings I had learned the average untrained bloke was soft in the belly, and the quickest way to stop a bush or city lair was to move in and hit him with everything you had, in the guts. This would generally bring his guard down and his head forward, so you could crack him on the jaw, then belt him in the belly again. These three punches won nine out of ten fights against average mugs.

If he came up after these three wallops, you still had the advantage. Most street fighters are suckers for a straight left. If he absorbed these, you could keep away and let him punch air; this will slow most fighters to a walk in no time. If he was still around after all this, you knew you had a bloody good fight on your hands.

On this occasion, I could see no reason why these tactics should fail with Potter. In addition, I had a good two-and-a-half-inch advantage in height and at least half a stone in weight. Things worked perfectly. I threw the left, crashed the right and then nearly broke my knuckles on my opponent's outsized jaw. From here on, however, things didn't go to plan, for in the next five seconds I was hit with a conglomeration of punches that seemed to come from so many angles I thought for a moment I was fighting half a dozen men.

It's hard to say what makes a fighter but one attribute must be a fighting heart and that's what this bloke had in large lumps. Fighting experience pulled me out of trouble over the next minute and I attempted to hold him off with straight lefts while I collected my scattered senses.

My lefts bounced off Potter's chin like peas off a brick wall, then he bored in, arms flailing. I hit him half a dozen times with my best Sunday punches,[6] but they had no effect. He threw so many punches he was hitting me six to one. I thought, 'I'll need an axe to stop this bugger.' I decided I was going to cop a hiding anyway, so I tried to match him punch for punch. A minute of this slugging had me buggered. I thought, 'I've had it', when a cold authoritative voice said, 'What's going on here?'

It was the Wingco. He looked at the dishevelled fighters, then at the silent gallery for a full minute, then said; 'You two men get dressed and report to my office immediately.'

Our interview was short and to the point. 'I don't care what you two were fighting about,' he stated, 'the main thing is I don't want to catch either of you two, or anyone else, fighting again, or believe me, you will be sorry. Now shake hands and forget about it.'

We shook hands, saluted and went out. Outside we looked sheepishly at each other. Potter said, 'I guess it was my fault. How about shaking hands again?' We did this and walked back to the flight.

If the boys thought there was going to be animosity and a return bout, they were disappointed. Hally and Blondie pulled me aside and asked, 'What was wrong with you? He was all over you like a rash.'

'There was only one reason,' I replied, 'why I didn't do him over.'

'What?', they asked.

'He was too bloody good.'

CHAPTER EIGHTEEN

We learned during the usual short arm inspection when we arrived on the squadron that the medico was an Australian. He was a tall, pleasant-looking fellow called Stanton. One morning after I'd been there for about three weeks I received a message to report to medical quarters, and was ushered in.

He said, 'I've been looking at your papers and noted you've been in Crothers to have flak splinters removed, and was checking up to see how the spots were healing.' In addition to this, he gave me a thorough medical check. After this was completed, he asked, 'How many operations have you done?'

'Twenty-two.'

'How do you feel?'

'Fit as a fiddle.'

'Nerves okay?,' he queried.

'Right as rain,' I replied, then asked, 'What's all this for, Doc?'

He thought for a while and said, 'This report states you were considerably shaken by your last operation. Twenty-two ops and a hundred and fifty four operational flying hours is a good effort. You can go off operational flying if you wish.'

'Yes, and be classified LMF,' I said.

'Nothing of the sort,' he said. 'You simply go on rest as having completed a tour.'

'Fair dinkum?', I asked in amazement.

'Certainly,' said the Doc. 'With not a stain on your honour.'

'You're different from the doctor on my last squadron,' I said warmly, 'but I feel okay. If at any time I feel I've had it, I'll report to you.'

That was the medical atmosphere that existed on this squadron. Stanton, like the medico at Crothers, looked on his charges as human beings, not as lead-swingers who were continually trying to put something across. Because of this the boys respected him. I would say with certainty no-one at any time tried to put anything over him.

An MO had the authority to override a CO. On this squadron it never would have been necessary. But in many instances, as far as I could see, the doctor did not have the guts to override his commanding officer.

As the weeks went by we began to develop a squadron spirit. Gradually the bomber boys forgot to mention their past flying experiences. As the nights lengthened and winter came on we heard the continuous drone of heavily laden bombers circling to get height and thought of the crews who would be riding in the darkness on their missions to Germany. On these occasions, if we were together, we would fall silent, thinking of Kiwi and the others, wondering if Ninnes and Jonesy were up there, plotting courses, preparing for the nine hour flight.

Day flying had many advantages, particularly with regard to leisure hours available. All duties usually finished at 3.30 pm, and we returned to the mess for tea at 4. The mess soon became aware that Australians, Kiwis and Canadians treated this as a main meal and did not bother to back up for the second lot. Thus we ate a combined tea and dinner. If anyone so desired, he could partake of a further meal at eight. This was usually only availed of by the Englishmen and a few hungry types. We then retired at, say, 4.45 pm to the main lounge where the gambling schools soon started. The Canadians considered straight poker a very tame game and introduced a new version called 'dealer's choice'.

The hard Australian and New Zealand gamblers took to these games like ducks to water and would not be bothered with straight poker; these were the big schools where you could win or lose fifty pounds in a night – big money in those days. Lesser schools contented themselves with minor games of slippery sam, pontoon or black jack.

Often these games started straight after tea and carried on till 6 am. It was during this period we made contact with Claude. He was in charge of the preparation of food for the mess.

Hally had been trying to make arrangements for him to serve tea and sandwiches to us in our night-long games at a cost of two shillings each. He came back after negotiations and said to me, 'Claude wants to see you. He's obviously a queen, so look out.'

I had found in my wanderings that my particular type of looks interested this type. Instead of kicking them out, the RAF drafted them to positions such as Claude's, or as hospital orderlies where their feminine instincts could be used to best advantage.

I had once heard a medical authority say 'the difference between a he-man and a queen, like that between a sane person and a lunatic, was only the width of a razor's edge', so I never had any desire to bash them up, which seemed to be the inclination of most of my companions.

I went out to see Claude and found him simpering like a shy school-girl and I quickly realised Hally was right. I had consumed quite an amount of grog and said, 'You look after us, Claude, and I'll look after you,' giving him a long wink.

From then on it was a case of me watching Claude. However, over the period I was in Beltwell I maintained his interest and hopes without becoming entangled in his desires, with many advantages to the card players in our all-night sittings. In addition, this deferred relationship helped the four musketeers, because at various times while Claude obligingly turned his back, I grabbed four-pound packages of marga-rine and complete roasts of beef and other hard-to-get delicacies from the kitchen.

These were taken to the haven where the roasts were sliced and grilled and often used as WAAF bait, particularly when they were mixed with the contents of parcels from Australia.

These months were, I think, the happiest I spent in England. If it weren't for the thought of what our sustained low-level training was for and the continued bad news about fighting on all fronts, particu-larly the Pacific, I think we would have been completely happy. Autumn came. Then winter; fortunately, not a patch on the preceding one. In November the tempo of our low-level flying was stepped up so that we flew, weather permitting, in echelons of six every day. Plants and factories were picked out as far away as Scotland and briefings were as thorough and definite as the real thing.

One particular sprawling factory in the Midlands was used several times and towards the end of the month we were adept at dodging chimneys and high tension wires in these mock attacks on individual buildings.

These tactics were mostly lost on the new gunners but Hally voiced all our thoughts when he said, 'I only hope the one they've picked for us is not in Germany or too bloody far away.'

On Sunday, December the seventh we were briefed. The target was Philips Radio Works, Eindhoven, Holland. Sunday had been chosen because a large number of Dutch workers would be absent. The Groupy stressed that this was an important and valuable target. If it could be put out of commission, it would be a real body-blow to the German war effort.[1]

Nine-tenths of our load was incendiaries. We were to contribute four boxes of six aircraft, the Kiwis three, and another Vent squadron three, making sixty Vents in all. Fighters were to go in ahead of us, stirring up the fighters.[2] We were to be covered by some hundred Spitfires fitted with long-range tanks; an innovation that would cause consternation, surprise and loss to our enemies.

The attack was to be entirely low-level. Flak opposition was to be expected crossing the off-shore islands and at odd scattered points, and was expected to be heavy over the target areas.

As we drove to our kites, Hally remarked, 'Well, it's something new, but I hope these bloody Spits keep close to us. I don't want to tangle with any Focke Wulfs in this bloody crate.'

I looked at the faces of these young airmen who were about to be blooded. They were serious and generally quiet. As each crew got out the rest wished them luck.

It was a fine, windless day with a slight mist. As we streamed across the flat Norfolk countryside the field workers stopped to wave to the modern cavalcade that rode the sky so close above their heads. The North Sea was grey and unruffled. We crossed it at zero feet. Our box was the tail-end of this bomber stream. Number One, the leader, had Number Two and Three on either side as support. Number Four flew just below Number One to miss his slipstream, and was supported by Numbers Five and Six. Thus, Number One flew at approximately twenty feet while Number Four (which was ourselves) was down to ten feet. Despite the nervous qualms at the pit of my stomach, I found this new experience exciting.

The low-level approach was intended to spoof the enemy radar. The idea was that the island defences would be taken by surprise and we would be across them before they recovered. What someone omitted to allow for was that the initial beating-up by the fighters and Mosquitos who had gone in ten minutes ahead would have the Jerry gunners right on their toes.

I heard Jack say, 'Enemy coast coming up', and then the sea beneath us began to churn white as the enemy gunners extended their welcome. Overhead, black smudges lined with red appeared as if by magic. Luckily, the heavies could not depress far enough down to get our range, but the concentration of Bofors, 20 mm and light flak was terrific.

Two tremendous splashes tossed water over our heads and marked the passing of two crews, then we were over the defenders. A little to our right a plane plunged into the earth, skidded into a strong point and exploded in a burst of flame and debris. It suddenly struck me that in this sort of flying, parachutes were useless; if you went in, there were no survivors. I sweated across those islands that day and anyone who says they were never afraid on ops is a bloody liar.

Suddenly we were flying across the mainland. A few black smudges chased us but it looked as if we had passed the strongly-defended coastal area. As we roared across the flat Dutch countryside the inhabitants out on their Sunday strolls waved frantically and jumped with joy. These Dutchies let it be known whose side they were on.

Bill had his head stuck out in the astrodome until the dome was blown away coming in over the coast without giving him anything worse than a scare. He returned to the front of the kite.

Suddenly Jack said, 'That's an aerodrome', and the next moment we were skipping across an excellently laid out drome. This was a costly blue on someone's part, because two more planes ploughed in with a smother of dust, flame and smoke. Probably this place had taken a beating earlier and was out for revenge. A cannon shell blew the perspex out on the starboard side of the cockpit, giving Bill his second fright but doing no damage.

The gunners poured a fusillade back without much apparent effect. A little farther we passed another Ventura burning fiercely. Four figures scrambling awkwardly away in their flying boots showed they at least had escaped. As we swept over them they turned and gave a forlorn wave.[3]

In all this excitement I had completely forgotten about the target. Wilbur's voice 'Target coming up' brought me back to reality. It would be hard to give my impressions over the next minute for the area was a nightmare of burning buildings, smokestacks and high tension wires.

Jerry gunners still manned their weapons on roof tops even though the windows belched smoke and flame. We went through so fast that it was hard to pick a target, so I put my finger on the tit and sprayed the entire area. How we missed the stacks and wires I'll never know. I saw a Vent veer crazily and hit a smokestack plumb in the centre and plunge downwards in a welter of dust, bricks and flame.

Jack screamed, 'Bombs away!', and we swung violently to the left. The clusters of incendiaries flew off at a tangent, travelling almost horizontally to smash into the front of the building in such a welter of explosion and fire that it really shook me. I knew why the place was so thoroughly alight.

We straightened up and missed a set of high tension wires by inches. I saw a burning Ventura that had smashed into a row of tenement houses. This, I heard later, was the only instance during the entire raid where civilian property was destroyed.[4]

The next moment we were doing a split-arse left turn as we went for home. It was only then that I noticed I still had my finger on the teat and that neither gun was firing. Around us, dog-fights were going on everywhere but enemy fighters appeared to have their hands full on that particular day.

We came out along a canal about three-quarters of a mile wide. Guns placed on either side turned in and churned the water white below us. Bill, who had gone to man the lower guns, had his third life when a shell hit both of them, curled them up in a 'V' but failed to explode.

Miraculously, no direct hits were scored on this fleeing target. A mile astern we saw a plane that turned out to be Pete the Canadian limping home. The German gunners concentrated on this inviting target but again, despite a hail of shell, the crew came through.

We came out over a marshy flat area without a shot being fired, which later prompted the thought, 'Why the hell didn't we go in that way?'. It was a badly mauled squadron that limped home. Because of the absence of runways, planes all pleading various emergencies landed everywhere. The place was a shambles.

Our petrol indicators showed empty five miles from the station and like everyone else we landed straight into the wind with another plane on our tail. While taxi-ing back on the tarmac we ground to a stop, completely out of petrol. At interrogation, I found the six bomber gunners had come through, which was almost a miracle.

A check showed our losses at six, as well as five Kiwis and four of our co-squadron. A total of fifteen out of sixty.[5]

A young gunner remarked, 'Well, that wasn't so bad.'

'Not bad?', said Hally dryly. 'Another three ops like that and we'll have completed our tour.'

The young fellow looked at him open-mouthed and said, 'But it's thirty ops for a tour isn't it?'

'That's right,' said Hally, patting him paternally on the head, 'only we won't have to go that far.'

On the way back to the mess we looked at each other and shook our heads. Smithy commented, 'Looks like a short career in TAF.'

I said, 'Bombers at their worst were never as bad as this. I hope to Christ they don't put on too many more do's like that.'

That night Groupy turned on a free party in the picture theatre for officers and sergeants. Strangely enough, these young fellows who had just completed an extremely tough mission seemed completely unaware of the importance of a twenty-five per cent loss and, possibly through nervous reaction, got gloriously full. Late in the evening Groupy announced that the attack had been successful and the entire target area was still burning furiously and that, as a reward, the entire squadron had been granted five days leave.

It wasn't until later we found that there wasn't a serviceable plane in the place, and that it was estimated it would take five days to get the squadron airborne again! As we staggered back to our quarters, sounds of revelry could still be heard from all sections of the station. Up in my room I thought I was seeing things when I spied a form in my bed.

'Jesus,' I said, 'what are you doing here, Maria?'[6]

A tousled red head supplied the answer. 'I had to see you, Johnny. I had to make sure you were alive.'

'If I was dead,' I replied, 'the bloody Committee of Adjustment would have been here by now.' I fell over in my haste to get my boots off and then found I couldn't make it.

'I'll have a little sleep,' I said drowsily, 'and then I'll come good.'

When I awoke it was daylight. Maria had gone and I had a splitting headache and felt awful.

During the morning we went out to see the photos which revealed the success of the attack. Our ground staff then advised that J for Johnny had 187 holes in it. They had calculated this by ringing each hole, large and small, with chalk and numbering them.[7]

The four of us decided to go up to London. Blondie said, 'Am I going to live up these five days. I've a feeling I won't see another leave.'

'Don't say that,' I said. 'Touch wood, you silly bugger.'

At the Boomerang Club we ran into a shining Dagworth, now a flight lieutenant. He told us things were going exceedingly well. His ferrying job, whilst being fraught with innumerable dangers, still offered compensating perks. If we cared to join him, he said condescendingly, he would be only too pleased to buy us a Scotch. We declined with thanks.

As we went on our way, Blondie growled, 'I'll bomp that bludger one of these days. He gives me a pain in the poofta-valve.'

That night, after a pub crawl, we talked our way into a so-called night club, telling the doorman, a tough-looking individual, we had been recommended by Joe.[8]

Safely settled inside, we were asked by a waiter if we would like a bottle of Scotch. It seemed a reasonable question. The only thing we forgot to ask was the price. This turned out to be five pounds, which caused some consternation as all we could muster was four pounds, five shillings.

A portly, benign-looking old gentleman with a platinum blonde companion came to our rescue by asking if he could have the pleasure, which was thankfully given. In a mater of minutes we had two more bottles of Scotch on our table, gifts of other kindly patrons.

The Scotch turned out to be firewater of the first order. We afterwards found that RAF bar stewards made pin money by selling empty Scotch bottles – complete with seals – to these joints for a pound or more. The result of the donations was so good that before the night was over we were dancing with the chorus who, on first sight, seemed a hard-bitten tough lot, but improved immeasurably as the night progressed.

Smithy tried to talk one sinewy chorine into taking him to her arms and bed and her retort was, 'Shucks, love, I'm old enough to be your grandmother. Why, me youngest is older than you!', which shows what a drop of good London moonshine could do.

We rolled back to the Lions Club at 6 am and the staff spent the rest of the day trying to wake us. One old cleaner, when she finally got us out after mid-day, said, 'Cor, what 'ave you boys been drinkin'? Metho? I 'aven't been game to light a fag all mornin' for fear of blowin' the place hup.'

Later we staggered down to Dirty Dick's, to be greeted with his usual question, 'You still here?' In sympathy for our woebegone looks he turned on a really good steak or whatever it was, that soothed our tortured stomachs.

These five days followed a fairly defined pattern; after breakfast at the club, a leisurely trip by tube to Boomerang House. There you were sure to meet some old acquaintances and learn of the doings of former course- and shipmates. Old Australian papers supplied some news of home: how surf clubs, cricket or football teams were faring according to the season and what was happening generally in that faraway island.

Pubs opened at about 11 am, which meant the drinkers departed to put the fires out. Staggered hours meant you could drink for most of the day and night. We soon got to know the hostelries and their hours and, if a real pub crawl developed, then there were still the dozens of small clubs, some reasonably sited, others in basements and back rooms that were only too anxious to make you an honorary member for a nominal fee. In most instances the females who frequented these dives were either part- or full-time prostitutes. We often wondered how they made a living because the competition from the amateurs was fierce. In the bars and night spots you rubbed shoulders with airmen, soldiers and sailors from every Commonwealth country, from America and from the free forces of nearly every nation in Europe.

Probably the most inhospitable of these fighting men, as far as the gunners were concerned anyway, were our own fighter pilots. These types were generally distinguishable by the way they aped their RAF counterparts, with scrawny moustaches and battered caps worn at a rakish angle. One day just after my arrival I walked into a bar where two of them were drinking. Being twelve thousand miles from home, I politely passed the time of day, only to be rewarded with a blank, icy stare as they returned to their drinks.

I can truthfully say at no time while I was in England did a fighter pilot say, 'g'day' to me. It was not unusual to see Aussie gunners and pilots at a bar, each ignoring the other.

A possible answer might be that the cream of the fighter boys had either 'bought it' or been moved back to Australia. Certainly no great Australian fighter name such as Bluey Truscott or Killer Caldwell came to light after 1941. Those left became more English than the English. This may sound like sour grapes but it didn't worry us a jot. Gunners had no reputations to keep and lived and loved for the day and night only.[9]

CHAPTER NINETEEN

We arrived back in camp full of speculation. It had been said that a ten per cent loss was more than the air force could stand. If this were so, we argued hopefully, there shouldn't be a repetition of the first op. However, the grim uncertainty remained.

That some indecision existed in the TAF was evident for the first few days, because even though the weather was good we stayed on the ground. Then some bright backroom boy got an idea. Four crews were called up for briefing and departed on their own. This caused some speculation till their return, when we found that they had been sent on individual train-busting sorties into Holland and Belgium.

This seemed to be a good way of committing suicide, though strangely enough all crews returned and reported they had seen no trains and no fighters. The weather closed down for a few days, then cleared. A runner announced that Smithy and I were wanted at the flight at 9.30 am.

The rest of the crews were already gathered when we arrived. We found at briefing that four planes were to go out on an individual train hunt. We were to fly at zero feet to mock the radar, stay together till the enemy coast was reached and then divide. Wireless silence was to be maintained. If we found a train, we were to attack and do as much damage as possible. If we saw any fighters we were to return immediately. Smithy muttered, 'If possible.'

'Rather like advising a surfer if he saw a shark to get out of the water,' and 'Do they think we're going to attack the flaming fighter?', were some of the comments.

The unknown always evokes more fear than the known. I was not happy with the mission. It looked too much like bearding the enemy in his den. Before we got into the bus we had a conference and decided in the event of trouble to use the clock system, because if attack came while we were flying in company, it would be each crew for itself.

As soon as we got under way, I started evasive action patter, interspersing sudden directions with long drawn-out ones.

A mist that reduced visibility to two miles hung over a leaden sea. The mist could be handy. Two miles is not far in the air. Fighters would find it hard to pick our camouflaged grey planes.

We came in over a deserted dune-covered coast without a shot being fired. This was heartening. I had imagined every portion of the west European coast bristling with soldiers, but this, when I later came to consider it, was a sheer impossibility. Anyway, no shots could mean no alarm.

Here we split, the two centre aircraft going straight ahead, and the two outer bearing left and right. As we were on the outer right we turned south and started a sweep, found the train line and followed it.

The land was flat and the soil a blackish grey. It appeared to be well-cultivated. In fact, a number of parties were working heads-down, bums-up. They didn't even bother to look up as we buzzed overhead, probably thinking we were Germans. One old farmer, working with a lethargic-looking horse, was galvanised into activity when the horse bolted and waved an angry fist at our retreating plane.

The stations were dreary and deserted. Bill voiced the opinion that either the service was poor or the trains, like rabbits, holed up during the day. We buzzed the line for half an hour over the countryside, drawing still further away from the coast until, finally, like music in our ears, came Jack's 'Have to turn back, petrol's getting low.' We came out the way we went in, with nary a sign of a Jerry and scooted across the sea towards home.

Two other planes were already in when we arrived and had substantially the same tale to tell at briefing. The fourth plane never turned up, which added a touch of mystery and tragedy to what appeared to be a very innocuous op.

That night there was some discussion as to what could have happened. That particular crew had taken the far northern beat. Perhaps they had met a fighter or run into an ack-ack group. One thing it did show was that train hunting wasn't without its hazards.

The next time the squadron tried this little stunt, two planes failed to return. What made these disappearances more mysterious was the complete absence of any wireless alarm that they were being attacked. Whatever got these planes was mighty sudden.

We were again called into the next briefing, only this time there were six crews and we were to work in pairs, keeping tabs on each other. If one got into trouble the other had to make for home. TAF was determined to find out what was happening to its planes.

Our partner was an English pilot called Petersen, a tall determined-looking joker with an all-Pom crew. The railway we were briefed to patrol had a line that branched north about five miles from its terminal. The instruction was, we were to start from the beginning or end of the offshoot and pick up Petersen at the main line. It would mean we would only be parted for a matter of minutes and would cover the entire system.

The day was a replica of the first. Same dead-dull sea, mist and grey fields. We found the little station that marked the terminal of our line and followed it towards our rendezvous. The grey fields slid beneath us. I was keeping a steady watch for snappers when suddenly I heard Wilbur say, 'There's a bloody train.' Swinging the turret around, I caught a glimpse of the long black goods train, snaking across the flat countryside. Wilbur altered course to bring it on our starboard side.

Jack said, 'There's Petersen.' We were flying a parallel course to the train at about fifteen hundred yards. Petersen's plane was streaking along to the left of the goods, with the obvious intention of either getting in first by giving the engine a burst from the rear, or flying ahead and coming back for a head-on attack. It was obvious he intended beating us to the first shot and the glory of chalking up the squadron's first engine.

Wilbur said, 'That bugger should be on the other side. He knows we have to come in on this bearing.' The Ventura was half-way along the train when, from the end, centre and front of the train smoke suddenly erupted and three lines of tracer converged on the low-flying Vent.

Petersen, sensing his danger, made a desperate effort to turn left, but in a matter of seconds the plane was literally blasted to pieces and plunged in a searing, rolling ball of flame into the grey fields.

It was like watching a drama from front seats. Here one minute was a plane and crew rushing in for a kill and, in a matter of seconds, a shattered rolling mass of flame and wreckage.

Jack's awed voice came over the intercom. 'Christ, did you see that?'

No-one answered. We were too stunned.

Wilbur said, 'There's the answer. That train's armed', and did a sweep left and came around in a wide circle.

'What are we going to do?', Wilbur asked.

'Let the bloody thing go,' I advised, 'and get cracking for home.'

'We could come in and make a fast attack on the engine from the side,' Wilbur said. 'We know the danger now, Petersen didn't.'

'Yes, and get a bellyful of lead,' I replied, 'those blokes are trained gunners. You've got to expose your guts no matter which way we attack. Let's get back and save someone else's lives besides our own.'

I knew his dilemma. A pilot is instructed to be aggressive at all times, to press his attack. If there were to be any reprimands or a bawling-out afterwards, he was the one who would cop the lot. Bill and Jack said nothing as we streaked by the slow-moving train at some fifteen hundred yards. I elevated my guns and gave the middle truck a long burst. It must have been good shooting because four streams of tracer snaked out towards us and kicked the dirt up under the plane. It stopped as soon as it started. I could imagine the itchy-fingered gunner getting a wallop from his superior.

Bill said, 'Cripes, that was close.'

We passed our target and commenced a wide sweep again.

Wilbur said, 'What do you think, Jack?'

'I agree with Johnny,' was his reply. 'Better to return with the news than go like Petersen.'

'How about you, Bill?', he asked.

There was a seemingly long silence, then, 'I agree with the other two', he replied. 'Those blokes have shown us that they can shoot. They apparently have multiple 20 mm cannons mounted in the rear centre and front. We wouldn't have Buckley's.'[1]

'Right,' said Wilbur. 'Let's get going. Give me a bearing, navigator.'

These were the sweetest words I had heard for many a day.

Back at base we made our report.

'Thank God you didn't go in,' said the Wingco. 'This explains the loss of our other machines. Train-hunting from now on will be a job for fighters.'[2]

CHAPTER TWENTY

Christmas sneaked up on us that year. By mutual agreement neither side is supposed to carry out offensive flights on this day of peace and goodwill. TAF must have received information that the Germans planned to break this tradition, so planes were bombed up and fuelled to retaliate in kind.

These arrangements had a sobering effect upon the station. However, the officers came over to the sergeant's mess in the morning and after healths had been suitably drunk, we all repaired to the airmen's mess to serve them the traditional dinner.

By afternoon the squadron, except for the teetotallers, was in no condition to carry out offensive duties of any kind. That night a riproaring party developed in the mess and the night resounded to the service songs, 'Salome, Salome', 'Oh, dear, What can the matter be, Three old ladies locked in the lavatory' and other air force favourites.

With the coming of the new year the squadron was given a new role. One morning we were called to a briefing and advised that our target was a locomotive repair works in France.

We were to cross the sea low again to spoof the radar, climb to six thousand feet crossing the coast and bomb from ten thousand. The Wingco said this was the ideal height, too high for light flak and not high enough for the heavy flak. We were to be given fighter protection so the op should be a piece of cake. The idea was to draw up fighters so the escort could deal with them. This sounded all right in theory, but as someone said, 'What if the escort does not deal with them?' [1]

This was one sortie that conformed to pattern. Probably to rebuild our morale after Eindhoven, Fighter Command sent out a packet of fighters. No flak was met over the coast, the target was lightly defended and we sailed in and walloped it good and hard.

Jerry fighters, probably feeling that discretion was the better part of valour, stayed on the ground. There were no losses and it was voted a pleasant do. This was the pattern we were to follow for the next couple of weeks. Our targets were either in France, Belgium or Holland. Our fighter escort kept the Jerry fighters engaged. Flak, though heavy in places, was not devastating. In five operations we lost only four aircraft. Life with TAF took on a new perspective.

'If these keep up it will do me,' declared Blondie. 'It's a piece of cake.'

But the German is a wily foe; just when you think you've got him beaten, he erupts. It was a day like the one when we did our first train hunt; visibility restricted to one-and-a-half to two miles. We had attacked a railhead in Holland and, after crossing the coast, came down to sea level, which was considered a good tactical move as fighters have a restricted advantage at sea level.

There were three boxes of six. Ours was leading when, out of the mist and flying right on the sea, came six Focke Wulfs with yellow noses, the badge of the dreaded Hermann Goering squadron, all picked and ruthless pilots.[2] They made one concentrated attack on the rear box, coming straight in from dead astern. In a matter of seconds three of our planes plunged with mighty splashes to their doom in the cold North Sea. The rest scattered.

When we got back we found it miraculous that the score had not been five, as two planes, including Blondie's, had great cannon holes in their wings and fuselage.

That night in the mess, the boys had their usual gripe about the uselessness of .303 machine guns and why the RAF didn't change them to .5 and give us real guns to fight with. At that time we had nothing to match the Focke Wulf 190 nor even the latest Messerschmitt 109. The .303 didn't seem to worry pilots in these fighters with their blunt noses. They seemed to bore in like a bulldog attacking a cat. You could see the bullets bouncing off them. Given these guns, .5s, early in the war, I feel casualties would have been cut considerably and we could have matched the enemy bullet for bullet. As it was, I never saw a day bomber shoot down even a Messerschmitt 109. Yet the RAF persisted with the inadequate .303 right till the end of the war.[3]

That event seemed to mark the end of our easy ops. Possibly the Luftwaffe had been sizing up these Venturas and found them singularly wanting, for on our next venture, an attack on an oil installation in France, the fighters came up in strength.

While battles flared around us in the blue sky, 109s broke through to attack the boxes. One daredevil attacked from below, shot up above us and dived straight at the group. This proved an effective way of breaking the formation as we scattered like pigeons before a hawk. Badly hit, one plane went into a steep glide. In a second it was pounced upon and blown to pieces.

Another 109, attempting the same manoeuvre on another box, either by accident or design, collided with a bomber so that they fell like a pair of whirling acrobats down through the clouds. Only one box out of the four bombed. The rest were scattered all over the sky and fought their way back in twos and threes. The tally that night, we found, was five out of twenty four, an exceedingly bad figure; an uneasy portent.

It was on an operation like this that Blondie went. We had gone into France to do over some secret installations the Underground had pinpointed. The inevitable mist lay over England but we climbed above it and came out into brilliant sunshine over the sea. Great canyons of clouds lay over the continent and between them our puny planes flew.

Over the target the flak was concentrated and intense. Two boxes each were to attack two separate targets. We had bombed and had turned for home when the other twelve planes which appeared to be a thousand feet higher came under severe ack-ack fire. We could see the planes weaving and dodging as they went in on their bombing run.

A bracket of these shots seemed to score a direct hit on the rear box. One plane appeared to disintegrate in the air and a second, its port motor aflame, turned away from the main group and headed for England pursued by venomous black puffs. As we watched, a white parachute opened just below the stricken plane, then farther down another. A burst of flak enveloped the top chute, which changed suddenly from a billowing white to an enveloping pink as the parachute and its burden fell with ever increasing velocity earthwards.

No more parachutes appeared, and the plane, still in a deep dive, disappeared into the clouds. The ack-ack battery concentrated on the lower chute, several bursts bracketing the slowly descending figure till it too disappeared.

Wilbur said with venom, 'Those bastards fired at those parachutes. Wonder who the poor buggers were.' Back home we learned that it was Blondie's plane that had been hit. Apparently it was the two gunners who had bailed out, the pilot and navigator staying with the plane in an endeavour to bring it home. We later learned it had crashed and both had been killed. Hally didn't say anything but stood apart as though in a daze. 'Blondie will be okay,' I said, but he didn't appear to hear me.

'Leave him alone,' said Smithy.

Going back on the bus, Smithy said, 'If either of those blokes were Blondie, I wouldn't give him a chance. The first was a goner when he went down in flames and the second was bracketed by ack-ack shrapnel. They're a lot of bastards to shoot at defenceless men.'

It was later confirmed that the Germans did shoot to kill para-chuting airmen. This typical ruthlessness was because there was a better than fifty-fifty chance of Allied airmen being rescued by Underground fighters once they reached the ground, and nearly all of these eventually returned to fight again.[4]

I could not help wondering at the time if Blondie was the man who had plummeted down, his parachute a mass of flame above him, and how this tough man had reacted. Did he scream? What were his last thoughts? What would I do under such circumstances? How long would you remain conscious on that last ten thousand feet death drop?

The mess was quiet that night. There was no card playing. The drinkers congregated in small groups. The usual light-hearted chatter and banter were stilled. Smithy, Hally and myself sat in a corner. Hally had given Smithy a fiver, saying, 'It's Blondie's, I borrowed it last night. Put it on the counter and we'll cut it out. It's the way he would have wanted it.'

Hally drank in a grim, intent way. We started at 5 pm. When the mess closed at 10.30, I said to Jonesy, the mess president, 'I know it's against orders, but give me a bottle of Scotch. We've got to knock this bloke flat somehow.'

Jonesy said, 'Come around to the back door,' and handed me a paper-wrapped parcel. We got Hally over to quarters. Smithy said, 'We'll drink this in our place. The Committee have been in. It'll drive him mad if he sees all Blondie's stuff checked and packed and, if he blows up, he's going to be a handful.'

We really hit him with that bottle. I'd say he drank most of it. He was as full as a man can be but wouldn't keel over. Suddenly he rasped, 'They're bastards; dirty, rotten, stinkin' bloody bastards. I'd kill every bloody German I could find.' As he said this, he staggered up, seized the table and with one mighty jerk pulled it apart; the chairs, the bed, everything in that room suffered the fate of the table. At the first signs of this upheaval, Smithy and I bailed out. To have tried to reason with him would have been like trying to pacify an enraged gorilla.

With the noise of splintering timber and shattered effects, lights popped on from adjacent huts and curious bods gathered to see what was afoot. They were met by two garrulous drunks and told to get back to their bloody beds. Gradually the noise of conflict died. There were a couple of reverberating whoomphs and then silence.

We looked in. The room sure was a mess. The only thing unbroken was the light – because it was recessed in the ceiling. Hally had passed out in the middle of the wreckage. We tried to lump him upstairs but, due to our inebriated state and his weight, found this impossible. Finally we cleared a space, made a bed on the floor and put him in, clothes and all. Smithy remarked, 'If he falls out he hasn't far to go.'

Next morning we made good the damage, snitching a table from one place, a chair from another. Hally, who was suffering a colossal hangover, made us laugh when he asked, 'What bloody clot bashed this place up?'

From that day on, Blondie's name was never mentioned.

CHAPTER TWENTY-ONE

Our ops through late winter and early spring seemed to follow a pattern. A couple of reasonably easy ones, then a real bone-rattler in which we would be met by everything Jerry could throw at us.

This lead to a rumour that there was an information leak somewhere. This was a distinct possibility as we seemed to run into some very well-prepared reception committees. Security was checked, special MI9 men appeared around the place, but still the unlucky break for Vents continued.[1] Many targets on which we were directed, often on information supplied by the Underground and our European agents, proved real hornets' nests. The two squadrons were thus constantly in need of replacement as planes and their crews fell in this high mortality rate.[2]

In early spring Group, in an endeavour to break this run of outs and to prove if there was a leak, directed us to targets in southern France. Because we did not have the endurance, we flew to dromes in the Dover or Cornwall areas in the late afternoon, spent the night and were briefed next day for targets.

As we passed out over the English coast on one of these trips, I looked down and saw an amazing sight; a real surf was rolling onto a white sandy beach guarded by towering headlands. 'Cripes,' I cried, 'there's a surf down there. What's that place, Jack?'

After a pause he said, 'Newquay.'

'That's the place I'm going to.' There were real howlers amongst those waves.

'Probably freeze your knackers off,' said Bill sceptically. 'I only tried swimming once over here and didn't know if I was Arthur or Martha when I came out.'

Nevertheless I tucked that name away in my mind. The old longing for the feel and thrill of a big wave under me was so strong that I felt I could surf even if there were ice floes.

It was on one of these away-from-home jaunts we were directed to a station somewhere in Devon. We were briefed as soon as we arrived. The target was an oil installation in the Bordeaux area. The intention was to get to bed early and take off at first light, which meant early rising, especially as clocks were forward two hours. We were to have an escort of sixty Spits from a very famous squadron, which sounded all right; even though they were only Mark V's their numbers should be able to take care of any trouble.

The gunners were bedded in cottages and retired to their quarters with the best of intentions until someone said, 'Do you blokes know there's a bloody pub next door?'

Investigations proved this to be the case. This was new to us. We later found that, as the air force took over farming lands and constructed dromes, they left the cottages and pubs, the latter being run by the owner who would be thoroughly vetted before being allowed to continue.

Someone suggested we go down and have a couple. The idea was enthusiastically taken up by about eight of the boys.

Hally said, 'No horseplay. We don't want the dicks on our tails. We're supposed to be in bed early you know.'

The bar was a small counterpart of those found in country pubs all over England. A group of five or six erks were playing darts and shove halfpenny, another three were drinking with four WAAFs, a civilian in a cloth cap was seated at the bar. The erks, particularly the three with the girls, viewed our boisterous entry with stony displeasure.

'Cor,' said the publican. 'Orstralians!', then bellowed, 'Ma!'

Ma was a large-bosomed, flinty-eyed female who took one look at us and started removing everything portable from the counter. Apparently they had unhappy memories of 'Orstralians' some time in the past.

Someone said, 'Three beers, Pop.'

'No beer 'ere,' said mine host.

It sounded as though we were being wiped off.

'What do you mean?' said Hally coldly.

'Only cider served 'ere.'

'Cider,' we echoed incredulously. 'But that's only lolly water!' said Smithy.

Both gave Smithy a withering look at this libellous statement. 'That's all we serve here,' the publican declared flatly. 'You can take it or leave it.'

The citizen who had been sitting quietly at the end of the bar said, 'That's all they drink here, Aussies. The cider from this part of the country is famous throughout England. In fact, it's a mighty potent drink, and if you haven't been used to it I advise you to take it easy.'

'Fair dinkum?', asked Smithy.

'I can assure you it's as far removed from the cider you know as milk is from water.'

'Here, Tom,' he said to the publican, throwing a pound on the counter. 'The shout's on me. Fill 'em up for these young gentlemen.'

Neither Tom nor his missus seemed over-enthused at the prospect of playing host to our party. 'Well, we don't want no trouble,' he declared.

As the first glasses came over he said, 'Now, no skylarkin' or fightin'. I don't want the provos around my ears.'

'That'll be the day when we start fighting on cider.'

The drink tasted something like slightly flat beer, but were we so used to numerous English brews we swallowed it without complaint. Someone shouted the second time and then before we knew it, there was a party in progress. After five or six drinks Tom Hedge, a fat slob who was a two-glass drunk, was giggling like a schoolgirl. Smithy said, 'I believe this bilge has got a kick.'

'Most certainly it has,' replied the farmer. 'In fact, there's a bet here that no-one can drink a pint of cider then walk a straight line to the door and back.'

'What?' said Hally. 'I could do it on my hands.'

'I'd advise you not to try it,' said our friend.

That was a challenge. Hally said, 'Give us a pint.'

Mine host was apparently not after trade. 'Why don't you go off to bed?', he cried plaintively.

'Give me a bloody pint,' said Hally, thumping the counter so that the glasses rattled. The pint was filled as someone drew a line with chalk from the score board.

The big gunner said, 'Here's mud in yer bloody eye,' drained the pint then started at a steady pace to the door, paused, and made a less steady journey back. Still, he made it.

I said, 'Give me a go.' It was a long drink; I had to take two cracks at it.

I made the door all right, but found the floor had a tendency to rise upwards on the homeward run. There was some controversy as to whether I had made it or not. Everyone was clamouring to have a go.

Things got a little hazy from then on. I don't know who started the fight but the next thing the bar was full of MPs in the charge of a very irate officer.

'Do you know you men have to be up at 3 am,' he declared. 'Now get to bed before I throw you all in the jug.'

As we started to leave he added, 'You'd better take this fellow with you.' Hedge was blissfully snoring under a bench. Someone tried to pick him up and fell on top of him. Finally two MPs picked him up by his arms and heels and carted him off like a sack of potatoes. As we left, the plaintive voice of mine host could be heard declaring that he had not wanted to serve us.

I got into bed, clothes and all, and seemed to do a horrible backward dive into a bottomless pit. I could have sworn I never even closed my eyes when I felt someone tugging at my arm and heard a strident Cockney voice in my ear bellowing, 'Come on, yer fugger! Wake oop! Wake oop!'

'What's the matter?' I asked, 'Is the bloody place on fire?'

'It's three fifteen,' he declared, 'Blimey, are you Orstralians hard to wake,' then, more kindly, 'Been on the cider, chum? I only 'ope you don't meet no fuggen Focke Wulfs today. You boys must have turned it on last night.'

From other points of the cottage came the cries of other runners, intermingled with curses and groans of the revellers. I had such a hangover I doused myself under a freezing cold shower.

As we went across to breakfast, Smithy said, 'I feel as though my eyes are falling out.' We all agreed that cider was a potent drop and was all its supporters claimed it to be. Most of us had cups of black coffee, averting our eyes from the fried eggs, turned on as a special.

Down at flight, Wilbur asked, 'What the hell have you gunners been up to? Weren't you supposed to go to bed early?' 'We did,' I replied. 'Trouble was, we got up again.'

'Bloody bad show,' he declared. 'You all look like something the cat's dragged in. How are you going to go if we run into trouble?'

'I hope the ruddy Spits get us out,' said Hally. 'They've got a name to live up to.'

We took off as the first faint light was appearing in the east. Although it was routine instruction that oxygen was not turned on under ten thousand feet, I plugged in and asked Wilbur to turn it on, as it was supposed to be a hangover cure.

There was silence, then Wilbur laughed. 'Okay, Johnny, have a suck. We don't want a half-dead gunner as a passenger.'

We were to fly to our usual plan, right on the deck for three parts of the journey, climb steeply to six thousand feet, cross the coast, bomb at nine thousand, cross the coast again at six thousand, then get smartly down to sea level. Red Box was some three hundred yards ahead, slightly on our starboard quarter. As the sun came up it cast a dazzling golden carpet across the uneasy sea. Sucking my oxygen I began to take an interest in things. The first layer of Spits was flying at about four hundred feet, with others above them to guard against surprise attack.

Obviously they were watching space and did not see three 190's, fighter-bombers intent on a sneak coast raid, drop their bombs and sweep in along that deadly dazzling carpet of light. The first intimation we had was someone from our box sounding the general alarm: 'Snappers, port quarter.' Swinging the turret around I saw three sinister shapes sweep around in an electrifying burst of speed like flying sharks and make a concerted attack on the first box.

Almost immediately our box had swung sharply to starboard and in a matter of seconds were beating it hell for leather for home. I don't think Red Box knew they were under attack until the first cannon shells smashed into them. As in a nightmare, I saw Numbers Four, Five and Six plunge with mighty splashes into the sea. 'God,' I said, 'that's Hally and Hedge.'

The other three planes broke formation and, twisting and turning, tried to shake off their attackers. One disappeared in a smother of foam. Two 190's, mindful of the umbrella above, broke smartly for their bases. The third continued, making at least five determined thrusts at its twisting, bobbing target. It was a masterly piece of evasive action. I thought, 'That's got the stamp of Smithy on it. I'll guarantee he's alive.'

At last the Spits tardily became aware something was wrong and started to join the fray but the Jerry pilot broke combat and scuttled eastwards showing the Mark Vs a clean pair of heels. The entire action had not taken more than sixty seconds. The surviving planes joined forces and, with a now compact cover of defending fighters, we returned to our base.

The two survivors asked for and got a landing priority, also requesting ambulance and fire wagon attendance. 'That's Smithy's plane,' I said. 'They must be shot up. Hope to hell they're all right.'

On our circuit we saw C for Charlie land first, skid along the runway, then slew sideways with the port wing dug into the soft earth. Four figures scrambled out and the ground crew did some good work in dragging the wreck clear.

Jack said, 'They can't be badly hurt, they can walk.'

At flight it was a sullen, angry group of airmen who faced the intelligence officers. Then we found all C for Charlie's crew had been taken off immediately to hospital, although we were informed there were no serious casualties.

A for Apple had come through with a cannon hit in the port wing. Apart from this, the crew were unscratched.

'Where were the fighters? What were they doing?', were the angry questions. How could sixty fighters let three 190's through to shoot down four bombers and so damage the fifth that it was a complete write-off, then allow them to get clean away? It didn't make sense.[3]

I kept thinking about Hally. It didn't seem possibly with his enormous strength and vitality that he could be lying fathoms deep in the cold Atlantic. I had a horrible feeling our impromptu party of the previous evening could have contributed to the tragedy. Hedge, as Number Five, would have been on the side of the enemy attack. Was it possible that he was asleep or dozing? Was the party responsible for the loss of four planes and sixteen airmen?

Later, the station CO addressed us and expressed his sympathy at our unexpected loss. He announced that we were to parade on the square in one hour's time. When we got there, the sixty sheepish-looking fighter pilots were lined up and for fifteen minutes were subjected to one of the most biting and scathing harangues I have listened to; but all the strong words in the world would not bring back our friends.

Before we left for Beltwell, we were told Smithy was C for Charlie's only casualty, and he was only slightly wounded by shrapnel splinters. The crew was, however, being kept under observation and would not return with us. Walker and his crew returned the next day with the information that Smithy had been taken to Crothers.

They said it was only Smithy's concise evasive directions that had saved them. Both the navigator and WOP declared what a horrible feeling it was to be seated virtually in the dark listening to his excited directions, feeling the impact of cannon hits and not knowing if the next moment would be their last.

That night we had a few quiet drinks in the mess. I think everyone who was on the previous night's party had a guilty conscience.

CHAPTER TWENTY-TWO

With the coming of spring we had completed sixteen ops as a crew and Wilbur asked me one day what I intended doing.

'Go through and finish this tour, of course. Then with fifty-two under my belt I can claim two tours. It might get me home.'

'It's okay with me,' he replied, 'but if you're going to stop on why don't you apply for a commission? You'd get it easily enough.'

I had never hankered to be an officer. Possibly some perverse streak in me subconsciously made me an officer-hater. My early air force impressions were of officers – some of them anyway – crawling like hell to get their commission. I put him off by saying I was losing so much money at poker, I couldn't afford to get a commission. 'Wait till I get a couple of hundred quid back', I temporised, 'then I'll have a go.'

A few days later I was called in before the adjutant. We had a pleasant chat on what I had done in civvy life. I don't know if he thought I was shooting a line when I explained that I had been a sales manager and earned about a thousand quid a year, but it certainly impressed him. I discovered he had been a school teacher on about five quid a week.[1]

He suggested I should apply for a commission as I was the only non-commissioned officer in our crew which, because of seniority and experience, must take a leading position on the squadron.

Also, my operational record marked me as a logical gunnery leader. He said Smithy, who had returned to the squadron that day after the extraction of various splinters from his person, was applying. Also, even though it wasn't official, the crew had been recommended for decorations.

I said I would think it over. That night I saw Smithy. He was thinner and there were dark shadows under his eyes. We went into the mess after tea and discussed the position. He said he had not given a definite answer. Like me, he felt no pleasure in leaving the happy-go-lucky atmosphere of the sergeants' mess.

Events were moving that were to change our respective minds. We received a group of reinforcements, the pilots and observers coming from the EATS in Canada. These new bods stood out as they wandered like lost souls in their new environment.

One day just after lunch I was going down to the village. At the main gate an altercation was going on and I found two of our ground crew boys being berated by a ginger-headed Australian flight lieutenant for not saluting. Coming to the rescue of the erks and seeking to put this sprog right, I butted in and told him that there was no saluting on an operational squadron; even the Groupy didn't ask for it.

At this interruption he swung around, looked me up and down and said, 'I suppose, sergeant, you would know your KRs?'

'I might,' I replied flippantly.

'Well,' he replied, 'do you know that section XYZ states when an officer salutes a subordinate, the latter must reply?'

'Ah! Wake up to yourself! You're not in some OTU in Canada. You're on an operational squadron, and no-one worries about such bullsh.'

'They don't? Well here's something for you,' he said, and flung me a humdinger, vibrating salute.

'Ah, go to hell!', I replied, and started to walk off.

The events of the next few minutes were unexpected and shattering. 'Guards, arrest this man for insubordination!'

The guards from the watch-house, who had gathered to listen to the back-chat, grinning broadly behind his back, suddenly snapped to attention at this unexpected turn of events.

'You're bloody mad,' I said. 'You can't do it.'

The sergeant came out from the inner office. 'What's the trouble?', he asked.

'Sergeant,' stated the flight loot, 'I order you to arrest this man for insubordination.'

The sergeant goggled. 'But he's aircrew,' he said. 'Been on the station a long time.'

'You know your duty,' was the reply.

The sergeant came across. 'Sorry, Flight,' he whispered, 'but he's got the drop on us.'

With a guard on either side, I was marched into the guard-house and placed in a cell. I was so astonished I hardly said anything. Then, as the door clanged behind me, I erupted. 'Get me Flying Officer Cronin,' I raged. 'I'll soon see if this bastard can do this to me.'[2]

Quite unperturbed, my adversary had the charge prepared, signed it and with a contemptuous glance in my direction, stalked out. When he was gone, the sergeant was most apologetic. 'He's a flight loot,' he said. 'I'm sorry, but what the hell could I do?'

'Get me Cronin and let me talk to him.'

It took some time to find Wilbur. When they let me out to the phone he was incredulous. 'What the hell have you been up to? It's only two. You can't be full yet.'

It took a while to get my message across. He was inclined to treat it as a leg-pull. Finally, when I convinced him it was no joke, he said needlessly, 'Wait there and I'll be down.'

In a matter of minutes the three crew members arrived and collapsed in hopeless laughter at my plight. When they got over their mirth, Wilbur asked, 'Is it true, sergeant, that my air gunner has been arrested for not saluting?'

'Yes,' replied that worthy. 'Here's the charge.'

Wilbur read it and said, 'See if you can get the Group Captain, will you?'

Luckily he was in his office. I heard Wilbur explaining the position. It must have tickled them both, for there was a lot of laughter. The Groupy asked to be put on to the sergeant, his instructions being to release the prisoner and to bring the charge sheet, witnesses and officer laying the charge immediately to his office.

It was a quick trial. The charge was read, then the Groupy delivered some very terse words of advice to a very red-faced officer to the effect that if he had wanted to get the tempo and atmosphere of an operational squadron he would have found saluting was dispensed with; also that he had brought an unnecessary charge against an aircrew member who had been with the squadron since its inception and before that had done a number of operations in Bomber Command. His decision was that the charge be dismissed. He also advised the thoroughly discomfited officer to pack his bags as he was being transferred from the squadron in the morning. Dismissing everyone else, he said, 'You stay, Beede.'

For a while he busied himself with papers and then, looking up, said, 'It's your own fault, Flight. Here are some papers. Take them up to the adjutant and fill them in,' and that's how I came to make my application for a commission. What I didn't know at the time was that the RAF wheels, like those of justice, grind slowly. After my forms were completed I thought, 'If I'm going to get my cash back I'll have to move fast.'[3]

But a lot of things were to happen before I put up my thin blue ring. The games still continued nearly every night and I was still placating Claude with promises of a night out and getting sandwiches and teas for the boys, plus a few extras from the kitchen for myself.

Then the news came that we were to be shifted from the gilded halls of Beltwell to a smaller satellite drome some five miles away. The Vents were in disgrace. They weren't fast or destructive enough. Their losses were too high and it took too many fighters to protect them. The truth was they should never have been used in the European sphere against frontline fighters like the 190s and improved 109s. Our drome was to go to a more important squadron.

This shift was in the nature of a demotion but the boys took it philosophically. Smithy and I were sorry to leave the pleasures of married quarters in one sense, but happy in another, for the place seemed to be peopled with the ghosts of Hally, Blondie, Hedge and others; everything reminded us of some event in which they had participated.

CHAPTER TWENTY-THREE

The main buildings of the new place were the inevitable Nissen huts. The quarters were quite reasonable, being weatherboard with separate rooms for two bods. We set ourselves up in one and with the practice born of long experience, soon scrounged a few extra chairs and tables to make the place a little more homey.

The living quarters were set deep in the trees and in place of the well-laid-out bitumen roads and paths of Beltwell we now had wandering dirt tracks. Dotted beside these byways were excavations ranging from six to ten feet deep left by the builders. These proved quite a trap on late trips back from the mess, particularly for unwise imbibers. Due to blackouts there wasn't a glimmer of light and, until the fellows got used to the paths and equipped themselves with torches, plaintive cries were often heard in the night as lost bods floundered in and out of holes or wandered completely lost in the darkness.

Those safely established in their beds thought it a helluva joke and left the lost souls to find their own way home. Several times inebriated bods were found in the morning sleeping soundly like modern babes in the wood.

This new location appealed to me. I had been reared in the country and the sighing of the wind in the pines had for me a soothing, indefinably sad note as though it mourned for all the young lives that were being lost in the titanic night-and-day aerial struggle over Europe.

Another pleasant feature was that we were now domiciled with the New Zealand squadron. Previously we had met only at odd mess get-togethers or when we played football. On these latter occasions we clashed as though deadly enemies and tried to pull each other to pieces.[1]

Living with our cousins we found them unassuming, pleasant fellows who could drink the grog, gamble and fit into the scheme of things better even than the Australians. The result was that we struck up a number of new acquaintances that rapidly developed into warm friendships.

The Kiwis had the same opinion of the Ventura; that it was not up to the fighting standard of the European theatre and should be pensioned off. Smithy and I developed special friendships with a young gunner called Rip, a big Maori called Bob and a long, stove-pipe of a gunner called Tommy. The latter was one of the most imperturbable men I ever met, with a dry unsmiling sense of humour that never failed even under the most adverse circumstances.

It was evident TAF was undecided what to do with us, because for the first two weeks in our new quarters, even though the weather was fine, we did no ops. We were advised if we had leave due, to take it. Never being reluctant in such matters, we took it.

Smithy and myself went to Edinburgh where we had the time of our lives in this beautiful, medieval Scottish city with its tree-lined streets. It was the only place in Britain where complete strangers stopped us in the street and asked us to have supper with them. We unanimously voted the auburn-haired softly spoken Scots lasses the most beautiful ever.

A few days after our return we were briefed for a raid on Dutch power stations. The Dutchies were asking for help because of the repressive measures the Nazis were using to break their strike. It was felt if we could knock out a few power stations, particularly with the workers absent, it would help their cause.

The first day we were about to cross our coast when we received a recall, the reason given being 'weather conditions bad on target area'. The following day we were in our kites, some having taxied to the take-off point, when the op was scrubbed for the same reason.

As we came back to flight, Jack said, 'I don't like this. Every bugger knows about this op; they should either choose a new target or scrub it altogether.'

On the third day, after standing on alert for three hours, word came through it was on. The force consisted of two boxes each from ours and the Kiwi squadron, twenty-four kites in all, with an escort of sixty Spits.

The low-flying mist had not risen appreciably and ground visibility was restricted at best to half a mile. Wilbur said, 'I hope it's better over the other side, otherwise this is one journey that's going to be unnecessary.'

Climbing a couple of thousand feet we came into clear blue sky and sparkling sunshine. The grey blanket persisted out across the Channel but as we came in to the enemy coast it began to clear so, as through gauze, we could dimly discern the outlines of shore and headlands.

That we were over the coast was verified by black splodges of hate which appeared as if by magic around us in the clear sky. The two boxes, battlewise, weaved their way through and all made the crossing safely. The two Kiwi boxes were half a mile away on the port quarter, about a thousand feet higher at eleven thousand. They were to go in first and we were to stoke the fires two minutes later.

The Spits had thrown out a protective umbrella and as usual were nattering incessantly. Wilbur growled, 'Why they make us keep complete silence while those bastards talk their heads off beats me.'

Jack announced, 'Ten minutes to target.' It looked like being another routine op. Suddenly, out of the ether, a precise English voice spoke with urgency, 'Red Box, can you see what's on the port quarter? I can't see for the sun.'

There was a short silence, then a voice screamed, 'Focke Wulfs, eighty plus, vectoring from the port quarter. Break! Break!'

In an instant the two boxes, realising the urgency of this alarm, started a split-arse turn to starboard. A voice said, 'Jettison', and the bombs plummeted earthwards.

As we came around the air about the Kiwis seemed to erupt in a maelstrom of cannon fire, tracer and twisting, writhing shapes. Relieved of their ironmongery, the Vents started in reasonable formation in a steep dive towards the coast. Everyone knew if we could reach sea level we might have a chance. Upstairs would be plain suicide.

In that mad dive gravity took over. Gloves and everything loose floated around my ears. With my head jammed tightly against the top of the turret, I couldn't even raise my hands. I thought, 'God, we'll never pull out of this.' Then, while the gunners were immobilised, like hawks sweeping on a flock of pigeons, three enemy fighters struck.

They hit the rear box in a paralysing burst of speed and spitting cannon fire. To those trained killers the fat Vents must have offered a perfect target. The first vicious attack accounted for three of the six planes.

Hard on their tails a lone fighter poured a stream of fire into our group, but the pilots, warned by the tracer and cannon fire, were already breaking formation and scattering. This decreased the target but robbed the box of its massed gun power. Every plane was on its own.

In these chaotic seconds, I had given myself up for lost. With my head jammed against the top of the turret and my guts in my throat I thought, 'This is it,' then with a swoop we came out, crossing the coast at such a bat the unprepared ground gunners were only able to fire a few wild shots.

As we skimmed to sea-level Jack said, 'You bloody beaut.' It was deliverance from certain death.

Immediately, from out of the mist at three o'clock, a yellow-nosed plane flashed, sighted us and came around on a vicious curve of pursuit. The intrusion of this peril, after our deliverance, made me hopping mad. After our escape, I'd felt nothing could stop us.

He came around in a perfect curve at six hundred yards. I bellowed my evasive order, 'Turn right, go.' In that moment of danger we were all on our toes as his gun began to spit. Like a rabbit twisting from the jaws of a greyhound, we came around in a turn so tight that it threw me sideways against the turret, and I lost him in my sights. He broke to my right and swept around in a perfect arc.

At my report, 'Attack broken', Wilbur had straightened and swung back on course. Like a hornet questing for his prey, the snub-nosed menace swung around. I sensed this attack wasn't going to be as impetuous as the first. The way the plane was handled showed this pilot was no mug.

He came in again from the same quarter but at what I felt was a reduced speed. I reported every movement to the tensed crew, who could see nothing and were only aware of their danger from my patter.

I waited till he was past the five hundred yard mark, but as I saw his nose straighten up I screamed the evasive order. Simultaneously with our turn the stream of explosive and tracer fire streamed at us. We came around in a violent turn, but instead of breaking to the right, the fighter came with us. I tried to keep my guns on him but again I was thrown to the side. I screamed, 'Keep turning, keep turning, he's still on us.' As his arc shortened, he swept away again.

The attack over, each member reported safe and sound. Wilbur said, 'I'm okay, but I'm afraid the port motor isn't. It's been hit badly. Where's that bastard now, gunner? If I could get half a chance I'd ditch.' Famous last words – to ditch we'd have to drop our speed by half and make a slow calculated approach. A hasty ditching at speed was suicide, the plane would disintegrate on hitting the water.

I said, 'He's preparing for another attack. Looks like dead astern.' For the second time that day, I gave myself up for dead. I said, 'Christ, where are the bloody Spits?' As though in answer to my blasphemous prayer, a grey shape swept into view and miraculously tacked itself onto the tail of our attacker. It was something like a hawk attacking a pigeon with a pee-wee on the latter's tail, offering a distraction. The Focke Wulf, with a speed of four hundred mph, had at least seventy on the Mark V Spit and, with one crook motor, at least a hundred and eighty on us.[2]

This attack would have meant curtains, but with the Spit on his tail, he had to rush it. Even on one engine the Vent performed creditably as Wilbur threw it into a corkscrew. I pressed the tit and gave him a long sustained burst till he broke off to starboard. I knew I must have hit him as he flew straight through my cone of fire without any apparent damage.

As he broke to the left, the Spit, perhaps two hundred yards behind, banked with its quarry and tried to get on his tail again. He had refrained from firing while we were in his line of fire. It was soon evident Jerry had decided to rid himself of this intruder, for he banked violently in an endeavour to get on the other's tail.

For the next couple of minutes I caught glimpses of this battle as the two planes flashed in and out of the mist. I felt there could be only one result as the Spit pilot was out-sped and out-manoeuvred by a faster plane and a better flier, but he had guts and stuck long enough to give us the break we needed.

A mighty splash in the leaden sea marked his end. I often think of that young fellow who lies beneath the cold dark waters of this unfriendly sea, truly might it be said that he lost his life in order that we might live.

I saw the Focke Wulf a few times questing around and then, no doubt mindful of depleted petrol supplies and with his ammunition low, he disappeared back to base. Wilbur said, 'I think one of those last shots must have holed the starboard petrol tank, it's getting very low. Send 'Mayday', Wireless Operator. How far are we from land, Navigator?'

'We'd be about half-way across,' said Jack. 'I got a bit mixed in those gyrations back there.'

There was a short silence, then Wilbur said, 'We'll have to ditch. I'll hold her as long as I can.'

'Jam the key,[3] Bill; you and Jack take ditching stations. When I say "go", gunner, scramble as you'll only have five or six seconds.'

I looked at the cold waters and thought, 'I bloody-well don't like this.' If we were to go in suddenly, it would probably mean a broken neck or back for me. On the other hand, I didn't like leaving the plane a sitting duck for some marauding fighter.

A voice said, 'Scramble', and I came out of that turret like a fireman coming down a greased pole, and in a split second had my back jammed against the bulkhead, my knees under my chin and my hands clasped at the back of my head, dragging it down.

I felt the jar as we hit, and a great swishing and splashing as we slid over the water. It wasn't as bad as I expected, not nearly as severe as that ground loop in S for Sugar. I thought for a second we might have skipped and there was a second crash coming when the cold water started to splash around my bottom.

I left that floor in a bound; twenty seconds was the estimated time we had to get out, and I had a horrible feeling I had wasted eighteen of them. A pair of blue-clad legs were disappearing out of the astrodome, which had been jettisoned before the crash. I tried to follow when I realised I still had my harness on. I hit the release button in sheer panic. The water was almost to the top of my boots as I came out of that hole like a rabbit out of a warren.

The raft had inflated and Bill and Jack were already in it.

Wilbur had hold of the cord. He said, 'Where the bloody hell have you been? I was just coming to look for you.'

I didn't think this merited a reply but scrambled smartly in. It tipped to one side and as it took my weight, Jack said, 'Sit down, you're rocking the ruddy boat.'

Wilbur cut the rope and we paddled away from the plane, which was already three-quarters under water. In a matter of seconds the nose disappeared, the tail rose momentarily in the air, and she was gone.

Jack, ever the navigator, said, 'Twenty-three-and-a-half seconds. The bloke who worked this out must have been speaking from experience.'

I said, 'Twenty-three-and-a-half seconds ... Christ, it seems like bloody years.'

Bill said, 'I don't know, it's just like pooping in bed, there's nothing to it!'

It was a poor joke, but probably from relief of the last fifteen minutes of tension and danger, we all started to laugh and were screaming with laughter when the sound of an approaching plane wiped the smiles from our faces.

Bill said, 'It's a single engine.'

We saw it flashing along twenty feet up. It was hard to pick its identity. Then I caught a glimpse of that unmistakable nose.

'It's a Spit!', I screamed, 'a ruddy Spit! You bloody beaut.'

Almost simultaneously he came around and swept over us, waggling his wings in recognition.

Jack said, 'What was that habit of yours that you were telling us about, Bill?', and we all started laughing again.

A short while after a second Spit joined our escort, which made us feel reasonably safe. Even if the Germans did send an E-Boat we felt we had a slight edge.

Wilbur said, 'That was a fine bit of evasive action you gave, Johnny.'

The other two agreed, and they sang 'For He's a Jolly Good Air Gunner'.

I was more than gratified, so said, 'May I say that was a masterly bit of flying, Wilbur, particularly that last bit on a conked-out engine.' This received general agreement, so we sang, 'For He's a Jolly Good Pilot.'

Jack said, 'I must commend our WAG for his brilliant execution of "Mayday", and his devotion to the noblest ideals of wireless operators as he was second out of the astrodome and first into the raft.'

This necessitated a dirgeful singing of 'The poor old WAG lay dying with a pisspot supporting his head.'

Bill responded by passing a vote of thanks to our efficient navigator who got himself lost in the melee, but crawled into the raft on his belly. It was a corny humour, spiced by good comradeship and that wonderful, indefinable feeling of being alive.

For my part, after twice giving myself up for lost in the last twenty minutes, it was a kind of bubbling ecstasy, a feeling that contained all the intoxicating pleasures you could think of. I felt I could sing, shout, scream with joy. It was during this unusual exhilarated state I got the idea I would survive the war. It was just something that came to me out of the blue, like the feeling you get that something is going to happen, a horse will win, it's going to rain, or some close friend is worried about something and you suddenly say, 'Don't worry, everything will be all right.' That was the feeling I got on the raft that day.

Apropos of nothing, Wilbur said, 'Johnny, how many ops have you done now?'

'Forty', I replied. 'Twenty-two on Wimps, eighteen on Vents.'

'You could retire, you know,' he said.

'What are you trying to do?' I asked, 'Kick me out of the crew?'

'No, I'm not,' he said, 'but after this, I wouldn't blame you if you took a rest.'

I thought this over. It was something I hadn't given any thought to. Then that feeling I had had earlier came, the surety that I would survive.

'No, Wilbur,' I said, 'I feel if we can all stick together we'll come out okay.'

'Thanks, Johnny,' he replied, 'I think all the crew would like to shake your hand on that.'

After a period, the elation wore off. Someone said, 'I wonder how the others got on.'

It was then I remembered the sight of the Kiwis smothered in fighters and cannon fire, the vicious attack on our planes on the way down, the scattering of our own box. It was a sobering thought. 'How many', we wondered, 'had survived?'

One hour fifteen minutes later, time check courtesy of our navigator, we heard the deep beat of a powerful motor. One of the Spits dipped down and flew a short circuit over us then, out of the mist, a white wave curling at its prow, came a low, powerful-looking speed boat. Sighting us, it performed a neat circle, cut its engines and came gliding towards us.

So neatly judged was its approach the raft hardly rocked. Ranging alongside, a clipped English voice said, 'Well, what have we here? Three kangaroos and a kiwi. Come on boys, all aboard.'

Strong hands reached down to pull us up. The officer said, 'Give us that rope, this little tub may come in handy again.' We were aboard in seconds. The raft was pulled in too and immediately deflated.

Almost as soon as we touched deck the muffled beat of the motor sprang to a full-throated roar and we were off. Once aboard we were whisked below. I had often heard of these Air Sea Rescue boats, but this was my first acquaintance. I was struck by their quiet unassuming efficiency. Apparently they were prepared for a badly shot-up, half-frozen lot of airmen. Instead, they found four healthy unscratched bods. They didn't let this deter them and without further ado, hit us with four powerful pots of rum.

The funny part about this was Bill was a non-drinker and Jack and Wilbur moderate ones. I'll never forget the look on Bill's face as, attempting to get his rum down his neck, he finally ended up in a paroxysm of choking coughs. Wilbur explained to our hosts he was a non-drinker.

This really shook them. A teetotal Australian was something they had never heard of. I fixed this by giving the officer a big wink and saying 'Give him one of those nice pink drinks. He'll like that.' Catching on, he poured a pink gin and Bill innocently drank these with growing hilarity on the one-and-a-half hour trip back to their base in The Wash.

Their hospitality was so good that we were a hilarious high-stepping group when we got off. Bill was particularly funny. A naturally buoyant, effervescent type, he literally bubbled with laughter and gin. The wonder was he wasn't flat on his back.

Conducted before the MO, we heard him say, 'What's wrong with that officer? Is he suffering from delayed shock?' The officer who had accompanied us in whispered something in his ear and they both laughed.

Darkness had fallen, so it was decided we would stop the night. A signal advised base that we were safe, who in turn told us to proceed to a nearby aerodrome early in the morning and we would be picked up. Apparently they were anxious to hear our story.

Not being an officer, I was directed to the Petty Officer's Mess. Wilbur tried hard to keep me with the crew, stretching the truth a bit by stating my commission was just about to come through, but with the Navy 'orders is orders', and he was told courteously but firmly this request could not be acceded to. To my surprise, he then declared that if I could not come into the Officer's Mess, the crew would come with me to mine. This really did cause some consternation as he was unusually belligerent and vehement about this point.

I thought, 'This is not like Wilbur' ... then I remembered the many drinks he had consumed. Things were developing into what might be termed a situation when I said, 'Bugger you blokes, you go to your own bloody mess. I'm going to have a bloody good time in the Sergeants'. Hooray.'

Famous last words – did I have a night and did those petty officers treat me well!

Next day they drove us out to the drome. The duty pilot was a new sprog, and he brought calamitous news. Only one Kiwi crew, the squadron leader's, had got back. Six planes, including ours, had failed to return from our squadron and as far as he knew, one Vent like ours had ditched near the enemy coast. Of the rest there was no news.

He told an incredible story which afterwards proved true, of the Kiwi Squadron Leader. Beset by German fighters he had dived to ground level, and instead of fleeing, had shaken off his pursuers and continued on to bomb his target.

I thought of our precipitous flight to sea level and our battle to get back. How about if we had gone the other way? Wilbur said, 'If that's true, he deserves a bloody VC'. And that is just what he got.[4]

Normally, our lone arrival back at camp would have created a furore, but so catastrophic had been the events of the day that our coming went almost unnoticed.

It took a while to sort things out. Then the horror of this catastrophe hit the squadron – eleven of the twelve Kiwi planes had been lost plus three of our own – a total of fourteen crews.

Fifty-six men ripped out of the station was something that just didn't seem possible. Where were Bob, Rip, Long'un, Snowy and dozens of other carefree happy blokes?

There were some amazing tales of luck and fighting prowess. Smithy's crew, like ours, had hit sea level and escaped across the Channel without a single shot being fired at them. Another crew had been involved in a melee in which three Focke Wulfs and four Spits had tangled. Both enemy and friendly shells had splattered around them and the fight had ended with two Spits and a Nazi in the drink and all fighters out of ammunition.

It was evident the RAF, despite German aerial superiority in planes and performance, had fought a valiant fight to protect the bombers. The unfortunate Kiwis had taken the full brunt of the first onslaught. The enemy had come out of the sun and their misfortune had been our good fortune, for it had given us a chance to flee, as well as bringing our own fighters into action.

The survivors and the rest of the squadron, ground crews and all, went into mourning and onto the grog. The next few days saw men who rarely drank hit the hops. The powers that be did not interfere. Perhaps they were on it, too. Gradually, after a couple of days, the station started to come out of it.

What really put us back on the wagon was the sobering information that TAF had decided the Vents had had it and were not to be used operationally again in Europe. This caused endless speculation. What was to happen to the crews? Were we to transfer to other aircraft or split up? Rumours swept the place, then officially it was announced that the pilots and navigators were to convert to Mosquitos. What was to happen to the WAGs and gunners was not decided.[5]

In addition, a new CO was to take over. His was a famous name in the RAF, a pilot with an unmatched fighting record.[6] When this was confirmed the squadron collectively went back on the hops again. The breaking up of crews is always a poignant moment and, in addition, for the gunners there was the unsettling speculation as to what was going to happen to them.

I personally thought it was a bloody nuisance. Forty ops could easily be classified as one tour.[7] My two tours seemed as far away as ever. If we could only have flown another ten sorties our crew could have signed off. Now I had to dodge the MO plus Kodak House to get another ten in somehow.

The arrival of the new CO didn't help any. He was an imposing figure of a man with an outstanding record, but lacking in tact. In the officer's mess he passed some remarks regarding the reputation of the Vents and the squadron's record. That didn't endear him to anyone, for what he didn't realise was that Venturas should never have been used in the European theatre and that the boys still remembered the loss of many close friends.

CHAPTER TWENTY-FOUR

One morning an announcement came over the Tannoy asking for volunteers to help bring in the harvest, particularly those who had had farming experience. This, to me, seemed to offer some variety. Smithy wouldn't be in it, stating flatly that he had been raised on a farm and he felt sure the English cockies wouldn't be any different to their Australian counterparts.

In vain I pointed out the possibilities of (A) Romance! The Land Army girls must simply be pining for some male solace. (B) Good food. (C) Fresh fruit. Smithy stated he could get as much romance as he could cope with on the station, the food was good enough for him, and he knew whatever fruit I got I'd have to bloody-well work for.

Undaunted, I put my name down and after a few days was called in and received directions to a farm some twenty miles away. I got my train ticket, rations and leave pass and was off.

I spilled out of a slow train at a sleepy little station and looked hopefully around for my host. There wasn't a soul in the immediate vicinity except a porter and myself. I asked directions and was advised the farm was situated on the other side of the village.

I thought, 'Perhaps he doesn't know I'm coming. I'll walk.' The walk turned out to be a two-mile effort, the day was hot and did I have a thirst by the time I located my objective.

The farm was situated beside the village and its tilled fields washed right up to the edge of the town itself, for, in the way of English villages and towns, there was no break of common land or reserves. The village ended and the farms began.

A cool little pub seemed to stand right next to the farmland itself, a handy little arrangement after a hot day in the fields.

It was just on two and closing time but the publican, a big, bluff looking man, condescended to pour me a couple of pints. I was sucking the second one down my parched throat when he asked, 'On leave, Aussie?'

'In a sort of way,' I replied, 'I'm giving farmer Giles a hand with his harvest.'[1]

He gave me what I could call a peculiar look. 'Friend of yours?', he asked.

'Never met him before. I'm doing a few days helping with the harvest.'

He gave a non-committal grunt and gently emptied me out.

The farmhouse was a double-storied structure, cool and shaded. The farmer's wife, a care-worn woman of perhaps fifty, welcomed me, asked me if I'd had lunch. When I said no, she set about getting me some.

Looking around the spotlessly clean kitchen, the thing that struck me most was the number of old-fashioned religious texts that adorned the walls, plus various illuminated addresses eulogising the services the farmer had given to the Ancient Order of Rechabites. He had served extended terms first as Secretary and then as President. This struck a dim chord in my memory. Must be a similar mob to the Ancient Order of Buffaloes, I decided.

Lunch over, she said, 'Sam is down in the fields, stooking'. It was said in such a way that I gauged she didn't really want me to go. The two pints and the lunch were amalgamating to produce a pleasant feeling of lassitude, so I felt it would be a pity to launch into my national service too soon; also I realised this woman was starved of someone to talk to.

Around 4.30 the farmer came in for tea. A tall, angular, stringy type who shook hands with me as though he had other things on his mind. Tea over, he said, 'You can help Alf, stook barley till supper.'

We found Alf in a field, busily tossing stooks of barley on a single horse-drawn cart. He was the picture of the English yokel – buck teeth, round face, protruding eyes. He wasn't as silly as he looked, however, as, after introductions, he continued to toss stooks onto the cart. This keenness persisted till the boss was out of sight, when he came to a full stop. He eyed me speculatively and then, in a guarded way began to cross-examine me as to why I wanted to work on the harvest for farmers in general and Giles in particular.

He seemed to have a suspicion I must be a friend of his boss and possibly planted as a spy. When I explained I had never met his boss before and had come of my own free will to work on the farm, he scratched his head in perplexity. 'It just don't make sense', he said. 'Farmer Giles, he be a hard man, he be mean, too. 'E'd skin a louse for its hide.'

On this basis I started to help with the work. I found the stooks unusually light for their size. We proceeded for perhaps twenty minutes on an easy working basis; Alf meditating in silence on the peculiarities of Australians. Then we stopped for a blow. During the ensuing discussion I found my companion bred rabbits as a sideline and learned to my surprise that nearly all rabbits sold in England were home-bred.

The small farmers could not afford to have wild rabbits on their properties so their warrens were dug out and the occupants eliminated. Wild rabbits were generally to be found only on big estates and were protected, and anyone shooting or trapping them could be had up for poaching, a particularly heinous crime, as a fat rabbit marketed at from twelve to fifteen shillings. Allowing for exchange, this was the pre-war price of an Australian sheep in many districts!

Rabbit-breeding, it appeared, had its problems and anxious moments, as only the previous night he had sat up till the wee small hours helping one of his favourite does in her labours.

The thought of someone sitting up ministering to a rabbit in the family way really made me laugh. Noting Alf's lack of appreciation at my merriment I hastened to explain that in the western districts of New South Wales, where I had once worked as a jackeroo, I had seen the ground moving with these pests during a rabbit plague as, by some mysterious motivation, they moved east.

I explained how we made wire netting tunnels to let the water-crazed creatures into the wire-netted dams by night and next day, four or five men armed with clubs had killed as many as two thousand trapped animals in the morning. I told of trails of poisoned bran spread across the country and how they died in their hundreds of thousands.

I'm sure Alf thought I was pulling his leg with tall Australian stories. Still, the time passed pleasantly, the only sour note being when the farmer returned and rolled an unappreciative eye at the half-loaded cart.

He must have decided we were a badly-matched pair, for he remarked on the way back to the farm that I would be working with his Land Army girls in the morning. This seemed a step in the right direction, as I had heard their frolicsome laughter in the distance, but anticipation is a wonderful thing, otherwise there wouldn't be half the marriages performed.

Even though I was up at dawn, I found to my surprise when I came down that everyone had breakfasted and departed for the fields. This put me at a slight disadvantage for I had to make my approach under the concentrated gaze of his three helpers. It would be unchivalrous to say what I felt when we met. Giles introduced us and they greeted me with a marked lack of enthusiasm. Apparently I didn't come up to their expectations either. Bertha, the oldest and largest, topped my five foot eight and a half inches by a good three inches. She was broad of shoulder and beam and weighed, at a conservative estimate, between twelve and thirteen stone. She eyed me speculatively and declared in a disappointed, rasping voice; 'But I thought all Australians were tall!'

Lizzie, her team-mate, tall, stringy and with the most muscular arms I've ever seen on any woman, grunted agreement. Peggy, the youngest, seemed a little more feminine, but as she also topped me by a good two inches, I could see I cut no ice in her eyes either.

They were, in fact, the toughest trio of amazons I'd ever met.

I was teamed with Peggy. Our job was to load a high-sided wagon with wheat sheaves. It didn't take me long to find loading barley was child's play to tossing these heavily-grained stooks that weighed anything from forty to fifty pounds.

It wasn't so bad in the early stages when the load was low, but as it rose, so did the energy and sweat required to hoist the wretched things up.

My amazonian companion tossed them indefatigably and gracefully but, as the morning wore on and my energy wore out, I began to understand, in its bitterest and fullest, the old saying about the straw and the camel. By mid-day I had the biggest crop of blisters in England.

After lunch it was agreed the girls (if so feminine a term could be applied to them) should attend to the building of the stack. I was appointed teamer, which I found meant that I had to toss the sheaves down to my fellow workers. I thought anything for a change from this back-breaking loading. It sounded a nice, light unskilled job, not requiring any intelligence. I however, started off with both wrong feet, for the first sheaf seemed by some mysterious means to be wired to the truck. While I was wrestling manfully with it, Bertha rasped scornfully, 'Get off bleedin' end of it, dolt.'

After ten minutes of heated and slow progress, it was unanimously agreed I should be middleman and the redoubtable Bertha took my place.

In my new post I found myself placed below the truck as the first receiver, the idea being that as the sheaves came down I should deftly toss them back to the others behind me who would build the stack.

I took my place and the next moment felt the whole truck must have collapsed on me, for I was inundated with fully eight sheaves in as many seconds. After being dug out and shifted back on again, I found the cause of my sudden eclipse. Bertha's method was a species of non-stop assault. The sheaves rained down like leaves before a southerly. Lizzie, now promoted to receiver, tossed them back with rapidity. By tea time I had been dug out a half-dozen times, and now had the biggest crop of blisters this side of the equator.

Those girls really dug me into the ground that day. I'd known hard work in my time. During the Depression I had cut ironbark sleepers, swung a banjo in a road gang under a notoriously tough ganger, cut scrub for a hungry station owner at a price that meant twelve hours solid work a day if you were able to make tucker, but all these faded into insignificance beside this work.

Giles worked harder than any of his hirelings. He was all over the place like a blue-arsed fly, stooking here, directing there, helping with the stack. He was a bloody marvel for his age and did the work of three men.

I always had some pride in my athletic prowess and it was probably this and ingrained male abhorrence of bowing to female superiority that kept me going. By 6 o'clock I'd had it and was wondering how the hell I could bow out with some shreds of male pride.

Fate came to my aid in an unexpected manner for, when staggering to the edge of the stack on rubbery legs to get down, I stood on what I thought was firm and somersaulted the twelve feet to earth with a bone-shaking thud. The amazons, I discovered, had a wonderful sense of humour, which found its fullest and most raucous expression at my predicament.

As I lay half-stunned, I thought 'The bastards!', then I made the discovery. I had a right shoulder, a relic of football days, which under some physical strain was liable to come out. On the football field my team-mates jolted it back into place and, except for a few moments of pain, I could continue with the game.

Giles was standing at the bottom of the stack as I hit the ground. The act I put on would have won me an Oscar. Luckily no-one knew the swift cure to my problem, so it took ten minutes to get it back into place. The excruciating pain I bore nobly with the odd, deep-throated groan. The shoulder back in place, I pronounced the arm as completely unserviceable, and requiring immediate hot foments. The farmer suggested a hot shower might fix it, and after that I could possibly apply myself to something not requiring a right arm. I smartly countered this by stating the pain was so excruciating I doubted if I could apply myself to anything.

On my way back to the farmhouse, a plan was already forming. I thought this bludger would find work for me if I had a broken back. I've got to get out of this place.

Back at the farmhouse his wife accepted my tale sympathetically. That shower was the most enjoyable I've ever experienced as I luxuriated my aching body under it for a prolonged period.

Safely in my room I dressed and then sat down. It would naturally take someone with a disabled wing a long time to dress. Through the day I had built up a prodigious thirst that neither water nor tea could assuage, but the plan had to come first.

Downstairs I explained to my hostess I was taking a walk to the village, which might help to relax my torn muscles. It was nearly seven, which meant I had two and a half hours to supper. I found the Post Office and put a personal call through to the sergeants' mess for Smithy. His peals of laughter when I explained I wanted him to call Giles' number as Adjutant and request my immediate recall, could be heard ten yards from the box. With some effort I got him to agree and explained I'd be back by 9 pm. My plaintive explanation that I'd had a bastard of a time only brought renewed merriment. I left the phone somewhat soured. It was the second time that day I had run into a misplaced sense of humour.

The pub was open when I came back. There was a woman in the bar and I'll never forget the delight of those first two pints. At the end of my fourth, I was still as thirsty as ever. I felt as though I had swallowed a block of rock salt.

At the end of the sixth, or perhaps it was the seventh, the publican walked in. He goggled at me. 'What the hell are you doing here?', he asked. 'I thought you were helping Giles with the harvest.'

'I was,' I replied, 'but at the moment I'm trying to quench the biggest thirst I've ever had.'

His voice was almost plaintive as he ordered me out of his pub. 'I've had enough trouble with him,' he said, 'him and his damned Rechabites.'

This struck a chord. I remembered the illuminated addresses on the walls and realisation came in a flash. Rechabites[2] – temperance – life member – secretary – past president – and it was then I realised the publican's predicament. That pub virtually in his front yard must have been an affront to Giles and his labours through the years.

I said, 'What's the time?'

Someone said, '9.30.'

In that convivial atmosphere it had simply bolted. I relieved the publican of my presence in a hurry.

As I walked into the dining-room I knew I had, in Giles' eyes, committed an unpardonable sin. The farmer was sitting stiff-backed at the head of the table. The meal was ready for carving in front of him. He looked at me and said, 'You are late. Supper has been held up.' Then, in more forthright tones, 'You have been drinking.'

At that moment the 'phone rang. He answered it and said, 'It's your station, it's the second time they have rung.'

I jammed the earphone right into my ear and said, 'Yes.' A medley of drunken shouts and laughter smote me. Smithy said, 'Where have you been, you bludger? This is my second call.'

I said, 'Yes, Sir, Beede speaking.'

Smithy, screaming with laughter, said, 'Cut out the bullsh, bludger and come home.'

'Very well, Sir,' I replied, 'I will catch the first available train back.'

A medley of yells and suggestions welled out of the earpiece. Someone yelled, 'How many of those Land Girls have you done?'

'Yes, I understand perfectly, Sir,' I said. 'A general recall. I'll find out when the first train leaves in the morning.'

Mrs Giles said, 'There's one at 7.30 and the next at 11 o'clock.'

'There's a train at 7.30 am, Sir,' I said.

'Get stuffed!' said Smithy.

'Goodnight, Sir,' I said. 'Yes, I'll be there.'

I hung up the receiver with my right arm. That's a blue, I thought.

As I turned back to the table the farmer finished his remarks. He said, 'I have never allowed drink or anyone who drinks to stay in this house. As you appear to be leaving in the morning, I will speak no further on the subject.'

I felt like telling him what he could do with his supper, but I was ravenous and where would I get anything to eat if I walked out at this hour, so I swallowed my pride and sat down. After grace, he sat with bowed head, probably saying a prayer for my salvation.

After I was served, both he and Bertha watched me with keen interest but one slip was enough. I started to hack into my meat with my left hand till Mrs Giles said kindly, 'Can I cut it for you?'

It was the most embarrassing meal I have ever sat through, for apart from this remark, not a word was spoken. After the meal was over, I thought, this is a poor show, this fellow has the courage of his convictions and I'm a low heel so as I was about to depart upstairs, I said, 'I'm sorry this set of circumstances has arisen, Mr Giles, apparently you have your opinions and I have mine, but as we appear to be poles apart in our convictions, it would be useless to discuss them.'

This might have gained me a point, but as I finished, I gave a terrific hiccough. This rather spoiled my apology and as my host made no effort to meet me, I left with my tattered dignity.

Just as I was about to scramble into bed there was a timid knock at the door. It was his wife, wringing her hands and looking fearfully over her shoulder.

'I'm sorry,' she said, 'he's a just man but he's a hard one.'

I said, 'Don't worry, mother. These things happen. Go to bed and forget about it', and added, 'Don't forget to call me for that train.' As she stood there I gave her a little peck on the cheek. 'Goodnight,' I enjoined; 'Sleep well.'

I slept like a log and when I woke the sun was shining and the birds singing. I looked at my watch. It was ten to eight. I thought, 'Gawd, I've missed the bloody train. What a pickle.' While I was trying to gather my scattered senses, there was the same timid knock on the door. It was Mrs Giles with a tray full of breakfast.

'You didn't call me.' I said accusingly.

'The war can wait for a few hours,' she said. 'I did come up to waken you but you were sleeping so soundly.'

As I ate she looked out the window at the yellow fields, then still not looking at me she said, 'Do not think unkindly of my husband. His father died a drunkard. As a child he knew poverty, hunger and want. Liquor is an obsession with him. He hates it so much he drove his only son from home.'

I knew then that she wanted to speak to someone to unburden her heart.

'Tell me about it,' I said.

It was the old tale of an uncompromising father, a young man of eighteen, kicking against parental restrictions.

One night, some five years before, after a football reunion, he had come home drunk and been caught by his father. The ensuing scene had been a violent one and in the morning he was gone. Somehow, by falsifying statements, he had joined the Army and been transferred to the Middle East. Caught in the war, he was still there, had been a Rat of Tobruk. His name was never mentioned in the home, and letters to the mother had to be addressed to a close friend.

I realised that was why she had not wakened me. Just for a while she wanted someone to mother and look after. When my time came to go I found she had packed me some cakes, preserved fruit and other delicacies.

She said, 'Keep along the hedge so Sam won't see you. I would not like to fetch him', and then, in defence of her spouse, 'He's a good man, but hard.'

I thought, 'He's an old bastard.'

As I sneaked along the road like a pariah, I thought of the farmer and the fact I had failed him as a worker and guest. Australians would be on the outer with him forever. I thought of his wife, her sorrow and her loyal defence of her helpmate.

Across the fields, the unmusical laughter of Bertha and her mates came to my ears. I decided, 'What the bloody hell am I worrying about harvests for? If those girls are my criterion, England should have no fear for her fields. Why should I impede them with my amateur frivolings?'

CHAPTER TWENTY-FIVE

Back in the camp I had to put up with a certain amount of chiacking, which I didn't mind. I was too happy to be there. However, I did notice there were no further volunteers to help with the harvest.

Life proceeded as of yore. The CO strode the earth like a God, disdaining to notice the lower forms of life. He did, however, give the pilots and navigators some hurry-up. They were embarked on an intensive night-flying program. The WAGs, for precautionary reasons, had to fly too. The gunners, being unnecessary cargo, were left behind.

The CO seemed determined to weld his crews into first-class disciplined tough airmen. As an instance, a Canadian Sergeant Pilot breached the censorship laws by writing home about the tough course they were embarked on. The CO considered that, if this information fell into enemy hands it would jeopardise the project. The entire camp – erks, WAAFS, fliers and all – were assembled in a full-dress parade. The charge was read by the Adjutant and the luckless airmen was stripped of his wings, buttons and even his Canadian insignia.

The station considered it a drastic and unnecessary action. As soon as the RCAF headquarters heard of this incident they recalled the disgraced pilot to London, granted him an immediate commission and shot him back in all the splendour of his new rank to collect his belongings, and then transferred him back to Canada on a special furlough. It was a slap in the eye for the CO and was intended as such.

One thing we admired about the RCAAF and the RNZAF was that they did not allow their members to be kicked around, which was more than you could say about our Kodak House mob.

Just after this episode I came up for interview on my commission. Smithy had already gone through and he and my crew gave me the gen on how to behave. My battledress was pressed. When I was ushered into the CO's office he was busily writing and didn't even raise his head. I saluted and stood like a ninny.

After a period, without even raising his eyes, he said, 'You have an application in for a commission. What makes you think you have earned this honour?'

I thought for a second, and said, 'Because I was advised by my former CO to do so. He considered I had earned it.'

'You have done eighteen operations.'

'Forty, sir.'

'Your record says eighteen,' he snapped.

I handed my log book across the table. 'I did twenty-two operations on Wellingtons prior to coming to the squadron.'

He took my book, looked at it, and for the first time looked at me. 'Why didn't you complete your tour on this squadron?' he asked.

I explained that three members, including the two pilots, had been killed on our last op and the rest had split up. He said, 'You could take a rest if you wish.'

'No,' I replied quickly. 'I would sooner continue with operations, sir.'

He looked at me with interest. 'Why do you want to carry on?'

'Because I hate the Nazis and all they stand for.'

I realised that it was on the false base of courage I could reach this man. I believed that, from his record, and this was borne out by the way he was to meet his death, that he was completely contemptuous of danger. There are a few men cast in this mould. It was a yardstick by which he measured lesser mortals. I expect he was surprised to find supposed evidence of it in such a low form of life as an air gunner. I do not know what actuates men like this. I certainly never got over fear of death or mutilation and sweated just as freely on my last as on my first op, and every other flier I spoke to privately admitted fear in the face of real danger. There were a few braggarts who claimed otherwise but I think for ninety-nine-point-nine per cent of men it is natural to be afraid of death.

After a few more remarks he curtly dismissed me, stating I would be advised when my interview with the Air Vice-Marshal was due. I knew by this I was through as far as he was concerned.

For all his faults I will speak of the CO as I found him. He was a wonderful pilot and airman. Strangely enough, after our interview, whenever we met he recognised me with a curt nod and I never failed to feel a sense of embarrassment, for I knew I was masquerading under a false flag. Although I did hate the Nazis, my immediate aim was an entirely selfish one, that of getting sufficient ops on the board to get back home.

I came up for interview before the AVM two weeks later. This man had a record second to none in the RAF. He had escaped twice, killing a few guards in the process. The Nazis had substantial rewards on his head. He was reputed to be a hard task driver, a brilliant organiser, an outspoken critic, but withal a human being, and because of this he received the full loyalty and co-operation of this staff.[1]

I marched into his office beside a ramrod stiff sergeant MP. Three hawk-eyed officers were sitting in various parts of the room. I knew they were there to note my reactions and behaviour. As I saluted and stood before him, he looked at me with keen eyes.

After a few preliminaries he shot the question I knew he asked every applicant: 'What would you do if you were escaping from the enemy and a guard stood in your way?'

'I'd kill him, if necessary,' I replied.

He looked at my records. 'I see you have played football, boxed and done some wrestling, all good tough sports.' He eyed me for a while and added, 'I also see you were born in Ireland. What part?'

This really shook me as I thought someone's let the cat out of the bag, but replied as nonchalantly as possible, 'Cork, sir.'

He then asked, 'If you're an Irishman, why did you join the RAAF, seeing that the Irish are neutral?'

I knew these officers were watching my reactions, so decided to bluff this one out. 'I left Ireland when I was three, sir. I feel I am now an Australian. All my roots are there. Besides, I hate Nazism and all its doctrines.' (This was true.)

He seemed keenly interested in my Irish ancestors. Had I been back? What did I think of the place?

I replied I had not been back, but intended going on my next leave. This interview was conducted on an easy conversational basis. I felt he was trying to find out something. At the time I was nonplussed and when he dismissed me forgot to salute. As I reached the door the sergeant murmured, 'Salute,' so I wheeled smartly and gave a ripper before I went out.

That interview had me worried. I had expected him to examine me on my operational life. His unexpected interest in my bogus Irish birthplace was disconcerting to say the least. It wasn't till I returned to the camp and discussed this matter with Jack and Wilbur that I learned he was a Southern Irishman and had been born in Cork.

After this the summer days went pleasantly. No-one seemed to be worrying unduly about us. We would report each day to flight and then discreetly take ourselves off to quiet retreats and our favourite spots, where we sunbaked – when the sun shone! – played cards and generally bludged. It was just what Smithy and I wanted, for it was a complete rest.

We filled in a week of this lay-off period by doing a two-week refresher course at the Group Training Station. This was later to pay dividends.

About this time a new sprog replacement pilot named Vincent Collins arrived on the station. He was built on Hally's lines and was the roughest bloke in speech and general behaviour that most of us had ever met. In addition, he used the two Australian adjectives with unusual freedom. He had originally been a steel worker in Newcastle. Just how he had graduated to a pilot was a mystery.

Someone said, 'He looks like a wild bull.' And 'Bull' he was henceforth.

He didn't take long to fall foul of the CO. It was rumoured, on being reprimanded for his language by the Wingco, that he had told him what to do. Whether it was his lack of social graces, his flying, his free use of the great Australian adjectives, or a combination of all three, he was banished from the squadron and immediately teamed up with the gunners – 'the only bastards,' he declared, 'who have any guts.'

He soon proved he was a worthy addition to our ranks by his drinking, fighting and leching abilities. In fact, it was agreed he had missed his vocation in service life.

Night diversions in the long twilight evenings consisted of visits to a nearby village and the pursuit of local wenches or, when the mood took us, adventuring by bike to the small country pubs whose drinkers were the local farm workers. These yokels rightly took a dim view of fur-riners drinking their beer. When aircrew were sighted the doors were locked and the publican would declare, despite the clink of glasses and sound of merriment from within, that beer was off.

A counter to this was to wait in the shadows till someone with the right knock came along and, as soon as the door was opened, to push in after him. Bull was the spearhead in all these forays and was he a fighter! I have seen him flatten three unsociable drinkers intent on tossing us out in as many seconds.

After a few such exhibitions it was obvious that he was the equal of Hally and in some respects even better. Had those two ever met in combat it would have been a fight of the century. Bull could drink prodigious amounts of beer and we found his tough, direct approach in matters of horizontal refreshment had amazing success.

CHAPTER TWENTY-SIX

On a three-day pass to London Smithy and I bumped into Clarkey in the Codger's Club. He still had his gunner's beret and sergeant's stripes and was drinking with three or four Kodak House types. The place was full of them. 'The Codger's Club?', commented Smithy, 'They should call it the Bludger's Club. Look at all those shiny bums!'

Clarkey came over. He was half-full and boastful. Life was wonderful, the rackets better and bigger and he had never had it so easy. 'Plenty of women, grog and opportunity.'

I said, 'If you're feeling so well, why don't you get back on to flying? There's plenty of room for a good gunner with guts.'

He was too full to see the insult. 'They'll never get me into a plane again,' he declared. He insisted on shouting and pulled out a roll of notes that made us both goggle. We knew he never gambled.

'Been skinning them at cards?', Smithy asked.

Clarkey gave a drunken leer. 'Cards, nothing; I'm on something better than that.'

We played dumb. Smithy said, 'I know you're a smart cookie. How about letting a couple of mates in on it?'

Clarkey looked around and then, dropping his voice, said mysteriously, 'Black market. There's a packet to be made if you know how.'

'But what do you sell?', I asked.

At this, a foxy-looking sergeant, who had been watching us from another group, came over. He had seen Clarkey flash his roll and realised he was full.

By way of conversation I asked, 'What section are you in?' The sergeant, Baxter, replied, 'Mails.'

Clarkey said, 'Beaut little working mate. Smart, too.'

The foxy one trod on Clarkey's toe but he was too full to realise Baxter was trying to shut him up. 'Get off me bloody foot!'

Baxter said, 'He's full. I'll take him back.'

'He's all right,' I replied. 'He's a cobber of ours. We owe him a drink anyway.'

It was obvious Baxter didn't want his working mate left alone, so he stayed on and, a short while after, led Clarkey away. 'I'd like to know what those bludgers are up to,' said Smithy. 'Obviously that sergeant didn't want to leave Clarkey alone with us.'

'Perhaps they're getting whisky or food from the mess,' I hazarded.

Next day when I was at Headquarters I called around to the mail section. The mail clerks there were very good and would go to no end of trouble to see if there was any mail.

There were no letters but there was a whopping big parcel from my mother. I picked it up and envisioned the delicacies inside. The clerk said, 'It's a beauty.' I weighed the possibilities of carrying it back to the station with me, but decided against it; after all it would only be a matter of four or five days' delay and would lose nothing in anticipation. I said, 'Send it on.'

Back at the station someone said, 'I see you're missing, presumed dead.'

'How come?', I enquired.

He showed me the paper. A Sgt. J. Bede was on the list. 'Strange', I said. 'There must be two dills in the Beede family, only this one is missing an "e".'

'Looks as though he's missing, period.'

As the days went by I looked hopefully for my parcel. When it hadn't turned up at the end of ten days I wrote to Kodak House querying its non-arrival. After a period I received a notice from the mail section advising that there was no record of any parcel being received at base for the past six weeks.

I then wrote direct to the Adjutant, stating that a friend and I had seen the parcel, the only reason I had not brought it back with me being its size and weight.

After a further period I received a second letter stating that after a thorough search and enquiry they were sorry to advise no record could be found of any parcel arriving at the time stated but they felt in view of the thoroughness of the investigation that the matter could now be closed.

I was as mad as a hornet, but what could I do? Both Smithy and I felt that there was a connection between Clarkey's drunken boasting and the missing parcel. If we hadn't seen the parcel we wouldn't have worried, nor been any the wiser if it hadn't turned up. Lots of letters from home referred to parcels but as the latter generally arrived months after the mail, it would be difficult to pinpoint a particular parcel.

However, we formulated a plan to see if we could get to the bottom of the mystery. Clarkey, given enough grog, we felt, was a moral to talk. As a part of the plan we procured a bottle of Scotch from the sergeant's mess at a prohibitive price and put it aside for future use.

About that time two events of importance came up. Smithy's commission came through and a week later I was notified that mine had also been granted. Almost simultaneously the gunners received orders to transfer. We were given the choice of going to the Middle East or to a TAF Boston squadron somewhere down in Surrey.

Smithy and I talked it over. The Middle East had its attractions, but as he had thirty-nine and I forty ops up, we thought it unlikely the RAF would be kind enough to release us as soon as we reached fifty, so plumped for the Boston Squadron. This good reasoning was later confirmed by the boys who went to the Middle East. These misguided souls, expecting to find glamour, mystery and exotic delight, found only sand, fleas, iron rations and in many instances, death.

While I do not think the flying in the Middle East was as tough as in the European theatre, at least we had some degree of comfort, good food, the fleshpots of London and adjacent towns. All you had to do to enjoy these delights was to stay alive.

After the big catastrophe there were sixteen straight gunners left on the squadron. Eleven of these fell for the lure of the East. Tommy, a Kiwi; another Tommy, a small Australian from Sydney; a big farmer from the Riverina called Stan, Smithy and myself made up the Boston contingent.

Prior to our departure, Smithy and I went up to London to be fitted for our uniforms and greatcoats. It appeared that before you could officially become an officer you had to be suitably attired as one. We were fitted by an exclusive tailor in Saville Row. In those days a budding officer received one very good light royal blue uniform and a second a little bit darker, plus a bobby-dazzler of an overcoat. It was 4 pm when the fittings were completed.

We had decided that this was an opportune time to test our Clarkey theory, so had taken our bottle of Scotch with us. We rang Clarkey and told him we had something we felt would interest him, and arranged to meet him at 5.30 at a little pub in Kingsway.

On the way, we dropped into Kodak House, where Smithy met an old school pal, saying, 'You go along and meet Clarkey, I'll be along in a few minutes.'

I arrived with our Scotch carefully wrapped. After a few grogs, Clarkey asked, 'What've you got that will interest me?'

I said, 'It'll keep. Let's have a few grogs.' I knew he was a two-bob drunk and felt sure of my capabilities, if necessary, to drink him under the counter. When he had been primed to my satisfaction I said, 'You told me last time we met, you were in the black. I can get plenty of Scotch, four or five bottles a week. Take a look at this one.'

He examined the Johnnie Walker with avaricious eyes. 'Gawd,' he said after a painstaking examination. 'It's genuine, too!'

'Of course it is,' I said. 'What's it worth?'

Without hesitation he replied, 'I'll give you six quid for every bottle you can bring along.'

As this represented almost two hundred per cent profit on the price I had paid, it was my turn to goggle. 'Right, I'll be in that. But before we strike a bargain I want to come in on the parcel racket too.'

Immediately, despite his half-lit condition, he was cautious. 'Where did you hear that rot?'

'Baxter told me,' I replied.

He said incredulously, 'Baxter! Why, that bastard's always on my back for talking too much!'

'He didn't talk too much,' I responded. 'The agreement is that I supply a minimum of five bottles of Scotch a week, but in return Smithy and I are cut in on the parcel proceeds. I've been cooking this up for some time. Perhaps you're not supposed to come in on the whisky deal. Maybe I'm speaking out of turn?'

'I'd bloody well better be in it,' he declared. 'I do most of the parcel work anyway. All he does is cop his share easy.'

'Sweet racket. Who thought up grabbing the parcels of blokes posted as missing?'

'Well, he did,' he said grudgingly. 'We get the various lists before they go into the newspapers, but I'm the one who disposes of the loot. He's clever. What I can't make out is how he came to discuss this with you. He's always telling me to keep our mouths shut.'

'How many in it?', I asked nonchalantly.

He was about to reply when he looked over my shoulder and said, 'Talk of the devil, here's the bludger now.'

I turned my head and, sure enough, there he was. Baxter came up to us in his unsmiling, foxy way. Clarkey said gaily, 'Hi, Bax! Just having a drink with our new partner.'

Baxter ignored the greeting and we nodded coolly to each other. It was my shout but I did not attempt to buy him a drink. What I wanted to do was get rid of him and concentrate on Clarkey. I said pointedly, 'We're having a little private chat. See you later, fellow.'

'So I see,' he said non-committally, but made no attempt to move. My companion must have sensed something was wrong; that there was a marked lack of cordiality between his partners. Perhaps he felt he was being frozen out.

He said, 'Johnny's just been telling me the news.'

'What news?', asked Baxter icily.

'You know what the bloody news is. And don't think you're going to leave me out of this deal. I'm the one who does all the work and takes all the risks; I want my share of the Scotch too.'

Baxter never took his eyes off me. He said, 'I think you must be drunk, Sergeant. I don't know what you're talking about. I've had no discussion with this person at any time and if he states differently he's a lying bastard.'

I thought, Where's bloody Smithy. I've got no witnesses. Fancy this bastard walking in at this moment.

In a split second I made my decision. 'Clarkey's just been telling me of your cute little brainwave of robbing the dead.'

He spat something at me and as he did I hit him with my favourite right rip to the guts. I wasn't worrying about his partner; I knew he was yellow. As Baxter crashed on his back I whirled to crown Clarkey but he was already in full flight for the door.

I knew I'd never catch him in the blackout, so in a desperate effort I clicked his heels together with my foot. As he skidded along the floor I took a brief look at Baxter. He was clutching his belly, trying to get up. I thought, 'He'll keep, I'll bash the illegitimate first'. I made a dive at the prostrate sergeant. I didn't make it; I was grabbed from behind by a pair of muscular arms and a burry Scotch voice said, 'Take it easy, Aussie. Take it easy.'

I made a valiant effort to toss the interloper over my head and, failing, tried to rake his shins with my heels, but he was a tremendously strong and skilful opponent and held me easily, making soothing Scottish noises. Clarkey picked himself up and dived into the night while his cobber, holding his stomach, his face contorted in pain, was close on his heels. Even after they were gone, I was still held in that vice-like grip.

The voice said, 'Fancy ye fightin' wi' yer freends.'

I knew I would never catch or find them now. 'Right, let me go.'

If I had any ideas of going on with it they were smartly doused when I turned around. He was a Scottish sergeant in kilts and six feet of muscle and brawn. An equally tough corporal nearly as big stood behind him.

'I'm sorry, Aussie, but I didnae want to see you fighting your friends.'

'Friends – nothing! They're the biggest pair of bludgers in the world; one is too yellow to fight and the other worked out a smart little racket of robbing parcels mostly, I would say, from the dead and missing.'

He said, 'It's fash I am at stopping yer wee brawl then; if I would have known that, I'd have helped you.'

He had an honest, craggy face and a friendly grin. 'Will yer have a dreenk with us?' he asked.

I found they were both in the 51st Scottish Division and had fought backwards and forwards in the desert and had been brought back for special duties.[1]

Next morning, Smithy, suffering a terrific hangover, explained he had fallen in with further friends from his home town and in the end had completely forgotten about our arrangement. He was particularly mad at the fact that he had not been present to give me a hand in the dust-up as he craved to hang just one on Clarkey. That he had escaped scot-free was a cause for singular remorse.

We discussed what we should do. That a racket was going on was obvious but then it was only my word against theirs. It was decided in the end that I seek an interview with the Groupy and lodge an official complaint for, if no endeavour was made to stop this little game, it would flourish unchecked. We both felt if the two birds were innocent they would lay a charge of assault, but if they laid low and did nothing they were obviously guilty.

If I had known what this decision was to let me in for I would have let the matter drop, and I didn't remember the old saying, 'Fools rush in'. We went up in the morning and soon found getting an interview with the CO was comparable to trying to see JC himself. It wasn't a case of just dropping in and spilling the beans to the big boy. Full details had to be given for reason for interview and it was no good stating ambiguously that it was a matter of grave importance, or for personal reasons. Finally, after a lot of backing and filling the reason went down as 'information of grave malpractices with regard to service mail', and I was told to be back at 3 pm.

Arriving on time I was kept waiting for an hour and then escorted into a room. There were two officers there, a Squadron Leader and a F/L. The former was a fat, bull-necked personage with a smug, self-satisfied air called Dale from the legal department, the other was a dark, sharp-looking type obviously there as an observer.

I was told to take a seat and naturally thought this was a preliminary to my interview with the Groupy.

The fat one advised that he was connected with the legal side of the service and if I had some information to give on the subject in hand to state it. If I had had any sense I should have stuck to my application and insisted on seeing the Groupy, but as Fatso seemed to be labouring under some deep emotion, and I thought this was the taking of preliminary evidence for a later interview, I started to spill the beans.

I had laid out my facts in some detail and I felt gave a coherent and lucid account of events leading up to my discussion with Clarkey the previous evening. While I spoke I noticed that the Squadron Leader did not even look at me but doodled viciously while his assistant lay back and watched me with hooded eyes.

I did not mention my attack and, after I had finished, there was what might be termed a pregnant silence. Then, my interviewer raised his eyes and said in a somewhat strangled voice, 'Is that all you have to say, Flight Sergeant?'

As the interview had progressed, I noticed his complexion had changed from a normal florid one to a deep purple and thought, 'This bloke is going to blow his top soon.' And blow it he did, but not in the way I had expected, for in the next five minutes I was subjected to a vicious tongue-lashing.

The gist of this diatribe was I was making vicious and unfounded accusations against conscientious and hard-working members of the Mail Service Department. My testimony had no supporting evidence except the vague support of a companion who was probably as drunk as I was. That a parcel of mine had disappeared had no bearing on the subject. This could have been lost anywhere along the line after it left Kodak House. My testimony of last night's discussion was of small consequence and even if it did take place, the two persons concerned were obviously pulling my leg.

After a lot more in this vein I was informed that (A) nothing further was going to be done in this matter, and (B) he understood I had recently been granted a commission and as my actions did certainly not constitute those of an officer and a gentleman, a heavy hint was conveyed that, if I was unwise enough to pursue the matter further, either at Headquarters or in my own private sphere, some unpleasant repercussions might come from it.

During the onslaught I went through a variety of emotions, in each of which I decided on a different course of action, ranging from the ridiculous to the sublime. Luckily, he talked so much when he made his final pronouncement I had my wits back, so when he advised I was dismissed, I said, 'I'm sorry you take this attitude, Sir, but as I considered this was a preliminary to an interview with the CO I have some evidence that completely refutes your attack on my motives. These I intend bringing forward at an appropriate time.'

I then saluted smartly and left the room. I thought as I went out, 'Even though that's all bull it will give the bastards something to think about, and should stop any precipitous decisions with regard to my commission.'

Smithy was waiting. He said, 'How did you go?'

I said, 'Up to poop. I took an earbashing, but if we're to get any mail at all we've got to work fast. Wait a while, then follow me into the mail section and discreetly ask me how the enquiry went, but loud enough for everyone to hear.'

I was at the counter when he came in and although I felt the young LAC attendants weren't in the racket I knew they would know something was cooking. My declaration for an interview with the CO would be common knowledge.

Smithy carried out instructions perfectly and asked the question. At this, silence fell over the room. I said, 'Good, they're putting the whole thing in the hands of the Service Police. There's going to be a few traps set. Someone's in for a rude shock, I think.'

I knew the grapevine would work smartly and that there would be some very careful people around for a long while.

We went to a pub and despite my wrath we laughed like hell. We felt we had won the last round anyway, but as an extra precaution decided to write home and request our people to number all parcels in the future.

Smith had got on to a couple of popsies the previous evening who had a flat and he had arranged to bring a cobber along. We still had the bottle of Scotch Clarkey had left in his hasty departure, so the future, despite a wasted day, was tinged with pleasant anticipation.

On our return we found things had moved swiftly. The pilots and observers were in the process of packing in preparation for their departure to a Mossie squadron. They were destined for Pathfinders. To me this was ominous news as I remembered Ninnes and Jones.

Wilbur came over and suggested that we go up to the local that night and have a few farewell grogs, stating Smithy's pilot and a few others were also going. The evening, despite half-hearted endeavours to create a party spirit, was a flop. There was an air of despondency over the gathering: a crew, once it has done a few ops and gone through a few shaky do's, develops a sense of comradeship that is hard to define. I couldn't get over the similarity of the parting with my last crew and a feeling persisted that this was indeed a farewell party.

Jack, at one stage, made a strange announcement; 'What are you looking so glum about, Johnny? I don't think you've got anything to worry about. But I'm not so sure about us three.' Someone said, 'That's a cheerful thing to say.'

Even a recounting of our adventures in Kodak House failed to raise a laugh, but it did bring a decision from all Australians present that they would arrange to have parcels numbered.

In the morning, word came through that the adventurers to the Middle East were to leave next day. They had already received various needles and carried out the intricate and involved proceedings that go with a movement from a station. This touched off a really riotous party.

Two days later the five gunners left for their new station and the Ventura squadron was no more.[2]

PART FOUR

BOSTON INTERLUDE

CHAPTER TWENTY-SEVEN

We travelled to our new location by train. Surrey was an entirely different neck of the English woods to Norfolk. In place of flat, almost treeless foodbowl space, this was lovely undulating woodland.

The station was situated about fourteen miles from a famous army training establishment.[1] The flying field sat on top of a plateau. The perimeter enclosed farmhouses and, what was more interesting, two pubs. The mess was two miles distant from flight and one of the pubs was about half-way between both. This was to prove an interesting obstacle for the boys in bad flying weather.

There were two squadrons on the field. Though they had separate flight commands, the crews shared the same mess and amenities. The only building with any pretensions was the officer's mess; the rest were the inevitable Nissen huts.

Even though we did not have our uniforms, Smithy and I decided to start our careers on the new squadron on the right note and presented ourselves at officers' quarters. We had removed our sergeants' stripes from our battledress and borrowed the thin blue braid that proclaimed our new status.

We found the other three gunners had been allocated to one squadron and Smithy and myself to the other. This raised the interesting question: who were we to fly with? This was settled the next day when we were called before our new gunnery leader, who proved to be a veteran in more ways than one. He had been a gunner in the first RAF which, even allowing for the fact that he was eighteen when the war ended, would make him forty-three. He was a dead ringer of the character in the Kruschen Salts advertisement seen jumping fences and was immediately dubbed Kruschen. He briefly welcomed us and then smartly got down to the subject we were to find dearest to his heart; physical fitness. We were subjected to a long-winded digression on the merits of physical fitness, so that it looked as if the Kruschen appellation was founded on fact as well as looks. After a suitable period I asked what crews were available. He said there were two vacancies; one to a Yank pilot who had joined the RAF early in the war, the other to a RAF pilot.

Smithy asked, 'What operational experience, sir?'

Kruschen dropped his bombshell. The Yank had eighteen ops, which was fair, the other crew, none. We both said incredulously, 'None?'

'That's right,' he declared. 'You can meet the crews now and decide amongst yourselves with whom you wish to fly.'

I said, 'But sir, we're both experienced gunners. We've each done forty operations. An appointment such as this means one of us will have to fly with an inexperienced crew.'

Kruschen agreed this was right, then brusquely stated we were in the air force to do our bit, not pick and choose pilots.

When we came out, we looked at each other. Smithy said, 'Ain't it a bastard.'

We agreed it was logical for both of us to want to fly with the Yank. I said, 'Let's go and meet them and we'll toss.'

The Yank was a hawk-faced flying officer with slightly buck teeth; his name was Tom Ryan but I never heard him referred to anything but 'The Yank'. His English navigator was a six-foot-five giant to whom we both took an instant liking called Stan Bell.

The sergeant RAF pilot was a chunky, serious-looking joker, his navigator a soft-voiced Scotsman. They were introduced as Bill Thomas and Jock McAlister. Both gunners were absent.

The Yank said with a pleasant drawl, 'From all reports, both of you boys seem to have tons of experience. For my part I'd be only too happy to have either of you in my crew and I know that goes for Bill here.'

Smithy said, 'I think the easiest way is to toss and the winner can have first choice. You can toss, Johnny, if you like.'

'We'll go outside,' I said. As we went through the door I said to Smithy, 'I know which way the penny is going to fall; you don't, so watch your step.'

Nine out of ten people will call heads, so the warning was warranted. I tossed the penny high in the air. Smithy said, 'Heads'. It fell a flat tail on the damp earth, then did a lazy flip and turned over heads.

The Yank said, 'Well, I'll be darned. I've never seen that happen before.' Smithy said, not without a small amount of triumph, 'I'll fly with you,' indicating the Yank. With minus-zero enthusiasm, I said, 'Right, I'm with you, Bill.'

We looked at each other speculatively. I knew he was aware of his lack of experience and sensed my disappointment so I tried to look happy. He slapped me on the back and said, sarcastically, 'Don't worry, Johnny, we'll try to bring ourselves up to your high standard.'

Later our WAG turned up, a tough-looking little Geordie with a broken nose called Fred 'Basher' Williamson. He'd been a professional pug fighting in London and the provinces.

In the afternoon, Bill reported we were to go for a flight, and it was then I got my second shock for the day.

The Bostons were two-engined bombers with a rakish upswept tail. The pilot's cockpit was forward, the navigator's under the nose. Each entered by separate doors and neither could get to the other; a nice thought if the pilot copped it. The gunners entered a trapdoor underneath the tail. The WAG sat in a small cockpit from which he rolled back a small perspex canopy, so apart from the top half and a couple of side levers which covered his head and protected his ears, he virtually sat in the open. He had two .303 machine guns and, as a precaution in violent evasive action, had a small chain called a 'monkey strap' that he attached to the back of his parachute harness.[2]

The straight AG's position was on the floor. He had a single .3 machine gun on a rack which protruded down through the trapdoor. Apart from this restricted downward view, he could not see anything going on around the aircraft. In the event of attack, all evasive action would be given by the WAG.

I kicked against this lowly position and ran smack into Basher's determined and obstinate opposition. 'By gum, that's my position and I'd be darned if I'm going to surrender it to any bleedin' Orstralian.' This was supported by Bill, who no doubt decided this was as good a time as any to put me in my place.

I was so mad I forgot to notice whether Bill flew well or not. I kept thinking, 'What's the use of all my experience if I'm stuck in this hole?' As soon as I got back I fronted Kruschen and tried to make my point. I was curtly informed that the RAF decided such matters as location of crew and any individual thoughts on the matter could be disregarded. My position was on the floor and that was where I would fly.

Smithy, I found, wasn't over-perturbed; he felt he could make a private arrangement with his crew to take over the WAG's position. I said, 'You'd better not let Kruschen know or he'll soon have you back on the bloody floor.'

That night I slept uneasily. The old bogey of the high mortality rate amongst new crews raised its ugly head. Here I was at the end of my second tour and virtually starting all over again, and in such a position in the event of attack I might just as well be blindfolded. What was worse, here was an obstinate WAG, supported by his pilot and gunnery leader, determined to hold his position. It was an outlook in which I couldn't see much future.

The following day Kruschen, no doubt wishing to assess the worth of his new gunners, announced he would hold a series of examinations on all gunnery subjects over the next three days. It was then that our revision course on our last station proved its weight in gold, for Smithy came first with an average of eighty-seven and I second with eighty-five. Our Basher had a staggeringly low average of fifteen while the Yank's WAG had thirty-five.

Kruschen was caustic regarding the general low averages of all WAGs and made threats that they would all have to do a gunnery course, which were never carried out. The main point was that he made no effort to put the gunners into their rightful places even though the radio sets were only used in emergency and all communication was by way of audio transmission, and even in emergencies the WAG could still use his set from the floor position.

On the strength of our WAG's abysmal ignorance on all matters pertaining to gunnery, I started a carefully planned campaign to sell the crew the idea of letting me take over the top position. To do this I knew I had to win their esteem and confidence, particularly Basher's. This was made more difficult by the fact that neither Bill nor Jock drank much, while the aggressive little gunner was suspicious and distrustful and, in true Geordie fashion, was careful and almost abstemious in his drinking.

One lucky break was that Smithy's crew, after the exam, had unanimously promoted him to the top position. The Yank and Stan agreed to carry on some useful propaganda on both Bill and Jock, which left me to deal with Basher. This job of selling extended over a week, and at the end I felt I had really won his confidence. Then I started on my theme that my main aim was to survive the war, which he agreed was the natural objective of every airman. Even at the end of this period, however, he declared himself unwilling to vacate what he considered was his rightful position. The Yank said that under their prompting, and particularly in view of their decision to let Smithy take over, both Bill and Jock were weakening.

In the final discussion with Basher I said, 'Fred, I want you to understand I do not want to do you out of your job, but I do want to see this war through and so do you. Your job is wireless operator, mine is gunner. If I did an examination on wireless I would get zero marks. You did one on gunnery with obvious results. It's a case of every man to his job, but in this game you don't get a chance to make a mistake. Generally your first mistake is your last, but unfortunately everyone else goes with you.'

Basher still was not sold, so we agreed to put it to our crew. He didn't know of the behind-the-scenes moves. We decided that each would state his case and if the voting was even we would toss for it.

I let him have first say. His main points were that the position was his by RAF regulation; everyone had to get experience; given time and practice he could catch up on his gunnery; we flew in formation anyway, under the leadership of a competent gunnery leader, so the position wasn't as serious as it appeared.

When I had my say I spoke from my heart and experience. I told them of the men I had seen die in the two years I had been in the air force; of a highly trained and implacable enemy who played for keeps; that it was my confirmed opinion that only the competent and highly trained crew had a chance of survival; a gunner's first mistake was usually his last; under no circumstances must we have a divided crew; instead we must use our combined strength and knowledge to its fullest advantage; a crew was only as strong as its weakest link; I felt literally hundreds of highly trained crews had gone to their deaths because, in attack, their lives and the plane had been passed over to the command of inexperienced gunners. I did not want to take over Basher's job as wireless operator because I knew nothing about it; on the other hand he knew practically nothing about mine; it was true we flew in formation, but what would happen if Number One plane was shot down or we were split by attack?; I had seen this happen a number of times and this only had to happen once; on the floor, all my experience would be useless; on top it could possibly save the plane and what was more important, all our lives.

We then took a secret vote and when they were counted I had all four. The first thing I did was to shake Basher's hand and genuinely thank him.

In the intervening period we had been doing quite a bit of flying and I began to realise Bill was no slouch when it came to handling a plane.

I do not know if he was a natural pilot, or whether he applied himself to it so assiduously he had little room for anything else.

The squadron was mainly engaged on low-level attacks, the modus operandi being somewhat similar to our first Vent do; that is, boxes of six in tight formation. These kites, however, were fifty miles an hour faster and were immeasurably nippier and more manoeuvrable.[3]

A fortnight after we had been on the squadron our names appeared on the battle order. Briefing was at 6 am and the target a railway workshop in France. Two boxes from each squadron were engaged. We were to go in at zero feet, the main objective being a round workshop building which was also used as a locomotive turntable.

As we took off once again I felt the butterflies in the tummy, the tightening of the muscles. Nestled in the Boston's belly were four five hundred pound bombs. At the height we were to fly it didn't give much room for error; a pranged kite would generally mean a defunct crew.

It was a beautiful summer morning and the sun glistened on the usually sombre Channel, giving it an unexpected silver lustre. We swept in over the sand dunes of the French coast and over some lovely wooded areas at treetop level. Fifteen minutes inland the target came up. The formations climbed sharply to five hundred feet and the bombs went down in a collective mass. Figures rushed frantically in all directions. The bombs were supposed to have a slight delay, but we were still over the target area when they went off. The planes rocked dangerously as the debris and hot blast climbed skyward.

One incident that caused some laughter afterwards was the sight of a familiar outhouse climbing almost intact into the sky before disappearing back into the maelstrom of dirt and smoke. I sincerely hope some poor Froggie wasn't having his morning movement at that particular time.

We came back over the familiar sand dunes and just off the coast a fleet of small fishing boats with brightly coloured sails popped up just ahead of us. As we charged over them, the fishermen jumped and waved, although some clot had to shatter this pleasant little scene by firing a burst of cannon fire at them.

Back at the station it was considered to have been successful and photos later verified this. Later that afternoon the blower advised that Smithy and I were wanted at the adj's office. We had fairly clear consciences, because if it had anything to do with the changeover of positions it would go before Kruschen.

The adj was a young flight lieutenant with an apologetic manner. After a bit of fiddling he advised that the CO had asked him to investigate whether we 'should be in officers' quarters'. We said we couldn't see why not as we had been told on our previous station that our commissions were granted and we had been fitted for uniforms.

'Have your commissions been officially confirmed?'

We admitted we weren't sure. 'Have you received officers' kit issue?'

It was the first we had heard of it. He then explained the reason for the interrogation was because papers confirming our new rank had only been received the previous day and that the CO took a dim view of our masquerade. We were to take off the blue stripe, put on our correct badges of rank and return to the sergeants' mess forthwith.

Smithy said, 'But you say, sir, the papers confirming our rank are here.'

'Yes.'

'Well,' Smithy declared, 'that means we are officers. Why shouldn't we remain as we are?'

This was a ticklish one. After a bit of hemming and hawing, he explained that the CO, by way of punishment for our transgressions, had decided to withhold our commissions for a week.

We took a dim view of this and told him so, then pulled the Happy act by declaring he had no authority to withhold our commissions and we would immediately refer the matter to RAAF Headquarters. This was an effective checkmate. The adj, being a diplomat, decided the easiest way out was to give us two days' leave to go to London to get our uniforms (as notice was also to hand that these were ready) and a decision would be made on our return.

In the interim we were to eat in the sergeants' mess but could stay in our sleeping quarters. This seemed reasonable as we didn't want to precipitate any head-on clashes. We had seen what happened to those in disfavour with the CO on our first station.

Up in London we filled in our time in the usual way. We met a few of the boys from the ship. They had finished tours with Bomber Command and were now on rest. As far as we could ascertain, not many of the bomber types seemed to have survived.

Bourke, it appeared, was living a life of ease. He had acquired an artificial leg, but because the leg was amputated above the knee, was having some trouble using it. He was, however, putting the middle one to its right and proper use, though at times it appeared there seemed to be some confusion amongst his admirers as to which was which. It was rumoured that a titled lady was willing to settle five thousand pounds a year on him provided he signed a ten year contract of service.

We returned carrying our new uniforms, which were really something, plus tailored overcoats. Coming back in the train we had decided it was wiser to make our peace with the CO, so reported to the adj on arrival. He told us we were to come up for interview before the CO in the morning and were for the present, sergeants.

In the morning we fronted, saluted and stood smartly at attention. Because he continued to write for fifteen minutes after our arrival we had plenty of time to study him. His lean face had a sour expression and it didn't take us long to realise we were in disfavour. Finally he looked up and said, 'Well?'

I said, 'We were told to report to you, sir.'

For the next twenty minutes he got stuck into us. He had a high-pitched, querulous voice. The guts of his schoolmaster-type lecture was that he took a poor view of our actions. He knew Australians in general and air gunners in particular were sadly lacking in discipline. This type of behaviour was not going to be tolerated on his station and anyone who felt he could do otherwise would soon change his mind.

We had decided to agree with him in every way: a case of mea culpa, mea culpa, mea maxima culpa, the theory being that if you demeaned yourself enough, there was no defence and no argument, and in the face of a complete lack of opposition the prosecution, having victory, would eventually fizzle out. This theory didn't seem to work with this bloke because the more we crawled to him the harder he got stuck into us.

I thought, 'Eating dirt doesn't seem to be the answer.' Also, I could see he was working up to a climax that boded us no good. He said, 'In view of your transgression I have decided … ' and paused ominously.

I thought, 'This is it', and said, 'I'm sorry we have earned your displeasure, sir, and can only assure you it was completely unintentional as we acted in the best of faith. However, while we were in London, we visited our headquarters to clarify our position.'

This stopped him. He said, 'You did.' Then, after a long pause, 'What was their report?'

I felt Smithy shiver beside me.

I replied, 'They stated that under no circumstances were our commissions to be held up. If they were, we were to let them know immediately.'

There was a longer pause, so I added, 'Neither Flight Sergeant Smith nor myself have any desire to precipitate this matter. We admit we were wrong and would like to apologise for our actions.'

He looked hard at us both, then said, 'I will accept your apology, but let me warn you both while you are on my station you will be subject to RAF laws and my discipline. Report to the adjutant.'

We saluted smartly and went out. Outside, Smithy said, 'My poor bloody nerves. What did you say that for?'

'Matter of psychological warfare. He won't carry this matter any further. He would only prove himself a dill. Besides, he was just going to wallop us. No good having a say after he's pronounced his sentence.'[4]

CHAPTER TWENTY-EIGHT

That morning we collected our officer's kit, which included two pairs of shoes and a new issue of underwear. New battle jackets were also included, but as the store only had a grey English issue we stuck to our blue until new ones could be forwarded from London. Resplendent in our new uniforms we officially entered the officers' mess for the first time. Previously, because of the uncertainty of our position, we had only eaten in the dining hall and discreetly adjourned to the local inns for beverage.

This transition from sergeant to officer was pleasant and interesting. The difference in service and cuisine was roughly that of a first and second class hotel; there was an air of deference in the attentions of the barmen and waiters. Silver pint pots on the shelves; the murmur of well-bred voices raised in genteel discussion; all reminiscent of a well-run club. There were other niceties that had us both declaring we should have been in it long ago.

The squadron leader's WAG, Des Holstead, a Londoner with a wide-mouthed grin, and his straight AG, Jack Stokes, a quiet, easy-going Canadian whom we had previously met at flight, joined us at the bar. In addition to being one-tour men, they were both gunnery leaders; that is, they had done the gunnery leader's course – a sound idea, because if one was knocked out the other could take over. There's no place better than a bar to get to know a man. We soon found we all shared a common bond of wanting to come out of this show alive.

They both showed keen interest in our previous experiences, particularly the fact that we had flown with Bomber Command. We gathered that they had a very high opinion of their pilot and observer. The squadron leader in particular, was considered not only a wonderful pilot but a jolly decent fellow. In civvy life he was a person of some standing in the community, being a gentleman farmer with large estates. His navigator had been doing engineering at Cambridge when war broke out. Later in the evening, because of our morning experiences, I casually asked what they thought of the CO. They looked at each other and laughed.

Jack said, 'He's a clot. You'll see in a minute. He'll be coming in with his retinue of bootlickers any moment. If you want to get anywhere on this station you have to crawl. He was a school teacher in civvy life and his service glory has gone to his head.'

'That accounts for the lecture he handed out this morning,' I said. Normally a Groupy would hand such ordinary matters over to a subordinate. At that moment, a noisy group of perhaps a dozen officers came into the bar. Like an Eastern potentate surrounded by fawning sycophants, the CO held pride of place. Outdoing them all in bootlicking was a small bloke who virtually raced around pandering to his superior's every wish.

'Who's the little runt?', Smithy asked.

'That's the MO,' said Jack. 'He outcrawls them all.'

'Makes sense, too,' I said. 'The MO generally patterns himself on the CO. If one's a bastard, so's the other. How is our little crawling friend?'

Des said nothing but expressively held his nose and pulled an imaginary chain. Smithy said, 'I notice the adj is mixed up with this mob. He seems a decent enough chap.'

'That's the shame of it,' said Jack. 'He's a damn nice fellow and the CO treats him like a lackey. Keeps him running like the office boy. I understand he comes from a poor family. It gives the CO a kind of perverted mental kick to wipe his boots on him. And the adj is afraid to kick for fear he'll get a bad report. Poor bugger, works himself to death doing extra work that the CO loads onto him.'

'The disgusting thing,' said Des, 'is that the CO himself crawls to our skipper and navigator like nobody's business because they have wealth and social position.'

'That's a laugh. And what do they do?'

'They can't stand a bloody bar of him. Still, it's very handy for us as we often get special treatment because of our crew association.'

A few nights later Des asked us if we would like to go down to the local with them as it was crew night. Enquiry elicited the fact that their skipper entertained the two gunners and his ground staff crew twice a month. Hearing of our experience they had invited Smithy and me to join the party. He was a big man with a prominent hooked nose and grey, piercing eyes. He looked a leader. Of such a mould, I felt, must have been men such as Drake, Cook and Flinders who had gone out into strange lands and seas to leave their mark.

His navigator, though not such an imposing figure, was the picture of the upper-crust Englishman who, because of his class rating, had no need to be anything but himself.

It was an easy, informal little gathering where the erks were as much at home as the skipper. Both being experts and keen rivals, the chief mechanic and the squadron leader battled out their game of darts, the deciding game being won by Chiefy amongst much light-hearted banter.

Des said, 'I'll bet you a tanner Lord Muck turns up before the night's out. He knows we're here and will decide to do a bit of slumming. You wait and see.'

Sure enough, as the party was clicking merrily along, the CO, followed by the ever-attentive MO, the glum adj and a couple of hangers-on, came in. He came across to our group but baulked when he saw Smithy and me. He said a few words, eyed us sourly and repaired to a civilian group which Jack declared included the local squire and the bank manager.

Their skipper looked at us both and said, 'You don't seem to be too popular.'

I said, 'No. We had a little upset a few days back.'

He laughed and said, 'Yes, I heard about it.'

From there the talk moved to our previous experiences. He was the type of man who could make you feel as though he was interested in you, and I like to feel he was. Des said, 'These boys have an idea on fighter control that seems good. I believe they used it on their previous squadron.'

We explained the clock system and the elimination of nautical terms in evasion patter. He evinced a genuine interest in this and asked his gunners what they thought of it. They both declared that it allowed for a more specific pin-pointing of the attack and that the terms right and left were more direct than port and starboard.

During the discussion, the CO sent the adj over asking the squadron leader to join his party, but he politely declined, indicating it was crew night.

Life in the officers' mess was in direct contrast to that in the sergeants' mess. In the latter you saw the top brass only at flight or at other odd places on the station. If you got full it was nobody's concern but your own. In our new environment, however, you fell over the powers-that-be at every step. Getting full or boisterous behaviour was frowned on, the CO considering the inhabitants of the mess should act as officers and gentlemen. The result was the Australians, except for a few drinks before supper, did their drinking in the local hostelries. In this respect the drinking habits of Australians and Englishmen differed widely; the Aussies, because of their six'o'clock-swill habits from home, drank before they ate; while the English, because of saner drinking laws, ate first and then wanted to drink afterwards.

The hotels were completely different from the yokel-filled ones of Norfolk. Here, in this lovely tree-covered country, they matched their surroundings. In each hotel there were at least three separate entertainment rooms, one with a piano, one for games, and a quiet retreat where you could drink and carry on a conversation away from the distractions of the other two rooms.

In these parts the femme interest was also bright and varied. Besides WAAFs, there was the local talent, Land Army girls, nurses from a nearby hospital, and a variety of others. One interesting facet of our new positions was the attraction that the officers' uniforms had for women. We found we had a ready entree to the company of females who would not have looked at us when we were sergeants. Few of them had a clue as to rank, and it was generally assumed that every commissioned officer flew a plane.

About this time three matters of internal interest claimed the attention of the squadron. One was the advent of the 1939–43 Star.

Fliers generally looked on this star with some contempt. It was awarded to all ranks, the only requirement being that you had been in some branch of the services in the European theatre between September 1939 and June 1943.

Aircrew felt the award of a Star for men completing a tour, with a bar for each additional tour, would have some merit, but we know of course the shiny-bums would not be in this as it would have sifted the fliers from the staff boys. Tommy the Kiwi said, 'They're like arseholes – everyone's got one.' We excluded the ground staff boys from the headquarters bludgers for, if anyone played a major part in winning the war, they did.

This Star was soon contemptuously referred to as 'spam', an ersatz and thoroughly disliked sausage and was unofficially banned by sixty per cent of aircrew, particularly the Canadians, New Zealanders and Australians. The only ones who put it up were the CO and his menagerie and some of the Poms who were used to following orders.

The CO got over this little problem by issuing an order that ribbons were to be attached as directed by a certain date. Anyone failing to comply with this direction would be confined to barracks, and so the red and blue star blossomed, as directed, on thirty or forty rebellious chests.

A few weeks later there was a funny sequel to this order. Smithy and I were up in London and ran into one of my former Sydney acquaintances who had just arrived in England, was not qualified to wear spam, but had obtained his commission in Australia. The three of us adjourned to a quiet hostelry to catch up on what was happening back home.

While we were quaffing beers, reminiscing and listening to what the Yanks were doing in Australia, a living example of English snobbery interjected. He was around the forty mark, wore the morning dress and spats of an English businessman, and spoke in clipped correct English.

He asked could we acquaint him as to what were the decorations we were wearing. Smithy, a hard-doer, took one look at him and said jocularly, 'Don't you know a VC when you see one?'

To our surprise he said, 'Really? May I congratulate you two officers on winning this highest British award for valour and bravery. May I buy you drinks?'

Smithy and I looked at each other in surprise and I was just going to make an explanation when Smithy shoved his heel down on my toe and said, 'I'm sure we'll only be too pleased to accept.'

Our new acquaintance insisted on turning on Scotch, advised us he was a barrister from the Inns of Court and most unfortunately had been too young for the first war and too old for the second, but was helping the war effort by keeping his practice going while his partner, who was in a not so fortunate age-group, did his bit in the Middle East.

We intended breaking the news to him but he turned out to be such an insufferable prig the explanation was deferred, particularly when, on learning we were flying officers, he declared despite our AG insignias, fighter pilots were the cream of the air force, and naturally socially superior to the common bomber or other air force types.

After that, we really took him for a ride, allowing him to do the honours for the rest of the night.

One funny aspect of our forced deception was when five RAAF types came in, all wearing spams, but our host was such a dill he didn't even notice them, although Smithy did an effective screening job. We often wondered what his reactions were when he got around to noticing the thousands of VC's adorning nearly every serviceman in London.

The second incident was when the CO decided some of the officers didn't measure up to his idea of officers and gentlemen, and to improve their manners and gentlemanly instincts, declared the first Tuesday of every month would be a full-dress dinner night, with all the trimmings.

The dinner edict met with just as much success as spam. The Groupy's cronies turned up in force but the Dominion blokes and a proportion of English officers who couldn't stand a bar of him stayed away. Finally the rebels were brought to heel by an order advising any officer absenting himself from the next mess dinner without reasonable excuse would be subject to disciplinary action. Everyone turned up for the next one, the rebels in self-defence, sitting together. These do's were tedious formal gatherings, beset with bull and long-winded speeches, which lasted up to three hours.

There was an old English custom we hadn't met before, and that was the passing of the port. At the end of the dinner the procedure was that the bottle or bottles were passed around and if you wanted some you helped yourself; if not, you passed it on. A rigid rule here was: the plonk must be passed from left to right.

To educate the ignorant newcomers, the initiates kept up a chant of 'Pass the port from left to right.' The Overseas, by unanimous assent, left the wine alone. Port, for my part, is one drink I could not stand, but these pseudo-English gentlemen seemed to consider they had to live up to the standards that gauged a man's social standing on his ability to drink one, two or even three bottles of port.

Thus, these sessions after dinner often lasted an hour, while the drinkers consumed from twenty to thirty bottles and were exceedingly tedious to the abstainers.

One night the non-drinkers chanced upon a diversion from the normal routine that, for a while, added a little welcome variety. The bottle had passed Smithy when he suddenly changed his mind and decided he would have some, so the diner, some two or three removed on his right, obligingly passed it back.

The effect on the gathering was spontaneous. There was a shocked silence, then a crescendo of 'Pass the port from left to right, left to right'. This change from the accepted practice so shook the gathering that Smithy declared, 'Let's try it again.'

From then on, every now and then, some ignoramus would belatedly change his mind after the port had passed till the Groupy, realising he was being taken for a ride, put an end to this little bit of fun by decreeing that the next man (not officer) that digressed from this hallowed English custom would miss out on his leave.

The third matter of interest was the coming of the Yanks. It was decided in higher places that we were to train four American crews a month in our low-level technique.

We found that with these crews the pilot and navigator were officers, the WOP and gunners were what was referred to as 'enlisted men', the officers presumably being volunteers, and that there was a deep class distinction between the two.

The two officers in each crew had a Jeep for their own personal use and, in addition, enjoyed rates of pay about four times higher than the Aussies and six above the Poms.

Two of the Yanks were domiciled in our hut. One was a tall, lean lantern-jawed Texan, the other an athletic six-footer from Carolina. We found these boys easy to get on with. Perhaps they had been well-briefed. Whatever it was, they refused to be drawn into these contentious issues, side-stepped arguments and proved such good fellows that they were soon accepted into the squadron. Soon, the blood of these newcomers was mingling with their instructors in occupied Europe.

CHAPTER TWENTY-NINE

It was lovely midsummer weather, and when our first leave came up I remembered the waves I had seen over Newquay. I broached the subject with Smithy. He was no surfer and I tried to talk him into it without success.

It was the first Saturday in August when I left, which didn't mean anything to me until I arrived at Waterloo Station to catch my train to Cornwall. Here I found to my astonishment great queues stretching for hundreds of yards and comprising a heterogenous collection of humanity. Then I found it was Bank Holiday, England's famous weekend when Londoners, as though drawn by some migratory instinct, make for the sea and holiday resorts.

The queue for my destination was four hundred yards long. To my amazement I found some of its weary members had waited patiently for as much as twenty hours, and even so it was uncertain they would get aboard the next train.

It was here I found the advantage of being an officer. I went along to the RTO and explained my predicament. His reaction was immediate. 'Just come with me, sir.' So, past the groups of tired travellers, squabbling kids and irritable parents I walked.

Near the top of the queue I passed a group of Australian erks and a strident voice demanded, 'Where are you going, bludger?' My escort didn't even deign to look back, but I turned and gave them a derisive fingers-up sign. At this an affected falsetto voice said, 'Oh, you ain't got no refinery!', and another said, 'He's a gunner. He wouldn't know any better.'

At the top of the queue, under the hostile glances of its long-suffering members, the RTO said to the attendant in charge of the barrier, 'Officer on operational transfer.' This worthy unlocked the iron gate and, opening it a few inches, let me slide through. I felt a heel and thanked the Lord for the Englishman's long-accepted habit of having his nose ground in the dirt by officialdom.

I had hardly gone twenty yards when I heard a clatter behind me and, turning, saw I had beaten the opening by only seconds and a surging mob of humanity was bearing down on me like a stampeding buffalo herd. That was enough for me and I kept going till the first surge, like a wave breaking over the shore, exhausted itself on the nearest carriages. I was inside and settled in a corner seat before the second wave broke into my carriage.

All my experience of Test Match crowds or the Easter Show push faded into insignificance in comparison with this tidal wave of English holidaymakers. No quarter was given and none asked by either sex. By judicious use of elbows, umbrellas, suitcases, pointed heels and sheer fighting spirit the women more than held their own. The train was filled in a twinkling. Compartments that normally held six and eight now housed sixteen and twenty. Corridors were packed tight with less fortunate but nevertheless triumphant travellers. The voices of innumerable mothers arose plaintively on the heavy air calling for lost young who howled dismally from all points of the compass. Outside, hundreds of the luckless sought to accomplish the impossible and cram one more sweating body into the now immovable mass.

Here and there arguments and an odd brawl broke out as disappointment, frustration and the rigours of their long wait proved too much even for English good humour and patience. Gradually, helpful police and harassed officials restored order and the unlucky ones were herded back into the interminable queue to wait a further ten hours for the next train.

While this commotion was going on outside, a reshuffling of bodies and all the paraphernalia that an Englishman takes on his holidays was going on inside. The carriage had packed to bursting point and I offered a cute little blonde a portion of my seat, and finally my knee. Everyone helped everyone else, so by the time the train started the mass had sorted itself into some sort of order and the cheerful British acceptance of the impossible had manifested itself.

Before long everyone knew everybody else, where they came from and where they were going. The blonde and her cobber, a brunette, were bound for Newquay. I said, 'That's good, I'm going there too.'

When I said I hadn't booked in to any place but was going down to take pot luck, everyone laughed. The blondie said, 'You're kidding, aren't you?'

It was then I learned that unless you booked twelve months ahead your chances of attaining so much as a bed in a bath, a place on a billiard table, or even a roof over your head were practically nil. Newquay at this time of the year was not full but overflowing.

I said confidently, 'I'll fix that with a bit of cold canvass.'

It was a tough trip. We arrived at our destination at 8 am next morning. I said goodbye to my fellow-travellers and set off with a light heart.

Two hours later, dirty and dusty, shoes trodden grey, I wasn't so optimistic. I had called on a hundred places and the unvarying answer to my unvarying query of 'Have you a room?' was, 'We are booked up till October … November … next year.' Well-meaning landladies sent me on wild goose chases with, 'I haven't a room, but Mrs So-and-So, now, she may have a room. I know her well, just mention my name.'

To add to my torments the sun, which had refused to shine while I was at camp, came out in molten glory. After three hours' fruitless effort, I was willing to admit defeat when I came to a tiny house, unpretentious, spotlessly clean. There was no 'Room to Let' sign, nor any other misleading signs by which Newquay taunts the weary tourist. I staggered up the steps and knocked. A silvery-haired old dear opened the door. To my croak of 'Have you a room?', she gazed at me – rather warily I thought – then gave me the amazing reply, 'I'll have to see my sister.' When the sister was produced she, too, subjected me to doubtful scrutiny, then asked, 'Are you an Australian?' I thought, 'Maybe I remind her of Ned Kelly!', and meekly gulped, 'Yes.'

Thereupon they retired for consultation to reappear with the magic words, 'We can let you have a room. Can you come back in half an hour?'

Mention of 'coming back in half an hour' rather dashed my hopes. I asked, 'Can I leave my bag?' When they graciously acquiesced, I went off, touching every bit of available wood for luck, wondering what the mysterious interval meant.

It wasn't till I returned and settled in that I discovered one of the ladies had given up her own room to me and the half-hour was needed to remove clothes. They were two exceedingly charming and truly English ladies. One was a widow and the other had never married, but with complete unselfishness they established me in their little home.

Arrangements were that I pay for bed and breakfast and forage for myself for other meals. This I felt I was quite capable of doing until I found residents got no extra rations to feed the multitude and, with its population swollen to ten times its normal size, queues were the order of the day. The locals moaned that the visitors, spurred by necessity, arose early and bought all available stocks. The visitors retaliated that they were charged exorbitant prices for everything from accommodation upwards and had to put up with much rudeness from tradesmen.

At this particular juncture, food problems were for me a thing of the future. The magnet was the heady smell of the sea and the thought of a surf. Directed by my landladies I made a bee-line for the beach. From the top of towering headlands which must have been two hundred feet high, I looked down on the beach below. The water, with a border-line of white, was a good mile out. Everyone seemed to be completely disinterested in it. On closer inspection, after climbing down a couple of hundred stairs, most seemed to be reclining on deck chairs, all with their backs to the water.

One bright spot was that there was really some fine sand; the sun was shining so that all that was required was to get the water in close enough to swim in it. Enquiries regarding dressing sheds brought blank stares; the beach didn't run to such conveniences, the procedure being you either wore your costume down under your clothes or wandered off into the innumerable caves and recesses that pitted the cliff base and disrobed there.

Lying on the sand with the warm sun on my back and appreciatively enjoying some really pretty holidaymakers, I found I could, with a dash of imagination, almost see myself back at Bondi or Manly; one big difference being the great patch of wet sand stretching out to the distant water. Watching this, I said to a fellow sunbaker, 'How the hell do you get a swim here?'

He looked at me in surprise and said, 'Ah, by gum, you wait till tide comes in, chum.'

'Does it really go out that far?'

'Farther,' he replied, 'it be on turn now. Water will soon be coming in.'

So it proved. In a matter of thirty minutes a small flood wave five inches high came rushing and rolling over the intervening sand. It was amazing to see the speed at which the tide flowed in. Within an hour, rocks that stood high and dry were under water and a real surf, breaking two hundred yards out, boomed and crashed into the caves and fissures in the cliff face.

Despite the fact that the water had, figuratively speaking, come almost up to their door, the sunbathers took no notice as they lounged in their canvas chairs, backs to the sea. A few children and adults paddled on the edge, but the rest ignored it.

I soon found one possible good reason for this strange behaviour when I wandered down to the edge of the tumbling surf. The water was freezingly cold. I had swum in Melbourne in winter but this water was colder than St Kilda baths in mid-August.

As the tide came in, it had engulfed the headlands so that the northern beach was a complete unit, probably four hundred yards long. The only solution I could find for a swim was to do a couple of vigorous laps on the beach and then go in by degrees. The water was so cold that I got wet by inches and could not get warm even on the swim out to the waves. The disconcerting part of this surf, besides the coldness of the water, was the eerie way the waves boomed into the caves in the headlands and cliffs. I cracked two waves and, despite my enthusiasm, had to give it away. Fifteen minutes was as long as I could stand.

Just after twelve the beach emptied as if by magic, in spite of the the brightly shining sun. This I put down to some strange English idiosyncrasy and stayed on while the sun and surf were good.

It was amazing the way the tide continued to come in; around about two when I decided on my last swim, there was only a strip of sand fifty yards wide. As I started my warm-up run I noticed that some of the chairs were, for the first time, turned towards the sea.

Even though the water was freezing I felt the old thrill of battling out through the turbulent water, felt the tug and drag of eddies as the waves crashed over me, the suck of the undertow as the big ones reared above, experienced again that exhilarating inward surge as I swam for a howler to come hurtling down the crest, the water sizzling from under my belly. It was living again. After a while the cold beat me and I came out with goose pimples on my goose pimples. A change had come over the weather. A cold breeze had blown up from the sea, the sun was obscured by cloud and I was chilled to the bone. A pretty femme said, 'That was marvellous, do it again.'

Through chattering teeth I said, 'Lady, I'm frozen to the bone. Wait till I get some breath and shake the icicles off and I'll give it a go.'

The promised surf never came off because the sun disappeared for good. The cold wind increased and the worms started to bite.

Getting dressed was really a problem. The surf had engulfed the caves and rocks. I solved this by retiring to the end of the beach, wrapping a towel around me and wriggling out of my costume and into my pants.

Up in the shopping centre I found the reason for the midday exodus. All the restaurants were either closed or had signs up announcing they were sold out. In desperation I went into a neat little fish food bar. The proprietor was a pleasant-faced middle-aged fellow. He said he was sorry, but couldn't serve any food until 6 pm. I felt a little salesmanship was required and explained my predicament – that I hadn't eaten since early morning, wasn't aware of the local eating rules, and was as hungry as a hunter.

He explained he had knocked back dozens and wasn't game to serve me. I declared I didn't care where I ate, in the kitchen, in the backyard, anywhere. Finally I prevailed on him to serve me a crab salad in the kitchen. During this surreptitious meal he explained there was only a limited amount of food available. The restaurants got no extra food and as most of the holidaymakers received only bed and breakfast and hung on to their ration cards, there just wasn't enough food to go round. He added that a similar position applied in the pubs and, if you wanted a drink, you had to be quick as the local hostelries stayed open only as long as their rations lasted.

He was a nice fellow who had known the Australians in the First World War. Before I left he gave me a note to take to the secretary of the local workmen's club, where he said I could get a comfortable drink should the necessity arise. However, he warned me they served a beer, significantly known as 'dynamite', which was not generally available in the pubs and, unlike the usual hogwash, really had a kick.

The transformation on the beaches was amazing. When I came out the tide was at the full, the central beach had gone, the ships in the little harbour were riding at anchor, protected from the waves that broke against its stout stone sides and rolled on to smash against the walls of the promenade. A sea mist had crept in, reducing visibility to a mile, and swimming for the day was over.

Strolling back to my lodging looking at the shops, I heard an excited voice calling, 'Johnny, Johnny.' It was the little blonde from the train and her dark cobber, the latter escorted by a sleek-looking civvie with a natty little moustache.

For my part, anyway, it was a fortunate meeting. The girls were racing back to their boarding house to be in the first sitting for supper. Food problems were just as acute on the boarding house front as for the freelance holidaymaker.

The blonde was tied up until 9 pm with a Canadian officer from a nearby station; this unlucky fellow had to be back in camp by 9.30 pm. I made arrangements to meet her in front of the local dancing Casino at 9.15. She gave my hand a squeeze and just that look from her baby blue eyes set my pulse racing. She was a cuddlesome little first-divisioner; the night promised its excitements.

I was in the first attacking wave at my lunchtime benefactor's food bar. He suggested I meet him at the workman's club at 7.30 and he would introduce me to the Secretary.

The six o'clock swill had nothing on the local pubs as the thirsty populace, its ranks swelled by thousands of visitors, struggled to get as much anaemic beer down their parched gullets as possible before the supply ran out. After struggling for half an hour to catch an elusive barmaid's eye I made for the workman's club. I had my benefactor's note clutched in my little hot hand and had asked to see the secretary, when the man himself walked in.

In a matter of minutes I was an honorary member and being introduced to his friends. It was a very pleasant set-up with plenty of good company, convivial companions and strong liquor. I disregarded Bill's warning and ordered pints. It was a pale draught and except for a stronger malty flavour, did not seem to differ appreciably from numerous other innocuous brews I had tasted all over England.

It was a complete surprise when the stewards started to warn us to drink up and get out. Then I found, to my horror, the time was 10.30. I also realised that I was very, very clucky, but the most horrible thought was I'd forgotten about my appointment. Clutching a very faint hope, I made for the Casino but there was no sign of the blonde.

Next morning my landladies, who had somehow managed to get me an egg, served me breakfast in bed. As the sun shone brightly I was on the beach early. There, later in the morning, I ran into my appointment of the previous evening. By her cool acknowledgment of my greeting I knew I had had it. Strangely enough, it's the girls you miss that you remember most.

Far out was a line of white water. As the tide came racing in it was evident there was a big surf running. From somewhere out in the vastness of the Atlantic those swells had been born and now they broke three hundred yards out, big fifteen foot howlers.

I wasn't game to go out to the big ones on my own, but ventured half-way in the hope that I would pick up a medium one. While I was there I got to thinking about the fin I had seen at the top of North of Scotland, as we were coming down the coast. It had looked uncommonly like a shark fin and even though I felt that any unlucky shark that ventured into the waters would assuredly die of pneumonia, the thought persisted.

While I was ruminating on this disturbing subject, three swimmers, two breast-stroking and one doing a powerful side stroke, went by making towards the big ones. I could hardly believe my eyes but smartly started after them. We were getting close to the first line when I spotted the crest of a whopper bearing in. At the sight of this wall of water the two breast-strokers turned for shore, stroking furiously; the side-stroker and I went forward. We both dived deep as its crest crashed and came up safely on the other side. Treading water, I told my companion he was the first swimmer I had met here who came out into the surf. He said he was stationed at the local heavy artillery garrison and had twice tried to swim The Channel. He stated his training for this arduous task was to swim five or six miles along the coast every day.

I asked him if he had ever seen any sharks. This was something he'd never apparently thought of and after a surprised pause, he said, 'No. I've never worried about them', and asked me what made me enquire. I stated I came from Australia where the sharks were always on our minds and also said I considered I had seen a shark's fin at the entrance to the Irish Sea as we were coming down The Channel.

As we were talking I saw a suitable wave forming. I was right on the spot and only had to turn and glide on to it. I rode it to within fifty yards of the shore and then dropped off as I was anxious to get back while I still had company. Halfway out, I met my companion swimming furiously towards shore. When he sighted me he stopped in amazement and demanded where the bloody hell I'd got to.

He was ashen-faced and stated we had been talking about sharks one moment and the next moment I had completely disappeared. He immediately decided I'd been grabbed by one and was making with all speed to the safety of the shore. His morale was so badly shaken I couldn't kid him into coming out again. I have often wondered if I spoiled the peace of mind of this marathon swimmer during his long jaunts along the coast, as he remembered the bleedin' Orstralian who had so unaccountably disappeared, and also the disturbing thought that perhaps sharks could survive in this supposedly warm Gulf Stream.

At the time, the thought of the fellow's consternation tickled my odd sense of humour so I ventured out, cracked another howler, and rode it on to the beach. Here I found this evidence of surf prowess really had the natives intrigued. As far as I could learn this was the first time anyone had seen a man ride a wave. To me it seemed amazing; that surf must have been rolling on to this beach for centuries and yet no one in the town, either local or visitor, had mastered the art of surf-riding.[1]

As the blonde was draped around some attentive swain and took some pains to let me see her, I was on the outer and palled up with a couple of femmes who wanted to know how I had learned this new art. They were both nice kids and we were later joined by a Scottish corporal. He proved a mighty interesting guy, was a member of the famous Black Watch and had been in the Middle East since 1938. The usual period was 2 years but with the outbreak of war they had been kept there. He had fought through all the Eighth Army battles, had been in Tobruk, had taken part in the famous Black Watch attack that had wiped out eighty per cent of their strength at El Alamein. On his return he had found his wife living with another man with three additional children added to his two. He had taken his wife's transgressions philosophically, stating he was bloody lucky to be alive.

I have always considered the Scotch and Australians to have a closer accord than with the English, Irish or Welsh. This probably stems from the kindred interests in fighting, wenching and drinking, plus their mutual dislike in the military sphere for bull of any kind. From the first day of our acquaintance his tough military training kept cropping up, and every now and then he would involuntarily call me 'Sir'. This would send the two girls into convulsions.

That night, I treated the dynamite with caution and met Scotty and the girls as per arrangement, and a pleasant and interesting time was had by all.

Those days on the beach at Newquay were some of the happiest I spent in England. On the last day on the beach the Mayor came down. He had half a dozen schoolboys with him. He introduced himself and explained that he had high hopes when the war was over of advertising the surfing attractions of Newquay. Would I be kind enough before I left to teach these young hopefuls the art of surf riding, so that they in turn could pass it on.

I tried to explain it took a number of years for me to become a competent surfer. I had started surfing at six and considered I was not a good surf swimmer and surfer till I was thirteen or fourteen.

I agreed, however, to take them out as they were selected swimmers. The only drawback here was all except one were breast or side-stroke swimmers. The exception was a solidly-built youth of about sixteen, who really showed some aptitude. He was the only one who could get through the breakers and doggedly followed me in attempts to climb on to waves, went down the mine, but came up for more. I hope with the few hints I gave him this young fellow in time became a competent surfer. When I finally left Newquay I was tanned and fitter than I had been for years.[2]

CHAPTER THIRTY

Life on the station was pleasant. With the coming of autumn the trees put on their mantle of gold and the lanes and highways were covered with a carpet of leaves. It was a new experience for the Australians; in treeless Norfolk we had never witnessed this lovely English transition from summer to winter.

With the shortening of the days we realised we were situated in a bad fog-bank area. These fogs weren't like the ordinary ones that lifted sometime during the day. They hung around for days, restricting visibility to a hundred yards, sometimes less.

No-one, except perhaps the CO, shed any tears at the advent of these grey clinging blankets. It meant you couldn't fly and no flying meant no ops. It was felt with the advent of winter they must get worse. This conjured up pleasant thoughts for all concerned. This didn't relieve us from being up at flight. Kruschen called regular rolls to see that his flock were not skulking in bed.

We did notice, on the odd occasions the fog cleared, an unusual amount of activity around the runways. We noted a small army of workmen busily laying an assorted collection of two inch pipes, for what reason no-one could guess.

Then one day, after a ten day lay-off, the fog suddenly cleared. Briefing was automatic. We were to attack marshalling yards in Belgium. Our track in was over a little fishing village which intelligence declared was undefended.

We roared in over the thatched rooftops without opposition, barely ten feet above the power wires which ran through the centre of the little place like a ribbon.

A few miles further on, still seventy miles from our objective, we ran into a wall of fog almost as dense as that which plagued our station. We hit it so suddenly that the attacking planes disappeared into its cloying greyness. It was an eerie experience; it was impossible to tell where the other boxes were. Luckily no collisions occurred. A general recall was announced. The Belgians, who had a few minutes before waved us in, had the pleasure of waving us back out.

Next day the met boys had the gen. The fog had disappeared and as our weather continued fine, it was on again. The squadron leader, who had only returned from leave with his crew the previous night, angled himself onto the battle order, to everyone's delight except the crew he pushed out.

With him back as leader the op took on a different perspective. The navigators were not called for prior briefing, which didn't cause any comment as the target was the same. It was Jock at general briefing who noticed the red ribbon showing the track in had not been altered. This was not a bright idea, particularly after our turn back of the previous day. No-one made any open comment. It did show laxity or laziness on someone's part.

The Squaddy and his crew were the only busy ones and were unaware that the route was the same as the previous day's abortive intrusion. Smithy, who was in the second box, had a crack at his navigator to bring this up. When he wouldn't be in it, I asked Jock to have a go. He wouldn't either. This had nothing to do with gunners. Perhaps everyone expected someone else to comment. In the end nothing was done.

As we were getting into the bus I told Des. He, in turn, told the Squadron Leader. I heard him say, 'Is that so?' He then asked one of the pilots if the information was correct. He snapped, 'You're a lot of bloody fools. Why didn't someone bring this up? There's thousands of miles of coastline. It's sheer bloody laziness. I'll have something to say when I get back.'

My butterflies were bad on takeoff and I had an uneasy feeling. 'Bill, I don't like this,' I said. 'Those bloody Jerries are one-track thinkers. We could get a hot reception over the coast.'

'I don't like it either,' Bill replied. 'I expect one of us should have spoken up. Perhaps we could take a different track in, anyway.'

Jock said, 'I don't think so. If anything went wrong he'd cop the lot.'

We were flying Number Five in the lead box; the other six were a little to our right at about six o'clock, six hundred yards astern.

Bill said, 'There's no doubt about the Squaddy. He flies like a dream. He's a marvellous leader.'

I looked at the compact box; the six planes flew almost as one unit not six feet above the sea. It was a marvellous example of precision formation flying. The thrill of this two hundred and eighty mile per hour rush dispelled my fears. Our leader, I felt, was capable of handling any situation.

Jock said, 'Enemy coast coming up.' I felt the formation rise slightly to skim the housetops and then the sky was full of flying tracer, smoke and fire. In two swift horrible seconds, One, Two, Three and Five had disappeared out of the sky. One, the Squaddy's, dived and hit power wires. The tail, whipping over like a giant catapult, shot Des through the air, turning somersaults where, for a few grim seconds he kept pace with our plane. Then, as the impetus of his two hundred and eighty mile an hour thrust lessened, he disappeared into the rooftops of the village.

The concentrated fire had come from our right. This had given our plane some protection. As we flashed over clear country I saw that we and Number Four were the only survivors. Behind us a pall of smoke marked the passing of four planes and sixteen lives. I saw the other box swing for home.

It was then I realised that instead of taking a wide sweep as a prelude to coming out, we were rushing inland. I thought, 'Jesus, Bill has frozen at the controls. We're bound for the middle of Belgium.' This was something I had heard could happen to pilots through shock. An answer to it, if you could get at him, was to wallop him over the ear, but this was impossible in a Boston. In a panic I called, 'Bill, pull out of it. We're going the wrong way.'

Then I heard his voice calling, 'Bobby, Bobby! Wake up! Wake up!'

A chill ran up and down my spine. I thought, 'He's nuts.' Basher, down in the dungeon, unable to see anything and sensing that something was wrong, was trying to force himself up.

I could see the tops of stunted trees under us, the pall of smoke was rapidly receding. It would be suicide to try to bail out, and still a voice was calling, 'Bobby! Bobby! Pull out!'

I called, 'Bill, Bill.' His voice said savagely, 'Shut your bloody mouth, will you.'

Then I saw we were flying beside the other survivor and enlightenment hit me. It was the other pilot who was frozen and our pilot was keeping with him, trying to pull him out. I saw the other gunner look over the side, evaluating a jump.

Suddenly the other plane came to life. Instead of its straight, rigid course, the wings dipped a couple of times. A voice said, 'I'm okay.'

Turning right, we came around in a wide sweep, Bill shepherding him like a sheepdog. All this, from the first fusillade of cannon fire to our turn, would have taken perhaps four minutes, but at close on five miles a minute we could be twenty miles inland.

Coming to the coast, Bill said, 'We'll climb,' and the planes rose to five hundred feet. The precautions were unnecessary. Not a shot was fired at us. All the hate seemed to have been concentrated over that little fishing village.

We had crossed the coast when two specks appeared behind us. They were possibly two miles astern but their slim silhouettes shrieked Me 109s. Luckily we still had our height. As I gave the alarm, Bill said, 'Jettison', and put the nose down into a shallow dive. He said afterwards the needle touched three hundred miles which wasn't bad for a light bomber.[1] I don't reckon those fighters gained much on us. They were still a mile astern when we were more than half-way across, and they decided to give it away, possibly feeling our calls for fighter protection would bring retribution.

Back at base we found the other box had landed safely, having smartly sheered off when they saw the fate of our crowd. All surviving crews were subjected to a searching interrogation. From the intensity of the fire we could only surmise we had run into a mobile twenty millimetre battery. Consisting of twenty to twenty-five trucks, each with four twenty millimetre synchronised cannons, these units were dreaded by low-flying planes. We would probably have run into a barrage of eighty to a hundred quick-firing guns. The point that no-one appeared anxious to pursue was whether they planted them in anticipation of our coming. This, on the face of things, looked likely; but the ultimate decision was that we had unluckily chanced on a marauding battery. In this respect, the base wallahs took some pains to protect each other, and we heard no censure on the dills who had been too bloody lazy to change the track in from the previous unsuccessful operation.

Coming back in the bus we agreed that nothing would be said about the other pilot's lapse, as we felt it was a certainty he would be classified as unsuitable for operations. One astute intelligence officer did get on to our late return but in the general flap we were able to broom this bloke. This decision proved a correct one as this young sergeant later received a commission and then won himself a very creditable DFC.

The loss of the four planes, particularly the squadron leader's crew, threw the entire station into deep mourning. The reaction was ground staff and air crew went on the grog and the Groupy, for once using tact, let them.

About this time the weather turned from balmy autumn to chilly winter. It seemed to happen overnight. All of a sudden the gold-clad trees were standing stark and bare against the sky and the night temperatures had dropped below freezing.

For a week after our unfortunate op the weather favoured the station. A damp cold fog held the area in its icy grip, which precluded flying and allowed everyone to drift back to normal. However, a few days later word went out there was to be a super panic and the station was to be cleaned from top to bottom. The reason for this was then given – we were to receive a visit from the King and Queen and the two Princesses.

I personally, and Australians to a man, had a profound admiration for this shy monarch and his able Queen who, despite the dangers of the Blitz and, later, the Buzz Bombs and V2s, remained with their people in London sharing their dangers, sympathising with them in their losses – this in contrast to the bulk of the supposed Blue Bloods who smartly took themselves off to their funk holes in the country and stayed there till the danger was over.

Their visit was an event, and the squadrons paraded with pride before their distinguished visitors.[2]

To help the gunners get back on their feet, Kruschen started a series of daily five-mile cross-country runs. The shrewdies soon woke up to the fact that, with visibility restricted to a hundred yards, all they had to do was get off the mark fast, disappear from sight, then make their way to a prearranged retreat for a game of cards, or some other relaxing notion, the midway publican proving very helpful in making a quiet back room available.

It was at one of these unscheduled bludging periods that the Rooter's Club was born. Its function was for a closer and more intimate relationship with all females. Membership was confined exclusively to gunners. It was innocuous enough, for during its short history, I would say there was far more boasting than fornicating. Its intended purpose was to take our minds off the grimness of operational life. The club operated for approximately five months before languishing, as most of its members were dead.

In the meantime, the small army of workmen had continued working on the strange pipe contraption. In the fog one day Smithy and I ventured across to inspect it. We found both sides of the runways were encircled by lengths of galvanised pipe joined in sections with holes bored at nine-inch intervals. They looked like enlarged gas stove pipes. We examined them with some interest till an authoritative civvy arrived and ordered us out of the area.

A few days later, while the fog still held, a dull glow pierced the gloom. We thought a kite must have pranged. It was then announced that this was the famous FIDO, Britain's answer to the fog problem. Oil was pumped through the pipes under pressure and automatically lit. The result was a four-inch flame from each hole. It was considered the heat generated would dissipate some of the fog and the burning oil jets would outline the runway and allow for take-off and landing.

The innovation was viewed with some scepticism and much resentment by the rank and file, as it looked like ending what had appeared to be a nice quiet winter operational period.

Our first op with the help of FIDO ushered in a new era. Visibility was about thirty yards on the ground. With some misgivings we were briefed for a target in France, bombing at nine thousand feet.

Getting to the takeoff point presented as many hazards as an op. If we weren't going up someone's bottom, someone was trying to go up ours. It was a time of blasphemy and frayed tempers. On the sides of the runway the oil fires burned murkily, adding their smoke to the fog. We seemed to fly into a wall of cotton wool, and I'll admit I said a little prayer of thanks as the wheels lifted. Five hundred feet up we miraculously climbed out of the swirling fog as the Met wallahs had said we would and into clear sunlight. It was a revelation.

The op wasn't bad, some light and heavy flak over the target. One unpleasant indication of things to come was the cold. On low-level ops we hadn't bothered to wear a lot of clothes; most crews flew in their battle jackets. No-one had issued any warning. The temperature on the ground was probably around 36°F but at nine thousand feet it would have been –20°F.[3] The gunner in a Boston was practically in the open air, the small canopy around his ears being the only windbreak. The floor gunner had to keep the bottom hatchway open to get his gun in place. This created a God-Almighty downward draught.

I thought I had been cold in Wimpys but this trip, in inadequate clothes, was a veritable freezer. My hands were so cold that in the event of attack it would have been impossible to use them.

Back over the drome the fog bank still held, but glowing murkily down below we could see the oil fires which gave some indication of the runway. Trouble was, pilots had to go down through the cotton wool, estimating the beginning and centre of the runway.

Everyone landed safely except one young pilot who hit the edge, skidded into the soft stuff, then ploughed through the pipes, the plane finally tipping over on its nose. In ordinary circumstances this would have been only a bad shaking for the crew, but in a matter of seconds the fire from the shattered pipes climbed up the fuselage and the plane was a raging inferno. The two gunners, being smart boys, got out and departed the scene rapidly, escaping with a singeing. The pilot got out all right but stopped to see if he could help his navigator until being driven back, severely scorched. The navigator, trapped in the shattered nose, was roasted to death, his screams being heard for some minutes till the smoke and flame overcame him.

This incident gave warning to pilots of the necessity of coming in on a straight and direct course, in which they were ably assisted by the bleatings of the sweating navigators.

Despite this tragedy the powers that be voted the pipes a great success. Any hopeful thoughts of carefree foggy winter days vanished.[4]

CHAPTER THIRTY-ONE

A three-day leave was due so Smithy and I decided to pay our usual respects to London. It was 7.30 pm when we got off at Waterloo Station and made our way up the stairs. A well-dressed, good-looking woman of twenty-five or so gave me that hard, direct stare that speaks volumes to a wide-awake male. She was in the night-fighter area. I felt she could be a lady of the night but, in case she wasn't, I stopped and said, 'Hello. Are you waiting for anyone in particular?'

She said, 'No.'

Acting on the axiom of nothing ventured, nothing gained, I asked her if she would like to have a drink with me. She gave me another direct stare, which I felt was meant to convey something, before answering, 'I don't mind.'

Unaware of this little by-play, Smithy had continued on. Finding me missing, he backtracked. His glance said, 'You bastard,' so I asked the femme if she had a friend. She hadn't, so I said, 'I'll see you at the pub, Smithy. I've met an old friend of mine.'

By the way he left I knew Smithy wasn't happy. As we went towards the entrance, I felt I hadn't got the message. Looking at her well-groomed figure I thought, 'She can't be on the street.'

It was evident she was no stranger to the district as we jointly made for the little working-man's pub tucked away in a side-street. Seated on a stool I ordered drinks and we formally wished each other luck. She was well-spoken and when I came to look at her closely, a very personable female. She had that indefinable feminine something that makes a man look twice. Perhaps it was the rounded bosom under the well-tailored suit, the straight direct frank gaze from dark eyes, the well-knit figure, the perky little stern, or maybe it was a combination of all these that made her an extremely intriguing and desirable person.

I firmly believe that four gins are equal to four months' acquaintance under normal conditions, so while we drank we got to know each other. She told me her name – we'll say it was Pearl. She was a tailoress. After a while, looking into her glass, she said, 'Johnny, are you interested in a really exciting night?'

'I certainly am.'

'Well, you can have it, but it will cost you money.'

This was a stumbler. I had always wondered how the ladies of the night in England made a living against the enthusiastic amateurs. From my viewpoint, paying cash for something that could be had for a little effort and initiative didn't make sense. Besides, a principle was involved.

'Pearl, I've knocked around this world a lot. I've never paid for my love yet, not in straight-out cold cash anyway.'

She said, 'I'm sorry. That's the way it is.'

I had a feeling the wisest thing to do was to buy her another drink and go, but this female intrigued me. There was an interesting story somewhere. I thought, 'A bit of salesmanship wouldn't hurt; I can always bail out.' My counter-proposal, backed by a bit of bull, was; we obviously got on well together, so she could have a night out on me, and the love side could be left in abeyance.

She agreed. Probably we both had our ideas on the ultimate outcome.

She took me around to an Italian restaurant where the food was good. It was a pleasant meal with all the trimmings. A mournful-looking Italian added a romantic touch by playing a squeeze-box and singing love songs in broken English.

Later we went to a night club, similar to the hundreds of others that had sprung up all over London where the payment of ten shillings automatically made you an honorary member and entitled you to drink, dance and sing to the inevitable piano till the wee small hours.

This wasn't a bad little club as they went. There were a number of pros, but I noticed with interest my companion was not known, not openly anyway, to any of this hard-faced fraternity.

It was twelve when we called it a night. We had consumed a lot of drink and we were in a very happy mood. If she had told me that was the end of the road I would have left with no ill feelings. As we came out into the blackout she linked her arm in mine so I tailed along.

After a fifteen minute walk we came to a quiet, modern-looking building. She turned in to the entrance. Without any query I followed. At her door I decided to test the atmosphere and pulled her to me. That kiss was a sizzler. I couldn't get inside fast enough.

The apartment was a well-furnished bed-sitting room with a

separate modern kitchen and bathroom. It was a palace compared to the usual dingy residential rooms in which most of London's love life was conducted.

It turned out to be a pleasant end to an interesting evening. Later, when we were having a little talk – there's no place like a bed for the sharing of secrets – Pearl said, 'I suppose you're wondering why I asked for money?'

I lied that I wasn't. She then gave me her explanation. She was married to a soldier who was fighting in the Eighth Army in the Middle East. They had been married only a month or so when he was called into the Army and shipped overseas. She said she found it impossible to do without men's company and, despite her many good resolutions, found she was an easy mark for any importuning male.

When she found she could not do without love she decided to cash in on it, so had moved from her Midlands home to London. Her objective was twelve pounds a week which, allowing for off moments, gave her a flat and five hundred pounds a year, all of which she banked. She declared she had close to fifteen hundred in the bank, and intended to establish her husband in some business when he returned. She was without embarrassment, explaining her position in plain, business-like terms.

She said she picked her lovers; had four regulars who paid well. This night had been a pleasant change. It reminded her of nights spent with her husband. She spoke in such endearing terms of her missing spouse that I asked, 'Do you love him?'. Her answer, which has had me pondering ever since, was 'Yes, I love him as much as a woman could love a man.'

Next morning she served a pleasant breakfast and tidied her flat. Before I left, even though it went against the grain, I said, 'Pearl, here's four pounds. Put it towards the rehabilitation fund.'

I wondered afterwards who had sold whom, but I sincerely trust her Tommy returned to his level-headed little wifey and they lived happily ever after.

I met Smithy at the club. He wanted to know where the bloody hell I'd been all night. I didn't discuss my unusual night out, only said I had had a most pleasant time. I could see he was not happy. 'He'll get over it,' I thought. He had done the same thing to me many times.

We met a few of the boys who had come over on the boat. They were generally survivors of tours but as far as we could find, only six of the gunners, excluding Clarkey, had come through, and about the same percentage of pilots and navigators. They were different fellows to the aloof, slightly supercilious shipboard mates. Some had done Bomber Command tours, others had finished on Beaufort torpedo bombers. There was a profound difference in the outlook and appearance of these young veterans, still in many cases just out of their teens. The strain of the many hours of operational flying was etched in the lines on their faces, in the hardness of their eyes.

They were interested to hear that Smithy and I were still on operations. Most had wanted to continue on and do their second tour after a rest, but Kodak House had cracked down on this. That we were approaching our fiftieth op, completed on three different kites, caused some discussion.

They wanted to know what we intended doing when we had reached our fiftieth. It was something I had thought of but never discussed with Smithy. I said, 'I think I'll go through and complete the full thirty ops and then they can go to buggery.'

Smithy, after a short silence, stated that this was also his intention.

We met a couple of the boys from the old Vent squadron. The pilots and navs were engaged on the famous little-advertised milk run to Berlin and adjacent German cities.[1] They told us Wilbur and Jack were missing but as yet there was no definite news as to their fate.

This didn't sound the best of propositions. The Mossies had only a crew of two, a pilot and a nav, carried a four thousand pound bomb, and were completely defenceless behind. Admittedly they had a fair turn of speed, but so did the latest 109s and Focke Wulfs. The Mossies operated on the nights after the big raids to keep the defences stirred up and the civilians out of bed. It meant that the enemy, instead of having six or seven hundred planes to chase, had only thirty or forty to get stuck into. I said, 'I don't like the sound of it; missing usually means dead.'[2]

It was a day of reminiscing and speculation. By evening we were bright. Towards tea-time a pilot said, 'Christ, look who's here!,' as a resplendent figure came into the club. It was Dagworth, full of his own importance, aglitter with his new rank of squadron leader. He descended on Smithy and me before we could get off the mark and condescendingly called us by our surnames until we reciprocated.

He was, he declared, engaged on a highly secret job of flying VIPs – couldn't tell us their names, but it was an extremely important job. He was wearing a beautifully tailored American overcoat, one of the perks of his ferrying work. He insisted on taking both of us for a drink, for at the sight of him the rest of his former shipmates had disappeared. Unable to think up a suitable excuse we went across with him to the little Scotch pub opposite Boomerang House.

Night and gloomy fog had fallen on the world's largest city. We had had a lot of drink but were not full. Dag insisted on shouting Scotch. It was a one-sided conversation. It got around to old shipmates and our host started enquiring about various members. Strangely enough, nearly everyone he asked about was dead or missing. Smithy became increasingly truculent; 'He's bloody well dead'; 'He's fugging had it.' I'm susceptible to atmosphere and realised he was fast approaching exploding point. If Dagworth had had any bloody sense he would have seen it too, but he was either too dumb or puffed up by his own importance and chose to ignore it.

He said, 'There's no doubt about it, you young fellows have all the luck. There's nothing I'd like more than to have a crack at the Nazis but,' he added piously, 'the powers that be seem to have reserved me for more important jobs.'

Smithy's reaction to this hypocritical tripe was surprising – for Smithy. 'What bloody bullsh. You've never done any ops, Dagworth, because you're yellow, you've got no guts. No-one can tell me a pilot capable of flying a plane across the Atlantic isn't capable of flying over Europe. You give me a pain because you've crawled and bludged ever since you came to England.'

Dagworth's mouth was a vacuous 'O'. He replied weakly, 'Remember you're speaking to a superior officer. I'll have you placed on a charge.'

'Superior posterior,' returned Smithy. 'This is what I think of you and your bloody whisky,' and he tipped it on the floor. Putting his face close to the other's purpling one he said, 'You can go and get fugged, you yellow bludging bastard.'

For a second I thought Dagworth was going to have a go. I said, 'I wouldn't do that, Dag. If you touch him I'll drop you.' I knew one good wallop in his big fat gut would stop him. On the other hand there was a world of difference between insulting an officer and striking him, so I didn't really want to see any fisticuffs.

He looked at us both and realised he was outgunned. Clutching his tattered dignity as he made for the door, he declared, 'You will hear more of this. I'll have you both court-martialled.'

Smithy's parting salutation was inelegant.

As Dagworth disappeared I said, 'I think we'll go, too.' RAF head-quarters was only fifty yards away and I could imagine him hotfooting across for MP reinforcements. But Smithy was obstreperous; 'I've been waiting to give that bastard the works. We know and so does he what I said is true. He hasn't the guts to do anything about it.'

It was only with an effort I got him out of the place and steered him down into the city. I knew if Dag could raise the bloodhounds he would cover all our usual drinking haunts nearby. As the night wore on we got fuller and my companion more difficult to handle.

Towards ten we had forgotten about Dag and were back in the Old Cock Inn in Fleet Street. I was of the opinion that Smithy was getting completely impossible and he probably had the same opinion about me. It's hard to remember what sparked the final upset. We had words, bitter ones. It would have developed into a brawl, which would have been all for the better – a black eye, a bloody nose gets rid of the tensions – but the drinkers broke it up.

He said, 'If I never see you again, Beede, it will be too bloody soon,' and disappeared into the night.

For a second I felt like following and attempting to make it up; then thought, 'Bugger him, he can come to me first.' What I didn't realise at the time was that he was only twenty-two and for the past two years had been on almost continuous active service. I was later to find there is a limit to most men's endurance and nerves on operational flying. At the time I felt only irritation at his perverseness.

A feminine voice beside me asked, 'Having a little upset, Aussie?'

I was aware I was full, but even allowing for the rose-tinted view-point this gives the opposite sex, she looked all right to me. She was a civvy in her thirties and seemingly endowed with all the things that make a woman a woman. To prove that she wasn't on the bot[3] she bought me a drink. Things got a little hazy after that. I remember taking her around to Dirty Dick's and then her suggestion that I come and have a cup of coffee.

I woke up next morning in unfamiliar surroundings. The time was 8.30. The morning light filtering through the blackout curtains showed I was on a double settee in a very tastefully decorated room. I looked at the sleeping female beside me with some anxiety. I had awakened like this before to some unprepossessing sights, but this one was above average. I tried to remember the night's doings. There was something oppressive on my mind. I finally traced it to my row with Smithy.

I couldn't remember her name. By a deal of tactful probing I found it was Beryl. She declared, 'Were you high last night! Had a fight with your friend and generally played merry hell!'

It was the beginning of an association that was to last while I stayed in England. She was a journalist and, I was later to find, a good one. She was a generous woman in every way and I think considered that part of her war effort was to keep a selected number of the boys happy. She showed her good sense before I left by advising to make up my quarrel with my friend.

I could not find Smithy around the club so I travelled back to the camp alone.

Meeting Smithy in the mess at tea, he proved his pilot's point by wiping me cold. He was certainly taking our quarrel to heart. I ran into the Yank and his navigator, Stan, and they both said, 'Have you and Smithy fallen out?'

'Yes, we had a little upset last night.'

'He's very crooked,' the Yank advised. 'I think the best thing is to leave him alone till he cools down.'

'We're both on the battle order tomorrow,' said Stan. 'Briefing's at 4.30 am.'

This was unusual. Stan voiced everyone's feelings when he added, 'I don't like the look of it.'

It was freezing cold when we were called at 3 am and some uncomplimentary remarks were directed at headquarters. Before briefing, security was in evidence for the first time since we'd been on the station. There were only six crews, three from each squadron, all experienced men. The curtain still covered the wall map so that we couldn't see our objective. Before the briefing started, the Groupy stated that because of the nature of the operation straight gunners need not go unless they desired. WAGs had to fly. He asked if any AG wished to withdraw. There were some enquiring looks and short consultations. I expect there were a few who would have liked to say 'no'. Smithy and I, because of our unusual set-up, had no option. Finally they all decided they would go.

There was an audible gasp when the curtain was pulled: the tape lead straight to the naval base of Brest, reputedly the strongest and toughest fortress on the European coast. Its very name was liable to send shivers down any thinking flier's spine.

After the murmur had subsided Groupy continued, 'My offer to gunners still stands. This is a low-level do and I can see no reason why straight AGs need fly.'

There was a silence, then a young Canadian and an Englishman said they did not wish to go. The CO said, 'Right! You will be under close guard till this is finished. You are excused.' They were immediately escorted from the room. I reckon the two men had more guts than the remaining four who sat terse and tight-lipped, held by false pride and fear of the opinion of their mates from accepting the virtual offer of their lives.

The objective was a merchant raider which had been damaged by a Sunderland and had put into Brest for safety and repairs. 'The target is of such importance that it must be destroyed no matter what the cost.' A pleasant declaration, these last five words, in terms of planes and young lives.

On the spectroscope we saw comprehensive pictures of the dog-legged breakwater and adjacent strong points. The raider, as shown by a last-minute photograph from a reconnaissance Mossie, was anchored in the middle of the harbour two hundred yards from the centre of the breakwater. Our plan was to leave an hour before first light, fly as low as possible and rendezvous at a given minute three miles from the harbour. Perfection of the plan required all planes to rendezvous on time, then immediately attack in line astern. Some were to carry short delay bombs, others incendiary. It was hoped sufficient hits with both would completely destroy the pirate.

The rendezvous was all-important for the success of the operation. The leader was instructed to do three short circuits of the area; two minutes after meeting, the available forces were to go in and attack. Anyone arriving late was to follow the main force, the equivalent of playing Russian roulette with all chambers loaded. In the event of a bad fog or mist we were to withdraw.

The Groupy finished on a highly emotional note, stressing the traditions and history of the squadron. His closing words had the unpleasant tinge of a farewell as though he never expected to see us again.

Going out in the bus we decided that, as we were third to take off and consequently Number Three in the attack line, it was necessary for Bill to keep in touch with the two preceding planes to the extent of following dangerously on their heels. To arrive late and not be a dingo would, in the face of the aroused defences, be suicide.

As we taxied around, FIDO's oil-fed fires glowed eerily through the envelope of fog which held the station in its grey grip. We took off so close behind Number Two that it looked as if we were racing them to the end of the strip. The advantage of this was apparent when we came out above the fog, for despite the flame arresters we could still see the glow of the exhausts in the blue-black sky. In a few minutes we also picked up Number One and never lost them for the rest of the journey.

Above the fog the night was clear and velvety black, the stars shining coldly through the frosty air. The temperature was minus fifteen when we took off; with the slipstream whizzing around our ears it was freezing. In spite of this, the anticipation of our impending ordeal brought on a cold sweat.

It was considered highly dangerous to go within three miles of this fortified strong point. We intended going right into its maw. It looked like curtains for most of the planes engaged. If I ever prayed for a real stinking yellow fog over the combat area I did on that one-hour trip.

Dawn was breaking as we came to our rendezvous. The light was strong enough to see the two planes ahead and two behind. There was a mist with visibility of two hundred and fifty yards, enough for the op to go ahead. We did three circuits as directed, then the leader waggled his wings to indicate he was going in to attack. As we straightened up I saw the sixth plane come out of the fog perhaps three hundred yards astern. There wasn't a chance he would catch us but he came in hell for leather after the echelon.

We were flying so low I felt and tasted the spray thrown back by the slipstream of the leaders. My guts were a solid ball of fear. Jock said, 'Here we are.' The broad breakwater flashed so close beneath us I felt I could have touched it. Out of the corner of my eye I saw the contours as it stretched away exactly as portrayed in the visascope. White streamers of flak were already whisking by. Someone said, 'There she is, bombs away', and the masts of a boat raced past our ears.

I anticipated the terrific right turn; as I felt the swing I grabbed the guns. For ten horrible seconds centrifugal force plucked at me with a mighty hand. I felt Basher rising below me, pressed up by this invisible force. Then the plane righted itself and the pressure was off. Behind us I saw a small vessel of perhaps a thousand tons wreathed in smoke and flames.

The sleeping giant was coming to life. A veritable inferno of flame and tracer poured in our direction. One of the rear planes did a crazy wobble, just cleared the causeway, then disappeared in a welter of spume into the sea; a second took a shell in the guts and disintegrated in the air. Below, the water was churned white as the defences reached out in fury at this audacious intrusion. The latecomer, still three hundred yards astern, took a pasting but came out seemingly unscathed.

The splashes dropped away. Suddenly, realising we had made it, I bellowed, 'We're out, we're out!,' and was immediately doused in a veritable wall of water. I thought for a second one of the planes must have gone in till I saw great pillars of white water erupting around us. Bill said, 'It's the bloody naval guns.' At this unexpected threat, we scattered to reduce the danger, but even after Brest had disappeared far astern into the mist those mighty guns continued to range and search for us, throwing their towering columns of water skywards. I suppose there wasn't much chance of their scoring a hit, but they kept up the tension.

It was here that Jock voiced the thought that was on everyone's mind; 'I don't think that was the raider at all. That ship was not more than a thousand tons; the raider is an eight thousand tonner.' In broad Geordie, Basher said fervently, 'Christ, I hope we don't have to go back.' It was a certainty the Jerries would not be caught napping next time.

As we regrouped, I noticed one of the planes flying on one engine; the port was feathered. It was not usual for a group to wait for a lame duck, but the leader must also have been feeling the relief of coming out alive, as he throttled back to let the tail-end Charlie and the damaged plane catch up. They flew at about seven o'clock a hundred yards away and, despite a two hundred and sixty miles clip, kept up with the box.

I could make out their markings and asked Jock, 'Who was flying M for Mary?'

'I think it's the Yank.' I looked across and gave a wave. I saw an answering reply from the Yank and Stan, and said, 'I believe you're right. Is he punishing that motor! God, I hope it lasts out.'

As we came in over our coast the Yank called and said that due to hydraulic failure he'd been unable to bomb and still had his lethal belly load. Bill commented, 'I hope his bloody landing gear works or it's curtains for someone.'

At base, the fog of early morning had almost disappeared. Despite quite fair visibility, FIDO still poured its dirty smoke skywards. The Yank called the control tower and explained his predicament and was given immediate priority. I could imagine the flap below, the marshalling of fire engines, ambulance and sundry staff cars. The control officer asked if his landing gear was working. There was a silence and then the Yank's nasal twang reported it was okay.

The rest of us were put into orbit; with the landing gear working there was little danger. A good pilot could land a bomb-laden plane on one engine without difficulty. Visibility was so good that I saw a second Boston cut in, in front of the Yank's. I said, 'What's that bastard doing?'

The intruding plane cut straight in ahead of the crippled bomber. Then the latter did an amazing thing; it turned left into its dead engine. For a second it seemed to hang in the sky and, in a twinkling, disappeared. Dumfounded, I said, 'I think they've crashed.'

Concentrating on his circuit, Bill said irritably, 'Who's crashed?'

'Smithy and the Yank.'

From behind the trees a black tell-tale pillar of smoke climbed skywards. Over the intercom a crisp voice said, 'All planes keep clear of smoke area. Plane with full bomb-load has just crashed.'

There was nothing we could do. There was still a faint hope that it wasn't Smithy's plane or that they had been able to break clear. The intruder was soon identified as one of the French planes. At interrogation the fact that we had bombed the wrong ship seemed of small consequence. The Groupy was ropeable. He didn't say much, but by his looks and actions intimated he was most displeased at our goof.

The only crew to receive any kudos was the crew who had gone in last. Admittedly they had been shot up but no worse than the rest. The crew's pilot, a flight lieutenant, belonged to the menagerie and was a particular toady of the CO's.[4]

After interrogations we waited for news of the crashed bomber. When it finally came through, it was a stunner. The plane had gone in from about fifty feet, crashed near a group of houses and immediately caught fire. An English erk home on compassionate leave to see his wife who had given premature birth to twins, had immediately raced across to the plane and succeeded in dragging Smithy from the blazing wreckage, when one of the bombs had exploded, blowing both the rescuer's legs off.

The explosion had kicked the three remaining bombs clear, which did not go up. The other three crew members had been incinerated. Showered with blazing petrol and peppered with blast and shrapnel, Smithy and his rescuer were not expected to live.

That night the rescuer died unhonoured and unsung. Smithy, from scanty information, was not far behind. The thought of burning petrol recalled those unfortunates at Crothers. I was physically sick at the thought of this young airman becoming a charred, walking skeleton.

I rarely prayed for my own safety during the war. I couldn't see how I could affront my God in everyday life and ask for his protection in battle. That night I prayed sincerely and fervently that Smithy's life be spared, that he be made whole and well again. I tried to get some information from our quack, but without result. In the end I went to see the Catholic padre. Smithy had been one of his flock. He was a good chap and gave me a daily bulletin. At the end of the week Smithy was moved from the local hospital to one closer to London.

The padre said, 'He's grievously wounded and terribly burned. Perhaps it might be better if God, in His compassion, took him to his reward.'

The two big questions from this tragedy were: 'Why did the bomber cut in ahead of a plane that had complete priority?', and 'How could an experienced pilot turn into his dead engine with a full bomb-load aboard, a flying manoeuvre calculated to bring almost certain disaster?'

It seemed a pointless loss of lives, akin to an infantryman surviving a tremendous land battle and, when safely back behind his lines, being shot by one of his own troops.

This flagrant breach of flying rules incensed the entire station to such an extent that it overshadowed the possibility of a return to Brest to try to finish the job we had botched. It was later learned the errant French pilot didn't understand a word of English and was unaware of his transgression.[5]

CHAPTER THIRTY-TWO

Smithy's accident really shook me. He had been as certain as I was he would come through, and I began to wonder if my premonition of survival was based on sound grounds. I had done fifty ops. 'This', I argued, 'was enough, but how the hell could I get out?' After some consideration I started to kid myself my eyes weren't too good. Prior to joining the RAAF I had used glasses for study and reading. I still had these with me. Furtively using them now and then behind a paper I was soon able to convince myself I was half-blind and a dolt to be flying at all.

It was a short step to a visit to medical with a complaint that my eyes were playing up. Our section did not have the means of a thorough test so I was despatched to the military hospital at Aldershot. The eye specialist was a grizzled colonel. Possibly in his day many thousands of applicants had had their hopes of a quick retirement from the services dashed against his rugged interrogation and knowledge. He asked why I felt my eyesight was not up to flying standard. I said my eyes had been playing up. I found it necessary to use my civvy glasses when reading.

He didn't muck around. 'I'm going to put you through certain tests; don't try to fake your replies because your answers will only laugh at each other.' At the end of the tests he deliberated for a while, then said, 'You say you use glasses for reading. Show them to me.' He tested the glasses and laughed.

'Do you know what they are?'

'No,' I said, with a sinking heart.

'You are one of the lucky ones in this world. You have almost perfect eyesight. These glasses are plain glass, so someone must have been having you on.'

I said, 'But I have to use them for reading.'

'Throw them away. How many ops have you done?'

'Fifty.'

We had a chat and I found he wasn't as tough as his exterior indicated. He said, 'It's not your eyes that are the trouble, it's your nerves.

I think you need a rest, Aussie. I could make a recommendation on these lines if you wished.'

I gave this some thought. It was a temptation, but I could imagine the boys laughing at me. Finally, I said, 'I don't want you to think I'm a hero or a fool as I don't think I am either. I'll push on for a while longer.'

A week later I was called in to medical quarters. The MO commented that I hadn't got far with my eye test. I said nothing, but looked at the ferrety-faced little chap with displeasure. As the interrogation progressed I realised his opening remarks were intended as an unpleasant crack and this was some sort of an interview for rehabilitation planning upon my discharge from the RAAF, because he was wading through a mass of questions. When I had got the gist of what it was all about I said, 'You won't have to worry about me if I ever come out of this alive.'

He said acidly, 'This is a test under the direction of the Air Board. Will you please answer the questions, Pilot Officer.'

When he asked details of my previous occupation, I said, 'Sales manager', and gave my firm's name. 'Salary?'

'A thousand a year.'

This might have been big-noting myself to a degree as the sum included some allowances. It was not till I thought the matter over later that I realised that a thousand pounds a year to the average Englishman at that time was a princely sum.

He looked at me with his beady eyes and said, 'It is intended that these questions be answered truthfully. You can forget the flights of fancy.'

I felt myself getting hot under the collar. 'I have no reason to exaggerate my earnings. They can be checked with my company. We have a branch here in England.'

He looked at my papers and said sarcastically, 'You are now twenty-seven. That means you were twenty-four when you came into the air force. They must appoint executives at an early age in Australia, Beede.'

'They do, Doctor. In fact, if a man has any brains and a desire to work he can almost write his own ticket. I have informed you that I am in no need of assistance when I receive my discharge. I would, however, suggest you give some thought to your own rehabilitation problems, as I feel you will be in need of considerable assistance when you quit the shelter of service life. Remember, you will not have the favour of a CO to carry you through. It is also possible you may even require some attention for your knees.'

They were insulting words. I felt he wouldn't have the guts to do anything about it.

He wrote across the form viciously, 'Officer refuses to co-operate', and, looking at me with smouldering eyes said, 'The interview is closed.'

I had an uneasy feeling that I had opened my mouth too wide. That night in the mess I saw the MO peering around at me as he poured his tale into the other's receptive ear. I thought, 'Damn 'em both. If I can come out of this alive these two bastards won't worry me.'

A few days later Bill and Jock went down with flu, both spending a fortnight in hospital. While I was grounded, the boys reported a strange incident while they were doing over a French target. They ran into heavy flak which concentrated on the rear box. One plane, badly hit, turned back. Two parachutes mushroomed below, showing the observer and bottom gunner Tubby Evans, had made it. The top gunner panicked and, instead of going out the safe bottom hatch, went out over the top, pulling his cord as he went, and became entangled in the tailplane. Unaware of his gunner's predicament, the pilot made an endeavour to crash-land the plane but smashed into the forest below, killing both himself and the trapped gunner. This unfortunate incident was to be the start of some strange adventures for the little Australian gunner.

In the meantime Christmas came almost like any other day, the only difference being the traditional morning in the sergeants' mess, and serving the airmen their dinner.

During this time we had some of the worst weather I'd seen in England – sleet, snow, fogs, in which long stalactites of ice hung from the telegraph and fence wires. The cold made life a misery and, what was worse, seriously interfered with the love life of the squadron, till someone found the flight buses offered a good refuge from the inclement ground conditions.

Tommy the Kiwi was an active member of the Rooters' Club. He was also a rabid card player and a mighty tippler. The combined effects of all these dissipations finally reduced him to a white-faced, shaky, bleary-eyed wreck. Having a minimum of faith in the local MO he waited until he obtained leave and went to his own headquarters in London in search of something, as he later explained, that would perk him up a bit. After the examination the amazed MO immediately classified him as a case of extreme battle fatigue. Within a week he was off the squadron and in less than a month on his way home. The rest of the boys looked on his good fortune with open-mouthed envy. As one commented; 'Its the first time I've ever heard of anyone rooting himself out of the Air Force.'

Just after Tommy's departure, Tubby arrived back on the squadron. He had a remarkable story to tell. After he had bailed out he had fallen into the arms of a section of the French Resistance while his navigator had been nabbed by the Nazis, even though they had fallen not more than five hundred yards apart. These doughty Resistance fighters had immediately spirited him away to a branch of the escape group who helped Allied airmen escape, generally through Spain, back to England.

At the first farmhouse he had been hidden in there was a French Canadian gunner who had crashed six months previously. This worthy had holed up with a very charming little French widow. He spoke French fluently and adamantly refused to budge from his happy little nook. A special officer, on his twelfth drop, had been parachuted in to dislodge this Lothario but, as far as Tubby knew, without success.

The men belonging to the special parachuting service were remarkable fellows. They travelled in and out of Occupied Europe as though it were peacetime, only now they came from the clouds. The reason for these frequent hazardous trips was to clear up little problems such as this, and to see that the escape route was operating properly and hadn't been taken over by the Gestapo. The penalty, if they were caught, was torture and death.

This little incident amused the boys. The picture of this gunner, happily holed up with this little French charmer and defying authority, tickled our fancies.

Tubby was loud in his praises of the courage and skill of these special men and the French civilians of the Resistance who risked extermination not only of themselves but of their friends and relations if caught. The Gestapo frequently dropped English-speaking agents dressed in RAF uniforms, who went the full length of the escape route and then handed the information gained over to this dread organisation. Despite such terrible reprisals as the wiping out of entire families, new cells would soon be formed and new escape avenues opened.[1]

Tubby, supplied with clothing and a false passport, had a remarkable but almost uneventful trip along the escape route that took him to Paris, by train to Toulouse, and finally a trip hidden in a hollowed bale of hay close to the Spanish border. Here he was handed over to a grizzled Spanish mountain guide who took him and an escaping fighter pilot by devious and secret paths up over the Pyrenees down into Spain. He told us the most dangerous part of this trip was when they had crossed into Spain, as Franco's gendarmes and tough militia, equipped with savage dogs, hunted the escaping airmen more relentlessly than the Nazis. It was God help both the hunted and their guides if they were caught in the inhospitable mountain highlands because nothing would be heard or seen of them again.

This part of the trip had taken them three weeks as they dodged patrols and made their way through these dangerous areas, helped by peasants and farmers, until they arrived in Madrid.

Even then the dangers were not over. The front of the British Embassy was covered by the militia, who were liable to apprehend any civilian whom they considered might be making for the Embassy. If caught by these toughs, it meant anything from six to twelve months in filthy, lice-ridden jails whilst the Ambassador sought their release.

In this instance a fake fight was started by some sympathetic friends of the guide, and whilst the attention of Franco's toughies was temporarily distracted, Tubby and his mate had slipped smartly inside. Even in the sanctuary of the Embassy it had taken a fortnight's planning to get them to Gibraltar and a waiting warship.

Tubby stated that in the sick bay of the boat was a skeleton-like lice-weakened wreck of a man, a New Zealand pilot, who had been grabbed in Madrid and had spent nine months in Franco's notorious jail. This poor wreck, then three-and-a-half stone, was normally a twelve-stone man. So much for Franco and his pleasant playmates.

The squadron had gone back to attacking ground installations. These were mysterious and extensive works reported by the Resistance. Sometimes these objectives were reasonably docile targets, while at other times they were veritable hornets' nests, ringed with concentrated and highly efficient ack-ack fire.[2]

It was on my fifty-second op that we struck trouble. We were to bomb at nine thousand feet. On the run in we struck a wall of highly concentrated flak. It was so close you could see the wicked red flash as the black rings mushroomed and smell the cordite and gunpowder. I heard Jock say, 'Bombs away,' and then felt the tremendous heat and concussion of a bursting shell. Bill said, 'Port motor out of action'. Jock reported, 'I've been hit by shrapnel in the face and shoulders' as, simultaneously, Bill said, 'Port motor on fire. I'm diving to extinguish flames.' Above us I could see the remnants of our box battling their way out.

Bill reported, 'Fire extinguished', and then, 'How are you, Navigator? Are you badly hit?' Jock's soft Scottish voice was full of agony as he replied, 'Aye! I've been badly hit.'

Then the disadvantage of the separate compartments of the Boston became evident because Basher and I, untouched by the blast, were unable to go to his assistance. It was a nightmare trip back. Twice more the motor caught alight and was extinguished by Bill's flying. Jock had lapsed into unconsciousness, now and then giving a sepulchral groan. It was almost a repetition of that nerve-wracking night flight across the channel in S for Sugar. By the time we reached our coast we were down to five hundred feet and Bill warned us to attach our parachutes in case the starboard motor gave out. He instructed, 'If I say "Jump", bail out immediately.'

We made the drome safely. Bill called and was granted an immediate priority. He said, 'I hope no bloody Froggie's going to jump our claim.'

'If he does I'll blow him out of the bloody sky,' I replied.

We made our approach. The motor appeared to be holding, the plane was straight and level, the trees slid below us. We were perhaps fifty feet with a thousand yards to go for a touch-down when the plane gave a peculiar lurch. For a matter of seconds I had a sensation as though I was going down in a fast lift. I never felt the crash; the world just seemed to black out.

It took me a long while to figure out where I was. I knew I was in a bed. I could see a dimly-lit high-domed ceiling. What I couldn't fathom was why I was in that particular spot. What was real was an all-consuming ache that seemed to envelop every part of my body. It felt as though someone had set to and belted me with a cricket bat.

The next time I looked at the ceiling it was daylight. I must have said, 'That's funny,' because a very English voice beside me said, 'He's conscious', and I became aware of a long serious face looking into mine. I went to turn my head but a terrific spasm of pain checked that.

The voice said, 'Don't try to move. You've been in a crash. Take it easy.'

I gave this consideration but it still didn't make sense, so I asked, 'Where am I?'

'Aldershot Military Hospital,' the voice replied. 'You crashed in a Boston in the hospital grounds.'

Then I remembered that momentary going-down-in-a-lift feeling and thought of Bill, Basher and Jock. 'What happened to the rest of the crew?'

The voice said, 'Don't worry about them,' and it didn't seem to matter much for I felt as though I were drifting away on a cloud. What I didn't know at the time was that they were pumping dope into me to soften the pain.

At the end of the week I had recovered sufficiently to start taking an interest in my surroundings, though I still couldn't turn my head. What I did find was that I was as near to black as it was possible to be. This, the doctor said, was extensive bruising from the shock of impact. I learned poor Jock had been killed in the crash. Bill had a broken leg and Basher, who was lying flat, had escaped almost Scot-free.

At the end of eight days I found, by careful manoeuvring, I could turn my head slightly to the left. In doing this it brought into view a somewhat remarkable-looking person propped up comfortably on pillows. A special bookrest with its own light meant he did not have to hold the book he was reading.

It was the face that interested me, elongated and horselike, of a purplish mottled hue. It was a caricature of the faces seen in cartoons of English aristocrats. What really highlighted this comparison was the fact that he was reading with a monocle. Now, how the hell could you read with a monocle?

Feeling the need for a little light conversation, I said, 'How are you?'

At my greeting, the horsy face turned toward me and stared in astonishment. The look was that of a well-bred collie gazing at a stray mongrel which had been so presumptuous as to bark at him. After a brief, cold survey he shook himself and, with an explosive, 'Hurump', turned back to his reading.

It was a dirty rebuff and I felt like saying, 'You snobbish bastard, what's biting you?'

With the passing of time the blue bruising started to turn grey. I had no broken bones, but as one doctor explained, extensive bruising often took as long to get over as a break.

One uncomfortable aftermath of the crash was that the right member of a pair that testify to one's manhood had swollen to the size of a cricket ball and refused to go down. This caused a deal of medical speculation and was the cause of some private joking on the part of the nurses.

One side of the ward was medical and the other surgical, which meant if a bed was transferred from the medical to the surgical side the unlucky occupant was due for an operation or amputation.

One morning, after I was able to sit up and give a bit of cheek, three straight-faced nurses came in and, after tidying my bed, wheeled it across to the surgical side. I said, 'What the hell are you putting me over here for?'

One said, 'Oh, specialist's orders.'

'But,' I replied, panic setting in, 'this is the surgical side.'

'That's right. I believe you're scheduled for this morning.'

'Like hell,' I replied. 'No-one's going to get me into any operating theatre.'

Then a nurse skipped into the ward and said, 'Matron's coming!', and back my bed went at the double to its correct side.

This little joke caused a laugh till my horsy companion reported the three jokers to Matron, declaring there was too much horseplay going on in the ward for proper discipline.

When I was able to use my hands I wrote to Kodak House enquiring how Smithy was. I didn't want to write letters if he was dead. After a period they replied, saying he had been moved to Crothers. I knew then that he was behind that wicket gate. I pondered for some days on what kind of letter I should write. I tried to imagine if I was in the same plight what type of letter would please me and came to the conclusion I wouldn't want any mail at all.

Finally I wrote a short note explaining my position and enquiring how he was doing. I didn't say anything regarding our last row as it now seemed so unimportant and foolish.

CHAPTER THIRTY-THREE

One day a team of some half-dozen doctors arrived and made a thorough examination of myself and two other patients in the ward. A short while afterwards special charts were set up over our respective beds and two nurses arrived with whopping great flat pills. I have never been able to swallow pills of any size, not even aspirin, as they stick in my gullet.

I said, 'Am I supposed to swallow that flaming horse pill?' The nurse said I was, so I popped it in my mouth, chewed it up and washed it down with a glass of water. This created some consternation so two doctors were called in for discussion and, after I had explained my position, agreed that it was okay for me to chew them first.

I was somewhat flattered by the attention and interest my method of disposing created. My temperature was taken every fifteen minutes and at least two doctors, plus a galaxy of nurses, came in to watch me. After a while I began to feel like a seal doing a fish-swallowing act.

My enthusiasm waned considerably, however, when one of the other pill-swallowing patients threw a mouth-frothing fit and turned a yellowish-green. This bloke was hastily removed and was not seen again.

After this incident the checks on the other patient and myself were doubled. Over a three day period I swallowed, literally, dozens of different coloured tablets but nothing happened to either of us and after a while they had a beneficial effect on my swollen testicle.

It wasn't till later I learned we were guinea pigs for the new sulphanilamide tablets. The bloke who turned the yellowish green was one of the unfortunates who was allergic to them.

Later I was allowed up to shave and bath. I found an interesting position existed with regard to my fellow patients who, with the exception of myself, were all Army officers. They were divided into two groups, the permanent or regular army and the men who had gained commissions in the field. Between these two was a solid wall of class distinction. The regular group completely ignored and even refused to recognise the amateurs.

I chummed up with a major who had won his commission in the Western Desert and was the holder of the inferior Military Medal (given only to lower ranks). This fellow had been a grocer before the war and, as he said, fell far below the social status of the professionals. He declared bitterly that these college-bred types, steeped in the learning and strategy of the 1914–1918 conflict, adamantly refused to listen to the practical experience of the so-called enlisted officers.

'How the hell England wins wars I'll never know,' he continued. 'The worst part about it all is that the poor bloody ordinary soldier has to take a terrific walloping whilst these college-trained military snobs are safely established at headquarters, well behind the lines, learning this new, fast-moving warfare.'

He told me my aloof bed-neighbour, the scion of a noble English family and a colonel in the quartermaster's department, was in for his alcoholic excesses, having recently suffered an attack of the DTs. 'Have you noticed how they put a screen around him a couple of times a day?'

I had.

'That's so he can have his ration of Scotch, being a part of the cure to wean him off the grog,' he said. 'He augments this daily ration with an arrangement with one of his officers. You have possibly noted,' he continued, 'that this fellow brings in the evening paper. In this is wrapped the extra drop.'

'This dipsomaniac,' he declared, 'was such a complete dill that 'even his associates speak contemptuously of him, and such a snob he refuses to speak to anyone other than his equal or superior. Because he's senior officer in the ward he has not spoken a single word to anyone except to reprimand the nurses or complain.'

My new and interesting friend said it was acknowledged in England that in the supposed blue-blood families the dill who was incapable of doing anything else qualified for the Army.

Being a neutral, I mixed with both groups and found some of the permanents nice fellows. One day I stumbled upon an easy formula to find out what particular category a fellow patient fell into. All one had to do was ask,'What did you do before the war?' This query brought two standard answers, 'Army, old man,' or the ranker-officer told you what he had been doing.

On the third Sunday some of the boys, including Tubby, came across with some personal effects. They said it had been a hard job planning the trip as visitors were not welcomed.

There was considerable laughter and light-hearted banter, particularly at the mention of my delicate injury. After ten minutes the colonel pressed for service and demanded to see the Matron. When she arrived he declared my visitors were creating an uproar, disturbing the patients, and demanded that they be ejected.

Poker-faced, the Matron said icily, 'If it's your orders, colonel, I'll ask them to go.'

'They are my orders.'

She used a lot of tact getting them out. Tubby, prior to his departure, asked, 'Who's that boofheaded old bastard, anyway?' It was an apt description, and from then on, first to a few and then to most, the colonel was known as 'Boofhead'.

During my stay in bed I had often heard the bark of staccato commands and the distant drumming of heavily shod feet. One day when wandering around I found a little balcony that gave a view of half of what I thought was a parade ground. What interested me was that the instructors out-numbered the trainees by two to one and, as far as I could see, all orders were executed at the double; everyone except the instructors ran.

I mentioned this to my major friend and he said, 'Oh, that's the punishment square. All those men are being punished for some misdemeanour or other and all orders naturally are done at the double.'

Next day I went to my lookout with some interest. I found there seemed to be several forms of punishment. Some offenders were put to work removing a large pile of stones or earth by wheelbarrow, over to another spot out of my view. After they had completed this job, they moved it back to the first area and vice versa.[1]

On this particular day four soldiers, laden like packhorses, were doing continuous circuits under the watchful eyes of three burly instructors equipped with truncheons or rubber hoses. As I could see half the area, I guessed that there were another three on the other side.

These four unfortunates galloped awkwardly around the square. If they looked like lessening their pace they received a good wallop with the truncheon over the legs or backsides. This really must have hurt as it galvanised them into renewed effort.

After forty-five minutes their pace really began to slacken. This brought their overseers swinging into action. As time wore on their energies began to evaporate; even the threat of the truncheons began to fade, but their oppressors countered this with stinging strokes as those poor devils began first to stagger and finally totter from sheer exhaustion.

There was one agile little bloke who must have had a phobia about being hit, because even the threat of a wallop galvanised him into nervous leaps forward. His sadistic tormentors realised this and every time he passed they would go to make a swipe at him. He must have been a power-house of energy because even after his three companions had collapsed insensible to the ground and were dragged away, he was still going.

Finally, even the nervous energy that propelled this harassed creature began to fade. His steps began to falter and then he started to stagger. Even though I was a hundred yards away I could sense his gasping breath, his contorted face, as he tried to gulp air into his over-worked lungs. It was then the instructors swung into action. I did not see the first stroke, but I heard the high-pitched cry. He came into view. The poor fellow was striving desperately to keep his stride. As he passed each MP, they walloped him and, as they did, he let out a piercing scream.

I watched this brutal, sadistic spectacle and found I was shaking with emotion and rage. The little bloke staggered out of sight and three more cries pierced the cold morning air. When he came into view again it was apparent he was at the end of his physical and mental resources and in attempting to evade the first truncheon swinger he staggered and fell in an exhausted heap.

The MP moved forward with the apparent intention of striking the fallen wretch again. It was then that an involuntary shout came from within me; 'Leave that man alone!', I bellowed.

The effect was instantaneous. He stopped in his stride and the three heads swung around simultaneously. They could see me on the balcony but couldn't make out who I was. I saw them look at each other and could imagine them saying, 'Who the bloody 'ell's that?'

The first bloke moved toward his victim uncertainly, so I shouted again, 'Leave that man alone.' I had the advantage of surprise, ano-nymity and the Pom MP's respect for an officer's command.

I could imagine them reasoning: 'It's coming from the officer's quarters, it must be a bleedin' officer,' so without further ado one picked up the fallen man by the shoulders and the other by the ankles and carted him out of sight.

Repercussions followed smartly on the heels of my intervention. An enquiry must have been started immediately to find who had given the unofficial and highly unethical order, and in a matter of thirty minutes I was summoned to the superintendent's office. A cold-eyed MP major wearing rimless glasses, who was a dead ringer for Himmler, was in attendance.

After verifying my name, designation and rank, the superintendent asked if I had been on a certain balcony some thirty minutes before.

'Yes.'

Had I interfered with the normal duties of military personnel by giving an unauthorised order?

I said I had.

My candid reply staggered them both. Whether they had expected me to hedge or lie I don't know. The superintendent looked in a non-plussed way at my papers. He asked, 'You are recovering from a plane crash, Pilot Officer?'

'Yes,' I replied.

He looked at his cold-eyed companion as if to say, 'The poor fellow's got wheels, he's mentally deranged.' Then he said, 'Your conduct is inexcusable and highly unethical. We do not want a repetition of it.'

The officer MP was more direct, declaring, 'You have interfered with the duties of members of His Majesty's forces.' He warned he did not want this to happen again, hinting darkly of unpleasant consequences.

Back in my ward my effort received a mixed reception. The amateurs were delighted, the professionals so extremely displeased they put me in the doghouse and refused to have any further truck with me. My friend the major confided to me that consensus of opinion was, 'The fellow's a damned Bolshevik.'

To make sure it couldn't happen again the door to the balcony was locked, so I never got around to seeing any more of the doings on the square, although from the commands and the pounding of heavily shod feet, it was evident the games still went on.

One day my old friend the eye specialist came into the ward on some duty. He must've had a good memory, for as he passed my bed he looked, stopped, and said, 'Hello, Aussie, what are you doing here?'

'Had a crash, sir.'

'You didn't take my advice, then.'

'I will now,' I replied. He was a nice fellow and dropped in several times after that to say 'hello' and pass derogatory remarks about Boofhead who received his cracks in stony silence.

Finally the time came for my discharge. I had been there a month and had made some good friends, but was still in the doghouse with the professionals. I had dressed and packed my bag and was making a last inspection of my locker to see if anything had been left.

The ward doctor was doing his rounds with two sisters and Matron in attendance. As I straightened up I found the colonel had turned his head and had me transfixed with his monocle.

Then, wonder of wonders, he spoke in stilted, clipped Army English, 'I wish to remark I view your going with extreme pleasure; the air in the ward will be the fresher for your departure. I am aware of your libellous comments regarding myself, and your reprehensible conduct. The full details will, in due course, be forwarded to your commanding officer.'

I looked at his glittering idiotic monocle, his mottled horse-like face. The doctor and his attendants were at the next bed and I thought, 'Why not?'

I spoke so that all could hear. 'You, my good major (that made him shudder) should have no anxiety about air because you pollute it with your whisky-laden breath. You have little to worry about, for there will always be a plentiful supply of Scotch for you and your kind, and an unlimited supply of young men from all over the world to fight the war while you lie in bed and bludge. I would, however, suggest to the doctor here, that he investigate the young lieutenant who brings in your supply of whisky wrapped in a newspaper every evening and removes the evidence by the same means next morning, because I feel your actions could lay a basis for a court-martial on a self-inflicted wound charge.'

The medical group, together with the rest of the ward, listened in open-mouthed silence to this exchange of pleasantries. As a closing shot I said, 'I'm sure you'll look into this matter, doctor.'

I got to the sliding doors, turned and looked back. All heads except the colonel's were turned my way. I gave them a nonchalant wave and walked down the corridor. The eye specialist had asked me to drop in and see him before I left. He said, 'A little drink won't hurt you before you go,' and mixed me a stiff whisky, adding, 'The doctor who has written your report is a friend of mine. He has recommended that you be given fourteen days' recuperation leave. Don't let them gyp you when you get back to your station.'

Back on the drome I got my leave and thought, 'I'll go up to Kodak House first and put in an application to go home.' Fifty-two ops plus my crash, in my opinion, constituted a good reason.[2] On the way up in the train I decided to add a compassionate one to bolster my case. My mother, a widow, was seventy-nine and had been seriously ill. I felt reasonably confident that with a little salesmanship I would soon be back in Australia, meeting friends and relatives, listening to the boom of the surf, feeling the surge of the big boomers once again. It was an exciting prospect – God, how I wanted to get home!

I found I first had to make a written application, stating reasons why I considered I should be granted a priority, and then wait for an interview. The latter, the sergeant clerk stated, might take three to five days. I solved this problem by passing over a fiddly, with a promise of a second if my call came up earlier. I was asked to come back later in the afternoon when I found my interview was listed for 3.30 pm the following day.

I was right on time waiting for my call. An orderly called, 'Pilot Officer Beede, interview with Squadron Leader Dale.' The name struck a chord – I stopped and exclaimed, 'Christ, not Squadron Leader Dale!' The orderly pushed me ahead, opened the door and said, 'Pilot Officer Beede.'

I looked at the fat figure at the desk; it was him all right. I thought, 'this bastard must fill every role in Kodak House.' He sat writing and ignored me for five minutes, the time-honoured custom of twirps. He finished, looked at me and said, 'Pilot Officer Beede.'

'Yes.'

'You have an application on compassionate and service grounds for return to Australia.'

'Yes, sir.' I thought, 'If I have to crawl to this illegitimate I'll get lower than a snake's belly.'

He examined my papers and asked, 'Are there any particular reasons why you feel your application should be considered?'

'Yes, sir.' I listed my mother's health, and that I had done fifty-two operations without rest and, finally, my crash and a month's stay in hospital.

He sat with his lips pursed, the tips of his fingers together. 'Yes, but have you any valid reasons?'

I had an uneasy feeling that I wasn't doing too well. 'Sir, I have done twenty-two operations on Wellingtons, half of the crew were wiped out on our last operation. I then completed eighteen on Venturas, the crew was disbanded because of the heavy loss of these planes, and the pilot and observer were dead. I then transferred to Bostons and completed a further twelve, and on our last operation the navigator was killed and the pilot broke a leg. I have now completed two tours. My mother is seriously ill; this can be verified in Australia. The reason I ask to be returned is because I feel I have done my bit, and also on compassionate grounds.'

He still sat with his fingers together. 'Beede, you don't seem to realise that there are thousands of young Australians in England who want to return home. I can nominate a hundred RAAF members in Kodak House who have service equal or better than yours. We do not receive applications from these airmen to return home.'

I thought, 'No, because the bastards never had it so easy.' Aloud, I said, 'But I have done it the hard way, sir; I have completed two tours.'

'Everyone has a duty to do. I have been in England as long as you; don't you think I want to go home? Don't you think 'X' (a high-ranking Australian officer noted for his amorous entanglements) would like to go home to his wife and children?'

At that particular period, 'X' was openly engaged in a romantic entanglement with the wife of a well-known London publican. I knew it was delicate ground but couldn't resist saying, 'I do not think "X" is missing any of the amenities of home life, sir.'

Dale looked at me steadily. 'I can see no reason at all why I should grant your request. Why, if I granted every request to airmen who want to run home to their mummies, we soon wouldn't have anyone left in England.'

I replied, 'Your simile is a little astray, sir, as my mother is seventy nine and has been seriously ill. This can be verified in Australia.' I knew I was fighting a losing battle. This was repetition, not salesmanship, and he knew he had the whip hand.

'That,' he said, 'is not of great consequence. There are literally thousands of seriously ill people in Australia; many close relations of men here in England. As for your fifty-two operations, you appear to have done these against the express orders of the RAAF. Just how you have managed this I don't know. As far as your records go, I will certainly recommend that they be treated as one tour.'

I looked at him and thought, 'Some day I'm going to meet you in civvy life and I'm making myself a solemn promise now that when I do, I'm going to get stuck into you.'

For the next fifteen minutes he proceeded to dress me down and cover my shortcomings as an officer. I had made unwarranted charges against members of the mail section and abused an officer in public (Dag's little episode); I was a troublemaker and generally not fit to hold the King's Commission. I felt at the time, and still think now, that he was endeavouring to provoke me into some unwise verbal and physical action. What I did was to stare stonily at him and say nothing, an effective counter to this type of person because where there is no argument they run out of words. He finished with, 'You will do your instructional period the same as all other one-tour air crew, so you can forget this application and, I warn you, Beede. Watch your step.'

I have a cobber in Australia who used to declare, 'Everything happens for the best.' That was the philosophy I tried to apply to this setback because I suffered a kind of nervous reaction. Perhaps it was a combination of the aftermath of the crash and all my hopes going bust but anyway, I felt awful, both mentally and physically.

It was then I thought of Mrs Weston and her quiet Surrey home. Luckily I had written to her from hospital telling her of my accident. I telephoned her from the club. She said, 'I've been expecting to hear from you. When are you coming down?'

There was magic in that soothing, motherly English voice. I said, 'Now, if I may.'

'Your bed is ready,' she replied. 'I'll meet you at the station.'

When I met her I said apologetically, 'I only seem to come to you when I'm recovering from something.'

'There could be no better time, Johnny.'

She had the car out and must have somehow begged or borrowed some petrol because the ordinary civilian did not get a petrol ration. In that quiet English home amongst this gracious family I spent the most restful ten days I had known for a long, long time. The woods were beginning to show the magical return of spring. I used to take my ground sheet out and watch the birds flit amongst the budding trees.

One episode that testified to the care and watchfulness of this woman was one day when I had gone to sleep, lulled by the sighing of the wind in the almost bare branches and the song of the blackbirds, I woke to find myself covered with a rug. How she knew where I was and that I was sleeping I never knew.

At the end of my leave I had got back some of my joie de vivre. When I thought of Smithy, Hally and Blondie, I realised I had nothing to beef about and could even reflect with wry amusement on Dale's bawling-out.

CHAPTER THIRTY-FOUR

When I returned to camp I found I was almost a stranger. In the previous six weeks a new crop of replacements had arrived. While I was busily hunting up my belongings, two new Australian gunners wanted to know if I had just joined the squadron. 'Christ, no,' I replied. 'I'm just getting out. I've finished my second tour.' Despite Dale's official statement, as far as I was concerned, it was going to be two tours for sure. This statement was received with some scepticism but, when confirmed, created quite a furore. A two-tour gunner was rated a very rare bird indeed.

In my absence, with the help of FIDO, operations had been constant; casualties, whilst not high, had been steady. What you have to realise is that even a five per cent loss per operation gives a constant cumulative loss of aircraft and men. Statistically, this should mean that at the end of twenty ops a squadron would be wiped out. It didn't work out this way, however, as the high losses generally came from the new crews.

Amongst the missing was Tubby Evans. Put in with a sprog crew, he had 'gone' on their second op, so that all his luck in parachuting safely and his trip into Spain went for nothing. Basher was crewed up again and very unhappy about his pilot; Bill was in a RAF hospital somewhere in the Midlands, his leg had been so badly smashed that complications had set in and, despite all possible care, had finally been amputated. He was very upset over this, but as Basher said, 'What the bloody hell. Even though his flying days are over, he's alive' – a condition, judging from his morose comments, he himself didn't expect to be in for long.

It wasn't till I talked to Basher and Bill that I realised I didn't have to fly again. I'd been so busy psychologically conditioning myself after my London interview I'd forgotten this angle and suddenly felt as though a great weight had been lifted. I thought, 'God! No more butterflies, no more sweating it out, no more freezing trips with the tears turning to ice on my cheeks.' Even though I wasn't going home, I was alive and well. What did I have to whinge about?

After lunch I received a message that the CO wanted to see me at 3.30 pm. This was a sobering bit of information; no doubt Boofhead's report had come through. Still, I thought, what the hell! Arming myself with my log book I presented myself on the dot. I could see he was in a stinking mood so let him do the talking.

'Your crew had an accident, Beede, and you have been in Aldershot.'

'Yes, sir.'

He fiddled with some papers and continued. 'You will be directed to a new crew. We have two who want gunners.'

'I'm afraid not, sir.'

He looked at me, colour rising in his cheeks. Probably he thought it was a case of rank mutiny. 'Why not?', he snapped.

'Because I have just completed fifty-two operations, or two tours, sir, and my headquarter's orders are that I am to go on an immediate rest.'

Evidently his records weren't up-to-date or he hadn't bothered to get my papers, but it gave me great pleasure to see his mounting irritation.

'You have only done twelve operations here.'

'That's true,' I replied sweetly, 'but I also did eighteen on Venturas and twenty two on Wellingtons. Here's my log-book, sir.'

He examined it for a while, grunted, 'Humph' and sat toying with his pencil; then said, 'Beede, I have a report here on your behaviour while you were in hospital.'

'A report?', I asked innocently.

'Yes, a personal report from Colonel XYZ who was, I understand, a patient in the same ward; in fact his bed was next to yours.'

As he spoke I could see his anger mounting. He informed me I was a disgrace to my commission and squadron, that he was indeed pleased I was leaving the station.

I used the same tactics I had with Dale – I didn't say anything. After he had disposed of this subject to his satisfaction, he continued, 'Also, there was, I believe, an infamous group of which you were one of the leaders, which had its primary aim the, er, ahem! debauching of the er, ah! virtuous women of this station.'

I nearly laughed at this and thought of an oft-repeated airman's joke that all the maidens of the station had got together to have a meeting but they were looking for a smaller room for the next one because they found the telephone box too large.

I thought of Happy's efforts on our first squadron and decided I'd give his tactics a go. 'Do I understand, sir, that you are accusing me of being a member of some group, or club, that has for its objective the moral downfall of the women of this station?'

He said flatly, 'I do.'

I was indignant. 'I take gross exception to your statement and intend to carry this matter further. I will, in fact, report your unwarranted accusation to my headquarters (if he only knew!) and I feel they will, without doubt, take this matter up for me.'

This stopped him and his back-pedalling merely confirmed my opinion of him – he was a gutless wonder. A strong officer would have battered me down. The main effect of this manoeuvre was to halt his dissection of my character and when he stated he was sorry he had wrongfully blackened my reputation we both let the matter drop.

Later, the adj told me I was being posted to the Group's rest home known amongst aircrew as Bullshit Castle. I lost no time getting my clearance in order and taking myself off to the train station.

One interesting piece of information I learned prior to my departure was that the crew who had tailed us in on the Brest attack had been recommended for decorations, then, after doing a further seven ops, had been taken off and been further recommended for bars to their DFCs.

PART FIVE

VICTORY IN SIGHT

CHAPTER THIRTY-FIVE

Bullshit Castle was an appropriate title. The station was situated in Norfolk and, while not headquarters for the Second TAF, was second in line. Its mess buildings were even better than Beltwell although single sleeping quarters were reserved exclusively for the base wallahs.

Temporarily retired aircrew quarters were still very comfortable. On an operational squadron an officer fended for himself, but here you shared a batman with another officer. Pete, a quiet, likeable Canadian navigator, and I held a joint interest in a middle-aged Scotsman called Scotty. Because I have always liked the Scots and treated him like a human being, he repaid it in a number of extra attentions which were often embarrassing.

Another feature of this establishment was the colossal amount of saluting that went on. For almost three years I had neglected this aspect of RAF life. I was brought to heel very early by a lecture from the adj on the necessity of setting a proper example to lower ranks and maintaining a standard of efficiency. Being aware of my shortcomings and having no desire to fall out with anyone, my arm worked like a railway signal at Clapham Junction.

A further function that had been missing from active service station life was parades. I would not have attended four in the past three years. Here they were a daily occurrence at 8 am, with roll-calls and all, till Pete and I hit upon the bright idea of appearing each alternate day and answering each other's name. This was later increased to include an English gunner which reduced our public appearances to one in three.

Despite these minor pinpricks it was a good station to be on. As usual with all headquarters the food and the mess arrangements were excellent. It was also a happy station – the transients were at least one-tour men, being blokes who were given to enjoying life. At night it was hard to realise you weren't back on a squadron. Card games, drinking and wenching flourished.

An interesting arrival at the Castle one day was the straight AG of the crew I had learned had been recommended for bars to their DFCs. He was wearing the bar so my information was right. We had always got on well together so he came across and told me his troubles. He was having a bad time as most of the boys were critical not only of the second award but that the crew had been credited with two tours after twenty operations.

'What the hell can I do? I didn't organise this racket.'

What he was really mad about was that the pilot and navigator had been posted direct to training schools. The WAG had gone on a special course and he alone was left to face the criticism from his ex-flying comrades. I had always found him a nice little fellow and could see his point of view. He further declared it was his intention, at the earliest possible date, to seek a new crew and do another tour, and so wipe out this slur on his fighting honour. I heard later that he did just that.

One evening as I was drinking at the bar a tall Wingco came up. I had seen him in the mess before. He had dark wavy hair, stood over six feet tall and looked like a matinee idol. 'Would you have a drink?' he asked.

What intrigued me was his accent, till I learnt he had been born in Northern Ireland, reared in England and had spent several years in Canada. His voice thus had a faint hint of the Irish brogue, coupled with the definite leavening of a Canadian drawl.

I should have wondered why the hell he, a Wingco, wanted to talk with me but he was such a pleasant bloke I merely thought he was interested in having a few grogs. I afterwards realised he must have known a good bit about me as he told me I had done two tours and even knew the squadrons I had been on. We had a pleasant session and by closing time I was, if not full, at least merry.

Around this time he revealed he was getting a crew together for a Mitchell squadron. He already had an observer and WAG but wanted a top gunner. Bars have always been my downfall in more ways than one; they seem to raise my fighting blood and drown my natural caution. I remember saying my headquarters had put me under the dog act and I was not allowed to do any more operational flying.

'If I could fix that would you fly with me?'

I thought of Dale and his sarcastic comments and replied, 'Boy, you would have a job in front of you.'

Before we left he got me to agree that if he could fix it with Kodak

House I would fly with him. Candidly, at the time I didn't think he had Buckley's.

I had completely forgotten my discussion with the Wingco when a fortnight later he came to see me in the mess and, with a wide grin, said, 'Well, I've fixed it.'

'Fixed what?'

'You're flying with me.'

I looked at him warily, 'It's not much good fixing it with Group, it's Kodak House who wield the stick.'

'It's okay with them; there's a signal through. You can check it in the morning.' This was a surprise as I didn't think he had a chance.

'Come and meet the crew,' he said, and lead me to two English airmen nearby. They rose as I approached. One was a six-footer with a lean, tanned face and the navigator's flying 'N'; his name was Ted Allington. He shook my hand firmly. He had a shy smile, something like Smithy's. I liked him instantly. The other was a well-set-up WAG with a DFM and an aloof English air. He looked me over critically, 'How many ops have you done?'

'Fifty two.'

'What on?'

I felt like saying, 'What the bloody hell has it got to do with you?', but in the interests of harmony told him. He replied, 'Hmm' in a way that suggested he didn't think much of my flying efforts. I thought, 'I don't like this bugger much.' The Wingco, sensing the rift, said, 'This is Fred Archer.' We shook hands diffidently, like two strange dogs exchanging perfunctory and slightly hostile greetings.

The Wingco said, 'Let's have a drink,' feeling, no doubt, a little grog would help matters. Archer in civvy life was a gentleman farmer and let us know it. In addition, he was a self-opinionated joker and from the beginning it looked as though we weren't going to get on very well. One point in his favour was he had done three tours; this would be his fourth.

Ted had done two tours in the Middle East, one on Blenheims, the other on Wellingtons. It looked like a gen crew. The only one who didn't give any details of his flying life was the Wingco, but I surmised he was reticent. You didn't get to being a Wingco in the RAF without some operational experience.

We grogged on till closing time; it was evident we all had one thing in common – a liking for the amber liquid. As we were leaving the mess the DFC and Bar English gunner pulled me aside and said, 'Are you flying with the Wingco?'

'Subject to a signal being in the office from Kodak House, I think I am.'

'Johnny, don't be a bloody fool, pull out. He's never done an operation in his life.'

The rest were going, so the Wingco called out, 'We'll see you in the morning.'

'What do you mean?' I asked. 'He's a bloody Wingco isn't he, and you don't get far in this outfit without doing your share.'

'He's never done an op,' he insisted. 'He was three years in Canada on the Empire Air Training Scheme; he was transferred across here and was in charge of some training base for another year. The RAF have now decided that to hold their rank, all flying personnel must do at least one tour. I know what I'm talking about, Johnny. Don't fly with him; pull out in the morning.'

This was disquieting news. I decided I'd resolve the matter next day. Before I went to sleep I gave the subject some deep thought. In the morning I went around to the office to see the signal. It stated I had permission to fly with Wing Commander Smith for the duration of his tour.[1]

I had long ago made a practice of putting my problems down on paper, listing for and against. I was getting tired of the bull-laden existence of the Castle and the prospect of returning to the carefree life of an operational squadron appealed to me. Also I felt this opportunity would not occur again; the signal specifically named the Wingco and this meant he had somehow pulled some strings somewhere, despite Dale's flat statement. Also, there was an elite amongst air-crew. The three-tour men looked condescendingly on the two- and one-tour boys.

A friend in Australia who evaded all service life declared that ego and personal aggrandisement were the motivating forces that attracted me towards the proposition, that I was subconsciously jealous of Archer's sixty-five ops and was after the public adulation that went to a man who could throw out his chest and say nonchalantly, 'I've done three tours.' There may be some truth in this. At the time I may have kidded myself three tours must put me in the front line for a return passage home. In addition they should keep me out of the Pacific War. When I got back I wanted to stop there.

The decision devolved on the pilot, so the best way to decide this was to see him. I found the Wingco at headquarters. I said, 'Could I see you, sir?'

He must have known what I was going to ask because he lead me outside. 'What is it, Johnny?'

'I might as well come to the point. I was told last night that you had no operational experience. Is that true?'

He thought for a while. 'In a way, yes. But does it make any difference?'

'Yes. Because I've survived fifty-two operations to date and don't feel like putting my neck out too far.'

'Look! If you have changed your mind and want to get out of your agreement it's okay with me, but let me tell you this. I have flown almost every plane in service with the RAF. I was a civil pilot and owned my own airline before the war. I have planned and taught both flying and evasive tactics for years. The day of the individual bomber pilot is over; today a squadron flies formation; success in this particular phase of aerial warfare depends on a pilot's ability to do just this. I'm after the best crew I can get and I feel you will fit into it, but it's up to you.'

His arguments were logical and convincing. To get to the rank of Wingco a pilot must have done a lot of flying.

He continued, 'I'm taking a plane up this morning. Fly with me if you like and make up your mind later – kind of try before you buy.'

The way he put it made me feel a heel. Not many gunners get a chance to fly with a wing commander. This position carries many privileges.

'No, I've made up my mind now,' I replied. 'I'll join your crew. The only point I'd like to make clear is that should I wish to retire when I get to sixty-five ops that I be allowed to.'

He replied, 'That's okay, Johnny. By then there should be some good gunners available. Let's go for that flip.'

He must have told the others of our discussion because when we went over to flight Archer, by a couple of remarks, hinted I was a choosey customer.

It was only a training Anson but the moment the Wingco took over the controls it was evident he knew his work. There's a feeling of surety and confidence about a capable pilot.

Back on the ground Archer said, 'Any complaints?' It wasn't said in a jocular way but I let it pass. I thought, 'this self-opinionated bastard and I are going to cross swords one day; it'll keep. No use having a stink now and getting myself tossed out of the crew.'

In the afternoon the Skipper – that was the term by which he was henceforth known – made arrangements to take up one of the two training Mitchells on a nearby satellite field. I had never seen one and was interested to find they were a solid American two-engined job with two .5s in an upper turret and two in a contraption under the plane that could be worked by the WAG for rear attacks.

I had never seen .5s before. Beside them the .303s looked like pea-shooters.[2] The Skipper was out to impress us that day. He took that kite off the ground so smoothly we were a hundred feet in the air before I was aware of it. He flew to about five thousand feet in a smooth, curving climb. After he leveled off he said, 'Hang on, I'm going to see if this kite can really fly', and for the next fifteen minutes he threw it around the sky like a single-engined fighter. He then took it earthwards at such a bat my head was forced against the turret perspex. Levelling off, he gave an exhibition of low flying, skimming hedges and trees, that was blood-tingling. Without a doubt this bloke was a champ.

For the next two weeks we flew on every available occasion. He seemed more than anxious to gain as much experience as possible prior to our transfer to the squadron. We also found as a formation the Wingco was without peer. Two other crews were in training and the three of us practised together. He seemed to be equally at home whether flying as Number One (leader), Number Two (left of leader) or Number Three (right of leader). He could tuck his wings in within inches of the other planes and follow every manoeuvre the pilots made.

During this period I expounded my thoughts on the clock system as opposed to the standard starboard and port terms. It looked like developing into a ding-dong argument as Archer espoused the old nautical terms till we learned TAF had swung over to the clock system anyway, and was to be standard patter.

After this little matter was decided we settled in as a crew. It was soon evident that, in addition to our pilot, we had a first-class navigator. Ted was, I decided, the equal of Ninnes. He had the same quick, sure brain; navigating came naturally to him. His pin-points, whether by day or by night, were always bang on. Archer, too, was a top-class wireless operator. We often had our differences on the ground, but in the air we were as one. This was really a first-class crew.

In getting to know each personally over this period I found the

Skipper was happily married with three children. Ted had married only five months previously on his return from the Middle East. His wife was already in the family way and he was still in the first ecstasies of his honeymoon. Archer was married but separated, which didn't surprise me at all.

One thing that stuck out was the Wingco's irresistible attraction for women. As with all headquarters, there were a number of WAAF officers in the mess, some of them top divisioners. The combination of rank, good looks, unusual accent plus a pleasant, winning personality had the girls in a dither and they flocked to him like moths around a candle. In this regard he was no slowcoach; he made Bourke Malloy look a rank amateur. It was never my good fortune to have females falling over themselves to please my slightest whim; I generally had to battle for my femmes. One result of his charm was, as he could only manage to accommodate one at a time, there were some very pleasant little crumbs to be picked up occasionally, especially as I had no competition from Ted, who was remaining faithful to his new bride. Archer was so egotistical and self-opinionated I could easily go under his neck. His mode of operation was to sit with his chest out and his chin in and expect the girls to fall for him.

Another interesting point was the Skipper's inexhaustible supply of money. He was as free with his money as he was with his love. There was the usual game of cards in the mess every night. Fortunately the players were not in the same street as Pete and his Canadian professionals, so that in a two-month period, aided by a lucky streak, I won close on two hundred pounds.

I had learnt something from Pete the Canadian. He believed in lucky runs and good and bad nights. If he sat in a game and played for an hour or so without winning, he would give it away. I never had the willpower to vacate a game even when the cards were running against me. On the bad occasions, however, I played it easy and did not try to push my luck. On the other hand, when the breeze was behind me I played it hard.

This two hundred pounds was a handy buffer for the Skipper's free-spending ways, and allowed me to come in on some interesting parties I would otherwise have had to stay out of.

At the end of a hard three-week training period we were posted to a squadron and here again the fruits of flying with a Wingco were shown as he wangled a seven-day leave pass.

CHAPTER THIRTY-SIX

Up at the Club one day I ran into six massive-looking AIF[1] types from Western Australia, and we got talking. They expressed some surprise that an aircrew type and an officer at that would speak to them, as roughly 99.99 per cent of those they had met at the Club treated them as though they didn't exist.

After a few beers they mentioned that they had a guide who was taking them on a tour of Soho, particularly through the male pervert areas.[2] I had heard of this part and knew it was out of bounds to all troops. I couldn't think of a better bodyguard than these six stalwarts, so readily agreed to go.

We met our guide in a pub in Piccadilly Circus. He was a podgy little Cockney called Charlie. A few beers later, he led us down into Soho.

At the first pub the publican, a bull-necked, pot-bellied individual, called us to one side. He said, 'Seven-eighths of this mob here are pick-pockets, thieves, cut-throats, prostitutes and pimps, the other eighth are murderers or worse. Watch who you pal up with – and your pockets.'

When we told him we intended going deeper into the wilds of Soho on a sight-seeing tour, he suggested caution, stating the locals didn't mind people who came to partake of the peculiar enjoyments they had to offer, but took a dim view of stickybeaks and sightseers. He said they all carried razor blades set in cork or other appropriate mediums, or carried other offensive weapons and would be decidedly dangerous if aroused.

Nevertheless, fortified by beer, we went on to the next pub. It was a murky-looking place with tables and seats set out in cabaret style. What we took to be females we soon found were males attired in feminine clothing and heavily made-up with rouge and mascara.

A French sailor was sitting at a table making passes at a be-wigged pseudo-blonde who laughed in a high falsetto. At another table two

Polish soldiers were drinking with two heavily made-up he's or she's. It was an amazing sight, all the stranger because this particular type of vice was so openly displayed.

We drank at the bar and tried not to appear over-curious. After a while, two heavily scented, garishly dressed bods came across and looked us over. When we showed no interest they drifted away.

Then the blackout curtains parted and someone – he or she – stood imperiously with hand on hip looking the scene over. The mob went wild, there were high-pitched squeals of recognition and delight; this was obviously someone of consequence. It was the strangest creature we had ever seen; a long, thin body; obviously masculine, but with shoulder-length black greasy hair framing a thin, line-ravaged face, heavily daubed with rouge, lipstick and mascara, the lanky frame encased in a kind of golden Chinese dress with two slits up the sides that came half-way up the thighs to reveal a pair of hairy spindly legs with an outsized pair of feet in golden flat-heeled sandals.

It was a spectacle and we gaped unashamedly. As he made his mincing, bottom-wagging way down amongst his wildly applauding associates, one of the boys muttered, 'Christ, now I've seen everything.'

The figure was hauled towards a piano on a raised dais; the reason for this public adulation was evident as soon as he sat down and commenced to play. I'm no highbrow but I know good music when I hear it. This joker was a champ and he held these creatures in his two hands as he played upon their desires and emotions. It was an amazing exhibition as his audience swayed and screamed with his playing.

The boys were not musically minded. One said, 'This place gives me the creeps, let's get some fresh air.'

Charlie said he was saving the piece de resistance for last. Here, he advised, we would find a 'one hundred per cent' gathering.

Bill said, 'Cripes, I'd say this joint would qualify in that respect.'

This hotel did not have the murky interior nor the garishly attired occupants of the last pub. There would have been from sixty to seventy in the bar, and quite a proportion were well-dressed well-to-do males. Big Bill said, 'This must be the headquarters of the Great Public Schools Old Boys' Association.'

Our arrival in the previous pub had not created much of a stir, but here it did. At the sight of the massive Aussies an audible sigh ran through the place and there were a number of whistles and squeals and invitations of 'Come over here, Aussie.'

We lined up for a grog and almost immediately eight pots appeared in front of us. When we went to pay, the barman said, 'These are with the compliments of the gentleman across the bar', indicating a tall, plump, well-dressed type, who gave us a greasy smile and an intimate wave.

'Tell him to stick his beer up his jumper,' said Big Bill. 'We pay for our own bloody grog.'

I could see that this bold statement had created a stir. A few minutes later Big Bill went up to the gentlemen's, which had to be reached by a narrow flight of perhaps twenty steps. Suddenly there was an outraged bellow from above. The next moment a figure came shooting down the stairs, two at a time. Behind him a second person hurtled down feet first on his stern, and behind them both appeared the massive gesticulating figure of Big Bill.

When he reached us he was exploding with wrath. He explained that he was just shaking the last drops off when a hand had reached around and grabbed him. He stated he had taken a swipe at this intruder, when a second hand had grabbed him from the right. At his violent reaction both had taken off, the second one being helped by a hefty kick on his rump which had precipitated him down the stairs.

As news of this altercation spread, complete silence fell over the bar. We noted everyone had left our area and congregated on the other side. The publican, obviously worried, came across and said, 'I would advise you to leave at once, because my guests have been seriously upset by your unwarranted attack.'

We were all full. I could see there was trouble brewing and remembered the first publican's warning about stickybeaks. 'Most of these blokes have knives or razor blades,' I said. 'Let's get out of here.'

As we went through the blackout curtain a glass shattered against the wall. A grey twilight covered the dingy houses and buildings. As we made our way along the narrow streets, a group of perhaps thirty figures followed us. By this stage, Charlie was really packing 'em and so was I.

When we came to a bombed-out building I grabbed a hunk of rusty iron pipe and the rest of our crowd armed themselves with pieces of wood. Despite these precautions the threatening group closed in on us till they were perhaps twenty yards behind.

Bill said, 'There's eight of us and about thirty of them. If they attack we'll put our backs against a wall. Don't swing at the first lot, jab them in their faces. What we have to watch is a sudden rush …'

Turning, he bellowed in stentorian tones, 'I'm giving you bastards a warning. If you don't fugg off we'll brain the bloody lot of you; you're dealing with fighting men. Now beat it before we get stuck into you.'

Fortunately for all concerned, this never eventuated. As soon as they saw we were prepared to make a stand, they stopped. But, as we moved off, they started following us again, menacingly, staying on our heels till we came almost into the city. There, before fading into the gathering gloom, a voice called, 'We'll remember you. We'll get you sometime, you dirty colonials.'

Did that bloke get a bronx cheer!

When it was clear they had gone, someone said, 'Well, guess we'd better get rid of our armament.' We were tossing it into a vacant allotment when a quiet voice said, 'What have you boys been up to?'

He was a large cop with a equally large offsider. We told them of our encounter with the mob.

He said, 'You know this area is out of bounds. It's exceedingly dangerous. There have been a number of instances of servicemen going in here who've never been seen again. Now beat it before I book the lot of you.'

I spent a night with Beryl. During the evening we were disturbed by two callers, who she explained were friends looking for cover. She said, 'It's funny these poor boys never seem to be able to get a room.'

It had been a tedious leave. Now that I had decided to do my tour I wanted to get on with it.

Next morning I went up to Kodak House to see if there was any mail, and intercepted a letter from Smithy. He was leaving Crothers to go to a hospital in Essex for skin grafting. He didn't discuss his injuries, but I knew he was as flat as a tack. He didn't expect to be in London for some time.

It was a short lifeless note that showed the mental turmoil he was in.

CHAPTER THIRTY-SEVEN

I arrived at the new camp in Surrey half a day early. We had been told the squadron was going over to field conditions; that is, we were to live in tents to acclimatise everyone for the coming Second Front and projected moves into France.

It was a huge, rambling place with crops growing right up to the mess walls. It housed three squadrons, two RAF and the other Dutch.[1]

When I presented myself at the office I was told I had a four days' extension of leave. The Wingco had evidently wangled this; the other two were contacted by phone but they had no means of informing me. Normally I would have relished this extra leave, but I'd had London and its fleshpots; besides, it didn't seem worth the struggle of going up and returning in a few days.

Most of the station were already in tents. I found a few odd bods, mostly airmen who had finished tours, getting clearances to go off the squadron which was still established in a huge ugly-looking mansion that crowned a hill overlooking the mess buildings. I was in no hurry to get under canvas, particularly without my crew, so settled myself in one of the many bedrooms that looked down on a lovely park. It was an amazing place; it had at least twenty outsize bedrooms and all the appointments that went with the opulent ugly early Victorian mansion.

The monstrosity belonged to the local Lord of the Manor who owned all the land the station was located on. He was related in very high places and, by general agreement of locals and the RAF, was a low illegitimate.

During my first night in the mess, I ran into Bill Fogg.[2] He had come direct to the squadron from Beltwell, was flying with a squadron leader, and had completed thirty ops, making a total of forty-eight. 'Why the hell don't you give it away?' I asked.

'The Skipper has an okay from the CO to do a further seventeen and I've decided to stop with him.'

'What's he like?'

'He's okay,' he replied, 'a bit mad, old English family and all that; ancestors have always been in the cavalry you know.'

'Hope he doesn't ride his plane like a horse,' I said.

He had news of Wilbur and Jack; their bodies had been recovered from a burnt-out Mossie some twenty miles west of Berlin. A Hun fighter had evidently jumped them on their way out. This shattered all hopes that they may have bailed out or crash-landed. It was depressing news, for these two young men had brains, ability, education, everything to make a success of their lives.[3]

We talked for a while of old times and Bill said, 'There's not many left, Johnny. I often wonder where it will all end.' Bull Stanton was on the station too. After his Ventura effort he had been banished to a training unit and was now engaged on his first tour. Bill declared he was as profane and wild as ever and still a bloody awful pilot.

Later at flight I met Bull, who was overjoyed to see me. He said, 'I heard you were bloody well dead, but I ought to have known they couldn't kill a tough old bastard like you.' His opinion of the RAF had not changed one jot. Since we last met he had, he declared, been fugged around by experts, but life on this station offered some compensations, particularly a hostel for Land Army girls on the other side of the drome. This, he declared, offered more smooey than you could poke a stick at.

The rest of the crew arrived four days later. I felt that there must have been some urgent family crisis to have kept the Wingco, but he was his old happy carefree self and made no mention of any family problems.

With the coming of spring the great aerial offensive that was to precede the opening of the Second Front had opened over Europe. By night the air vibrated with the drum of the mighty air fleets of Bomber Command as they went forth to pound Germany and her satellites. No two-engined obsolete Wellingtons these, but four-engined giants such as the Lancasters, Halifaxes and Stirlings, capable of carrying a twelve thousand pound bomb load.

When these returned in the early morning the Fortresses took up the offensive, circling and climbing in their hundreds in the clear spring air to gain height till their vapour trails criss-crossed the heavens.

Supporting these, the mediums – such as our own Mitchells, Bostons and Marauders – drove across the Channel, escorted by hundreds of fighters, to attack railway depots, bridges and any installation that would be of assistance to Hitler. Truly might it be said that the Nazis had sown and reaped a whirlwind of destruction.

In our own little world, our Skipper didn't seem to be in any hurry to join the fray, which didn't worry the other two one jot – they were already home! We did a few training flights and it looked as if we were destined to fiddle around indefinitely till the Groupy cracked down.

Under RAF protocol the Skipper should have been immediate leader, but in this case, here was a pilot who hadn't even done an op. A sprog starting in such circumstances would have to fly in positions Five and Six; if he survived long enough he would rise to Four, then Two and Three depending on his ability, then finally to Number One. The powers that be solved this problem by deciding that we would fly Number Four in our first do and after he'd cut his teeth and learned the ropes the Skipper was to take over leadership of a box. Due to his excellent training form at the Castle I had no qualms that he could cover this position. He showed a marked lack of enthusiasm at the prospect of his coming operational baptism. He displayed little interest in the briefing. You would have thought he was just finishing his tour instead of starting one.

Coming out of dispersal he ran the port wheel off the concrete runway onto the soft ground. When it started to dig in, instead of waiting for the tractor to pull us out, he revved forward so that the bomber, with its two thousand pound bomb load, bogged in to the axle. This unexpected upset caused a panic. Queries and commands crackled from Control. Operations, due to fighter protection and group arrangements, are a matter of split-second timing. The officer in Control must have been a beauty. There was always a second kite bombed up and ready to go kept for such emergencies. He set a series of commands and instructions going and, in a matter of minutes, a bus was alongside our bogged plane and we'd piled out.

The Chiefy, a hard-bitten Australian warrant officer, took one look at the immobilised bomber and made a cutting motion with his finger across his throat.

I said defensively, 'The wheel slipped off the runway.'

'Pig's bum,' he replied. 'The greenest sprog wouldn't do this – it was done intentionally.'

I made a very rude reply, scrambled into the bus and we were on our way to the spare. I did notice our Skipper didn't look his usual happy self. This I put down to a combination of first op jitters and the mix-up. Group would want to know what the hell caused the delay.

We took off thirteen minutes late, which was no mean feat. It was a tame op on some of the mysterious installations. There were no fighters, no flak, but in spite of this our Skipper, from the time we got near the enemy coast, flew like a hairy goat. Gone was the perfect synchronisation and steady co-ordination; in its place was an unusual up and down undulating movement, which threw Five and Six out of formation and must have been a headache to those two pilots.

As we came in to bomb we bloody nearly ran under the top three; luckily things straightened themselves out sufficiently for all six planes to bomb. It was a rotten bomb pattern and a lousy display of flying.

When we got back four hours later, Chiefy and his crew had just managed to pull the bogged bomber out. He was as mad as a hornet and most profane. His opinion on pilots, Wingcos or not, who bogged planes, was completely unprintable.

That night, the Skipper got the car out and we went into Guildford. He was his old happy self again, without a care in the world. His poor exhibition of the day seemed to be completely forgotten.

Guildford was a garrison town, that is, the permanent Army officers and NCOs had their homes there, in which the wives and families resided, whilst Poppa was doing his bit in various parts of England or the globe. No doubt a big portion of these femmes stayed at home and virtuously looked after the home and the kids. On the other hand, a fair proportion frequented the pubs looking for convivial male company.

The Skipper made a contact with an extremely presentable blonde, who attracted three comrades in a kind of chain reaction. They were well-dressed and well-spoken and a pleasant party eventuated. When the pubs closed, the Skipper piled us all into the car and arrangements were made for him to pick us up at midnight.

My companion was Betty, a presentable dark Spanish-looking woman in the twenty-eight to thirty age group. Ted had her cobber. By a kind of tacit agreement we went to my companion's home, which turned out to be quite a pretentious double-storied establishment. We both thought we were going to have supper, however Betty said, 'We'll leave these two down here and go upstairs.' It was as easy as that.

In the in-between confiding period, she advised her husband was a Major in the permanent forces. She had a boy of twelve who went to a nearby boarding school and came home on weekends. Her husband was an easy-going kind of person. She stated she neither loved nor hated him. Married at eighteen she was now really enjoying life. She, however, had her scruples. She only cohabited with officers, with the qualification she had to like the man.

At midnight an alarm shrilled, set, I found, prior to the fun and frolics. These girls were really organised. 'You boys had better get cracking,' she said, 'your Skipper will be waiting for you.'

Our chauffeur was late. During the wait Ted was plunged into the depths of remorse. 'A man's an animal,' he said. 'Here I am cohabiting with that slut, while my wife is at home expecting my child.'

'It doesn't look as though you had much choice, those girls would seduce a saint,' I replied.

I wasn't feeling very proud of myself either; the photos on the mantlepiece and in the bedroom had shown a likeable kind of a bloke. Still, I thought, what the hell, if it wasn't me it would be someone else.

The aerial offensive mounted in intensity. That the Huns were more concerned with damage to their homeland than occupied Europe was exemplified on our second operation. We had been briefed to attack a target in Holland at nine thousand feet.[4] It was a beautiful fine summer day. As we went in over the coast, away to our left and at least fifteen thousand feet higher, two formations of Fortresses gleamed in the bright sunlight. These groups flew in battle formations of thirty-five each. They had strong fighter protection as dozens of smaller planes could be seen circling above and below. Fifty miles in from the coast, German planes attacked the two groups in strength and the air was filled with the turmoil of men trying to annihilate each other, five miles above the earth.

Despite the fact that the Mitchells would have been an easier target, we weren't touched. We were flying Number Two, so my search area was in that quarter and I had a full view of this grim aerial battle. In spite of the fighter protection the attackers broke through the protecting ring again and again. In the half hour period I watched, until we bombed and turned for home, eight Fortresses, streaming smoke and fire, had plunged earthwards, and I could imagine the dry taste of fear in the mouths of those airmen far above us, with at least another hour to the target in Germany, and then a four hour trip back. For mine I'd sooner do it under cover of darkness.

On the trip we met neither flak nor fighters but despite this, as we got near the target our plane started to undulate like a ship in a rough sea. This, I decided, was the Skipper's idea of evasive action, only there was nothing to evade.

These ops, to my way of thinking, were exceedingly easy. With the memory of Wimpy operations over this area two years before and even the Ventura ops a year later, it didn't seem possible that you could fly a hundred and fifty miles into Holland and not have a single shot fired at you in anger. This seemed to be the time to get as many in while the going was easy.

That night I expressed the opinion to the Skipper that this state of affairs would not last; as soon as the second front opened we would run into tougher opposition, so we should take advantage of this easy phase to do as many ops as possible.

Despite the favourable operational conditions, our Skipper didn't seem anxious to hop in and follow this good advice. But, like a king born to a throne the day arrived when he had to take his place as Number One. The target was a factory in Southern Germany, not an easy target. It meant we had to cross France and, using the Black Forest as a final marker, go in and hit the target.[4]

Intelligence stated the target had a priority as it manufactured component parts for a new German fighter. We were told we could expect some flak, and possibly fighter resistance. A strong escort would neutralise the last problem.

Met promised thunderheads and cumulus clouds with a base of twelve thousand feet but, as we were to fly at ten thousand, it was thought they would not worry us.

Going in over the coast, three guns away to our left opened up. In addition to the range being too far, their shooting was so poorly directed I didn't report it. The Skipper must have because he threw the plane into violent evasive action so that for a while it was like riding a bucking bronco. This, in turn, gave the formation a torrid time as they sought to keep formation behind him.

After this little effort he asked, 'Did you see the flak?'

When I replied that I had, he tore a strip off me for not reporting it. He was savage over the matter and advised me to keep my eyes open and not go to sleep.

'What's wrong with this drongo?' I thought, but said nothing.

It was a fantastic flight, the huge billowing cumulus clouds with bases at ten thousand feet, and thunderheads at twenty, came up as Met had predicted and through the valleys and canyons of this aerial fairyland we flew. Despite their beauty these cloud formations could serve as a cover for marauding enemy fighters. The Wingco seemed uneasy in this respect. His first 'Are you watching, gunner, can you see anything?', evoked a standard reply, but when it was repeated twenty to thirty times, it became a bit monotonous.

Our navigator, despite frequent deviations to evade threatening cloud formations, brought us bang in on course. I heard him say 'Black Forest coming up at one o'clock, five minutes to target'. More out of curiosity I swivelled the turret around to see these historic woods that had figured so frequently in the history of Europe.

Ted said, 'Three minutes to target, Pilot', and gave a slight course correction.

It was then the flak came up. It was obviously predicted and fairly accurate. I got halfway through 'Flak at nine o'clock' when the plane seemed to fall away from beneath me. We must have fallen two hundred feet. For a second I thought 'God, we've been hit.' It wasn't till we started to rise again I realised it was evasive action, the only trouble being we were rising bang under our formation. I could see the bottoms of the planes and the whirling propellers rushing towards me and let out a God-Almighty yell.

The result to this timely warning was as unexpected as our Skipper's reaction to the flak. Our plane broke away sharply to the right while the box, minus their leader, turned left. I saw them disappear behind a bank of clouds and there, right over Southern Germany, we were on our Pat Malone.

Under normal conditions we should have been able to pick our mob up again but when they disappeared behind the clouds it was the last we saw of them. There were some panicky requests on the part of our Skipper asking where the formation had gone to, but when it was evident they had disappeared into the blue and we were all alone, his thoughts immediately turned to beating a retreat back to England.

The logical plan from my point of view was to make this as unobtrusive and quiet as possible. There was enough cloud formation around for us to skip from bank to bank and make a quiet exit. But to the amazement of the crew, as Ted gave a course for home, we flew about a thousand feet under the cloud base, and in addition he started a bleat on open broadcast 'Leader Black Box calling, we are all alone. Where are angels?'

This, in layman's language, meant a broadcast to our escorting fighters advising we were alone and requesting their protection, but the only flaw in this appeal was it was also monitored by the Germans, so they also knew there was a lone bomber stooging homewards unescorted.

So strong was the belief in the infallibility of pilots he made at least half a dozen appeals before Ted voiced a protest and said, 'I consider we should keep quiet, Pilot, we are only advertising our position.' Our Skipper did not acknowledge this remark, but sent out another call for protection.

I thought, 'Bugger it, it isn't often a new crew member, let alone a gunner, advises a pilot', but I felt this was an emergency, so I reported, 'Gunner to Pilot. May I suggest all outward calls cease and that we get up into cloud cover? We're sitting ducks for any fighter attack in our present position.'

This message was not acknowledged, so like a lost lamb bleating in a forest full of wolves, we flew across France, a thousand feet from cloud cover. Three times I saw fighters take off, but still consider the Jerries thought it was such an obvious trap we were not attacked. I could imagine them evaluating this lone tempting target, the bleating pleas for fighter protection and saying the Teutonic version of 'Like bloody hell. What's in the clouds above?'

Just the same, someone's guardian angel worked overtime that day, for when we crossed the coast we ran out of clouds, but made the fifty mile sea trip without molestation. It was bloody-well incredible. We arrived back over base twenty minutes ahead of our formation.

It would have been funny only for the serious implications, for the box, bereft of its leader, had also turned for home without bombing, so that six bombers and their crews, plus a highly organised fighter escort, had made an eight hundred mile return trip with all its perils for Sweet Fanny Adams.

Chiefy was on hand as we parked our plane, bomb-load and all. Ground crew took a fierce pride in their efficiency and manifested as big an interest in bombing results as air crew, so that they felt any goof was a reflection on their work and ability.

When I said we lost the formation, Chiefy said incredulously; 'But you didn't bring your eggs back!'

I was feeling a bit tense myself; a crew shares its captain's inefficiency. There were a hundred and one reasons why you might not bomb; also, I felt there was no reason why I should account to a Warrant Officer Chief Mechanic, so replied, 'Of course we didn't bloody-well bomb; in fact we're lucky to be here.'

He said; 'That bastard's yellow. I could have told you that when he bogged that plane. You're a bloody fool to fly with him. He'll prang as sure as eggs.'

We had some uncomfortable moments when the rest of the boys returned. That night, despite a freezing atmosphere, the Wingco was in the Mess. The events of the day seemed to have had no effect upon him, and he was his charming natural self. It says a lot for his personality that by the end of the evening he was back on drinking terms with most of the mess.

The Wingco's lack of fighting heart must have set the Groupy a problem, for here was a top-ranking officer whose position by all flying protocol should be at the head of his squadron, and was not suited for the job. If he had been an NCO, he would have been disposed of smartly by being classified LMF, but this derogatory term could not be applied to a Wingco.

We sat on the sidelines for a few days while the powers-that-be chewed the matter over, then our names appeared on the battle order again; this time, we were flying as Number Four.

The do was almost a repetition of the previous fiasco, our pilot did reasonably well, until we started our run-in and the inevitable flak came up, then we started to buck around the sky like a buck jumper at a rodeo. The result was Five and Six couldn't keep formation and it was a bloody awful pattern. There was no doubt our Skipper was a bloody menace to everyone and more help to the enemy than the RAF.

Safely back on the ground he seemed to be able to revert to his old happy-go-lucky self and be completely impervious to the cold reactions of his flying comrades. Strangely enough, as a crew, we stuck by him.

That night we went into Guildford and hit the grog, and when we got back to camp we were full. He invited us to help him knock over a bottle of Scotch, but the other two declined. Hoping to get him drunk enough to talk, I went along with him. About three-quarters of a bottle later, he said, 'You think I'm a coward, don't you, Johnny?'

It was a delicate question. I said, 'No, Skipper, but I think you're a bit flak happy. Actually, it's the least of our worries. It's the fighters you've got to worry about.'

I won't repeat our conversation. The main point he made was he intended seeing the war through, and he didn't give a bugger what anyone thought. His three little girls and his wife, he declared, were his main consideration, for despite his philanderings he was very much in love. His transient loves meant nothing, they were a part of a war-jumbled world. He had never wanted to fly operationally and didn't give a damn if he was removed from the squadron.

He declared he wasn't built for war, and I thought of poor Mac. There was nothing maudlin in this discussion. He stated his case and I couldn't see anything wrong with it. Three years previously I might have, but I'd seen a lot of men die since then.

Next morning we looked at each other sheepishly and I said, 'What we discussed last night, Skipper, is between you and me.'

CHAPTER THIRTY-EIGHT

After these operational blues the Skipper again made no attempt to get back into the fray. We sat around the station for a few days, then he announced we had a six-day leave; this was unusual as it only came up every six weeks. Ted decided to go home to his wifey. The Skipper and Archer plumped for London. I'd had a few bad nights at cards and wasn't holding too well, but the Skipper said, 'Come up for a few nights, you can sleep in my suite.' I thought he was bulling but when we got to London he had a suite booked in one of the leading hotels, which was costing him seventy notes a week. It was a sumptuous place; you sank up to your ankles in the pile of the carpets. The appointments were splendid.

In the cocktail bar we fell in with three well-dressed females, one of which turned out to be a countess. They were class with a capital 'C', but turned out to be sisters of very ordinary mould when the party was continued in the suite after the lounge closed.

The Skipper, being of senior rank, copped the countess and the double bed. Archer ensconced himself on a divan and in his usual style argued with his partner all night. After unsuccessfully trying a narrow couch I grabbed a couple of pillows, a counterpane and made a sort of nest on the sumptuous carpet.

My well-bred low-heel declared it was the first time she'd been done on the floor and voted it an exceedingly diverting experience. Next morning the girls looked slightly the worse for wear and decided to slip off before the staff arrived, but made arrangements to meet us that night.

After two more nights of similar frolics I was in to the Skipper for about twenty quid. Those girls were certainly expensive, so more for financial reasons than anything else I decided to pull out.

As I was leaving, Skipper said, 'You'd better ring up before you go back. We may get an extension.'

I looked at him hard and said, 'When are you going back to do some ops?'

'Bugger the ops', he replied, 'this life will do me. As far as I can see we won't be doing any ops for quite a while.'

I spent a cheap night with Beryl. With womanly intuition she asked what was worrying me; 'You're not your old bright self.'

I told her my problem. She replied, 'Why are you so anxious to get your tour over?' I explained I felt this was an opportune time and my third tour was tied up with my chances of getting back home.

'If your pilot won't fly, why don't you fly with someone else?'

I started to explain that this wasn't done, and then thought, 'Why not?' On every squadron there were spare gunners filling in for regular members who for various reasons couldn't fly. I had the credentials, the only trouble was to get an okay from the Skipper.

Next morning I went back to the hotel and asked him for a private chat. I put my cards on the table, explaining the only reason I was doing my third tour was to tie it up with an application to go home. My point was if he intended flying I would be with him, but if he didn't, I wanted to fly freelance.

He wasn't happy. It was a blow to his ego, but finally he reluctantly agreed. Ted took a dim view of this decision and declared as far as he was concerned I was out of the crew for good. I told him I wasn't worried about what he thought and if he wanted to make something of it we could settle it right there. The Skipper squashed any chance of a brawl by declaring there would be no fighting in his suite.

As I was walking up Kingsway I saw a familiar blue-clad figure ahead and thought, 'By cripes, that's Smithy!'

I passed him and looked sideways to make sure. It was him all right, but a battle-scarred, battered Smithy. A jagged red scar which the plastic surgeon's skill could not erase ran like a bolt of lightning from his forehead down over his nose to his lip, where it struck right across his cheek, lifting the side of his mouth in a fixed, sardonic leer. Even his cap pulled low could not hide the disfiguring burn scars which covered the upper part of his face and puckered the skin on his left cheek. He had no eyelashes and his eyes looked out from hairless lids. He was a stone lighter. Gone in that crash was the boyish charm that had rattled a hundred English feminine hearts.

We looked at each other in surprise. The shock must have shown in my face, but I said, 'How the bloody hell are you? I didn't expect to see you here.'

His eyes skidded off me. 'I'm all right,' he declared defensively.

For a moment I thought he was carrying on our last argument. Then I realised this young airman was embarrassed by the unsightly gash and burns that covered his face. His attitude said, 'Why the hell don't you leave me alone?'

It was a time for tact. I said, 'I'm sorry about our last argument, it was my fault. I would like to apologise.' He looked down at his feet and said, 'I've forgotten about that, Johnny. A lot of water's flowed under the bridge since then.'

To my suggestion of a drink, he responded, 'I don't seem to be able to drink like I used to.'

'Let's have a cup of tea, then.' I steered him towards a small cafe but at the door he backed out. 'No,' he said. 'We'll have a drink.'

I didn't seem to be able to get to him; there was a defensive wall between us. As I looked at this young, old flying veteran with the disfigured face, I felt like saying, 'Bryan, those are honourable scars. The ugliness is only in your own mind. Wear them with honour.'

We had a beer, then he said, 'I think I'll have a soft drink.'

We spoke in fits and starts. I didn't seem to be able to get his wavelength. He was still in hospital but Kodak House had advised he was to be transferred to a squadron converting to Lancasters in the near future.

'You're what?'

He repeated his statement.

'But why the bloody hell are they doing that?', I exploded.

'Well,' he replied slowly, 'when I came up on this trip I went in to see them about getting home and this was the result of the application.'

'You saw Dale?'

'That's right.'

I said, 'He's a pure unadulterated bastard. He's still got his knife into us both. Anyway, you won't have to do any more flying.'

'That's the bloody trouble,' he replied. 'How can you do a conversion course without flying? I don't know if I'm to go there as an instructor or to join a crew.'

I remembered my reactions after my accident and looked sideways at this battle-scarred warrior. By everything that was right and decent he should have been on his way home, or at least on complete rest. We wandered out of the pub. It was getting towards six. 'How about coming down to the club?', I suggested.

He side-stepped this. 'No, I've had that bloody place,' he declared flatly.

We settled for a picture show. I knew I still hadn't got through to him. Apart from his scars he was a totally different Smithy to the one I had known. During the two-hour period we were together he had not laughed or even smiled.

Neither of us had made any plans to stop in London that night. After the show we made our way up to the Strand Hotel. I knew the receptionist and she gave us a double room with twin beds.

It wasn't until he started to get undressed I realised what was worrying him, for even after he had removed everything but his singlet and underpants he still had his cap on. I think he would have worn it to bed only it was virtually impossible to pull a woollen singlet over a RAAF officer's cap.

He turned his back while he pulled it off but I saw enough to realise the whole of his head must have been scarred and burnt by the petrol flames. The skin specialists had done a good job; the top of his head looked like a suet pudding with clumps of hairs pushing up like lawn through top dressing. I knew I could not act as though I had not seen it. This was obviously the reason why he would not go near Boomerang House and why he had kept his cap on till the last possible moment.

I chose to act differently. 'Those skin boys have done a marvellous job on you, Smithy,' I declared. 'I wouldn't have thought it was possible.'

He kept his back to me and said, 'Don't bullsh to me – I know how I look.'

'No! Fair dinkum. You're a thousand times better than I expected. You're like the bloke with a front tooth missing; you think everyone's looking at you.'

I knew I was on tender ground but at least it made him talk about himself.

Later, when the lights were out, I learned something else. He was terrified of flying again. He said, 'I sweat blood every time I think of it. Christ, Johnny, I just don't seem to be able to get over this.'

I could have said, 'See the quack and get him to take you off flying,' but knew what his answer would be. He was wearing an honourably won DFM. He was a veteran of fifty tough operations. This should surely entitle him to complete rest and a berth on the first boat to Australia.

'What really gets my goat is that both Dagworth and Clarkey are on their way home,' he said.

'They're what?' I spluttered in disbelief.

This was true. He had learnt it at Kodak House that afternoon.

'Then there's no bloody justice in the world,' I declared.

CHAPTER THIRTY-NINE

During my absence from flying a drastic change had come over the operational sphere. Both TAF and Bomber Command had started the pre-invasion round-the-clock bombing of marshalling yards and other key points of the network or railways the Germans had at their command. The intent was if not to paralyse, at least to seriously impede the German's ability to bring up troops and reinforcements when the invasion started.

Recognising these portents and in an endeavour to lessen its effect, the Nazi High Command had moved in army anti-aircraft units. These forces, unlike their civilian counterparts, were showing such unexpected accuracy it was decided they must be using some new direction-finding equipment.

The disquieting part of this new peril was that their first shots were usually bang on target; there was no warning. Also, they ranged on Number One, which meant the percentage of hits on box leaders was unusually high. After a while it was considered a highly dangerous occupation to fly with the leader. Having no desire to terminate my flying at this stage of the game, I chose my pilots where possible and evaded the One, Two and Three positions.

While there was slight fighter opposition, the RAF and Yanks dominated the skies. When enemy aircraft did break through their attacks were only half-hearted, proving either that the calibre of the pilots was poor or, what was more likely, they didn't relish the combined fire power of twelve .5 guns spitting cannon shell at them. It was a long cry from the days when they brushed .303 fire aside like peas from a pea-shooter and pressed their attacks viciously right on our tails.

One occasion when I couldn't miss out flying with a leader was when the CO asked me to fly with the Dutch Wingco. The squadron by this time were using OBOE, a radar system worked by two stations in England which sent out radar pulses. These pulses were received by the aircraft and sent back to the ground station. The navigator, using this equipment, tracked in on his target, following a defined path with dots on one side, dashes on the other. When the dots stopped he pressed the teat and bombed. In good or bad weather it was supposed to give a hit or miss error of fifty feet. Its use necessitated an extra bod who sat in the second pilot's seat and industriously wound a handle which activated some part of the mechanism.

I had heard of some of the idiosyncrasies of this pilot. One was that he was completely contemptuous of danger, the other that as soon as he had cleared the enemy coast on the way back he put his aircraft on George, the automatic pilot, sat back and sucked a large meerschaum pipe. I found these things to be true. This flier was one of those people who had no nerves; coming onto the target, despite concentrated and accurate flak he flew straight and level for a good thirty seconds which, while securing a very accurate bombing pattern, was mighty hard on the nerves. Because he had a record of some hundred and forty ops I could only conclude he was very lucky.

One interesting fact I learnt about the Dutchies on this trip was that, unlike the RAF, they had no rest period after tours. A Dutch pilot was a trained navigator and the navigator a trained pilot, which must have made them the most efficient air force in the world. All they did after they had completed thirty ops was to swap places and do another tour. I never found out how they calculated their tours, but as I was finding it mighty hard work to get through three, I could only conclude they had not operated over Germany. Nevertheless, they were doing a mighty job, extremely co-operative, and were gentlemen of the first water.

An aftermath of this trip was that the Dutchies, who had taken over a large barn-like building and turned it into a mess, invited the Australian officers to a Bols night. For the uninitiated, Bols to the Dutch is what aqua vitae is to the Swedes, vodka to the Russians, beer to the Australians. There is only one true blue Bols and that is made in Holland and bottled in earthenware jars. To get the fair-dinkum product they flew a plane to Spain every two weeks for supplies. How they got over Franco's peevishness with all things democratic I never knew. Perhaps by this time he had seen the writing on the wall and was more kindly disposed toward the Allies.

We never knew if our hosts put one over us. At the party they reckoned there was only one way to drink Bols: neat and fast! It was the nearest thing to firewater I ever drank; you could feel it burning right down to your kidneys. I didn't wake till 4 pm next day then, as I went to get up, suffered such paralysing neck and head pains that I thought I had polio. It wasn't till I found all the other Aussie imbibers were similarly smitten that I realised it was a Dutch hangover.

About this time a strong rumour came out of occupied Europe that Hitler had a fanatical force of some fifty thousand parachute troops who were to be dropped into the Southern Downs in suicide forays as soon as the Second Front began. The intention of these troops was to do as much damage as possible and fight to the death.

The High Command must have felt there was some truth in these reports because the tents were uprooted from their open paddock positions and replaced in woods. In addition, all flying crew were issued with .44 revolvers and twenty rounds of ammunition and some ground crew with tommy guns.

The only time any of us had seen a .44 was at the films when they appeared to be used with great accuracy and nonchalance by both goodies and baddies. A close personal acquaintanceship with these portable howitzers revealed them to be great cumbersome pieces of ironmongery with which it would be difficult to hit the proverbial haystack at nine paces. The thought of meeting a highly trained, murderously inclined Nazi parachutist didn't appeal to anyone and I'm certain if the threatened drop had eventuated they would have had to be Olympic champions to have caught most of the station personnel.

While we had our six-shooters there were some highly exciting and funny incidents, bearing in mind that most of the men had never handled, let alone fired, a revolver. The result, after one week, was two fingers and a toe shot off, and various narrow escapes as guns exploded unexpectedly by night and day.

A lanky Australian pilot called Bluey chanced upon one of the ammunition boxes containing .44 ammunition and grabbed a fistful, then passed the word onto myself and this little Aussie gunner, a bloke called Murph, and we too helped ourselves.

Often aircrew walked back to the mess taking a short cut through a pretty little wooded depression in which blackberries grew and rabbits abounded. We had tried unsuccessfully to snare this furry mutton. Now, with plenty of ammo, we started taking pot shots at these difficult targets. The odds against hitting a moving rabbit even with a rifle are high but with those cumbersome pieces I'd say they were astronomical.

One evening, reinforced by three of the boys who had been let into the know, we decided to see if we could really bag a bunny. We split into three pairs and started a stealthy stalk. After several ineffectual pots, there was a yell from Murph. Sure enough, he had scored a direct hit. We were all gathered around viewing the still-kicking victim when out of the woods stepped a gamekeeper and his henchman.

This bloke put on an act as though, as Bluey said later, we'd shot a bloody bullock. The gamekeeper declared the rabbit belonged to His Lordship and our action constituted outright poaching, a culpable and punishable offence. He demanded we hand over the property. One of the boys told him to go to buggery. We moved off carrying the evidence and the gamekeeper withdrew, declaring he would immediately report our unlawful actions to his master.

We debated whether we should dispose of the evidence by tossing it into a clump of blackberries. Murph said, 'Why don't we eat the bloody thing! His Lordship won't be able to put his bloodhounds on the trail until tomorrow anyway.'

That night we partook of barbecued rabbit and, while there wasn't much for each of us, it was very tasty.

Still later proceedings were enlivened by a duel between two very full Australian sergeant gunners. These two fell out and decided to fight it out with .44s in a wheat field near the tent area. As this was a courting area used by the boys and Land Army girls, some consternation was caused as the two duellists, thirty paces apart, started to blaze away, each shot being punctuated with such pleasantries as 'Missed, ya bastard!' and 'Cop this, mug!'. Because one bloke's fire was direct into the camp area, everyone hit the ground until they ran out of ammunition.

Our landlord visited the camp next day with his hirelings while we were absent on a sortie and put on a fair old yike. He demanded the squadron be paraded so the miscreants who had shot his rabbit could be identified and punished. The CO had first tried being conciliatory; finding this unsuccessful he had really got stuck into him, asking him didn't he know there was a war on; telling him the men who had shot his miserable rabbit were now flying over Europe risking their lives. Finally, the Groupy point-blank refused his request for a line-up and told him to go to buggery; at which the Lord of the Manor departed, loudly declaring he would take this matter to higher quarters.

That afternoon, Blue, Murph and I received a message to parade before the CO. He looked annoyed as we marched in and saluted. 'Did you men shoot a rabbit yesterday afternoon?'

We said, 'Yes, sir.'

'Would you please leave his bloody rabbits alone,' he said. 'That goat hasn't found out there's a God-damned war on yet,' and returned to his papers.

We waited expectantly. He looked up and said, 'What are you waiting for? You can go.'

Three days later an order came through we were to hand in our revolvers. Whether headquarters decided we were an untrustworthy mob with arms or the order stemmed from His Lordship's complaint we never discovered.

The aerial warfare was rushing towards a climax as the date for the invasion neared and the squadron flew daily in good or bad weather, often squeezing in two ops while the long daylight hours lasted.

If flying was the order of the day, l'amour reigned by night. The wheat was ripening in the fields. This we soon found was an uncomfortable base for such recreation. The procedure was for the boys to take the femmes of their choice and a blanket each to the nearest field, trample an area flat, lay the blanket over the hay and they had an excellent couch for love-making.

For those who favoured this particular type of outdoor entertainment there was no lack of partners as the WAAF and Land Army girls were very generous. As an instance, it was said one pretty blonde in the sergeants' mess entertained a new lover every night. Let me hasten to add, new areas were not trampled every time, as most had their favourite spots and returned to them whenever possible.

A week after the rabbit episode His Lordship decided to retaliate and sent his servants forth to stop this crop-trampling pastime. They had done a few amorous couples over when they chanced upon Bull who was entertaining his piece. The modus operandi of these fellows was to wallop the offending airmen over the bottom with a cudgel and tell them to get the hell out of the place. Lesser souls slunk off in embarrassment. Bull was made of sterner stuff and reacted violently to the wallop across his stern. His roars of rage could be heard for a mile as he chased his assailants across the fields and through the woods, bellowing murderous threats. After that, the outdoor lovers were left severely alone.

CHAPTER FORTY

We knew that D-Day was at hand. A few days before the big event the squadrons were switched to night ops. Very few crew members were trained for anything but day flying. There wasn't a gunner except myself who had a clue and I was rusty.

In addition, the weather was lousy with cloud base at twelve hundred feet and ceiling of twenty thousand. This meant we flew at twelve hundred feet as it was impossible to navigate, let alone bomb, through ten-tenths cloud.

The first few nights were reasonably easy. Then Jerry, relieved of the dominant swarming day fighter escorts, started to shift his night fighters in. This was a sphere in which they reigned supreme as nearly all their fighter strength was trained in this defensive arm. In addition, Bomber Command had swung a big proportion of strength away from the nightly bashing of Germany proper and was concentrating on key railway points in France.

As an indication of this stepped-up night aerial activity, on the night before D-Day, flying with Bluey we had four fighter encounters. I found these defenders did not press attacks as they had over Germany. Possibly they looked for easy pickings. When they found an aircraft on the alert they passed on to something easier. As an indication of this rising fighting tempo the squadron lost three out of sixteen kites on the first night and five out of twenty on the second.

D-Day, for us, was an anti-climax. We had returned from a bridge-bashing do at 4 am and were eating breakfast when the Groupy came in and announce, 'It's on, boys. The first troops went ashore in France early this morning.' There were a few tired claps and someone said, 'About bloody time.'

We took off again in the twilight to attack bridges well to the rear of the battle zones. Cloud base was at fifteen hundred feet and we flew just below it. Despite the cloud a nearly full moon gave fair visibility.

We crossed the coast well away from the battle zone and had two fighter encounters. If the first fighter was easily discouraged, the second, a two-engined job, evidently a JU88, stuck persistently. There were planes everywhere so that collision, particularly when doing evasive action, was almost as great a danger as the fighters. We finally lost our persistent pursuer and then were walloped by a flak ship as we came over the coast.

The losses that night were six planes of the twenty engaged. Among those lost were Bluey and Murph. This marked my sixty-fourth op. As things were working out exactly as I had expected I decided to call it a day. The Groupy raised no objections and offered his congratulations. 'Sixty-four is near enough,' he said, and added, 'Do you know your crew is going back on ops?'

I said, 'I didn't know.'

'I think the Wingco is hopeful you will fly with him.' We looked at each other and laughed.

At the midday session the Wingco came across and shouted me a beer. I anticipated him by stating I was through with flying. He didn't say anything for a while, then asked had I completed my third tour.

I said, 'My bloody oath. It's strictly terra firma for me in future; the more firmer, the less terror.'

We had a few more grogs and he said, 'We're going on to night ops and are looking for a gunner who's had night flying experience.'

'You'll find they're as scarce as hen's teeth on this squadron. All the boys here are strictly TAF types,' I said, adding, 'I'll give you a tip, though. Whoever you get tell him to keep his eyes peeled.'

He thought for a while and said, 'You wouldn't like to do a few more ops, Johnny? With Ted, Archer and you, we'd have a first-class crew.'

I looked at him. He was a likeable bloke. He knew he had come to the end of the road. He either flew now or had to get off the squadron in disgrace.

I said, 'No thanks, Skipper. I feel I've done my share. If, however, I had ops to do, I'd fly with you.'

That night I learnt from Ted that they had resolved their problems by recruiting a new WAG and Archer the farmer was to take over as gunner. Ted said, 'I'm not very keen about this. He's such an egotistical bastard he thinks he's the best gunner in the world but this is the first time he'll have flown in a turret.'

'My advice,' I said, 'is that you go out and get some practice. Things are really hot in the air over there. Tell him to get his patter right, and synchronise with the Skipper, because those boys play for keeps.'

'I know it's good advice,' he responded gloomily, 'but how can you get it across to him?'

That night I got so full I didn't remember going to bed. Strangely enough I wasn't elated over the completion of my flying term. I puzzled this one out till I realised it was the sixty-four ops that was the focal point; sixty-five ops was the norm for three tours. It was like scoring ninety-nine runs in a Test and retiring, or getting to match point in a tennis match and giving up. I felt I would never be able to say truthfully I had completed three tours.

On D-Day plus five, Bill Fogg came to me with a solution for this problem. His crew were to take three journalists – two English and one Dutch – on a special night flight, the intention being that they would give the public an article on TAF's doings. Would I fly with them as tail gunner? Bill was highly excited over this chance for some free publicity. However, they wanted a properly trained tail-end Charley and I was the only one on the station who fitted the bill.

I said I'd think it over. At midday I hit myself with a few sherbets. They were enough to tilt the scales, and when Bill and his pilot came across I said, 'Yes'.

Special intercom connections were to be put in for our visitors so they could listen in to our discussions. At briefing, I found we were to carry an extra navigator as the standard one was to be fully engrossed with OBOE. Four extra bods was a helluva lot. I sincerely hoped we didn't have to get out in a hurry or someone was sure to be killed in the rush.

Five planes were briefed for a bash on a railway junction. In addition to OBOE, two Mosquitos were to drop markers on the target five minutes before we went in, thus ensuring a hundred per cent success – and good publicity!

The journalists didn't seem over-happy with their assignment. One, a sombre looking character, asked me had I much experience. I told him this would be my sixty-fifth op. 'I suppose,' he asked with a nervous laugh, 'we can expect some flak and fighter opposition?'

'You can certainly expect fighters,' I replied. 'The place is lousy with them. Flak's generally of minor consequence.' I asked, 'Have you done much flying?'

'Oh, yes, I did a couple of trips to Paris before the war.'

'How about your cobbers?'

'The Dutchman has flown quite a bit, but Tom,' indicating a fair-haired, stoutish character, 'has never been up in a plane before.'

'Have they shown you how to hook on a parachute?', I asked.

'We've got the harness and all that. You don't think we'll be needing it, do you?'

Our pilot was like a cat with two tails. He sprouted false heartiness. He was already reading the headlines in the newspapers. I recalled my first impression of him as a gong-hunter and hoped he wasn't going to put on any special acts for his passengers. I found before we took off that our extra navigator was a complete sprog, on his first trip, but thought that OBOE plus the Mossie markers would offset him.

Because twilight held till close on 11.30 pm we took off at 11, the idea being that by the time we hit the enemy coast it would be dark. A solid bank of cloud extended from twelve hundred feet to twenty-one thousand so we flew just below it. As we progressed, the wonderful panorama of sea might the allies had gathered for this greatest sea invasion of all time unfolded itself. Under cover of darkness this great concourse of ships was ferrying reinforcements, ammunition and supplies to extend the slender foothold they had gained. They sailed in groups of approximately fifty vessels and stretched as far as the eye could see in almost every direction.

We were about a third the way across and passing over one of these convoys when the first tracer spiralled up towards us. I reported, 'Flak from the ships dead below.'

The pilot said, 'Fire the colours of the day smartly, Second Navigator.'

By this time we had passed over this trigger-happy group who, even though we were out of range, continued to reach us with their fiery fingers. The Skipper said, 'We're coming up on to another group. Be ready with the colours, Navigator.'

As we passed, this mob, taking their cue from the other, let us have it. It was bloody hot. The pilot said savagely, 'Have you fired those colours, Navigator?'

Over the intercom a timid voice said, 'I forgot to bring them, sir.'

There was a silence while the pilot threw the plane into some sharp evasive action. As we passed out of range, he said sarcastically, 'I suppose you forgot your parachute too!'

There was a momentary silence, then the timid voice replied, 'Yes, sir.'

I reckon this was one of the smartest crossings of the Channel on record for a Mitchell. Every time we got anywhere near one of these groups we copped the lot. Sometimes in trying to miss one we would end up between two fires. There were some unprintable things said about Royal Navy escorts that night.

As a result of these upsets we hit the enemy coast earlier than we should have, not a pleasant thought. It meant we'd be stooging around in dangerous skies for an extra ten minutes.

We skirted the narrow perimeter of the battlefield. It was alight with the eerie glow of battle as two mighty armies tried to grind each other into the ground. Out at sea great flashes showed the presence of battleships pouring in their contribution to this upheaval of fire and steel.

It had been decided that should anything go wrong with the Mosquito arrangements we would bomb on OBOE. The navigator soon reported sustained and effective jamming and that he was unable to get anything.

Simultaneously, at five o'clock and about four hundred yards, I saw a JU88 banking gracefully. The pale moonlight glinted on its wings. I reported immediately and said, 'I don't think he's seen us.' Bill said, 'I can see him, Johnny.'

The pilot said, 'Give him the works, gunners.'

I thought I was hearing things and said, 'Don't fire at him, Bill, he's moving off.' It was a commonsense rule that you didn't reveal your presence to a fighter. If he didn't want to have a go you left him severely alone.

A few minutes later we had our hands full. A single-engined fighter flashed by us and came around in a neatly executed curve of pursuit. I'll say this for our pilot, he could fly. He beat two smart passes then skipped into the clouds. When we came out a few minutes later for a look-see he was gone, but in the confusion of pursuit we were flying west, into the incoming aircraft stream. I heard a startled squeak from someone and a great black four-engined bomber flashed past feet above us. We rocked in its wash as it disappeared into the night. It couldn't have been closer.

The pilot asked the number one navigator if he had picked up anything. He reported continued jamming. He asked the second nav for a course but, because of our gyrations, he was completely lost and admitted it. The pilot had a few uncomplimentary things to say but it wasn't the sprog's fault. Better and more experienced navigators than he would have lost themselves in these circumstances.

After a period the OBOE operator said he had a signal and considered we should be in the target area. The time was right for the markers, but where the hell were the Mossies? We stooged around waiting for the markers to give us an indication. It later turned out they didn't show up. I could feel the note of frustration in the pilot's voice. Here he had everything lined up for a perfect line-shoot and everything seemed to be going wrong.

We had come down to five hundred feet in an endeavour to locate our target. Then Bill announced a line of twelve vehicles at three o'clock. In the dim light it was impossible to see what they were, but even at a distance of six hundred yards they looked big enough. We did a circuit and the pilot said, 'Let's beat them up.'

It didn't make sense to me. We hadn't reached our objective, still had a full bomb-load and here he was talking about attacking another target. Besides, this was my last op. I put my spoke in and said, 'I wouldn't advise it, sir. We haven't bombed yet.'

He said, 'Are you afraid, Beede?'

I replied, 'No, sir, but commonsense dictates we bomb and get back by the shortest and quickest route.'

He said, 'Prepare plane for action, we're going to attack line of vehicles at nine o'clock.' We came down to two hundred feet. He said, 'Let them have it.'

I'll never know what those things were, but for every shot we threw at them they threw fifty back at us. We seemed to be completely enveloped in tracer. Boy, was it a surprise packet. We broke that engagement smartly and I felt like saying, 'Serves you right, you know-all bastard.'

Time was running out. Our bombing time had passed. The pilot said, 'We'll have to find a secondary target.' We stooged around and finally laid our eggs on a road junction.

OBOE was still on the blink so he asked second Nav for a course home. He gave one with a complete lack of confidence. The pilot said, 'We'll fly under the clouds, let's hope we don't strike too many fighters.' Bill spotted the JU88 as it whirled around us and came in from seven o'clock. He was a persistent cuss. He made four attacks before we lost him by seeking cloud cover.

The pilot said, 'I'll stick in here for a while. Give me a course,

Navigator.' He gave one by guess or by God. After a while the pilot said, 'I'm coming out. See if you can get me a pinpoint.'

We got it all right, a forest of searchlights and a hail of flak. We were bang over Dunkirk, an unhealthy spot at the best of times, but doubly so at the moment. The Skipper showed commendable tactical sense and put the plane into an almost vertical dive and we crossed the sea front at less than a hundred feet. Luckily it was mostly heavy stuff which, unable to range, burst above us. The cones of searchlights could not hold the swift-moving target. A flak ship anchored off shore gave us a pasting in the short time we were in its vicinity and I felt the plane shudder as 20 mm cannon shells struck.

As soon as we were clear of this pest the pilot called for a report from all crew members. The only one that didn't answer was Bill. He called him twice, then said, 'You had better check the mid-upper turret, rear gunner, and if the gunner is incapacitated, take over.' I felt like questioning the wisdom of this move. If Bill had had it, it meant the plane would be defenceless while I made the transfer from rear to mid-upper. On the other hand, I realised he could be hit, bleeding to death. The journalists, if they were alive, could come in handy here.

I came out of my rat hole backwards. My feeling was one of urgency. The transfer was made more difficult as the pilot, once he had cleared the flak ship, climbed steeply to cloud base. This, in view of our reception coming across, was a wise move.

What I did not know was that in the wild dive to sea level Bill had pulled out his intercom plug. Just after I started my retreat along the pitch black tail he rectified this and reported himself as being right. It was just as well he was because I had almost reached the turret when a fighter, either attracted by the Dunkirk commotion or called by the defence, attacked viciously from seven o'clock. The pilot, in answer to Bill's evasive order, threw the plane into a sharp diving turn to the left. The first intimation I had was that the plane seemed to fall away from beneath me. I had a momentary feeling I was falling and then collided with a bone-shattering bang against something very solid.

The journalists told me afterwards I had collided with the flare chute and was knocked cold for twenty minutes. In that period we shook off the attacker and, free of Nazi jamming, the navigator set a course for home. I came to with my head propped on a parachute.

Not being plugged in, I still didn't know the score. All I could remember was the urgency of my mission. I could dimly discern the bulk of the turret above, so climbed up and tentatively pulled at a leg that was hanging down, and nearly had my teeth knocked down my throat for my pains. Bill was obviously not only alive but kicking. Although I wasn't feeling it, I climbed back to my hole and reported in.

The pilot said, 'Where have you been, Rear Gunner?', even though one of the passengers had reported my accident. I replied, 'I'd like to ruddy well know myself.'

We landed without incident. The kite had half a dozen whopping holes in it and innumerable small ones. How the hell someone wasn't killed or seriously wounded I'll never know. This, I knew, was the end of my flying.

The journalists' reaction to the pilot's efforts was the opposite of what he expected. By unanimous consent they declared he was bloody well mad. The article eulogising our flight was never published.

Next morning I could hardly get out of bed. I had a terrific headache almost as bad as the results of the Bols party. In addition, I had very bad bruising on my left side which extended around to the back. I must have walloped that flare chute hard.

At lunch I asked Bill how many ops he had done. He said that was his sixtieth. I said, 'Why don't you give it away? You've done more than your share.'

'We have only five more to do and that'll finish our second tour,' he said.

I didn't mince my words. 'Bill, that silly bastard thinks he's flying a fighter. He should be reported for some of the things he did last night. He was not only risking his own neck but those of his crew. A good bomber pilot doesn't take unnecessary risks. If he continues to fly like that he'll go and so will you.'

Despite my efforts he would not be swayed. 'No, Johnny, I'll finish the tour with him. I feel everything will be okay.'

Two nights later they went out and never returned. Red Cross and German reports after the war showed that they had crashed in flames and the entire crew burnt to death, the only evidence left being Bill's Australian buttons and their dog tags.

In the mess that evening the Wingco came across. He was very subdued. On the previous night they had tangled with a fighter. He said, 'I wish I had taken your advice, Johnny, and done our ops while the going was easy. It's a sight more dangerous now.'

I said, 'It's all right, Skipper, if there's complete understanding between yourself and the gunners. Night flying, as you've probably found out, is the opposite of day. In day you have a dozen pairs of eyes searching, in the night you have four and no fighter protection. Your safety lies in the alertness of your gunners and your own quick reflexes.'

He seemed to want to talk. He spoke of his wife and family. He was the complete opposite of the easy-going, fun-seeking Skipper I had known. I felt he had something on his mind. Finally, it came. 'Johnny, you didn't have any feeling about me when you decided to finish your tour on your own.'

I didn't catch on, then woke up. 'Good God, no. If you had been flying I'd have been with you all the way.'

'I was just wondering, sometimes we Irishmen feel things deeper than the average person,' he said.

I knew then he felt he had a premonition and I felt it too. It was the same feeling I had had when I said, 'Goodbye' to Ninnes and Jones and later Jack and Wilbur, but I said, 'I wouldn't worry about that. Many a time I've felt it was curtains but everything turned out right. But I would suggest that you get a damn good accord with Fred and your new gunner. That's the secret of survival in this business.'

Later on I had a grog with Ted. I said, 'The Skipper seems in low spirits.'

'Yes, he's been like that for the last couple of days.'

I felt like telling him my thoughts but decided not to. Hunches were twopence a dozen in the air force.

A few nights later they went out and nothing was ever heard of them again. Whether they were jumped over the sea or hit by flak and ended in the drink, no-one ever knew. I do know this: the Wingco knew that night in the mess, that come what may you cannot evade your fate. I feel certain when his time came he died with credit and honour.

CHAPTER FORTY-ONE

My headache persisted. I had a nagging pain down my left side and back where I had struck the flare chute. I boiled myself under the hot shower to no avail. My camp companion finally remarked irritably, 'What the hell's wrong with you?'

I explained what had happened and he had a look at my back. 'Gawd, you've got a tremendous bruise down your left side and back. If I was you I'd go and see the quack.'

'I'll be okay when the bruising wears off.'

I staggered around for two days. At night, I couldn't sleep unless I was propped up with a miscellaneous collection of clothing. If anyone bumped me or touched me I'd yell with pain. After these two days of agony I made for the MO's caravan. He gave me a perfunctory examination and said, 'It's just a bit of bruising. You'll be right.'

I put up with this for another four days and went back to him again. I said, 'Doc, I'm no whinger but I can't sleep with this damn thing. If anyone touches me on the chest, side or back it's bloody painful. I'm sure there must be something wrong.'

He was a fat slob; he prodded me in a few places again and said, 'It's only bruising. You'll be sweet in a few days, boy!' For over a fortnight I suffered agonies with this thing and then it began to ease.

Now that I was free of ops I felt I could really enjoy myself. However, a strange condition began to manifest itself. I was all right till I started to drink. I was okay for the first two or three but after that I would black out. The strange part about this was that I would remain on my feet and be mobile, but from all reports I was a cranky, abusive, unstable fighting bastard.

During the next couple of weeks, despite my handicap, I set about having a mighty good time. In a couple of blacked-out sessions at poker I won a packet. After one game, of which I didn't remember a thing,

I woke up next morning on my stretcher with my pockets full of notes. A count showed ninety-eight. I had an uneasy feeling I might have robbed a bank until my tent mate informed me of my phenomenal run of luck the previous night. On other occasions I would wake up stone, motherless broke.

I palled up with a couple of young Aussie gunners who had pooled their resources and purchased a car, which they ran on purloined aviation spirit. As their financial resources were low I came in as a paying third party. They were a couple of lads. The driver was a little bloke called Tom Francis. His mate Jim Gazzard, Gazz for short, was a big shambling type. They had an act in which they imitated the yells of a dog in mortal pain, Francis taking the high notes, Gazz the yelping undertones. It was a bottler and guaranteed to stop cars, trucks or buses in a matter of seconds, while the imitators busted themselves watching the drivers look for the cause of this canine agony.

My Guildford associations paid off here. We used to make the twelve-mile journey in twelve minutes flat, with my heart in my mouth most of the way. The return trip, according to odd bods we picked up, was a damn sight worse, but as I was usually blacked-out I never knew anything about it. They told me I continually demanded that the driver take his foot off the bloody brake.

During this period we enlarged our contacts amongst the gay wives of the town. One declared that no man living could satisfy her desires. The point here was, although we may not have succeeded, it was a pleasant challenge to take up.

There was another female called Suicide Sal. Association with her was considered to be fraught with peril. Her husband was not only suspicious but a violent character. Arriving home one night and finding the connubial couch occupied, he had pursued the luckless lover with a blazing .44. It was conceded that any relations with this female were better conducted in the park.

On several occasions I awoke in her establishment with the previous evening a complete blank, but judging by the breakfasts that were cooked and the tender farewells given, I came to the conclusion I must have had a wonderful time, the only trouble was I couldn't remember anything about it.

A few weeks later I received a letter from Smithy. He was at a place called Hatfoss doing a six week gunnery leader's course.[1] The direction from Kodak House had been so sudden his station had had to fly him across to be in time to start. This move seemed to be for the better. His mental attitude was on the way up.

His first impression of the place was that it had more bull than Homebush.[2] Equipment and instructors were the best he had ever struck; the CO of the gunnery course was a Wingco straight air gunner with a DSO, DFM and bar, which would make him the only one in captivity.

In the ensuing weeks I had reports on his progress. This school, he declared, relegated all previous courses and retraining schools he had attended to the kindergarten class. Hatfoss was known as the air gunner's university. It had modern bombers and fighters, and highly skilled pilots for fighter affiliation. The equipment had to be seen to be believed – all the latest electronic stuff. I could read his enthusiasm in his letters.

He had one big query; why hadn't the gunners been put through a school like this before going on operations? Most of the trainees were one or two-tour men. What a difference it would have made to The Mob and thousands of other young gunners like them who had been sent out to face a highly-trained, ruthless foe with hardly a clue. A course like this would have meant not only that a percentage of the dead gunners would now be alive, but also the crews that had died with them.[3]

Three weeks after I finished ops I received a summons to Kodak House. I felt this could only mean one thing, return to Aussie.

I was ushered into the office in which I had suffered my reverse some four months before, but instead of Dale another officer greeted me. He was a pleasant flight lieutenant. We discussed a few commonplace matters. He had only just arrived from Australia.

I couldn't resist asking, 'Where's the squadron leader gone?'

'Oh, he's back in Australia by now.'

I didn't bat an eyelid. 'He deserves it. He had a hard tour of duty.'

The Flight Lieutenant looked at me squarely, but said nothing. No doubt he had already seen my papers.

The crux of the discussions was that I had not done any instructing while I was in England, and before consideration would be given to returning I would have to do a gunnery leader's course. I tried to argue that I had completed three tours, but he was adamant. Arrangements had been made for me to do the six week course at Hatfoss. They would advise me of the date.

Good behaviour, he warned, and strict attention to air force protocol, played as big a part in getting a pass as aerial warfare knowledge.

Back on the station I wandered around like a lost soul. I found I had nothing in common with the eager-beaver young airmen who nattered incessantly of their doings in the mess. I was like a washed-up pug. I had no crew and such was the tempo of the war and loss of crews I hardly knew anyone. In my absence Tommy Francis and his cobber had 'bought it' and the Committee of Adjustment were trying to apportion the car.

It is not generally known that in the initial three months after D-Day the RAF and USAAF lost over twelve thousand planes but such was the reserve of planes and crews it was said they could have doubled this number and still had plenty.[4]

One evening after dinner the mess orderly told me I was wanted on the phone. I knew there was an operation on but such was their confidence they hadn't even cut the phone off. It was Smithy ringing from London. He had completed his course with an A pass. He was bubbling with excitement but wouldn't tell me why. Could I come up tomorrow?

'I don't see why not. I'm like a shag on a rock here.'

'Right. I'll see you at the club tomorrow for lunch.'

This was news. Last time I had seen him I wouldn't have been able to drag him there with a team of wild horses.

He was seated in a large armchair near the door, waiting for me. The scar still ran in a jagged line across his face. More hair had pushed its way through the patched skin on his scalp. It wasn't these things I specially noted, but a fair replica of the old Smithy grin that greeted me, a crinkle around the battered eyes that spoke louder than any words.

'Gee, I'm glad to see you, Johnny. Come and have a grog.'

I knew he had news and guessed what it was. I let him do the build-up. Then it was out. He had received his notification to go to Brighton – he was going back to Australia. I said, 'Good luck, boy. You've bloody well earned it.'

He had a plan. Why shouldn't I have a go at getting back on the same draft as him? I had earned it too.

I remembered my interview. 'I don't think I'd have Buckley's.'

He said, 'If you don't have a go, you'll never know. Let's have a crack at this new bloke together – he's different to Dale.'

We went in together and joined our arguments and entreaties. He was a decent bloke and said, 'It's not me that makes the decisions, boys, but I'll see what I can do.' I sent Smithy out and continued the assault. This was something I wanted more than anything on earth; his final decision was that he would do all he could to help me.

I was coming down the steps when I met the doctor from Beltwell. The surprise was mutual. He asked me what I had been doing. I explained I had just completed my third tour. He declared, 'You're a bloody fool. It hasn't got you anywhere.' I explained why I was here and told him of my interview.

He looked at me keenly and said, 'You don't look too good.'

I told him of my last accident, that I was still tender in certain spots. It was a fortunate meeting for he said, 'I've been transferred here. Come up and I'll look you over.'

After half an hour's examination and probing, he said, 'You are lucky. You've had two ribs broken and one badly bent but they appear to have mended naturally.'

He asked me who the station medical officer was, then said, 'Better take a couple of fire flashes back and put them under him, he needs livening up.'

I explained my strange blackouts and propensity for violence when I was in them, the sudden twinges in my back and a few additional fancied ailments for good measure. I nearly over-sold, for he said, 'I think you should have X-rays and a complete rest.'

I smartly back-pedalled. 'Doc, all I want is to get back home. I'm a poor old washed-up gunner. Can you help me?'

I think he saw through my ruse, but he was a cracker-jack. 'I'll have a go. I think your record of sixty-five ops plus your injuries and black-outs could constitute a good case of battle fatigue. Leave it to me. I'll write a report.'

CHAPTER FORTY-TWO

That evening in September 1944 we witnessed a strange phenomenon. There were two sharp, almost simultaneous explosions, different from anything we had heard before. Seconds later the cloudy sky was suffused with a pink glow and, after a pause, there was a sound like that of an express train travelling at tremendous speed overhead. About a minute later, this performance was repeated. The Londoners looked at each other and asked, 'What the bloody hell's this?'[1]

No-one except the High Command knew that these were the first V2 rockets, the forerunners of some eleven hundred missiles that were to add another burden to the ordinary Englishman's life until the advancing Allied armies were able finally to over-run their launching bases.

Unlike the V1 buzz-bomb, the V2 gave no prior notice of its arrival and the three thousand people killed would never have known what hit them. In my opinion, this event marked the end not only of the air gunner but aircrew, and was a grim portent for the unarmed populations of the world of what another – a nuclear war – holds for them.

Next morning Smithy left to start packing prior to his move to the pre-embarkation depot at Brighton. He was a new man, his 'A' pass, removal from all flying and transfer home, were triple tonics that were working wonders. 'Jeez,' he said, 'I only hope we can go back together.'

The station was in a state of flux, getting ready to transfer to France. I sweated it out for a week, waiting and wondering. I must have been a burden to my fellow-men because, sitting in the mess behind a paper, I heard a young Australian officer say, 'Who's that garrulous old bastard who gets around on his own?'. His companion laughed and said, 'Oh, he's supposed to have done three tours and is waiting for the magic word. From all reports, he's a bit flak-happy.'

One day when I went up to the mess the letter from Kodak House was there. I was afraid to open it. What if they decided to send me on this bloody course?

I retired to a corner and looked at it for five minutes. Finally I plucked up courage. 'Well, Sydney or the bush.'

It read in part, 'You are to report to the pre-embarkation depot at Brighton in six days time.'

There wasn't anyone around I could share the good news with, so I made a quick trip to London. There were a few goodbyes I wanted to say. I dropped in to thank the doc. He declared he had had little to do with my transfer. I said, 'Like hell! But someday I may be able to do you a good turn too.'

I left many friends in England, both in civil and service life. I do not think I was a shrewdie, or trouble-maker, possibly because I was years older than my young flying companions, and had knocked around a lot before joining up. I couldn't stand the phony grandeur with which some officers invested themselves. These dills were in the minority, the top operating echelon were down to earth good fellows.

Brighton was a staging area for incoming and outgoing Aussie airmen. Nearly all of the big hotels on the sea front were occupied by the RAAF. Here you met the young enthusiastic newcomers anxious to be in the fight before it was all over and the sober young-old men who had done their one, two, and in some cases three tours, the ordeal of battles over. Europe was reflected in their eyes and faces.

It would be hard for the average person to calculate what a tour of thirty operations meant. Air Vice-Marshall D.C.T. Bennett, the father of the Pathfinder Force, speaking in his book of that title, stated, 'I believe that particularly in the other services, and indeed amongst the public, it is seldom appreciated that an ordinary bomber pilot (which included the crew) was called upon to do about thirty operations and that each of these operations was equivalent to a major battle which, in either of the other two services, would be regarded as the experience of a lifetime.'

After I had found my billet I went in search of Smithy. I found him in his room flat-out asleep and tickled his nose with a feather pulled from a pillow.

He opened his eyes and looked at me blankly for a second, then yelled, 'Johnny, you bloody beaut. I knew you'd make it.'

There were some three hundred bods comprising pilots, WAGS, observers and gunners marked for embarkation. Happily enough, the old class distinction of the early years was gone; the gunners were accorded an honourable place in this company. As an indication of this, we became good friends with two fighter pilots who had completed a tour on Typhoons and two Pathfinder boys who had completed seventy-five operations.

As though it was a judgement for the tale I had tried to put over the doc at Kodak House, the pain in my back, which had worried me only slightly, now began to increase in severity. It wasn't till I started to pass blood I realised something was radically wrong.

I thought this would happen to me. If I go to the quack I'm a moral to go into hospital, miss the boat and perhaps be stuck in England for another three months.

I conferred with my mates – two were in favour of my going to the MO but Smithy and the two fighter boys said, 'Why not stick it out for a couple of days, it may clear up.'

At the end of this period I was worse. Then one of the crowd had a brainwave. He said, 'I know one of the medical orderlies in charge of prescriptions. We'll have a few drinks with him tonight.' He was a ginger-haired Queenslander who listened sympathetically to my problem. He advised me to see the quack. 'Sounds like kidney trouble,' he said. 'Sulpha tablets might fix it temporarily till you get on board the boat, but I'm not sure of your reactions.'

I recounted my pill-swallowing efforts in hospital. So it was decided to give them a go. In appreciation I handed over a quid and received thirty pills, to be taken at the rate of three a day. If anything unusual happened I was to go to the doctor immediately. They must have been just what he would have ordered, for they stopped the discharge and relieved the pain considerably.

It is not my intention to bore the reader with my aches and pains but, believe me, while I waited for that embarkation order I was a miserable poor coot.

At last it came. We were told to be ready the following day. The only trouble was we had to carry all our goods with us. My mates were champions, they shared most of my heavy gear between them.

The rumour was we were to board the Queen Mary at Liverpool. We entrained at dusk. As the train started to glide through the quiet countryside, I thought of a trip so like this one, more than three years before, only that time we had been moving south instead of north and this little island had been a hard-pressed fortress.

Today the picture was completely reversed. A million troops had already crossed the Channel; something Hitler, with all his might, had never been able to accomplish. With Russian troops hammering from the east and Allied armies pushing from the south and west, it was now Germany which was the beleaguered fortress.

I looked at the little hamlets flashing by, with the untiring workers in the fields. I saw in my mind row upon row of sleeping forms in the underground stations. I thought of the thousands of flimsy shelters in the back yards of hundreds of thousands of homes in London, into which the families crawled as the buzz-bombs beat their staccato way across the skies by day and night.

The indomitable spirit of the English working man and his family was something that Hitler had been able to bend but never break. These people had stood steadfast during five years of tribulation and destruction, joining the endless queues for their meagre rations, suffering bombs, fire, buzz-bombs and V2 rockets. They were the solid base on which certain victory had ultimately been built; had they failed, everything would have been lost.

The blackout curtains should have been in place, but so remote was the chance of an air raid that the conductor had not bothered to tell us to pull them down. The lights shone dully in the windows, and as I looked out into the darkening countryside I saw, as though in a dream, my mates again, not as they were now, lying in their graves on alien shores or resting at the bottom of the cold North Sea, but rather in the full vigour of their youth and strength, with all the joy of living that is the birthright of the young. There was Hally with his bear-like hug; Blondie with his deep, grating laugh; Mac with his sad, dog-like eyes; Happy arguing his political points; Aub with his heart-warming smile; ebullient, happy-go-lucky Kiwi. I saw them all as I had known them, was it three or thirty years ago?

So clear was my vision that I raised my hand in an involuntary salute.

Then, in a moment they were gone, lost in the mist and shadows of the gathering dusk.

APPENDIX ONE

Operation Oyster,
Philips Radio works, Eindhoven, 6 December 1942.
Cusack's First Raid and Beyond

With so many of its young men away in Europe as the Japanese threatened, as in the Great War, Australian newspapers and magazines published as much as they could about their boys fighting back. What follows is a compilation of excerpts from John Cusack's letters home to Dymphna Cusack and Cath Gunn as published in two Australian newspapers, as well as relevant excerpts from contemporary newspaper articles.

December, 1942: The trip to Eindhoven to attack the Philips' Radio Works was our biggest to date. There were more than a hundred bombers; Bostons, Mosquitos and Venturas. Ours, the Venturas, were to go in last, with our plane the last of the lot. We planned to fly as low as we could and pack as tightly as we could, skimming trees and houses.

My trip was destined not to be a pleasant one, for on testing my guns just after leaving our coast, one jammed, and for the next twenty minutes I sweated and swore while I tried to fix it. I was so busy that I failed to notice that we had reached the Dutch coast. I was wakened to the fact by the hundreds of white streamers that started to streak up past us. I had seen flak before, but never as close as this, as we were only a few feet above the heads of the gunners. The heavy flak is something like a black mushroom that grows and expands when it bursts; the light stuff is like white streamers sailing by. Our wireless operator had his head in the Astra hatch during this little interlude, and a shell blew the glass dome off without even scratching him. As may be guessed, my efforts to get the gun going ceased, and I concentrated on the other, which luckily functioned, so I proceeded to pay back their attentions in kind.

Across these islands and on the mainland the defences are heavy and the shooting good. It shakes you to see planes dive, possibly with your own cobbers aboard dive and become rolling balls of flame. Still, once we left the heavy coastal defences behind we struck flak only in patches.

But one incident rather tickled me. We skimmed over some trees an on to an aerodrome. The defenders gave us merry hell, but as we flashed past I noticed one gunner nonchalantly leaning against his machine-gun and taking no part in the plastering. I gave him a fleeting wave, and he waved back. At the height of tense activity I had time to think, 'That bloke and I have the same ideas on this ruddy business!'.

Flying low like this through heavy flak, we do what is known as 'evasive action', which means the pilots set their planes weaving and dodging in what I call 'The Dance of Death' – a mad capering that frightens the seven daylights out of each other as we're all close together and there isn't much room for manoeuvring. As we skimmed over towns and villages, Dutchmen out on their Sunday strolls waved to us. It was an oddly cheering sight.

Coming in last to the target, I saw everything. On the target we did such a violent evasive action that I walloped my head against the top of the turret. Our incendiaries made a helluva mess, and we skimmed in over the tops of the blazing factory buildings from which German gunners – still at their posts – were giving us hell. One kite here with a particular friend of mine in it blew up in mid-air. The only merciful thing was that it was all so quick they wouldn't have known anything about it.

I was trying to get a shot at the roof-top gunners when, to my horror, my other gun jammed. I've never been so scared in my life: I broke into a cold sweat. To make matters snappier, just as we got off the target I spotted a Focke Wulf chasing a Mosquito. As they were about a hundred and fifty miles an hour faster than we were, I hoped they'd go on chasing.

By a miracle, we didn't see another fighter coming out, though in one spot, coming down a channel about a mile and a half wide, we were plastered by batteries from both sides. I didn't think it was possible for planes to live in such flak; it churned the water into a white mass of foam. One shell twisted our bottom guns round like a corkscrew, but, luckily for us, didn't explode.

Luck was with us all the way back, and the whole crew came out without a scratch, despite about thirty holes in the plane. Never thought I'd be so happy to see any place as I was to see England. We landed with the port engine conking and with only petrol for another five minutes. There were bits of a tree and leaves caught in the port engine.

Several other newspapers reported the attack on Eindhoven differently; these quotes are from the Herald, Daily Telegraph *Service and AAP:*

Bombers of the Australian Lockheed Ventura Squadron, on their first raid on Sunday, flew so low they ran into flocks of birds frightened from marshes and fields in Holland.

Pilot Officer Leigh Rule, formerly of Scotch College, Melbourne, said today, 'Birds crashed into the planes like bricks hitting windows. One front-gunner got a black eye and an observer's hand was badly split. The fuselages in a few seconds looked as though the crews had been pillow-fighting – every plane was holed or dented where the birds hit us like flak.

Sergeant Cecil Goldstiver hit ten birds, which tore out the Ventura's landing lights. 'It was my crew's first attack, and everyone mistook the birds for shells,' he said. Sergeant Goldstiver had a second scare. When he was bombing the Radio Works almost at roof-top height, a giant chimney loomed through the smoke. 'I lifted the port wing and missed the chimney by inches,' he said.

Describing the attack on the Philips Works, Sergeant Donald Marshall, an air-gunner, of Bexley (NSW) said, 'I could see the high walls of the factory crumbling down to nothing as our bombs rained down.'

Pilot Officer Lloyd Alley, of Braidwood (NSW) said, 'Eindhoven looked like a total casualty. It was a magnificent kick-off for our squadron. Sergeants John Cusack (Coogee), John Webb (Manly) and Arthur Galley (Balmain), all air gunners, said the Philips factory was bristling with guns.

All the Australians paid tribute to the bravery of the German gunners, who coolly and accurately fired at the raiders from buildings which were already burning and were likely to blow up at any minute. Pilot Officer Rule, a veteran of 17 raids, said, 'Don't under-estimate those Germans in the occupied countries. They've got guts!'

February, 1943: Five operational flights in ten days have kept us pretty busy lately. First to Abbeville, where we bombed an aerodrome from ten thousand feet and struck nothing worse than flak, although that was pretty accurate. The next two were aerodromes, and then to Cherbourg and Bruges. 'F for Freddie' now has the greatest number of operational flights for the squadron.

We are just back from a raid on an inland target. As the black, ugly blobs of flak broke around, I saw one of our formation hit in the port engine, losing height. Soon three little black specks hurtled from it, and then three white mushrooms opened one after another, drifting down into the clouds. The pilot apparently made an effort to fly the plane back on his own, and the last we saw of it was with one motor billowing black smoke and wreathed in a circle of ack-ack fire. Suddenly, instead of black blobs of flak, we began to see reddish-tinted ones – a disturbing sight, for that is the method the Germans use to call and direct their fighters. Almost three-quarters of the way back to the coast I spotted a blunt-nosed aircraft speeding along under us. Things began to happen, and the sky seemed to be full of twisting black shapes. Three made a vicious attack on our formation, a decidedly unorthodox one, diving under from astern and up and over in front. Evasive action and luck saved our machine, but Number Two went down in flames.

Dog-fights were going on all over the sky between our fighters and the Germans. We ourselves had to beat off two more savage attacks before we got to the coast. It seemed impossible to live in the hail of tracer bullets, but luck was still with us, and we came down in a fast dive to sea-level, leaving the fighter boys behind, still embroiled in battles without end. All agreed that we had no time to be scared in the battle, but all had a bad attack of the jitters when the reaction set in.

Another newspaper clipping reports: 'Targets raided by the RAAF Ventura Squadron in daylight recently included aerodromes at Coen, Abbeville and Maupertuis (France) and engine sheds at Baugh. After the attack on Maupertuis, the Wing-Commander of escorting fighters reported, "Excellent bombing". Main buildings, hangars and dispersal huts were hit and debris was flung sky-high. The anti-aircraft fire was heavy and five Venturas were hit, but all aircraft in the squadron succeeded in returning to their base.'

March: An armed merchantman, attacked in the Channel, put into Dunkirk, and the authorities decided it had to be sunk. Dunkirk is about the unhealthiest spot on the whole coast, but away we went. Three times we tried, and could not even see the town for clouds. On the fourth trip the weather was beautiful and the French coast came up tranquil and serene. Dunkirk, scene of history and of horror, looked a little Toy-town. In one shattering burst the illusion was swept aside as flak came up in one tremendous curtain. The concussion threw the plane all over the sky, but we managed to get in, drop our bombs and start to streak for home. On the way back we watched planes crash-landing on fields and aerodromes all along the line, but 'F for Freddie' came back right on the dot, and with no more than a dozen holes. Adding insult to injury, photographs next day showed that the damn thing hadn't been hit, although there were some near misses.

May: We began one of our toughest flights the other day by soaring above cloud formations of incredible beauty, towering masses of fleecy fantasy. Near the enemy coast they cleared, and we meandered serenely over a Europe bathed in peaceful sunlight.

Wicked red splashes awoke us to reality with a shock. The formation slipped and weaved in a crafty dance, but did not deviate from the course. From my lofty perch I watched the bombs go, following them down until they merged with the landscape and were lost. Then from the target arose small columns of smoke that spread and mingled until the whole place seemed to be erupting.

The formation turned for home in a wide sweep. Then out of the intercom came the blood-chilling words, 'Fighters on the red quarter'. Black specks multiplied and became larger, the gun-leader's voice gave out 'evasive action', and the formation twisted and turned as one. Combination and concentrated fire-power were our hopes: the unfortunate straggler had no chance.

Suddenly, out of the blue like avenging angels, plummeted the high-flying escort of Spitfires, and a series of dog-fights and pursuits swirled at a terrific pace over the whole sky. Some of the German fighters engaged the Spitfires, others hammered away at their quick-breaking attacks on our bombers, the main target. So we battled our way back to the coast, and far back over the sea.

The squadron did not come off a hundred per cent best that day, but I guess we gave as good as we got.

The best account of Operation Oyster and the raids in which the author participated in in 2 Group is found in Chaz Bowyer, 2 Group RAF. A Complete History: 1936–1945, *Faber, 1974; 'Twenty three aircraft were damaged in bird collisions during the operation …' (p. 280). Readers keen to read about one of the most extraordinary low-level raids of the war could look to James Dugan and Carroll Stewart, Ploesti.* The Great Ground to Air Battle of 1 August 1943, *Jonathan Cape, 1963].*

APPENDIX TWO

Bomber's Leave – Surfing in Cornwall
by 'Pilot-Officer John B. Cusack'

Mid-summer in England! A few days operational leave, and my thoughts turned to Newquay, on the south coast of Cornwall.

There – so some of my Australian pals told me – you could get a surf and, if you were very, very lucky, some sunshine! To Newquay I decided to go.

I started off in a happy nostalgic dream of long days on Coogee Beach, and quite oblivious of the newspaper stories about over-crowded trains and holiday crowds. Official injunctions to stay at home seemed hardly meant for me. Innumerable posters pointed accusing fingers at me, asking, 'Is Your Journey Really Necessary?' and 'Why Not Stay Put?'.

I arrived at Paddington station two hours before the train was due to leave to find a mere two or three thousand lined up. One look at the swaying jumble of humanity, suitcases, umbrellas and other weapons of assault, shattered my happy dream. I tootled off to a sympathetic RTO and explained that I was on operational leave. So, just before the train drew in, he escorted me to a place of vantage, and I beat the flood of humanity that flowed over officials and barriers. All my experience of test match crowds, bargain-hunting gangs and Easter Shows faded into insignificance before this tidal wave of English holiday-makers. No quarter was given – and none asked – by either sex. By judicious use of elbows, umbrellas, suitcases and sharp-pointed heels, the women more than held their own. The train was filled in a twinkling. Carriages that normally held six to eight now housed sixteen to twenty. Corridors were packed tight with less fortunate though, nevertheless, triumphant travellers. The voices of innumerable mothers arose plaintively on the foetid air, calling for lost young, who howled dismally in reply. Outside, hundreds of luckless would-be travellers sought to cram just one more sweating body into the now immovable mass.

Disappointment and the rigours of their long wait were too much even for English good-humour. There were violent arguments, short but vicious bouts of fisticuffs, incessant clamour. Gradually good-natured police and harassed officials restored order and the unlucky ones were herded into another interminable queue that would not find relief for ten hours!

Eventually all my low cunning went for nought, for a grey-haired old lady, who had been up to London to see her wounded soldier son in hospital won both my sympathy and my seat, and I stood – or rather was held up – for eleven hours to Newquay.

During the long journey I heard hundreds of tales of holidaying in Newquay – all with one main motif, namely, that unless you had booked at least twelve months before, your chance of attaining to so much as a bed on the billiard table was nil. I had made no arrangements, and when I alighted, I set forth, dirty and bewhiskered, in search of a bed.

The unvarying answer to my query, 'Have you a room?', was 'We are booked up till October, or November, or next year, or the millennium'. To add to my sufferings, the sun – which had perversely refused to shine for the past two or three months – came out in molten glory.

Reduced by now to a dusty, thirsty mendicant, I came at last to a tiny house, unpretentious, spotlessly clean. There was no sign of 'Room to Let', or any of the misleading notices by which Newquay taunts the weary tourist. Still, more out of habit than hope, I staggered up the steps to meet a silvery-haired old dear who opened the door to my question.

She gazed at my appearance, then gave me the amazing reply; 'I'll have to see my sister.' The sister, produced from the innermost regions, subjected me to a doubtful scrutiny and then asked, 'Are you an Australian?'. I thought I probably reminded her of Ned Kelly, so meekly gulped, 'Yes.' Thereupon they retired for consultation, to reappear with the magic words; 'We can let you have a room. Can you come back in half an hour?' I said, 'Can I leave my bag?' and, when they graciously acquiesced, I went off touching every bit of available wood for luck, wondering what the mysterious interval could mean.

It wasn't till I returned and settled in that I discovered one of these old ladies had given up her own room to me, and the half-hour was needed to remove her effects. And there I remained – the white-headed boy!

The difficulty of reaching pleasure resorts in war-time is only excelled by the difficulty of surviving in them if you get there. The local residents get no extra rations to feed the multitude, so that queues are the order of the day. The locals complain that the visitors arise early and buy all available stocks. The visitors reply that they are charged exorbitant prices for everything from accommodation upwards, and have to put up with much rudeness from tradesmen.

And there really was a surf there, with waves curling at least two hundred yards out.

Crowds lined the beach to watch the 'mad Australian' crack the combers; for I seemed to be the only one to put the surf to its proper use. I must admit it was sometimes only vanity (personal and national) that got me in at all, for the water – in mid-summer – was so bitterly cold that I had to do at least a four-hundred yard run to prepare the circulation for the shock. But, as a result, the waistline diminished, and the elasticity returned to the step (bombing is such a sedentary occupation!) and I was in good condition to fight my way back on the long journey to London.

APPENDIX THREE

John Beede's War – and John Bede Cusack's War

John Bede Cusack's semi-fictional creation, John Beede, was an air-gunner in four types of twin-engined aircraft, each designed before World War II. This appendix puts the experiences of the author and Beede into the context in which they found themselves.

Beede relates his expectation that he was training for the RAF's Bomber Command. However, it is important to understand that '… the RAF started the war with a bomber fleet that was totally inadequate to carry out its own stated aims … the gap between what was expected of the RAF and what it could in fact deliver was enormous.'[1]

On one raid in December 1940 the Luftwaffe shot down 12 Vickers Wellingtons and seriously damaged another three, proving beyond doubt that Bomber Command's bombers, despite pre-war optimism, could not out-fight or out-run Luftwaffe fighters. Bomber Command, in the main, switched to night-bombing.

'Too many aircraft designs in the 1930s were compromised in the end because of uncertain specification writing and … of subsequent changes in operational requirements … [these were] symptoms of a lack of direction … the Typhoon might have been available in 1940 had the Air Ministry not persisted in sponsoring an engine, the Napier Sabre, whose unreliability took some time to cure.'[2]

For example, the breakthrough jet-powered Gloster Meteor only came into service in the last months of the war; had sufficient attention been paid to Geoffrey Whittle's work in the mid-1930s, his engine would have been with the British considerably earlier.

Geoffrey De Havilland's Mosquito did not respond to an Air Ministry Specification because the company's claims for the abilities of the aircraft were simply not believed – de Havilland met stiff Air Ministry opposition. The 'Mossie' finally began offensive operations 'twelve months later than it need have done if de Havilland's performance forecasts had been accepted. What a punch squadrons of

Mosquito bombers and fighters could have packed in 1940 – when they certainly could, and should, have become available.'[3]

Bomber Command's switch to night bombing continued inauspiciously for over a year. Until the advent of such electronic navigational aids as Gee in March 1942, OBOE in December, and then H2S, Bomber Command experienced great difficulty in locating their targets. Until late 1942, 'German targets were sometimes unaware that they had been the subject of an attempted attack ...'[4]

Bomber Command were also losing aircraft at an unsustainable rate. Apart from operational losses, they lost them in training accidents, to other theatres such as North Africa and the Mediterranean, and to other expanding parts of Bomber Command such as Training or Pathfinders as well as 'rival' Commands such as Coastal and Ferry. Wimpys were even adapted in the Med as torpedo bombers (for which they were manifestly not intended) and by Coastal Command for magnetic mine-clearing (sporting an enormous hoop girdling the entire horizontal diameter of the aircraft).

Another loss was simply 'too many ops'; the aircraft were built with calculated obsolescence in mind, not longevity. Ops pushed aircraft well beyond peacetime safety specifications and they were not expected to survive more than a few months. Aircraft which survived more than, say, forty ops, were a rarity. Beede's Wimpy, S for Sugar, is described as 'a comparatively new machine, her paper run into France having been her first trip'; however it doesn't take too many weeks before the same aircraft is a 'wornout kite' to whom losing 'a thousand or two feet' in altitude was 'not ... unusual'. Although Cusack did not fly ops on Wimpys his observation is, in the main, correct.

Yet by March 1941 Bomber Command was also expected to be hitting oil targets and cities, U-Boat construction yards, U-Boat ports pens and the factories where their parts were made, and the sailors themselves, as well as German battleships *Scharnhorst* and *Gneisenau*, lay mines at sea, drop propaganda leaflets and convert to the newer, better bombers coming on-stream. It was an almost impossible task.[5]

Cusack wonders why more appropriate training wasn't provided, observing bitterly that better training could have saved many lives. He is correct; however Britain and its colonies were very, very unprepared for war on the scale which eventuated, so the answer is partly poor forward planning and little military spending in peacetime. Then, as now, neither were in great supply, particularly in England. Also, 'electronic equipment' as described above existed only in rudimentary, underfunded development when The Mob were training; they didn't begin to eventuate until about the time Cusack – not Beede – arrived in England.

When Beede arrives in England in late 1941, it is a full year after Bomber Command began night operations. Front line bomber squadrons were equipped with Vickers Wellingtons, Bristol Blenheims, Handley Page Hampdens, Armstrong Whitworth Whitleys and the new Avro Manchesters and Short Stirlings. Each Group, comprising of many squadrons, generally used only one aircraft – for example, 4 Group used Whitleys for night raids, while Blenheims were used by 2 Group mostly for daylight raids on precise, nearby targets because of their short range, comparatively low speed and lack of defensive armament.[6] We shall return to 2 Group when Cusack joins them.

Beede's first squadron, then, we assume to be No. 12, part of 1 Group. His first aircraft was the Mark III Vickers Wellington or, more affectionately, the 'Wimpy' after cartoon character Popeye's chubby sidekick, the hamburger-addicted J. Wellington Wimpy, who 'would gladly pay you Tuesday for a hamburger today'.[7]

The Wimpy's range was about 2,000 miles with a bomb load of 1,500 pounds. The Wimpy had a maximum speed of about 250 mph at its average height of 12,500 feet, but was slower at its top height of 22,000 feet. As with all aircraft of the period, 'power steering' did not exist; it took physical strength and determination for a pilot to man-handle the controls which manipulated wing-flaps and tail-rudders. Fortunately, the Wimpy handled well on one engine.

Several squadrons of Wimpys had been formed before the war; with four .303 machine guns in the rear turret, a maximum bomb load of 4,500 pounds, the Wimpy was considered the RAF's most promising bomber and was thought to be an effective weapon with the range, speed and guns to deal firmly with any Nazi.

The Wimpy's criss-cross girder-like frame was termed 'geodesic' by its designer, 'boffin' Barnes Wallis[8] (who later developed the 'bouncing bomb' of Dam Busters fame). This was covered in stiff dope-covered fabric, allowing the Wimpy to take enormous punishment and return with the crew more or less intact, and was relatively easily repaired. Astonishing photographs exist of Wimpys after a raid with large chunks of their fuselage missing, or without large swathes of burned-off fabric; the stark framework makes the aircraft look peculiarly strong yet fragile. Cusack's description of Beede viewing his crew's aerodrome through the holes in their Wimpy's fuselage is not unique.

The Wimpy's flying characteristics were unusual if not slightly bizarre (like standing in the middle of a bendy-bus), the geodesic framework moving with the winds. This took a little getting used to, particularly if the aircraft turned sharply as you were waddling down the walkway. The 'wings and tails seemed to have a strong desire to flap, controls tended to wander off of their own accord in the cockpit …'[9]

The Wimpy was the first aircraft to bomb Germany and the first to drop the 4,000 pound blockbuster 'cookie' blast-bomb, (while Beede was en-route to Halifax). Three months later the Wimpy became the homely, heroic face of Bomber Command when 'F for Freddie', pilot Charles 'Percy' Pickard and RAF personnel (various) starred in the enormously popular propaganda film 'Target for Tonight'. By the third year of the war Wimpys were being phased out of the front line. The Wimpy had remained on night ops far longer than it should have because the RAF didn't have enough new aircraft; the Short Stirling and the Avro Manchester both carried more bombs further. Due to the shortage of aircraft and the plethora of jobs requiring aircraft, Wimpys remained useful everywhere from training, controlling raids via radar, to parachutist-training and glider-tug, to Coastal Command spotting U-Boats using the very successful Leigh light coupled with its own radar. In 1942, Wimpys bluffed the Italian fleet away from the remains of Operation Pedestal's crucial convoy to Malta with a few parachute flares and bombs – and well-timed plain language radio messages.[10]

The bombing war was a long period of attrition and adjustment to new science and new developments. During 1942 'area bombing' came to be perceived as the only way to combat the Nazis at this time, and became the norm for Bomber Command. The Air Ministry wrote that 'the primary object of your operations should now be focussed on the morale of the enemy civilian population and, in particular, of the industrial workers'.[11]

Area bombing, while clearly dreadful, was fired by many understandable emotions, especially when you consider that:

In the summer of 1942 four hundred million people in Europe lay under the yoke of German rule. The empire of Adolf Hitler, then at its greatest extent, stretched from the Mediterranean to the Arctic, from the English Channel to the Black Sea and almost to the Caspian … in the ancient capitals of Europe – in Athens, Rome and Vienna, in Paris and Prague, Oslo and Warsaw – all other voices were drowned by the voice of Nazi Germany.[12]

John Bede Cusack was never a part of Bomber Command's area bombing campaign. Instead, he joined 2 Group in August 1942.

By then, 2 Group had fought an array of battles from England, Africa and the Med with the Bristol Blenheim, an aircraft billed before the war as 'the bomber which was faster than a fighter'. Combat conditions quickly revealed inadequacies in range, speed, and defensive and offensive armament. However, the Blenheim continued to be used on ops because there was simply no ready replacement. 2 Group's crews were to suffer greatly;

> One disadvantage that Bomber Command had to struggle with for most of the war was the multiplicity of aircraft types that it had to operate at any one period and the high proportion of those types that were always obsolete and unsuitable but which had to be employed until better types became available.[13]

It was now time for 2 Group to replace the Blenheim. Mosquitos would have been ideal, however production was only just beginning and there weren't enough to go around. The Air Ministry only issued a specification to replace the Blenheim in 1940, manifestly insufficient time to develop a replacement aircraft which was urgently needed before the specification was written.

Almost unbelievably, the Air Ministry proffered the Armstrong Whitworth Albemarle to 2 Group; no other Group would have even looked at the Albemarle, yet 2 Group took the time and trouble to test it out, losing a pilot and an aircraft in the process. Upon testing, if not viewing, the Albemarle was rejected as thoroughly unsuitable.

2 Group appear to have been the underdog; during the first quarter of 1942, 'the very existence of [2] Group [had been] considered and finally it was decided to maintain it for the day when it would afford close support for the Army in the essential invasion of Europe'.[14]

Now with legendary Air-Vice Marshal Basil Embry as Air Officer Commanding, 2 Group now left Bomber Command – and its area bombing policy – on June 1, 1942. Now, as part of the Second Tactical Air Force, 2 Group's brief was to provide diversions in support of the main bombing force, army support, attacks on merchant shipping;

precision attacks with copious fighter support termed 'Circuses', and night intruder operations to destroy Luftwaffe night-fighters either on the ground, as they were landing, or adjacent to their aerodrome.

By August 1942 the tide of the war was turning, although it would clearly be a lengthy struggle. There was the 'raid in force' on Dieppe, the battle for Leningrad had started and that of Stalingrad about to begin; the Battle of Midway, one of the key battles of World War Two, had been won by the Americans. Back in England, 2 Group began to develop, adding new squadrons and replacing the Blenheim with a scant few Mosquitos, the Boston III, and the Lockheed Ventura.

Lockheed's Model 18 Lodestar civil airliner had been converted to a bomber and was ordered by the Air Ministry woefully late, in 1940. The Ventura was certainly an improvement over the Blenheim, however the Vent was a stop-gap light bomber entering a conflict for which it was not properly designed. In short, it was the worst of 2 Group's new aircraft. Regarded as a thirsty aircraft with leaky petrol tanks, cantankerous vacuum pumps, poor manoeuvrability and short range; to top it off, no navigator was happy with their position.

Air-cooled 2000 hp radial engines shoved rather large 'paddle-bladed' propellers around, giving the Vent a unique, turbulent sound when airborne. With a cruising speed of just under 270 mph at 9,500 feet and a maximum of 290 mph at 16,000 feet, the Vent was a little faster than the Blenheim's maximum, although the Vent's cruising speed (on weak mixture) was some 50 mph faster. Its top height was just under 25,000 feet.

Because of their civilian-based design the interior was quite large, but could not accommodate more than 2500 pounds of bombs, usually four 250-pounders and three 500-pounders. With a range of around 900 miles (half that of the Wimpy), the Vent was always going to be used on targets relatively close to England.

The pilot sat next to the navigator, who also doubled as bomb aimer; behind them sat the wireless operator/ forward air gunner. The mid-upper gunner manned a turret which could fire, as Cusack says, 360 degrees and still not blow off the rudders on the twin tail. The two fixed electrically fired .5 guns at the front and three pairs of .303s were no match for the faster, cannon-equipped fighters of the Luftwaffe.

One feels for the erks as one gazes at the short gap between the Ventura's belly and the ground; it is easy to imagine their curses as they struggled to load the 500 pounders. Although some photographs show a tidy little winch, these seemed to be in short supply, resulting in use of the Mark One Back: an erk would get on his hands and knees while two others would heave a bomb onto his back, then the first erk would stagger up, the others manhandling the heavy, awkward thing into the aircraft, struggling to hold it in position while attaching it to the bomb rack.

The Vent handled well enough, as a civil airliner should, although the Boston III was considerably swifter and more manoeuvrable. At low level the Vent flew at 190 mph across the sea and climbed, at best, at 170 mph, considerably slower than 2 Group's next best new aircraft, the Boston; dictating ops by the Vents' slower speed meant their close escort was not the fast Spitfire IXs, which were a match for the current FW 190s, but the slower Spitfire Vb's.

However, it was either the Ventura, or nothing. Bostons and B25 Mitchells had also been ordered for 2 Group as a similar stop-gap measure as, once again, there were only so many aircraft to go around.

Following a week's gunnery practice at Stormy Downs, Cusack joined 464 Squadron three weeks after it had formed on 1st September. 464 was part of 140 Wing, which included 487 (NZ) and 21 (RAF). Although 'by late September 1942, further questions were asked as to the aircraft's suitability for employment as a bomber ...',[15] on the 8th October ten Venturas had arrived at 464 and nine at 487, and training for low-level daylight ops was under way. 21 Squadron, with 22 Vents, found their training for night intruder ops dropped by November.

This agglomeration of varied aircraft prevented 2 Group from operating effectively as a unified force on any one specific raid – as Operation Oyster proved. Consequently, decisions had to be made about how to best utilise the aircraft they had, and (again) what role currently best suited 2 Group.

As 464 converted to two-man Mosquitos, Cusack's services were no longer required. In the wider world, Mussolini was thrown in jail; Sicily was completely occupied by the Allies; the bombing of the Romanian oilfields at Ploesti resulted in the loss of 53 B24s and the bombing of Schweinfurt lost 60 B17s; Bomber Command attacked Peenemunde, the V1 and V2 experimental site with 560 aircraft, losing 40; shortly afterwards Italy capitulated but remained occupied by the Nazis.

Joining No. 107 Squadron the following month after completing 19 ops, Beede's third aircraft (and Cusack's second) was now a veteran of 2 Group and looked, at first glance, a little like the Ventura. The first bomber with a retractable tricycle undercarriage, the Douglas Boston III's low-altitude airspeed was a little over 300 mph, dropping with altitude. Although the Boston had a 25,000 foot ceiling, it struggled to make 270 mph at 14,000 feet. Still, with twice the power of the Blenheim it was faster and carried more bombs (2000 pounds), had a similar range to the Vent and also handled well on one engine.

As with many aircraft of this period, the Boston possessed idiosyncrasies which proved problematic; the tricycle undercarriage required practice, as did start-up procedures and take-off. Cusack mentions the Boston's lack of move-around (and escape) space and the inability of anyone to take over the controls in the event of pilot injury; hardly reassuring for crews going into action at low level against lively German flak.

With four fixed .303 guns in the nose, two .303 guns in a dorsal turret (i.e., further down the aircraft's back) two fixed .303 guns in the bomb-aimer's section, and a ventral .303 gun (i.e., firing backwards under the belly), the Boston arrived at a time when combat expectations had been considerably raised.

Cusack is not the first to question the wisdom of using the Boston; however, 'it filled the gap between Blenheims and Mosquito VI's, [and] to crews who had been operating or training on Blenheims, the Boston III was a very pleasant surprise'. Wing Commander Pelly-Fry commented: 'Extremely comfortable and beautiful to fly. It bred self confidence and you could fly it as easily as a Tiger Moth … and perhaps most important of all for a twin-engined bomber, it was extremely manoeuvrable.'[16]

Initial Boston operations were maritime, followed by 'Circus' type day ops bombing airfields, ports, power stations and factories with the intent of bringing up the Luftwaffe to play with their Spitfire IX fighter escort. Significant Boston raids included an attack on the Poissy Matford factory, the raid on Dieppe on 19 August 1942, and Operation Oyster at the Philips Radio works in December, as well as numerous raids on V-1 sites (referred to as 'installations', 'works' or 'No-Ball' in many an airman's logbook). Roles were found for the Boston in the Middle East and they proved extremely effective on the Russian front; on D-Day Bostons were to be found laying smokescreens in support of the landing craft.

Cusack left 107 Squadron in January 1944, during the preliminary stages of air operations to support the Allied invasion of Europe,

'Overlord'. He returned to duty at Swanton Morley, as the preparatory stage to support Overlord began in March 1944 and was shortly afterwards transferred to 98 Squadron at Dunsfold, now with 31 ops under his belt. The battle of Monte Cassino was still under way as the Allies landed in Italy, at Anzio and Nettuno; the siege of Leningrad was lifted.

Cusack's last aircraft was the B25, justly famous for the first bombing attack on the Japanese mainland in February 1942, barely two months after the Japanese attack on Pearl Harbor; the Doolittle Raid. Sixteen converted B25B Mitchells were launched from the aircraft carrier USS *Hornet* to bomb Tokyo, most crews landing in China to travel back to the US. This raid sealed the fate of the Japanese invasion of the Pacific because it led directly to their approval of plans centring on Midway. The B25H, a later variant, holds the distinction of being the first aircraft to sink a destroyer using only its guns; however, Cusack flew in the B25J variant, the Mitchell II.

The twin-ruddered tricycle-geared B25 also had a move-around (and escape) space problem. However, behind the pilot, copilot and bomb-aimer, and adjacent to the gunners, was nearly half an inch of helpful armour plate. With a low-altitude airspeed of about 300 mph, with a 25,000 foot ceiling, the Mitchell also had the same range as the Vent, but carried more bombs (4000 pounds) and handled well on one engine.

The Mitchell II had a .303 gun in a ball-and-socket mount in the nose with 600 rounds, which could be aimed and fired by the bomb-aimer. About mid-way down the fuselage, just behind the bomb-bay, was a retractable turret with two .5 guns with 350 rounds each which could be aimed by a kneeling gunner through a periscopic sight. Just behind that was top power-operated turret with two .5 guns with 400 rounds each. The B25J could fight back more effectively than either the Boston or the Vent; a much more encouraging weapon to take to war against the Nazis.

By the end of April, with 36 ops, Cusack transferred to 180 Squadron, still with his Wing Commander, still on Mitchells, where he completed his two tours; his final op was from half-past midnight until three am on D-Day, June 6, attacking a crossroads south-east of Le Havre.

Although Beede finishes his third tour on the Mitchell, it is important to remember that Cusack did not start ops in 12 Squadron, but with 464 on Vents. Beede's final tally of ops was 65, technically a third tour. However, Cusack actually completed his second tour with 53 ops, and, unlike his creation Beede, finished his obligation as a gunnery instructor … in the Wimpy Mark III at Catfoss.

Training establishments such as Catfoss, as well as Heavy Conversion Units, were easily recognised from the air by the significant number of adjacent crashed and burned-out aircraft. Aircraft used in gunnery training tended be operational survivors, therefore old and cantankerous and often downright dangerous. It was not entirely uncommon to see the remains of two aircraft welded together and expected, by the CO, to fly normally. Under these circumstances we can better understand the author's desire to write his character out of what he might have regarded as a hazardous, thankless, necessity.

Operationally, as with the majority of those involved, John Cusack's contribution to the war effort was of course quite minor; to pretend otherwise would be mendacious. However, his greater contribution is to Australian literature and our personal understanding of the nature of war. Quite apart from his remarkable survival of two full tours, spread over four squadrons, particularly in such trying circumstances, he was lucky to survive his final tour as an instructor, so it is to his considerable credit that he could then write such a unique memoir as *They Hosed Them Out*.

Robert Brokenmouth

GLOSSARY

The Adj: adjutant; the superior officer's assistant – handles communications and orders, correspondence. Like a military secretary or personal assistant.

AG: Air Gunner.

ASR: Air Sea Rescue. Small ships which rescued aircrew from the waters around Britain.

ATS: Air Traffic Service (i.e., Air Traffic Control).

Australia House: On the Strand, handled all Australian service personnel.

AVM: Air Vice-Marshall.

Batman: Servant to officers, usually shared between several.

Bods: service personnel (from 'warm bodies').

Boffins: backroom experts.

Boomerang Club: excellent Australians-only service club on the ground floor at the rear of Australia House.

Boston: the Douglas Boston III, an American RAF twin-engined bomber. The Havoc was the American variant.

Bought it: killed (Americans used to say 'bought the farm'; see Chuck Yeager and Leo Janos, *Yeager: An Autobiography*, Century Hutchinson, 1986, p. 28).

Buckleys: 'Buckley's (chance)'. A forlorn hope: Australian: from c. 1875.

Chief, Chiefy: Chief Mechanic.

Circus: RAF term; 'to harass the enemy … by bombing and to destroy enemy aircraft in the air …' or on the ground and to harass enemy aerodromes.

CO: Commanding Officer.

Combats: attacks from fighters, attacks between fighters and other aircraft.

Dicing: flying on operations. From 'dicing with death'.

Dirty Dick's: a somewhat contraband-y cafe in London.

DFC: Distinguished Flying Cross, awarded to officers.

DFM: Distinguished Flying Medal, awarded to non-commissioned officers.

Dingo: Australian slang; one who is reluctant to contribute to the group.

Do: an operational sortie.

Drongo: Australian slang, an idiot or fool.

EATS: Empire Air Training Scheme, initial training of aircrew in colonies such as Canada or Australia.

Erks: RAF ground crew.

Fiddly: Australian for a pound note (i.e., as a bribe).

FIDO: Fog Intensive Dispersal Operation. Pipes pumped with oil lit at strategic points to 'burn off' fog on a runway.

Flak: Anti-aircraft fire. Cannon.

Flight: place of assembly for aircrew, short for Flight Dispersal.

Focke Wulf; Focke Wulf 190: German single-engined fighter made by Focke and designed by the delightfully named Kurt Tank.

Geordie: someone, usually a man, from the north-east of England, usually near Newcastle-upon-Tyne. Their accents (and other things) are unique.

Gen: top rate. Also; information, or knowledgeable (for example, a 'gen crew').

Get the chop: shot down in flames (or, more commonly, killed in action).

Gong: a flying decoration, a medal.

Groupy: Group-Commander, commanding officer of a station.

Halifax, Hally or Hallibag: RAF four-engined bomber.

Hampden: early RAF twin-engined bomber.

ITS: Initial Training School.

Kiwi Squadron: 487 Squadron, one of six New Zealand squadrons in the RAF.

Kodak House: On Kingsway, RAAF Headquarters in England.

KRs: King's Regulations – summary of RAF law.

LAC: Leading Aircraftman.

Lancaster: RAF four-engined bomber.

Land Army: Women who worked on the land, helping farmers, breeders etc.

Line-shooting or Line-slinging: boasting.

LMF: Lack of Moral Fibre. RAF code for cowardice or a victim of battle fatigue. Still a controversial subject.

mea culpa: Latin for 'through my fault'.

Messerschmitt 109: German single-engined fighter.

Met, Met boys: Meteorological staff, Meteorological Officer.

Mitchell: Douglas B-25, RAF twin-engined bomber.

Mossie: De Havilland Mosquito, RAF twin-engined bomber which flew fast and high.

MP: Military Policeman.

MO: Medical Officer.

Nav: navigator (formerly observer).

Night Fighter: (1) a fighter that flies at night; (2) a prostitute.

NCO: Non-Commissioned Officer (a sergeant).

Ned Kelly: well-known Australian bushranger.

Operations, Ops: bombing sorties.

OTU: Operational Training Unit.

Pathfinders: New bomber group which marked targets with precision.

Popsie: a young, attractive woman. From poppet, nursery slang for youngster.

Pot: A Brisbane or Melbourne term for a glass of beer (10 fl oz or 285 mL). The same glass is a middy or half-pint in Sydney, Canberra and Perth, a schooner in Adelaide, a handle in Darwin and a ten in Hobart.

PR: Photo Reconnaissance.

PTI: Physical Training Instructor.

Quid: Australian slang for a pound note.

RTO: Rail Transport Officer.

Second Dickey: co-pilot.

Short Arm Inspection: medical inspection of the privates.

Six O'Clock Swill: The licensing laws in Australia allowed pubs to be open only between 5 and 6 pm, which meant that everyone attempted to cram an evening's drinking into a very short space of time. Women were segregated from the front bar at this time.

SL: Squadron Leader.

Smooey: The vernacular for either women's genitalia or the women themselves, similar to the American term 'pussy'. Possibly from 'smoot': a narrow passage (Lincolnshire, arch).

Snappers: enemy fighters.

Sprog: 'n. A recruit: RAF: since c. 1930; by c. 1939 also – via the Fleet Air Arm – used occ. by the Navy … Origin obscure and debatable ... In the Navy the term means an infant.' Partridge, op. cit.

Stirling: RAF four-engined bomber.

Sunderland: RAF four-engined long range flying-boat/ bomber used by Coastal Command for Air Sea Rescue and anti-U-Boat work.

TAF: Tactical Air Force, usually referring to the Second Tactical Air Force, a bomber and fighter group designed to get the Luftwaffe up into the air to be destroyed prior to D-Day, the Allied invasion of Europe.

Tannoy: public address system.

TOT: Time scheduled to arrive On Target.

Trips: ops.

Twirp: Beede's original definition is 'a spiteful person', an interesting variant meaning distinctly different from that of someone weak-minded and silly.

U/S: Unserviceable; also, useless.

Ventura: RAF twin-engined bomber.

VC: Victoria Cross, the highest award for gallantry that Britain can bestow.

Wellington (Wimpy): Vickers Wellington, early RAF twin-engined bomber.

WAAF: Women's Auxiliary Air Force (referred to as Waffs, and their places of residence, Wafferies).

WAG: Wireless Air Gunner.

Whitley: early RAF twin-engined bomber.

Wingco: Wing Commander.

Winter's: Australian Initial Training School station.

W/O: Warrant Officer; between a non-commissioned officer and a commissioned officer, a W/O holds their office by warrant.

WOP: Wireless Operator.

WRNS: Women's Royal Naval Service (who were referred to as Wrens, and their places of residence, Wrenneries).

In every branch of military service, and increasingly in modern work-places, there develops a kind of 'masonic dialect'. For further elucidation, see Eric Partridge, *A Dictionary of RAF Slang*, Michael Joseph, 1945 (and recently republished by Pavilion), and Bernard and Jean Beadle, *War Speak. A Collection of Slang and other words used in the RAF during the 1939–45 War*.

NOTES

Dedication page

Randall Jarrell was an American poet who served in the USAAF. His first two books were *Blood for a Stranger* (Harcourt, 1942) and *Little Friend, Little Friend* (Dial, 1945).

Introduction

1   For more on the ABS, see pp. 129–168, Jack Beasley, *Red Letter Days: Notes from Inside an Era*, Australasian Book Society, 1979. Although the ABS was formed with a broad platform, it has been said that it would have been more successful (with greater longevity) without its public Communist Party of Australia influence. The ABS never had much over 3000 members.

2   Weary Dunlop is too well-known to footnote, however Kristen Alexander, *Clive Caldwell, Air Ace* is definitive and well worth a read.

Chapter One

1   The ship was the *Ceramic*, sailing in Fast Convoy HX.201 from Halifax on 2 August 1942, arriving apparently intact at Liverpool on 14 August 1942. See www.convoyweb.org.uk/hx/index.html or www.warsailors. com. While some ex-servicemen have told me they never heard the word 'fuck' used during WW2, Campbell Muirhead's *Diary of a Bomb Aimer*, Spellmount, 1987 (being an actual 1944 diary) makes it clear that it was a word of very common usage. While some maintain 'fugg' is a contraction of 'fucking bugger', most of the fuggs here imply, by their context, self-censorship on the part of a publisher not willing to raise further ire in a more conservative society.

2   U-Boats, German submarines, sunk hundreds of Allied vessels in the North Atlantic; the U-Boat crews called June 1940 – February 1941 'the happy time', and January – June 1942 'the second happy time'. See, for example, *Convoy, War For the Atlantic* (DVD), Darlow Smithson Productions and Cream Productions, Special Broadcasting Service Corporation, 2010. The first hint that *They Hosed Them Out* cannot be regarded as strictly factual comes as one realises that there were no U-Boats in the Caribbean in April 1941; only after 7 December 1941, when Germany declared war on the USA. Joseph Goebbels was the Nazi 'Minister for Propaganda and Enlightenment'.

3   Plimsoll. The plimsoll line, invented by Samuel Plimsoll, is the waterline, positioned amidships, showing the legal limit that that ship could be loaded for specific water types and temperatures. Watersiders were the men who used to be called 'wharfies' who loaded and unloaded ships.

4   Fo'c'sle. Navy term for forecastle, an interior of the ship toward the bow.

5   Observer. In April 1942 the role of observer (the identification badge sported an 'O' with a wing on the right side – a flying 'O' or 'flying arse-hole') was split into two separate roles, Navigator (flying 'N') and Air Bomber (i.e., bomb aimer – flying 'AB').

6   A classic institutional procedure found in schools and the military; with insufficient bods to make up the correct number, the officer selects random hapless bods and informs them that they have 'volunteered'.

Chapter Two

1   Hydrophone. A passive listening device used by submarines, it converts acoustic energy into electrical energy.

2   Guns. Oerlikons, Swiss 20 mm cannon, designed to be operated and maintained by non-gunners. Bofors is the Swedish company who designed the extensively used anti-aircraft 40 mm autocannon.

3   Davits. Devices used to lower lifeboats, rather like long steel arms.

4   For details on the actual losses, see www.warsailors.com; search for convoy HX.201.

5   Twenty thousand pounds would, in 2012, be worth about half a million UK pounds.

6   Nautical term also applied to aircraft. 'Starboard' means 'right', 'port' means 'left'. The Kurier, FW-200 or Focke Wulf Kondor, was the Luftwaffe's only operational four-engined bomber. Based at Bordeaux, it could fly almost 600 miles out into the Atlantic, also liaising with U-boat 'wolf packs'. See Martin Middlebrook, *Convoy*, William Morrow, 1976.

7   A common mistake although, ironically, many European boys would not have made it as many had extensive shrapnel collections.

8   Aldis lamp. A large, shuttered lamp which enabled ships to communicate visually via Morse code.

Chapter Three

1   Although this is the equivalent of thirty-four to forty-three thousand pounds today, the amounts would also represent between four and six times the average yearly wage of the day, about two hundred and seventy pounds, which would be equivalent to seven thousand, seven hundred and fifty pounds today. Clearly, the pound bought more at the time, or 'went further', than the dollar does today.

2   Winter's ITS was the first step in the Empire Air Training Scheme. See John McCarthy, *A Last Call of Empire. Australian Aircrew, Britain And The Empire Air Training Scheme*, Australian War Memorial, 1988.

3   Obsolete before they were ordered, the three-man Fairey Battles were slow and inadequate as a fighter or bomber and were relegated to a training role only after providing – or causing – several VCs, usually to the pilot of the aircraft leading the charge ... see Flight Lieutenant William Simpson, *One of Our Pilots is Safe*, Hamish Hamilton, 1942. The Vickers machine gun was a water-cooled, reliable .303 machine gun heavy enough to need several men to carry it, in service with the British Army from 1912 to 1968. The .303 Cusack refers to is a Lee-Enfield.

4   Cusack originally varies Dagworth's name between 'Dagworth' and 'Dagworthy', however, he was introduced as 'Dagworth' so he can stay that way. Cusack knew this name would have raised a smile in Australia: a 'dag' is Australian slang for a bit of excrement clinging to the rear wool of a sheep so also meant a 'shitty hanger-on'.

5   Mix-up. Meaning 'fight' or 'brawl', not 'confusion'.
6   Navvying: building a road or rail-line. Boxing and fighting bouts were popular entertainments around Australia, not least for the gambling opportunities.
7   Every seaside town in England was fortified in this way, with similar results and similar sticky ends.
8   Bullsh. Cusack is referring to the various formalities of military life from saluting to guard duty. In *Down and Out in Paris and London* (Gollancz, 1933), towards the end of Chapter 22, George Orwell sums up a contemporary view of the ruling class: 'I believe that this instinct to perpetuate useless work is, at bottom, simply fear of the mob. The mob (the thought runs) are such low animals that they would be dangerous if they had leisure; it is safer to keep them too busy to think.' Orwell has more to say on this subject, and is a recurrent theme for Cusack.
9   Untaped. All windows were to be taped with a cross to minimise blast damage caused by flying splinters.
10 Lord Haw Haw was the German radio announcer, Irish Nazi sympathiser William Joyce. Cusack is mimicking his bizarre, cold, upper-class voice.
11 Shouts. Australian term for 'a round of drinks'.
12 Further reading: Brown and Barrett, *Knowledge of Evil: Child Prostitution and Child Sexual Abuse in Twentieth-Century England*, Willan Publishing, 2002.

Chapter Four

1   The Lady Ryder Hospitality Scheme provided accommodation for airmen. Many families opened their homes to airmen on leave.
2   See Constantine Fitzgibbon: *The Blitz*, Macdonald, 1957; reprinted in 2010 by Faber and Faber.
3   The Boomerang Club was on the ground floor of Australia House (which was, confusingly, referred to as Boomerang House), which resided in Australia Square on The Strand. The Boomerang Club housed a tailor and a barber's, but as the tailor had a dodgy reputation not everyone used him (including the author); a branch of the Commonwealth Bank was also nearby, as were the many – usually full – hotels.
4   Policemen's torches were dimmed by a black cover allowing only a thin strip of light.
5   Illustrations of typical scenes can be seen in Henry Moore, *Shelter Sketch-Book*, British Museum, 1988; or Maurice Gorman, *Londoners*, Percival Marshall, 1951.

Chapter Five

1   Cusack's logbook describes Stormy Downs, 7 Air Gunnery School.
2   Double British Summer Time has given historians many headaches.
3   Borne out by Cusack's logbook, this is a scathing comment for late 1942 (as opposed to the book's fictional late 1941). Cusack's gunnery practice was in Whitleys and Boulton-Paul Defiants, and an intriguing line on 27 September 1942 reads 'Lysander washed out'. Looking a little like a Hurricane with a drag-inducing rear turret, the Boulton-Paul Defiant's improbable design screamed obsolescence; the Westland Lysander was a useful Army co-operation aircraft which was superb for clandestine drops and pick-ups behind enemy lines. Neither aircraft were suited for outright combat, hence their training roles. There are few Defiant survivors;

one account may be found in Chapter Five, 'Les Smith', in *Flak*, Michael Veitch, Macmillan, 2006. Compare Cusack's gunnery training with that of Mike Henry's *Air Gunner*, GT Foulis, 1964.

Chapter Six

1 England's varying dialects confuse the English, never mind Colonials. British Rail announcements sounded, as Anthony Buckridge put it, 'as if the announcer was speaking whilst eating a packet of crisps'.
2 From Cusack's descriptions of Wellington missions and losses, many have assumed he is describing 12 Squadron (in No. 1 Group), then based at RAF Binbrook and known as 'the chop squadron' because of their dreadful losses in the 1940 Battle of France. Certainly there are many similarities between 12 Squadron's operational record and Cusack's account, which argue that he later referred to a cobber's log-book and recollections. I partly agree, but suspect much of what Cusack writes in Part Two is also an amalgam of his own experiences, aircrew talk and hearsay. See Flying Officer T. Mason, *Leads the Field: The History of No. 12 Squadron*, [The Squadron], 1960, and Chaz Bowyer, *Wellington at War*, Ian Allan, 1982.
3 Designed by Major Nissen for temporary troop accommodation in 1916. Most Nissen huts on ex-RAF 'dromes have decayed; some have been redesigned into family homes. An igloo hut is a smaller version.
4 Dickey pilot. Eric Partridge, *A Dictionary of Slang and Unconventional English*; Routledge and Kegan Paul, 1961; 'A pilot flying with an experienced pilot for instructional purposes, RAF; since c. 1930. He occupied the dickey seat.' Either Snowden or Cusack is confusing the seat with Williams' role of co-pilot, which was later altered to flight engineer to avoid unnecessary training of pilots; on the other hand, each station used slang variants unique to itself.
5 This appears to have been the case in 12 Squadron around October-November 1941. Crews did not always fly in the same 'kite', but even so this is a chilling statistic.
6 RAF slang for the Army was either 'brown types' or 'brown jobs'; both are also slang for excreta. This is partly why Army types were also referred to as 'pongoes'.

Chapter Seven

1 Most crews loathed mine-laying and leaflet ops; certainly many bundles were dropped unopened.
2 C.F. Andrews and E.B. Morgan, *Vickers Aircraft Since 1908*, Putnam, 1995 gives the Wellington a service ceiling of 18,000 feet; presumably when not burdened with bombs and a full load of petrol. See Appendix Three.
3 Four thousand pounds is equivalent to eighteen hundred kilograms.
4 Hence the old joke in bomber messes; 'Can I have your eggs if you don't come back?', as seen in the 1957 film *The Dam Busters*.
5 'The casualty rate in Bomber Command was the heaviest of any British service in the Second World War ... the average casualty rate for the year of 1943 was 3.6% of all aircraft that took off for operations ... from these figures it can be calculated that 33% of the crews which flew in 1943 could survive their first tour and only 16% would survive both first and second tours.' From *The Battle of Hamburg: Allied Bomber Forces Against a German City in 1943*, by Martin Middlebrook, Allan Lane, 1980 (p. 39).

Chapter Eight

1   The first thousand-bomber raid was on 30/31 May 1942 against Cologne; see *The Thousand Plan. The Story of the First Thousand Bomber Raid on Cologne* by Ralph Barker, Chatto and Windus, 1965.

2   Schemozzle. Confusion, possibly from the Yiddish word *shlimazl*: misfortune.

3   Also flying on this raid were the 'heavy' bombers or 'heavies'; the new Lancaster, its widow-making precursor the Manchester, and the older Stirlings and Hudsons.

4   This sequence, when compared to Cusack's earlier prescription to evade enemy aircraft where the enemy aircraft is on the starboard side and the pilot is ordered to 'Turn starboard, go!', is contradictory. The idea is to turn toward the attacker and fly past him, minimising the period of contact rather than flying in the same direction as the attacker, which gives the attacker more potential contact and opportunity to destroy your aircraft.

5   1,046 aircraft took off on 30 May. Although 41 aircraft were lost (7 crashing with all or almost all of the crew killed or wounded), this loss rate of 3.9% was acceptably low and, for many reasons, then and now, the first Thousand Bomber Raid was a success. However, 12 Squadron suffered the most casualties on this raid; of the 28 which took off (a squadron record) four aircraft and crews were lost (14%) so, coupled with Cusack's description, it seems clear that he based his account on that of someone on 12 Squadron at the time. 'The Committee of Adjustment' were often taken from existing crews. One moving account is found in Muirhead, (op. cit., pp. 91–93).

Chapter Nine

1   The RAF clock system, as Cusack describes it, was initially used by RFC artillery spotters in WW1, and was in use by Fighter Command for years before it was adopted by Bomber Command.

2   Epidiascope: or opaque projector, a device similar to a slide projector. Cusack uses a different term each time he describes the same device.

3   Cusack's chronology certainly serves his story; here, the Thousand Raid of 30/31 May 1942 occurs a full year before the Nazi's invasion of Russia – on 22 June 1941.

4   No 4 Group was then based at Linton-on-Ouse, Yorkshire, operating Halifaxes and Whitleys; all Group HQs operated bomber aircraft.

Chapter Ten

1   These facilities sound like relics from peace-time, if not WW1.

2   A shag is a bird, often to be found perched on a rock on a cold miserable coast. Expressively, 'a shag' is also English slang for 'a fuck'.

3   Presumably the Johnny Walker Red label (Churchill's favourite). At the time there was also Johnny Walker Swing or Johnny Walker Black; the Black was reserved for higher-ranking officers. 'Three-quarters full' means the stewards would be able to claim they'd accidentally broken an already-opened bottle.

4   'You may be a bit stiff'; '… -4. Penniless: Australian: C. 20 Ex stiff, n., 7, q.v. – 5 ? hence, unlucky; mostly Australian and New Zealand, from c. 1910.' – Partridge, op. cit. Now-archaic Australian slang.

5   LMF. See Edgar Jones, 'LMF: The Use of Psychiatric Stigma in the Royal Air Force during the Second World War', *Journal of Military History*,

Volume 70, Number 2, April 2006, pp. 439–458; or Allan Douglas English, *The Cream of the Crop: Canadian Aircrew, 1939–1945*, McGill-Queen's University Press, 1996 (chapter 6).

6 Patrick Bishop in *Bomber Boys: Fighting Back 1940–1945*, Harper, 2007, p. 80, quotes Michael Wood in 106 Squadron at about this time; 'there was a story going around that the accounts related by one of our crews was suspect and did not tie up with the accounts of the target area put forward by the rest of the squadron. The CO became suspicious and arranged to plot the course of the aircraft in question. From the information gathered, it transpired that the aircraft was flying up and down the North Sea dropping their bombs in the drink and, after the necessary time lapse, flying back to base.' Bishop adds, 'Wood never verified the story. But the fact that it was doing the rounds was indicative of the low mood.'

Chapter Eleven

1 Premonition. The autobiographies of Bomber Command veterans are filled with individuals who experience a convincing foreknowledge of disaster. Sometimes this foreknowledge is averted, more often the individual's aircraft fails to return. For example Patrick Bishop, (op. cit., Chapter 12: The Chop).

2 'somewhere in England': all place-name signs had been removed to hamper the enemy, so radio broadcasts of military activity always took place 'somewhere in England'; this became a wry joke.

3 Packing them. Packing the shits, i.e., so terrified you can barely hold your shit in. Australian slang.

Chapter Twelve

1 Cookies, the most common of the High Capacity blast bombs, were introduced in the spring of 1941.

2 This list of towns and cities were certainly bombed by 12 Squadron during the latter part of 1941 and early 1942. (Mason, op. cit.).

3 Goering's boast was made as he addressed the Luftwaffe in September 1939, 'No enemy bomber can reach the Ruhr. If one reaches the Ruhr, my name is not Goering. You may call me Meyer'. This lead to many German underground jokes featuring 'Meyer'. See Nicholas Fleming, August 1939: The Last Days of Peace, Peter Davies, 1979.

4 'The vast majority of those who were removed from flying duties were stated to be suffering from 'neurosis' rather than cowardice. The proportion was roughly eight to one ... the punishment for LMF was shame. Officers and NCOs alike were remustered as Aircraftsman Second Class, the lowest rank.' (Bishop, op. cit., pp. 249 – 250)' Despite what Cusack says, officers were certainly charged with LMF. As individual station commanders often approached the problem differently, I suspect Cusack and/or his informant simply experienced a CO who favoured officers as Cusack describes, and took the CO to represent the entire RAF.

Chapter Thirteen

1 It would have been most unusual for a single aircraft to receive more than one night-fighter attack at this time, so we must assume Cusack means that he would see up to six night fighter attacks per op. The Battle of the Atlantic was ongoing and ever-present, reaching a climax around March to May 1943.

2   There were no pyrotechnical flying drums known as 'scarecrows'. What the crews saw was other planes blowing up, often with a full bomb-load.
3   I./Nachtjagdgeschwader 2 handled long-range intruder attacks over England using a few flights of Bf 109s and a flight of Do17s. Although between October 1940 and October 1941 over 90 RAF aircraft were lost to intruder night-fighters, Hitler stopped these attacks because he didn't believe they were getting results. See Heinz Rokker, *Chronk I. Gruppe Nachtjagd-Geschwader 2 – I./NJG 2*, Heinz Nickel, 1997; or Simon Parry, *Intruders over Britain: The Luftwaffe Night Fighter Offensive 1940–1945*, Air Research, 1987. Parry demonstrates that only one Wimpy from 12 Squadron was shot down by an intruder (on 14 August 1941); also, the German's only large, well-planned intruder raid took place on 3/4 March, 1945 ('Operation Gisela').
4   Although we might find it hard to believe that such a large percentage of German bombs would be defective, Stephen Ambrose quotes a most fortuitous dud German bomb on p. 155 of *Pegasus Bridge. D-Day: The Daring British Airborne Raid*, Pocket Books, 2003, and James Dugan and Carroll Stewart, in *Ploesti* (Jonathan Cape, 1963, p. 67), remark that 'the Americans only had general-purpose bombs, and recent tests on a US proving-ground had determined the dismaying fact that 50% of the 1000 pound bombs failed to detonate and a quarter of the 500 pounders did not go off'.

Chapter Fourteen
1   Dicky. In the sense of 'dodgy', 'unreliable'.
2   It's also likely front gunners didn't survive bail-outs from a Wimpy because their escape hatch was placed in such a way that they'd have to dodge a spinning propeller while hurtling through space.
3   'Crothers' is probably the nearby Ely Hospital. There is a list of WW2 RAF Hospitals in Mary Mackie, *Sky Wards: A History of the Princess Mary's Royal Air Force Nursing Service*; see also Nicola Tyrer, *Sisters in Arms*, Weidenfeld and Nicolson, 2008.

Chapter Fifteen
1   The men being treated for burns are members of what was called 'The Guinea Pig Club'; the remarkable man who pioneered plastic surgery for severe burns was Archibald McIndoe. Hugh McLeave, *McIndoe: Plastic Surgeon*, Frederick Muller, 1961. For a first-hand account of what some burns victims experienced, see Simpson, op. cit.

Chapter Sixteen
1   12 Squadron moved to Wickenby in September 1942; their last Wellington op was 9/10 November. They then converted to Lancasters. A first tour in Bomber Command at this time was thirty ops (not including returns or 'scrubs'). Aircrew then went to instruct at a training unit, returning to a squadron for a second tour of twenty ops; after fifty ops, aircrew could not be asked to do further ops and were usually posted.
2   See Donald Bennett, *Pathfinder*, Frederick Muller, 1958.
3   The Pathfinders tour was initially sixty ops, with your previous ops counting towards it. A similar discussion, with a different outcome, occurs in John Bushby, *Gunner's Moon*, Ian Allan, 1972. The number of Pathfinder ops later settled to 45 with your previous ops, at least fifteen, counting towards it. The 45 ops counted as two tours as opposed to the

more usual two tours of 50. See both Harold J. Wright, *Pathfinders Light the Way*, McCann Publishing, 1983 and Ted Stocker, *A Pathfinder's War*, Grub Street, 2009.

4 5 Group HQ were based at RAF Mildenhall, Suffolk, operating Wellingtons. Cusack stated earlier that this incident occurred at 4 Group HQ.

Chapter Seventeen

1 Cusack is now drawing on his log-book; he flew with 464 Squadron from late 1942 to early 1943. Beltwell is actually Feltwell, which sounds like a ribald jest. 'Fugg 'em all' is also a popular and vernacular rendition of 'Bless 'em All'.

2 Six of the remaining nine of the original 32 gunners from Winters ITS were Beede, Smithy, Hally, Blondie, Bourke and Hedge. Clarke is not included in this list. The Lockheed Ventura was developed from the Hudson; both were originally passenger aircraft. See Appendix Three.

3 487 Squadron.

4 Cusack had two hours' gunnery practice at West Raynham on Boulton-Paul Defiants in November 1942; Cusack's description of the gunnery leader almost fits Frederick Barker, DFM, who had 12 kills, and was posted to the Middle East in 1942.

5 A stone is 14 pounds, or about 6.3 kilograms. Hence 10–5 means 'ten stone five pounds', etc.

6 A Sunday Punch is the best punch a boxer can throw, intended to either knock the opponent out or put him on the floor. Incidentally, the boxer Cusack fought may well be Leslie Feighan, who became National Australian Professional Featherweight Champion in 1943.

Chapter Eighteen

1 Operation Oyster was a famous precision raid, essential to 2 Group, and was Cusack's first operational flight. See Appendix One and Mark Lax and Leon Kane-Maguire, *The Gestapo Hunters, 464 Squadron RAF 1942–1945*, Banner Books, 1999.

2 'Stirring up the fighters'; i.e., get the defending fighters up in the air early, so that when the bombers arrived, the defending fighters have little fuel left and are obliged to land, preferably while the attacking bombers are doing their job. The TAF was used for several jobs, chief of which was the continued attrition of the Luftwaffe in preparation for D-Day.

3 The crashed aircraft was presumably SB-N, flown by Sergeant Stan Moss. Lax, op. cit., p. 42; 'The Venturas had unfortunately strayed south of their intended track, making landfall at Walcheren [where] as a result, they flew directly over Woesdrecht airfield where flak caused the next loss ...'

4 Lax, op. cit., p. 46; 'many Dutch homes in the near vicinity had also been hit, but as the raid had occurred on a Sunday, only about 25 civilian casualties had been recorded'. Of the 36 Venturas which attacked the target, 8 were lost (22%). By comparison, of the 34 Bostons which also attacked, four were lost (12%).

5 Cusack's figures here are incorrect, but I doubt he had much access to accurate sources.

6 No context for Maria was provided in the original manuscripts.

7   J-Johnny (i.e., SB-J) was not the Ventura Cusack flew in on this raid; that was SB-C, although he and his pilot, Flying Officer Phil Kerr, usually flew in SB-F.
8   This sort of low dive was infamously popular in London, seeping into the fiction of the day. See Gerald Kersh, *Night and the City*, Simon and Schuster, 1946.
9   Perhaps. See Stewart Wilson, *Almost Unknown. The Story of Squadron Leader Tony Gaze OAM, DFC, Australian Spitfire Ace and Racing Driver*, Chevron, 2009. With a tally of 12.5 kills over 488 combat operations, Gaze is the only Australian to win a DFC and two bars, was the first Squadron Leader of an Allied jet wing (flying the Gloster Meteor) and the first Australian to shoot down a jet (an ME 262).

Chapter Nineteen

1   'Buckley's (chance). A forlorn hope: Australian: from c. 1875. C.J. Dennis. 'Buckley was a declared outlaw whose chance of escape was made hopeless', Jice Doone. (there have been many other explanations)'. Partridge, op. cit.
2   This story of train-busting is not chronicled as such in either Lax or Chaz Bowyer's *2 Group RAF. A Complete History: 1936–1945*, Faber, 1974. By the end of 1942, the three squadrons equipped with Venturas which fought together, Numbers 21, 464 and 487, had lost a total of 13 Vents, an unacceptably high percentage (over 15%). 'It meant that the Ventura was not suited to continental daylight bombing operations, but before a new type would arrive, Ventura operations would have to change in the new year.' Lax, op. cit.

Chapter Twenty

1   From Lax, op. cit., p. 50; morale 'must have nose-dived once crews found out they were to be used as German fighter bait … Circus operations were designed to bring enemy fighters into action where they could be engaged by Allied fighters, and hopefully, destroyed in the air. It was up to the bombers to lure the German defenders into the air and survive their initial onslaught.'
2   It was a commonly-held belief that all yellow-nosed Focke Wulfs out of France were from the Hermann Goering squadron. Not true, but an interesting example of effective propaganda.
3   A long-held opinion amongst flyers and gunners from Fighter Command to Coastal Command, ever since the Battle of France was, 'give us cannon, not pop-guns'. Allied fighter pilots found that even though they were hitting the enemy with eight .303s, they weren't destroying the enemy as easily as the enemy, equipped with cannon since 1940, destroyed them. Some types of RAF aircraft were fitted with cannon; by 1944, for example, cannon-equipped Beauforts laid considerable waste to Axis shipping, but in the main, bombers were stuck with .303s.
4   These chances of evasion seem disproportionate at this stage of the war. Also, much flak was radar-directed ('predicted flak'); parachutists would not show up on radar. From Cusack's description it seems like a bracket of already-fired predicted flak caught the first unfortunate escaping airman. Although a parachutist is a small target moving significantly differently from an aircraft, once the gunners had the range of the first parachutist it would be fairly easy to visually bracket the second. Certainly some gunners and pilots – on both sides – shot parachuting aircrew, however this was

not routine; on the other hand, German snipers deliberately aimed at the wounded and medical staff at an aid station adjacent to Pegasus bridge on D-Day (Stephen Ambrose, op. cit., p. 146).

Chapter Twenty-one

1 Cusack probably means MI5, which is military security. MI9 and SOE handled foreign affairs and so forth. However, perhaps MI9 got the job as MI5 were too busy.
2 By this time '464 Squadron had 14 members killed on active service and four others were now prisoners of war' – Lax, op. cit.
3 This story does not appear to correspond with Lax nor, at a casual glance, with Cusack's logbook, although the action – and the story – does seem credible.

Chapter Twenty-two

1 Lax describes Cusack thus: 'Flt Lt John Bede Cusack, RAAF No. 411873. b 1 Oct 11, Sales Manager, Coogee, NSW. 464, 107 and 180 Sqns, 139 Wg. 464 Sqn – 30 Sep 42 – 7 Sep 43.'
2 In peacetime, as W/O Chris Dunne explains at www.army.gov.au/traditions/documents/OriginsofSaluting.htm, 'the salute is a symbol of greeting, of mutual respect, trust and confidence initiated by the junior in rank, with no loss of dignity on either side'. He continues, 'Returning a member's salute is not only acknowledgment of a salute to the officer personally, but a recognition of the fact that, through an officer, members have given an outward sign of their loyalty ...'. Cusack could have returned the Flight Lieutenant's salute, then mentioned it to someone superior to the F/L, who could have then sorted the problem out. Incidentally, saluting, because it was so unusual on station, had become a way of getting someone's attention if you wanted to talk to them; WAAFs, for example.
3 Cusack is mixing his metaphors – 'the wheels of justice' with 'the mills of change (or God) grind slowly, yet they grind exceeding small'; the ancient Greek later paraphrased and made famous by Longfellow. Interestingly, the 'wheels of justice' version is now far more common.

Chapter Twenty-three

1 'Football' being either Australian Rules or Rugby, not Association Football (i.e., soccer).
2 The Focke Wulf 190 was certainly a bit over 400 mph, but the Spitfire Mark V (Cusack is probably referring to Vb's) had a top speed of closer to 375 mph (depending on altitude).
3 'Jam the key'. Wilbur meant the WOP to lock or jam the radio key down, ensuring the radio key sent out a continuous signal (until the aircraft sunk) to pinpoint their position as an aid for Air Sea Rescue.
4 Squadron Leader Len Trent won his VC on 3 May 1943. As to the presence of the Focke Wulfs; 'Unbeknown to Group, a convention of [enemy] fighter pilots was taking place at Schiphol, into which many of the best pilots in the West had flown. This assembly was then held on alert during a visit of the German Governor of Holland to the town of Haarlem – which lay on the Ventura's route to Amsterdam.' Bowyer, op. cit., pp. 309–314. The Spitfires of 11 Group turned up a full thirty minutes too early, with the result that 70 enemy fighters were scrambled, FW190s for the Spitfires,

the Bf 190s for the bombers. The aftermath was grim; 'This was the fourth time that an entire squadron had been virtually wiped out in one operation'.

5 It was always 2 Group's desire to phase out the Vents and Bostons and replace them with either Mitchells or Mosquitos; Group understood that the Vents in particular were inadequate for the task set them. It is likely that the results of this raid speeded the process up.

6 Wing Commander Henry John Walter 'Jack' Meakin, DFC, RAF was CO of 464 from 27 April 1943 to 5 January 1944. Given that Jack Meakin died in 1989, and Cusack refers to 'the manner in which he met his death' back in 1965, relatives of Jack Meakin should note that it would seem Cusack has created an amalgam of characters; at this remove it is of course not possible to ascertain with any degree of reliability whether it is Meakin to whom Cusack refers during the rest of his time with 464. The 'remarks regarding the reputation of the Vents' attributed to the new CO were also commensurate with those made by the head of 2 Group, Air Vice-Marshal Basil Embry (who died in 1977).

7 No; forty ops could not be classified as one tour, only one tour and further operations.

Chapter Twenty-four

1 'Farmer Giles' is an affectionately contemptuous English name for their farmers; all apparently taciturn, surly and determinedly unworldly. The caricature was soundly based, however; and is also rhyming slang for piles.

2 The Independent Order of Rechabites came into being as part of the temperance movement in England as a Friendly Society in 1835.

Chapter Twenty-five

1 Air Vice-Marshal Basil Embry. His book, *Mission Completed*, Hutchinson, is worth a visit; as is Anthony Richardson, *Wingless Victory: The Story of Sir Basil Embry's Escape from Occupied Europe*, Odhams, 1950. Incidentally, Embry was born in Gloucestershire, not Cork.

Chapter Twenty-six

1 The 51st Highland Division's 'special duties' were preparing for D-Day; they landed in Normandy on D-Day Plus One as part of 1 Corps and quickly saw action.

2 464 Squadron then converted to Mosquitos.

Chapter Twenty-seven

1 At this time Cusack's squadron, No. 107, shared Hartford Bridge with No. 88. The 'famous army training establishment' is probably Aldershot.

2 A hold-over from biplane days, the monkey strap kept the gunner in his seat. Unless the chain snapped.

3 The Boston was considerably more manoeuvrable than the Vent, and was supposed to be a little under 30 mph faster. However, combat conditions alter the ability of an aircraft – Cusack earlier refers to 'old' aircraft which can only be less than two years from the factory, which we would regard as almost new today.

4 107 Squadron's CO from April to October 1943 was Wing Commander R.G. England, and from November 1943 to July 1944 was Wing Commander M.E. Pollard. Since Cusack joined 107 in early September and left in March 1944 and keeps one CO throughout his 'Boston Interlude',

I suggest his often scathing descriptions of the CO may well be colourfully embellished descriptions of a 'type' rather than that of any particular individual. There is no way to determine the truth of the matter with any accuracy now.

Chapter Twenty-nine

1   See www.theblackwatch.co.uk.
2   The Newquay Board Riders are one of many current surf associations in Newquay, which is now a prime destination for British surfers. I am sure Cusack would be pleased to know that they even have a surfing school there.

Chapter Thirty

1   If the Boston's needle touched 300 mph, that's still below what the Boston was supposed to be capable of; how many aircraft of the day tested when new, compared to how they performed in combat as a veteran, were often very different. These kites were not built to last.
2   Cusack was in 464 Squadron not, as he relates, 107, when these events occurred. 464 was visited by the Queen on 26 May 1943. From an Australian newspaper cutting: 'On her visit to overseas fliers serving in Britain, The Queen and Australian Ventura crews talked ... of the bomber men's experiences. Her Majesty chatted for some time with a veteran Australian crew, of which Sgt J. Cusack ... is a member. After questions about letters from home, the talk revolved around the flier's experiences in raids on Eindhoven radio works (Holland) last December, and in recent attacks on a chemical factory at Ostend (Belgium), marshalling yards at Caen (France), a whale oil factory ship in dry-dock at Ijmuiden (Holland) and marshalling yards at Abbeville (France). Group Captain Edwards, VC, of Western Australia, introduced Her Majesty to his pilots.'
    This letter was later published in an Australian newspaper: 'Flt-Sgt John Cusack, with a Ventura bomber squadron in England, to Miss Catherine Gunn: "We had a great day a few days back, a visit from their Majesties the King and Queen, and what a to-do for days before – bags of cleaning, scrubbing, scouring and what have you. When the big day arrived our kites were lined up most impressively, with ourselves in front of them. Was introduced to King George, and had quite a chat with Queen Elizabeth. She certainly is very nice and very natural. She's got a very infectious grin, or, should I say smile, and is a most gracious person".'
3   36°F = 2°C; –20°F = – 7°C.
4   FIDO (Fog Intensive Dispersal Operation) indisputably saved many lives and aircraft. However, the waves of heat coming up from the flames were difficult to negotiate; this was not the only example of an aircraft crashing and burning in FIDO's flames. Cusack is describing RAF Foulsham, which is about 15 miles northwest of Norwich, built for 2 Group and equipped with FIDO. Cusacks' next two squadrons, Nos 98 and 180, had their home there at this time.

Chapter Thirty-one

1   A milk-run was slang for an easy op; Cusack is being sardonic as the brutalising Battle of Berlin, roughly from November 1943 to March 1944, was in full swing and was anything but easy; see Martin Middlebrook, *The Berlin Raids. RAF Bomber Command Winter 1943–1944*, Viking, 1988. It is worth

mentioning here that the German night intruder operations recommenced in August 1943.

2   Further reading; Chaz Bowyer, *Mosquito at War*, Ian Allan, 1973.

3   'on the bot': on the scrounge. 'bot: to borrow money; (usually bot on) to sponge or impose on (others); Aust'n and NZ slang; since c. 1920' Partridge, op. cit.

4   This may be slightly unfair; it took courage to fly into the barrage of flak in any circumstances, particularly at low level. Also, the last pilot in line, watching the rest of the squadron cop it before you went in, would seem to me to be at the very least equally brave. If every pilot who died because they stayed at the controls of a crippled (if not burning) aircraft to let the rest of the crew escape were awarded what they deserved, there would have been a great many more VC's awarded.

5   The Free French Squadron which shared the drome (also flying Bostons) was No. 342. The reader may find it incredible that a pilot who did not have sufficient command of English would be let up in the air by the RAF, however the Free French proved rather a blind spot for the English, who let them get away with things which they would not accept from other allies. On the other hand, some of the ops in this chapter appear to be amalgams of other ops and other flier's experiences; for example, while Cusack was in 107 Squadron, his logbook indicates he did not fly to Brest, although he and his brother squadrons certainly flew similar missions.

Chapter Thirty-two

1   See John Nichol and Tony Rennell, *Home Run: Escape from Nazi Europe*, Viking, 2007.

2   These 'works' were V1 launching sites, also referred to as 'installations' and 'No-Ball' sites.

Chapter Thirty-three

1   A punishment also used by Nazi concentration camp guards. See Olga Lengyel, *Five Chimneys*, Ziff Davis, 1947.

2   Air Chief Marshall Harris had ruled that a tour was 30 ops; the airmen then became eligible to do six months as an instructor. Anyone finishing this first tour was only required to do 20 ops on a second tour. See Bishop, op. cit., p. 226; although anyone reading Guy Gibson's *Enemy Coast Ahead* will realise that there were ways of avoiding instructing if one was so determined.

Chapter Thirty-five

1   Cusack's log-book does reveal a likely candidate for 'Wing-Commander Smith', however it's probably best to follow his lead on this and leave him in the mists of history. It is not, of course, Basil Embry, who used this pseudonym to fly on ops against orders.

2   Although the Ventura did have a fixed .5 in the nose, the B25H Mitchell II had four .5 guns and a .303 gun in the nose.

Chapter Thirty-six

1   AIF stood for Australian Imperial Force, although Cusack is using the term to denote Australian Army.

2   It is worth mentioning that homosexuality was illegal in England at this time and punishable by a substantial jail term, which is an improvement

on the punishment of death, which remained in England until 1861. Homosexuality was decriminalised in England in 1961, however the legalisation of acts in private between two men 21 years or over did not extend to the Merchant Navy or the armed forces. For more on Soho, a good starting point can be found in Barry Miles, *London Calling*, Atlantic Books, 2010 (Chapters 2 and 3).

Chapter Thirty-seven

1 The author's new squadron is No. 98 at Swanton Morley, near East Dereham in Norfolk in March 1944, moving to Dunsfold in southern England by April 1944. The two other RAF squadrons were No 226 and No. 88; the Dutch squadron was No. 320. Dunsfold Aerosdrome is still used today, not least because it is the test track for the Reasonably Priced Car in television's popular Top Gear program. Recollections of a Mitchell pilot contemporaneous with Cusack can be found in 'Nevin Filby', the second chapter of *Fly* by Michael Veitch (Penguin Viking, 2008).
2 Flying Officer Bill Fogg: Wireless Air Gunner. 'an open-faced, bubbling, enthusiastic Australian', last seen in Cusack's 464 crew.
3 In Mosquito HX912: SB-F, F/L Phil Kerr and F/O Jack Hannah were 'last seen in a shallow dive near the target ... the aero-engine works at Woippy near Metz, France' (Lax, op. cit., pp. 93–95).
4 Cusack's logbook makes it clear that, while at both 98 and 180 Squadrons, he did not fly any missions to Holland, nor to Germany.

Chapter Forty-one

1 Hatfoss is a thinly disguised Central Gunnery School, Catfoss, established in 1941.
2 Homebush was the site of a major Sydney abattoir. The phrase would have been a commonplace, if rough, exclamation; 'bull' being short for 'bullshit'.
3 See Appendix Three.
4 Not correct. Bomber Command and the TAF would have lost a little over a combined total thousand planes in this period.

Chapter Forty-two

1 The first two V2 rockets landed London about 6.30 pm Friday 8 September 1944, in Chiswick and Epping, and were initially explained for the public as gas main explosions. About 1400 V2s were launched at England, and while about 290 went astray or blew up en route, the rest killed an estimated 2,754 people and seriously injured 6523. Over 1200 V2s fell in and around Antwerp. See Norman Longmate, *Hitler's Rockets: The Story of the V2s*, WW Norton, 1978 and J.C. Masterman, *The Double-Cross System in the War of 1939–1945*, ANU Press, 1972.

Appendix 3 — John Beede's War and John Bede Cusack's War

1 Bishop, op. cit., pp. 10 and 70.
2 Sir Charles Webster and Noble Frankland, *The Strategic Offensive Against Germany 1939–1945*, HMSO, 1961, Vol IV, p. 144. As quoted in Middlebrook, (op. cit.) p. 24.
3 L.F.E. Coombs, *The Lion Has Wings. The Race to Prepare the RAF for WW2: 1935–1940*, Airlife.
4 Chaz Bowyer, *2 Group RAF. A Complete History: 1936–1945*, Faber, 1974, p236. Compare the Air Ministry specifications and subsequent orders for

the likes of the Ventura and Boston to the then current progress with de Havilland's Mosquito.

5   The interested reader may like to examine *Bomber Command. The Air Ministry Account of Bomber Command's Offensive Against the Axis, September 1939-July 1941*, HMSO, 1941, for an excellent example of how data mixed with optimism and determinism can produce propaganda.

6   Hughie Edwards won his VC in 2 Group in a Blenheim; see Arthur Hoyle, *Hughie Edwards, the Fortunate Airman*, Canberra, 1999; at the time the author was in 464, Edwards was CO of 2 Group's adjacent 105 Squadron, which flew Mosquitos.

7   Almost every aircraft type in World War Two was varied to meet operational needs; there are multiple variants or 'Marks' – actual performance figures for each Mark are quite specific, and tend to be confusing to the casual reader.

8   Barnes Wallis had prepared designs for the Tallboy bomb, to penetrate thick concrete submarine bunkers, and the 22,000 pound Grand Slam 'earthquake' bombs years before they were produced.

9   Chaz Bowyer, *Royal Air Force. The Air Force in Service Since 1918*, Hamlyn, 1981.

10 Peter Shankland and Anthony Hunter, *Malta Convoy*, Fontana, 1963, pp. 134–137. Also, it is highly unlikely that Cusack could have avoided the extraordinary influence of *Target for Tonight*.

11 Bishop, op. cit., p. 70.

12 Chester Wilmot, *The Struggle for Europe*, William Collins, 1954, p. 17.

13 Middlebrook, op. cit., p. 33. Compare Mike Henry's experiences in a daylight ops Blenheim squadron (op. cit.).

14 Bowyer, *Royal Air Force. The Air Force in Service Since 1918*, Hamlyn, 1981, p. 241.

15 Lax, op. cit., p. 31.

16 Harry Gann, *Aircraft in Profile*, Volume 9, Profile Publications 1971, pp. 258–259, and Bowyer, ibid, pp. 262–266.

    See also Charles A. Mendenhall, *Deadly Duo. The B-25 and B-26 in WWII*, Specialty Press, 1981. The *Aircraft in Profile* series, published by Profile Publications from the late 1960s to the late 1970s, provides a good mixed-bag of aircraft to investigate.

ABOUT THE AUTHOR

A memoir by his daughter, Kerry McCouat

John Bede Cusack, the author of *They Hosed Them Out*, was born on 22 February 1908 in West Wyalong, a country town in New South Wales.

Both sides of his family came from Irish rebel stock. John's paternal grandfather, Michael Cusack, had migrated from Ireland in 1854, sponsored by a 'ticket of leave' uncle, Timothy, who had been convicted as a rebel and transported in 1827. John's maternal grandfather, Michael Crowley, a member of Sinn Fein, had escaped to Australia after being sought for his part in rebel activities.

John's mother Bridget (nee Crowley), had been a governess before her marriage. His father James, a sheep farmer, was 14 years older than his wife. John was the second youngest of their six children.

At the time of John's birth, West Wyalong was somewhat of a boom town. The 1893 discovery of gold in the district had transformed it from a sleepy hollow to a thriving centre with a population, at its peak, of about 12,000. Gold had also transformed the Cusack family's fortunes – James had successfully joined the rush by pegging out the productive *True Blue* goldmine right in the main street of the town.

This time of relative prosperity for the family came to a sudden end in 1914, when the seam of the *True Blue* ran out. James Cusack soon found himself bankrupt and the family was forced to move to Sydney, where they set up an inner city boarding house. Unfortunately, however, James exhibited an almost pathological jealousy of any male boarder, and Bridget was forced to leave him. She and the children moved to Coogee, a seaside suburb, where she set up another boarding house. From then on, James played no further role in the family. John was only about six at the time of the break-up and there was no mistaking where his sympathies lay. He adored his mother but would never have a good word to say for his father.

Growing up in Coogee

The break-up and upheaval was no doubt traumatic, and placed the family in a totally different environment. Coogee would become the family's base from then on, and the centre of John's social life. It was at Coogee's famous beach that John's long-term love of surfing and surf clubs started.

Then, as now, Coogee was one of Sydney's prime seaside attractions. Apart from a 150 foot Canadian toboggan slide on its northern hillside, Coogee's most distinctive building at the time, and the hub of its social activities, was the Aquarium Baths. Built at the northern end of the beach, with a distinctive large dome modelled on those in English seaside resorts, it housed a collection of exotic fish displayed in glass tanks surrounding a large dance floor.

There was also a large swimming baths. These would later become famous in the 1930s when a shark, newly captured and placed on display, disgorged the tattooed arm of an unfortunate individual who had been murdered and thrown into the sea. The 'Shark Arm Case' made international headlines and, decades later, even formed the basis of an episode of the television show *CSI: Miami*.

Coogee's attractions multiplied further in later years, when a pleasure pier was opened, and a shark net securing the southern half of the beach was installed. The pier's attractions included a large theatre, a ballroom and an upstairs restaurant for 400. The shark net was revolutionary for its time and attracted 10,000 people to the beach on its first day. It also allowed for night time swimming.

Despite the family's reduced circumstances, they were happy in Coogee. With their mother placing a particularly high value on education, all of the children attended and matriculated at local Catholic schools, and distinguished themselves in various ways.

John's oldest brother, Leo, reportedly became the youngest wireless operator in the British and Australian navies in World War I, later becoming involved in the early days of wireless communication between Australia and England. John's sister Margie became a nursing sister, eventually owning a nursing home on the hill between the Coogee Bay and Oceanic hotels. Due to health issues, his sister Dymphna (Nell) lived from an early age with an aunt and uncle in the country but later won a Teachers Training scholarship to Sydney University. As we shall see, Dymphna would later go on to a distinguished writing career. Molly became an outstanding tennis player and, as detailed later, Beatrice (Bea) assisted John in his early writing efforts.

The Irish influence in the family was strong. One night, during a period when Grandma Crowley lived with them, everyone in the household – other than Grandma – was startled by an unnerving shriek. The next day, it was discovered that Grandma had passed away. The cry, it was agreed, must have been the wail of the Banshee which, according to legend, presages death and is heard by all but the victim.

'On the wallaby'

John finished his education at Christian Brothers, Waverley, but by this time, in the late 1920s, work in Sydney was becoming hard to find. When opportunities dried up altogether during the Great Depression, John and a mate applied for a 'work for the dole' scheme. They spent a year in Tuena, a small town west of Sydney, panning for gold and learning a lot about life in a country town. However, the pickings were meagre. By the end of the year, the sum total of John's efforts went into the making of a gold ring for his mother. Years later, he would return with his wife to revisit his old haunts in the town. The visit was highlighted by a bizarre incident where – to everyone's amazement – John killed a snake in the main street.

After John's Tuena stint, like thousands of fellow Australians, he took to travelling the countryside, 'on the wallaby', looking for work. Through a fellow surf club member he obtained a job in a shearing shed as a piece picker, which paid well for those days – 3 pounds 10 shillings ($7) and keep. He also cut timber, ringbarked and felled scrub for little more than the cost of his tucker. He tried his hand at professional boxing, where the going rate was from 10 shillings to one pound a round – less if the crowd was poor.

At one stage, he even took the position of coach of a country rugby league team, though this ended up with almost a fight a day, when the local footballing lads, hearing that John had been in the fight game, had a few beers and came forward to try him out. He even spent six weeks on the infamous Boggabilla Railway where, as he later described it, the dregs and scum of the out-of-work labour force had gathered.

John returned to Coogee in 1932, but work was still hard to find, and he decided to move down the coast to Stanwell Park. Here he survived by living in a tent, and made a modest start to his literary career, optimistically writing stories and articles for magazines and newspapers. Using up to six different names enabled him to submit multiple articles to editors on such occasions as Anzac Day and other national events. Younger sister Bea helped out by typing the stories up, and they shared the slim proceeds. (Some years later, when Bea's marriage broke up, John returned the favour by encouraging the rest of the family to put in money for her two children's education.) During this difficult period, elder sister Dymphna would also send John money whenever she could. It was support for which he would always be grateful.

Birth of a salesman

Things started looking up in 1933, when John saw an advertisement in the *Sydney Morning Herald*. Its message was compelling: 'Do you want to earn 8 pounds to 12 pounds a week? Many of our men are earning 15 pounds a week!' The prospect of good regular pay saw John present himself, crumpled suit and all, at the city office of Electrolux. Today, Electrolux is known as one of the largest electrical appliance manufacturers in the world, but in those days it had just recently started its Australian operations and was only selling vacuum cleaners.

The interview went well, and the next day John started at their training school. Everything proceeded smoothly until our budding salesman was asked to put theory into practice by simulating an approach to a customer. The problem was this. John had a secret which he had somehow failed to mention at his initial interview – under pressure, and in some circumstances, he stuttered. In fact, he attributed his fighting abilities to this affliction, as in his early school days he had got 'stuck into' anyone brash enough to imitate him. (Later, in England, his stutter would be noticed by the Queen Mother when she and the King visited the Squadron. She was able to put John at his ease by revealing to him that her husband also had the same affliction – itself later depicted in the 2010 film *The King's Speech*).

The stutter initially looked like making John's sales career a very short-lived one. Nevertheless, his mother encouraged him to keep trying, and John persisted, travelling by tram round Sydney, and carrying his demonstration products in a reinforced cardboard Globite case. It was a tough job. At the time, vacuum cleaners were still novelties, and most homes did not even have refrigerators or other electrical appliances. As he recounted in a sales manual which he wrote much later, he had to overcome a number of objections wherever he went: '*My mother cleaned the house with a broom and lived until she was 88, so dirt can't be dangerous*'. '*Every Spring we put the carpets on the line and my husband beats them – he's the best vacuum cleaner in the country.*' And so on.

After a very dispiriting two weeks with no sales, John decided on one last door knock. As the front door opened, his heart truly sank. The house had no carpets or mats at all. There were not even any power points. He realised he would have to pitch his demonstration solely on the basis of the vacuum cleaner's many fancy attachments. With the help of an adaptor which he plugged into the hallway light socket, he used the floor brush to vacuum sweep the floors, showed how the utility nozzle could be used for cleaning mattresses, blankets and suits, and demonstrated the 'Insector', which blew paradichlorobenzene into the atmosphere to eliminate cockroaches and fleas. His hopes weren't high but, to his amazement, he found that he had impressed the housewife and her tram conductor husband. They decided on the spot. He had made his first sale.

His first taste of success buoyed him along. He became an eager pupil, accompanying and observing the company's top sales performers. He learned to be a salesman, not just a demonstrator. Within a year he was the fourth most successful salesman in Australia, second the following year and in the next he was promoted to supervisor and transferred to Queensland. With his new found prosperity, he traded in his old second hand car, and bought a new Ford sports roadster, later replaced over the years by a series of Oldsmobiles. (Despite the fancy cars, however, it has to be said that John never showed any mechanical or handyman abilities whatsoever.) Later, John's burgeoning Electrolux career took him to various other managerial roles in South Australia, Victoria and New South Wales.

Off to war

One day in 1939, when John was in Grafton establishing a couple of sales agents, he met two air force officers on a war recruiting campaign for the RAAF. At this stage, the 'phoney war' that preceded the real outbreak of hostilities in the Second World War had been in progress for three months. John had given some thought to joining up, but couldn't see any urgency. However, during a rather riotous night of drinking with the air force men, John and five others signed up.

At the time, the Air Force had an age limit of 25 which should have made John, at a ripe 31, ineligible. This barrier was overcome by one of the RAAF men suggesting that John put back his age and claim that he was born in Eire, a neutral country where they apparently had no birth certificates. All John needed to do was sign a statutory declaration.

As it happened, the ruse proved to be unnecessary. Two months later, when the call-up papers hadn't come through, he went down to the RAAF headquarters at Rushcutters Bay in Sydney. Strangely, they had no record of his enlistment. The clerk simply asked him if he wanted to join up, and the answer was 'yes'. He was accepted on the spot.

After training in Australia, being 'volunteered' as an Air Gunner and travelling to England, he started flying in March 1942. His wartime activities from then on are, of course, the inspiration for *They Hosed Them Out*. After many operations over Europe he had his last flight on 1 September 1944. He sailed back to Australia, stopping in New York where he and his fellow airmen were billeted with local families for a bit of rest and recreation (R and R). John found himself staying on the country estate of a wealthy New York family, complete with pool and tennis court. He later described how he and his friends awoke one morning to find a string of polo ponies tied up outside the house – a birthday gift from the lady of the house to her husband.

Home again

John arrived back in Sydney in December 1944. Two weeks later, he married his long-time girlfriend Cath Gunn at St Brigid's Church in Coogee.

Cath had grown up in Melbourne as the oldest daughter of the nine children of Dan and Tottie Gunn (nee Reilly). A mix of Scottish and Irish backgrounds, Dan and Tottie were an enterprising and hard-working couple, with Dan having to work multiple jobs during the Depression to feed and clothe his large family.

One family member recalls that he once asked the meaning of the distinctive imprint on the family crockery. Dan promptly told him that it was the Gunn family crest. The true situation was revealed a number of years later when it was realised that the initials RMJC on the plates actually stood for Royal Melbourne Jockey Club, one of Dan's many workplaces.

Cath worked as a photographer, and had first met John when he was working in Victoria before the war. As the story goes, Cath was at a dance at the seaside town at Lorne. Owing to the competition for girls, the young men who had accompanied Cath and her friends formed a protective semicircle around them. The first that Cath saw of John was when she saw his arm come through the human barrier and a disembodied voice asked, 'Can I have the next dance?'

Cath's oldest brother was Terry Reilly, the well known welterweight boxer and referee. With four young sisters to protect, Terry cast a stern eye over any visiting boyfriends, but John evidently passed muster.

John, despite all his reported wartime liaisons (later described by him as 'poetic licence'), was greatly intrigued by the independent-minded Cath, who was seven years younger. For her part, she thought John had that touch of magic. But their relationship had to overcome several hurdles. Before the war, with John travelling a lot in his job, much of their relationship was conducted by telephone – not the best medium for a stutterer. And later, of course, the war intervened in a major way. But despite having a number of boyfriends – and several marriage proposals – Cath corresponded with John for the duration and decided to wait for him.

Once married, they had to find somewhere to live. However, in 1945, with the Pacific War still in progress, accommodation in Sydney was hard to come by. A small block of flats that John had purchased in Kings Cross before the war was no longer available, having already been sold by Dymphna under a power of attorney that John had previously given her.

The circumstances surrounding that sale were revealing of the times. Dymphna had always been a harsh critic of racism, sexism and political complacency – a feminist before the word was popular. So, when she found during John's wartime absence that the block of flats had become filled with prostitutes and American servicemen, she took to 'cleaning up' the residence with a vengeance. Later, the Japanese submarine attack on Sydney in 1942 prompted her, along with many others, to vacate Sydney and she sold the flats for way below their real value. Dymphna had of course acted from the highest of motives, but with property values subsequently spiralling upwards, it was an unfortunate setback for John's hopes of future prosperity!

Nevertheless, John was able to use his pre-war contacts to secure a bed-sit back in the Cross. It was so small that the bed had to be pulled down from the wall. Cath's good-natured mother, Tottie, was most intrigued when she visited later and was given a bed on the window seat of a bay window, with only a pull-across curtain to separate her from the newlyweds.

Before the war had started, the Cross had been the most densely populated area in Australia, with flats, hotels, shops and restaurants in profusion open at all hours. It was the home of artists such as William Dobell and actors like Chips Rafferty. The combination of businessmen, confidence men, ladies of quality and ladies of the night made living at the Cross a real experience. Well-dressed and cultivated 'Reffos' (refugees) from Europe's troubles added to the mix. John had always loved this cosmopolitan and bohemian atmosphere and had many friends there from all walks of life.

Much of the background for John's later book *You Can Only Die Once* comes from his experiences in the Cross during that era. He once told of being invited out one Friday night to accompany his 'copper friends' from the Vice Squad. His friends spent the night visiting the brothels in the area, collecting their hush money and being entertained by the madams and their girls. (Much later, it was these connections that, in the 1950s, enabled John to obtain a range of gambling equipment which he and Cath used to run fund-raising nights for their daughter's school.)

Getting back to normal

John and Cath's stay in Kings Cross was followed by a period of house swapping and an interlude in Melbourne. They later moved back to Coogee, where they bought a house on Bream Street. In 1947, I was born, their only child. My first memories are of the moon rising over Coogee bay, of night swimming during heat waves, and fish cooked fresh on Coogee headland from the local fishermen's catch.

Despite John's upbeat nature – PMA (Positive Mental Attitude) was his favourite byword – the stress of the war years and his crash landings continued to take their toll long after the war had ended. He had alarming nightmares. Cath would be woken up by him standing on the bed making plane and gun noises. One night he grabbed her by the foot thinking she was an escaping German soldier. During the day, he spent a lot of time at the beach, just lying on the edge of the water allowing the waves to wash over him. Unable to return to full-time work, he starting selling real estate part-time. It was not until 1948 that John's full fitness finally returned and he rejoined Electrolux.

John had always been a natural at most sports. He had played first grade rugby union for Randwick, the Galloping Greens, after leaving school. But surfing was his first love and also his therapy. He belonged to Coogee Surf Life Saving Club – the Penguins – from an early age and was always down there for the Sunday races and drinks afterwards.

Even when he was transferred to Newcastle for 18 months, I remember that we returned to Coogee every weekend (a 200 mile round-trip) to stay in the flat underneath our Bream St house.

John's next transfer was to Brisbane as Queensland manager, where the locals proved to be very welcoming, The Electrolux crowd became family friends and our large old Queenslander house was the scene of many happy parties. The girls all brought a dish and each bloke was given the chore of looking after one girl's drinking glass. If he was forgetful and the glass became empty, he was fined. The money went into the 'whale's eardrum' – a souvenir from a family visit to the still active whaling station on Tangalooma Island in Moreton Bay – and was invested in a lottery ticket for all the party goers. The evening usually ended with everyone on the floor playing dice – 'up and down the river', poker dice and so on.

Brisbane was a hot city in those pre air-conditioning days and it was also 60 miles from the nearest beach. Undeterred, John organised the family to travel every weekend in summer and every second weekend in winter down to Surfers Paradise. Over the Christmas holidays, my mother and I, along with our wire-haired terrier Curly, would spend six weeks in a rented house with John joining us for his annual three week holiday.

Surfers was like our home away from home. Today, of course, it is a famous resort, but in the 50s and 60s it was just a friendly local village. The beach had a PA system with a resident disc jockey. Mutton bird oil was sprayed on the sun worshippers by John Paterson, a regular sight with his big tanned belly and pith helmet topped with a stuffed mutton bird. It seemed that half of Brisbane migrated there in the summer for the cooling ocean breezes, and half of Melbourne – including some of Cath's old beaus – migrated there for the winter sun.

The shark bell went off at least once a day in the summer. Any sharks that were caught were put on display in the boatshed and an entry fee was charged. Paula Stafford's bikinis also made their first appearance in that era. John usually gave me the task of alerting him to any 'good sorts' that might appear on the beach while he was occupied reading his newspaper. At midday, everyone would repair to the Surfers Paradise Hotel beer garden where Melbourne band leader, Stan Bourne, and his musicians were in residence. I remember John partnering one of my girlfriends to win the twist dancing competition one year.

All his life John was happy to pick up hitch hikers, even people who were at the local bus stop on his way to work. As most of the young lifesavers hitched from Brisbane to their clubs on the Gold Coast every weekend, we always had two or three in the back seat. In his best story-telling way, John would spend the journey regaling them with colourful details of his life adventures, while my mother and I listened patiently to the familiar tales.

John's stories and general conversation were always peppered with colourful terms. Characters were criticised for being *dill brains* and *drongos* as well as *whingers* and *earbashers*, while *bright sparks* got the *thumbs up*. *Acting like a big girl with no pants on* or being *full as a goog* was not a *good look*. Enthusiasms were marked with *you beauty!* and *whacko the did (diddle-oh)*. *Bloody* was as far as he went with regard to actual swearing, at least in my hearing.

John and Cath spent a lot of time raising money from the local businesses and beachgoers at Surfers to build and equip a new clubhouse with bunk beds for the Brisbane boys. John's salesmanship talents were put to full use. He became president of the surf club and, no doubt, a role model for many of the boys.

John was always 'John' to everyone – including all my friends and even me from a very early age. When my mother asked me why I didn't call him 'Daddy', my reply was that he didn't act like a Daddy, he was simply John.

He was an indulgent and enthusiastic father. Despite the fact that he probably would have loved to have had a son, I was always taken out the back in the surf, and to a local pool in Brisbane two or three mornings a week. Queenslanders hate the cold, and every winter Brisbane pools were closed down – except for one winter when one of the city pools opened. As it turned out, John was their sole customer, earning him a photo in the Courier Mail.

The origins of *They Hosed Them Out*

Although life was going well, John continued to suffer from insomnia and recurring war-related nightmares. On the advice of his local doctor, he started writing down the stories of his air force days, hoping to purge the old memories. For a number of years, this became his ritual, each night before he went to bed.

Fortunately, writing came easily to him. During the war, with Dymphna's assistance, he had already had a number of articles published in the Sydney papers (see Appendices 1 and 2) and had even been dubbed the 'official' Ventura historian. Gradually, as his nightmares slowly diminished, the pile of foolscap pages mounted in the guest bedroom of our Brisbane house.

As chance would have it, Dymphna was staying with us at the time, waiting to travel overseas on a passenger freighter, her preferred mode of travel. Dymphna by this stage had become quite famous as the author of a number of books, all with a focus on social and political issues. Her best-known, *Come in Spinner* (later a television mini-series), was inspired partly by her Kings Cross experiences, and told the story of three young women set in the wartime Sydney of black marketeers, abortionists and R-and-R Yanks. The book won Dymphna and her co-author, Florence James, the Sydney *Daily Telegraph* prize in 1948 – a real feat for women in that chauvinist era. The fact that they entered the competition using assumed gender-neutral names no doubt helped. Dymphna's other works included *Say No to Death* (about the death of her friend, Kay, from tuberculosis) and *Southern Steel* (about Newcastle, where she taught during the war).

Her books were also published overseas in 15 different languages, and were particularly popular in France, Eastern European countries, the Soviet Union, North Korea and China. As royalties in many of these countries were not transferable, she and her husband Norman Freehill, a financial journalist and Communist, lived an exciting and nomadic lifestyle travelling in these countries. In 1956, they were invited to China and spent over two years there. Dymphna wrote *Chinese Women Speak* after interviewing women from a variety of backgrounds, including Madame Mao. Perhaps not surprisingly for those times, both she and Norman had ASIO files and were never allowed into the USA.

On this particular occasion, as it happened, a dock strike had delayed Dymphna's departure, so she took the opportunity to read through John's stories. She soon realised that he had the makings of a book, and she introduced him to contacts at the Australasian Book Society. Later, the massive chore began of editing 250,000 words down to a manageable size. The book was finally published as *They Hosed Them Out* in 1965, under John's pen name John Beede. To John's delight, the book was greeted with a mass of favourable reviews, being praised as 'a minor war classic' (Max Harris), 'outstanding' (*Daily Telegraph*) and 'of the stature of Hersey's *The War Lover*' (*Australian Book Review*). It has since been reprinted a number of times (including under the title *Rear Gunner*), with the present expanded and annotated edition being the sixth.

Settling in Sydney

Although Brisbane had been enjoyable, John had welcomed the news that he would be transferring back to Sydney in 1962. This time it was as Electrolux's NSW manager, a prize position. It meant a return to his old home ground at Coogee and we rented a house there. Cath, however, had other plans in mind. After months of house-hunting, she managed to talk John into buying a block of land in Mosman overlooking beautiful Chinamans Beach in Middle Harbour. Despite John's misgivings that he might find himself surrounded by 'a bunch of snobs', it turned out that a lot of our neighbours were from John's old stamping grounds.

Wherever we lived, my parents made friends with the neighbours. Many a barrier was broken down by John's standard response, 'Let's have them in for a drink, Cath'. I don't think I ever heard John offer any guest a cup of tea. If they arrived anytime after midday, they were given a beer.

During the week, John was rarely home on time, as drinks with the Electrolux boys at the Petersham RSL Club were nightly occurrences. Cath had become used to this routine over the years and fined him if he didn't ring her before 7 pm. John's other extra-curricular interest was gambling on the horses. He had always had an SP bookie and listened avidly to the Saturday races on the radio. However, his success at punting did not match his enthusiasm. Once, when we were in Newcastle, Cath decided to stem this steady outward flow of money by setting herself up as John's bookie. The extent of John's lack of punting prowess soon became undeniably clear. He refused to place any more bets with her after she had accumulated enough winnings to buy herself a fur stole!

John eventually retired from Electrolux in 1973, with many farewells. His going away card from his work colleagues was festooned with a big 'Merci Bucups' on the front (John's version of 'merci beaucoup'), one of his favourite expressions.

In retirement, John always had itchy feet, saying that he wanted to fit in as much travel as possible. He didn't want to become 'one of those old buggers' he used to see travelling round the world, hobbling on a walking stick. Trying to encourage him into a more relaxed mode of travel, Cath rather cunningly used to book them on cruise ships. Even on these, John was always up at the crack of dawn walking round the deck, playing table tennis and joining in any competition in the pool. Inevitably, he was the first to arrive at the Captain's cocktail party, and the last to leave.

At about this time, I had moved to London on an extended working holiday. Cath and John came over on one of the Women's Weekly World Discovery Tours and we met up there. My boyfriend (and future husband) Philip's introduction to John occurred when I took him up to their hotel room. As soon as we knocked, John's arm appeared through the half-open door, brandishing a welcome can of ice-cold VB beer.

Cath and John also took off on a number of European tours. Cath had to shush him on the Rhine cruise when he kept audibly recalling many of the towns which he had previously flown over on bombing raids. As he always had an excellent memory for dates, he was able to add that helpful detail as well.

Back home in Mosman, John spent his retirement swimming locally, with Cath keeping an eye out for sharks from the balcony. He quickly became an outstanding local lawn bowler and did some beach fishing. At one stage Cath even found him a job as a 'messenger boy' at a large city bank. After befriending everyone there, he said he'd never experienced such an easy time earning money.

Despite his cheerful and party going disposition, John retained a number of health problems from the war years. There were mentions of 'those bloody Repat doctors' who refused to acknowledge that any of his conditions were related to the crash landings and the stress of all those wartime ops. His athletic fitness and PMA probably helped him to stay on top of most of his injuries.

John's problem with insomnia was notorious. As a teenager, I could never sneak in late at night, as he awoke at the slightest sound. Cath's plan of a lily pond in a sunken bath in the garden came to an end when it attracted 'those bloody noisy frogs'. Onion and potato plants sprouted around the pond as a result of these vegetables being thrown from the balcony to quell the nightly noise. Many a frog ended up in a jam jar in the kitchen awaiting a ride across the Spit Bridge.

A serious blood disorder finally caused John to spend a lot of time in isolation in hospital. He kept the staff entertained with his stories, and inspired all of his specialists to read *They Hosed Them Out*. In the winter of 1979, yearning for some warm weather and sunshine, John talked Cath into going to Cairns where he had spent some of his early years.

He died suddenly from a blood clot soon after his return. He was 71. He had donated his body to the university and his ashes are interred in the war veterans' cemetery in Sydney.

Dymphna died soon after receiving her Order of Australia in 1981. John's grandson Nicholas was born in 1982. Cath, despite losing her 'dear John', enjoyed life for another 20 years, a time spent with friends, playing golf and indulging her grandson.

Kerry McCouat (nee Cusack)

Wakefield Press is an independent publishing and
distribution company based in Adelaide, South Australia.
We love good stories and publish beautiful books.
To see our full range of books, please visit our website at
www.wakefieldpress.com.au
where all titles are available for purchase.

Find us!

Twitter: www.twitter.com/wakefieldpress
Facebook: www.facebook.com/wakefield.press
Instagram: instagram.com/wakefieldpress